Dedication

This first book could only be for My Darling

Acknowledgments

To the family and friends providing my everyday reasons for existing--my eternal thanks for your endless support.
You know who you are.
To the family and friends providing the fodder that fuels my evil imagination--my infernal thanks for your endless good humor.
You know how I am.
To the lovely people giving me expert advice, reading my unfinished manuscript, sharing their thoughts with me, and writing reviews--please read the above starting with,
'To the family and friends...'
To Nana—wherever you are, can you feel the love?
Tracy Ellen

Table of Contents

Table Of Contents

Prologue

Chapter I

Chapter II

Chapter III

Chapter IV

Chapter V

Chapter VI

Chapter VII

Chapter VIII

Chapter IX

Chapter X

Chapter XI

Chapter XII

Chapter XIII

Chapter XIV

Chapter XV

Chapter XVI

Chapter XVII

Chapter XVIII

Chapter XIX

Chapter XX

Chapter XXI

Chapter XXII

Prologue

Monday, 11/19/12

To: anabelSR38@yahoo.com
From: anabelJR83@gmail.com
Subject: What I did last weekend

Dearest NanaBel,

I'm hoping this email finds my favorite camel jockey in her usual fighting form? My mind pictures you lingering over an exotic drink by an oasis wearing a pith helmet and jodhpurs while surrounded by exotic men in long, white robes.

Meanwhile, back here in the tundra, we're finally getting the snow predicted for the last two days. It's really coming down, so I'm expecting a slow day at the store.

I've finished customizing the last report on the new inventory system. Total pain, but it should pay for itself in the short run. I'm flooded with data to analyze and trying to not wet my pants in excitement. Also, YTD numbers are kicking major butt over last year.

Now, don't fall off your hump when reading this, but I actually took this past weekend off to have fun. I know, right?

I'm sure my weekend fun didn't come near to comparing to the splendors of exploring the deserts of Ancient Egypt, or the splendors of exploring the personal tent of a Bedouin Sheikh. (Woman, thy name is Jezebel!)

Since you've asked repeatedly what I've been up to, and since I am a most dutiful granddaughter, and since I know you'll hear twenty different versions from twenty different people, and since we're speaking of jezebels…

On Friday night, I stayed home and was minding my own business when I fell asleep reading…

Chapter I
"Free Your Mind" by En Vogue

Friday (technically Saturday morning), 11/17/12
2:30 AM

Before realizing I was even fully awake, I found myself sitting up at attention with my instincts screaming and adrenaline racing through my veins. My heart was beating so loud I couldn't determine what roused me over the pressure of the blood pounding through my head.

I live alone. I had spent a quiet Friday night at home by myself to start my weekend off from work. The last I remembered was lying on my bed, surrounded by several fluffy pillows for protection, and reading a surprisingly good zombie book. I must have dozed off despite all the grisly excitement.

My room was pitch black. To get my bearings, I glanced at the clock on the bedside table and saw the faint illumination of red numbers reading 2:31 AM. Okay, the power was working. I didn't recall doing it, but before falling asleep earlier I must have set aside my book and turned off the lamp.

I concentrated on breathing to settle myself down. After a few seconds of breathing slowly I could hear again. I held perfectly still and listened intently.

My bed faces the open doorway. There are no windows in the hallway outside my second floor bedroom. It was a yawning darkness offering no clues as to what had catapulted me from sleep.

I was beginning to think it was a zombie-induced hallucination that had scared me awake. I was cussing myself out for reading a scary book right before bed when I heard it again. On the floor near my bed is a register vent that allows me to hear noises on the ground floor below me. Straining to listen, I recognized the sounds of the hardwood floorboards squeaking in the main entrance lobby. The noise was distinctly audible as footsteps, if you knew what you were listening for. I have lived in this apartment since I was a kid and now own the entire old building. I know every squeak of every floorboard in the whole place--I know what to listen for.

'What the hell...? Had someone really broken into my building?'

I quickly pictured the layout downstairs. The entrance lobby is a large, rectangular room situated in the northwest corner of the building. In the lobby are three doors. The first is a main set of double doors leading to the outside sidewalk at the corner of Division Street and Fourth Street in downtown Northfield, Minnesota. A similar set of interior doors opens into my shop, Bel's Books. The bookstore encompasses the entire ground floor of the building. The third door is the entrance to my place. This nondescript, steel door opens to the stairway leading up to my second story apartment over the book shop. All three of these doors are locked.

I sat frozen unable to move. I was still in denial over the sounds I'd identified and not yet reacting. The soft squealing noise I heard next meant the intruder had somehow unlocked the door leading up to my apartment. The acoustics of the high ceiling in the open staircase amplified every sound.

Now I was reacting. I was whispering out loud, "Oh my god, Oh my god!"

I had been meaning to get someone to fix the sticking door for the last week. Thanks to being a slacker, I knew someone was coming up the stairs.

Anytime I've been in tight spots in my past, I'm perfectly willing to bargain my soul and convert right then and there. I vow fervently to be a good girl for the rest of my life. In my head, I recited my lifetime litany of these negotiations.

'Oh, please, please! Get me out of this in one piece. I swear I'll never do anything bad again...'

It seemed like I waited an eternity, but it was probably only another heartbeat before my brain took over my wimpy, codependent subconscious and shouted, *'Get your butt up and do something yourself!'*

Thinking weapons, my next immediate thought was to grab my gun from the nightstand drawer. A stellar idea except for the fact my Glock 9 mm was currently with my cousin on a gun safety and handling retreat up north in Duluth. I swore silently at the irony Candy was learning how to safely use my weapon while I had to handle a home invader with my good looks.

My mind racing a mile a minute, I pushed aside the chenille throw I had been dozing under and reached for my phone. In the dark, I patted all around the surface of the nightstand. I felt my book and my empty gelato bowl, but no cell.

Then I remembered what I'd done and it made me want to throw something in a frantic panic. I'd left my cell sitting in the bathroom down the hall on the vanity, plugged in and charging. The bathroom was located across the hall between my room and the stairs, but closer to the stairs. I couldn't take the risk of trying to sneak over there without being heard and possibly intercepted. Also, my phone had been dying intermittently lately and I may need a new battery. It was possible even if I did make it there

A Date with Fate

without being heard, I could end up being trapped in the bathroom with no cell signal or weapons.

With a heart beating a frenzied double time in my chest, I tried not to feel cursed.

I stood up and concentrated on listening. There's a full flight of hardwood stairs, a landing, and then a switchback up another shorter flight to reach my foyer. It wasn't long before I detected another stealthy sound. The creak I heard was near the landing.

'Crap, crap, crap!' I bit my lip, hurriedly thinking over my options. I desperately needed a plan right about now. The urge to freak out was not a plan. I suspected it was not a good idea to give in to the temptation to lie on the floor and play dead like I do in bad dreams when monsters are chasing me. I could hide, but probably would be easily found since my bedroom has no great hiding spots; like a secret panic room complete with a big, red button.

I am majorly bumming I didn't pay more attention when my girlfriends were talking about the importance of always having an aerosol can and a lighter within easy reach. Tipsy on vodka tonics at the time, it had seemed unwieldy, and a tad brutal, to choose to set someone on fire with a Rube Goldberg flamethrower as a defense when you could simply shoot them. What I wouldn't give now for a supersized can of Raid and a Bic.

Sadly, I'm not a secret ninja or a supernatural female. All 5-foot-1-inch and a hundred and four pounds of me is an entirely mortal, girly-girl. The odds are decidedly stacked against me winning over most men in a physical fight. No matter how I looked at it, without my gun to scare off the intruder, I was screwed.

A flash of inspiration had me dropping to my knees on the rug. I urgently felt around under my bed for the forgotten weapon of choice before I purchased my pistol.

'Yes!'

I sprang back up. I immediately felt a little tougher with the Louisville slugger in hand. A crack with a bat could give me some time, although not as much as a bullet in the chest. If anyone came into this room my plan was a simple one; hit and run.

Outside my bedroom windows were bright streetlights. I need total darkness to sleep well. At night, lined draperies were always pulled tightly closed across the windows on either side of my bed. Right now, I was really happy with this quirk of mine. As long as the intruder wasn't wearing night vision goggles, the blackout conditions could give me the advantage of surprise.

On TV, it shows green lights flickering around their heads like lightening bugs if people are wearing those creepy, alien-looking goggles.

In that event, Plan B would be to flip on the overhead light, blind them, and then continue with my Plan A of hit and run.

I felt a bubble of hysteria rising in my throat when realizing I was basing my escape on the accuracy of a freaking television show.

'Why would green lights be flickering around anyone's head if they were wearing NVG's? Wasn't the whole blasted point to have the advantage in the dark, not be lit up like a neon sign?'

I was losing it and seriously contemplated nailing myself in the head with my own bat, so I could pass out to avoid whatever was coming my way.

Standing there, I was chilled and shaky, goose bumps popping up all over. I'm not the type that gets cold easily. I knew it was from being hyped-up. It didn't help my long hair was still damp from my earlier bath, and I was wearing a little nothing of a nightgown so short it barely covered my shivering butt. I almost shrieked when hearing a faint rustle of clothing and a definite creak of the top stair. The sound galvanized me into action.

I swiftly crossed the floor of my room while making sure to stay on the thick pile of the area rug to avoid noise. I stood slightly behind the halfway open door. I didn't want to try and close the door; it would serve no purpose. It didn't lock and was squeaky like everything else in my old building.

I hefted the bat in readiness. It was possible I'd only get one, good swing at the intruder and I needed to make it count. If I missed--well, my mind wouldn't even go there.

A few agonizing seconds later, I heard the intruder pause on the threshold of my doorway. I held my breath. I heard a soft footfall, and then another. With the third step, he was now squarely in my bedroom. My eyesight more adapted to the darkness, I guessed it was a man by his general height and width of shoulders. His vague outline seemed tall, but it was hard to be sure. Even under the best of circumstances, most men seem tall from my vantage point.

I tried to ignore my churning gut and keep a level head. Would projectile vomiting the bowl of caramel sea salt gelato I had earlier tonight be a turn off, or just make me easy prey? I didn't know the right answer, but I hate puking. I swallowed my saliva and strove to feel a little calmer, more coherent. I've always sworn I wouldn't be that girl that fell down in her high heels and cried when being chased by a bad guy. Now was the time to prove it.

These thoughts were all a quick flash across my racing brain as I acknowledged one, indisputable fact with a gut-tightening sensation. By coming straight to my room as he unerringly had, this person proved he meant to come after me.

Within the first moments, I realized it was too iffy to go for his head in the dark. I readjusted my aim and went for the vicinity of his knees. Even as I swung the bat, I sensed movement in the air around me. My swing was prematurely halted against something solid with a loud WHAP! It sounded like an open hand. My heart plunged. I had somehow broadcast my intent. I felt a sharp yank and the bat went flying out of my slippery grip. I heard the muffled thud of the bat when it landed on the rug somewhere in the dark room. My only weapon may as well be on Mars.

Above me, a man's voice softly hissed, "That wasn't a very nice way to greet me."

'Holy Freakin' Moly!'

I didn't wait around to chat. I pivoted and took off running for the open doorway behind me. I hadn't gone two feet when I was caught mid-stride by arms locking around my waist like bands of steel. I let loose with a startled scream as I was swung around like a rag doll. My feet were off the ground, and my back was pulled tightly against a chest that felt as hard as granite.

My attacker started to walk with me, carrying me easily back into my bedroom. I fought against him while shouting for help at the top of my lungs. It was a knee-jerk reaction. My building is located on the main street in Northfield, but it is mid-November and both my windows were closed tight. Even if I could be heard, there is no foot traffic in downtown this time of night. It's a college town, but last call was long over. The bars stop serving at one in the morning and there are no all-night diners nearby.

I knew it was me against this man.

My next move was another knee-jerk reaction; it was a Déjà vu move from my childhood fights that always resulted in a quick getaway. I pried up one of his fingers at my waist with both of my hands. I wrenched it backwards with a jerk.

"God*dammit*!" his voice spit out in the darkness. He snatched his hand away from mine.

'It worked!'

Unfortunately for me, it didn't work for more than a second. I had no chance to get at his other hand to free myself before he quickly maneuvered and repositioned his hold. He now entrapped both my arms against the front of my body. One of his arms was across my chest and the other around my hips.

I kicked at him backwards as hard as I could. I tried to twist my body to knee him in the jewels. Like a vice, his arm clamped across my hips prevented that move. I couldn't get at him. If his low laughter was any indicator, kicking him furiously barefoot wasn't doing him any damage but really hurt the hell out of my toes.

He stepped us nearer to the vicinity of my bed. Right at that very instant, I learned something new about myself I've never before had a reason to know. I hated being bound without the use of my arms. My response came from deep within me at some primal level never consciously experienced. Instinctually, my reaction was to fight like a wildcat. I bucked my body, kicked my legs, and tried to smash my head back against his face—anything to throw him off stride and give me an opening to get loose.

He made a mockery of my efforts by easily controlling my frenzied attempts to get free. As if to emphasize this total power over me, my attacker put his hand over my breast and squeezed. Throwing my head wildly around didn't stop his tongue from licking up my throat to my ear.

He growled, "You aren't going anywhere, little girl, but fight me all you want."

His touch and guttural voice held me frozen in suspended shock for an instant. This was really happening to me.

I didn't answer. I saved my breath for battling him. I knew my struggling was turning my assailant on big time. I could feel him hard against me from behind while I strived to get free. I tried to ignore this as I fought him, but it was like trying to ignore a red-hot poker.

I used every trick I had ever been taught to break his holds. Too bad these tricks were from years ago, and against my sisters. I hadn't been in an actual physical fight since I was thirteen. I could verbally slay Hannibal Lector into a blubbering fool without breaking a sweat, but I am not a kick-ass fighter against a man. I was captured with no use of my arms. I was unable to turn my hips, so my legs were useless, too. I still had a functioning brain, though. I allowed my body to relax and go heavily limp in his arms, as if in a dead faint.

My attacker didn't care if I was dead or alive, but instead took advantage of my feigned slump. He stuck his hand down the front of my nightgown; cupping and rubbing my breasts. His other hand on my hip moved to my naked butt, and he pinched me hard.

Unexpectedly shocked from my coma, I inadvertently yelled, "Ouch!"

He laughed at my pained reaction. Until I jumped up and snapped my head back, catching his mocking mouth with the top of my skull. It felt like his front teeth were embedded to the gums in my cranium. I didn't think grown-ups had soft spots, only infants. Apparently, mine had never fused. I didn't receive much delight from his moan of what had to be a mouthful of hair-filled agony since my own moan of throbbing hurt was louder.

My attacker recovered quickly. With a bounce, he hoisted me up higher against him. His hand roved all over my butt and the back of my thighs. He held me close against him to limit my range of motion. His mouth was hot on my ear whispering words I couldn't distinguish, or be sure were even in English. I hoped I'd loosened his front teeth.

I wrenched my head away as far as I could to avoid his mouth, but couldn't move my hips enough to avoid his busy hand. I felt his fingers

A Date with Fate

strumming boldly down my rear end. Then I felt those fingers move between my legs, and the vibration of another mocking laugh against my neck.

The touch of my attacker's invasive fingers drove me over the edge into a mindless, uncontrolled frenzy to escape his touch. I erupted and fought against him like a woman possessed. Blindingly out of control of anything I was doing or screaming, I was only dimly aware of kicking and scratching, head butting, throwing myself from side to side, and even snapping at his face. Had he come within range, I would have ate his face off zombie-style and then asked for seconds. I don't know how long it took before his excited laughter started to penetrate my futile haze of bloodlust to kill him.

I could hear the underlying, sexual tension in his voice as he held me to him, goading me on, whispering he was stronger and would always win. He was a predator and the harder I fought the more aroused he became.

The next thing I knew, I went sailing though the air in the darkness. I landed on my bed so hard that I bounced not once, but twice. My antique bed springs were squeaking protests louder than my own shrieks. My attacker had snapped on the bedside lamp and tore his T-shirt off over his head by the time I came to a stop from bouncing. I was disoriented at the sudden blaze of light and struggling to catch my breath.

Breath or no breath, I couldn't afford to lie there on my back, on my bed, and at his mercy. I hurriedly rose up, but didn't get much further than my elbows before his hand clamped around the front of my neck and pushed me back down against my pillows. He kept me there.

The black dots hadn't disappeared in front of my eyes from dazedly staring at the sudden burst of lamplight a moment ago. My attacker was a fuzzy blur as he stood next to the bed. I pulled with all my strength on his hand casually surrounding my throat. It wasn't even a huge, monster hand. This guy was seriously strong, or I was incredibly weak. Either way, I couldn't get free of him.

His hand slid off my neck and glided slowly downward. My nightgown is more like a longish, tight tank top. It's made of a stretchy lace material with an elasticized neckline cut straight across and held up by thin spaghetti straps. He spread his hand, fingers dipping under the gown's neckline. His splayed hand was lying across the top curve of my breasts, and exerting no apparent effort, held me firmly down on the bed. Unbelievably, I was unable to do much more than lift my head from the bed pillows.

Inside my head, I was calling him every foul name in the book and some that hadn't been written. In my bedroom, my hitched breathing was the only sound in the silent night around us as we continued battling. I soon realized it was a one-sided struggle because my attacker was doing nothing but standing next to the bed and holding me down. He was probably getting off on the view every time I lashed out at him with a kick. I couldn't let that stop me.

He blocked my attempts to maim him with kicks by using his left knee to pin down my thighs. I got a quick glance of a bare foot. Knowing this meant he had taken the time to remove his shoes and socks made me shudder. He had planned out this assault. His right foot stayed planted on the floor by my bed.

During this time, I still couldn't see the predator's face as he was a shadow backlit by the light from the lamp. Even with my vision restored, my damp hair lying across my eyes in tangles made trying to see a nightmare version of peek-a-boo. I was out of breath, and I could feel my nightie was twisted up above my hips from thrashing around.

I'm sure it would matter later I was partially blinded, winded, and so blatantly exposed to him, but not right this minute. The man was lifting his hand off my chest and I knew it was my golden opportunity.

I went for his balls.

With a surprised grunt, he adroitly avoided my fist by turning his body towards his right. This caused my punch to bounce harmlessly off his left thigh, but I had anticipated this move and my left hand was already in motion.

I was an inch from my goal of causing a painful distraction so I could get away when his right hand shot out. He grabbed my fist in a tight grip and thrust my arm off course, causing me to cry out. Not so much in pain, but in total frustration at the lost opportunity to nail him. He released my fist quickly but kept hold of my wrist.

My attacker gave a little shake to my hand in his grip and mockingly made a "tsking", chiding sound, as if disappointed in me for missing.

He then laughed like a demon, in obvious delight with his own prowess.

I ignored his taunts, focusing on pulling my hand back out of his grip.

He responded by forcibly lifting my arm up, and then over my head. He pried open my clenched fist and pressed my fingers firmly around one of the iron bars of my headboard. He kept his much larger hand tight around mine.

His free hand went for my other wrist. My free hand knocked his away. He kept coming back and grabbing for me. I kept batting his hand away. It was a Three Stooges moment. It would have been funny if it wasn't so serious, and if I got to be Moe instead of Curly on the receiving end. He managed to capture my wrist with a hand as tight as a manacle. He made this hand hold another bar on my headboard. Now both of my hands were covered by both of his.

A Date with Fate

My assaulter sat down alongside my prone body, leaning across me to keep my hips pinned to the bed. I'm in good shape but I have to admit, no matter how fit you are exercise alone doesn't prepare you for this kind of battling. My arms were held up high, and my hips and upper thighs were trapped under the weight of his angled body.

I was panicky at the vulnerability of my position and I was suddenly exhausted from battling him so ferociously. That tiny voice popped up again, the wussy one that prays for help. Wussy voice whispered insidiously how easy it would be to give in, admit defeat, and let my attacker win with no more fight from me.

'Yeah, right!'

I laid a smack down on that little cowardly voice and took several, calming breaths. Surrender is not a word in my vocabulary.

I concentrated on my next move, or tried to come up with one. I didn't have many options to choose from. I knew I'd have to be ready to act when I got the chance. I needed to face who I was up against.

I briskly shook my head from side to side to remove my mass of long hair from my eyes.

My attacker was no longer backlit by the lamp. I could see him. The left side of him was bathed in shadows, but not so much that I couldn't tell what he looked like.

In the swift, comprehensive glance I stole before veiling my eyes beneath my lashes, I observed a few things about the predator holding me captive on my bed. He wasn't too ugly or scary looking, and could pass for attractive in a dark, rugged way. He had a short, black beard. He wasn't as tall as my earlier impression before the light was on. His raised arms were flexed with muscle. No wonder I couldn't move him; the man looked strong.

Another thing I had noticed in my brief glance, Muscle Man wasn't paying any attention to what I was thinking. He was absorbed doing his own reconnaissance.

Now that I was held down and temporarily still, I was acutely aware of the fact I may as well be nude for all the cover my nightgown afforded. In his position of leaning against me, he was intently checking out what he could easily survey above and under the sheer lace, namely most of my breasts.

'Oh, my god!'

I squeezed my eyes tightly shut. Based on his earlier grabbing and now his intense expression, my attacker seemed to have a thing for boobs. I really, really wanted to wipe that arrogantly leering expression off his face. I took a fortifying breath and made myself focus on how to get away, determined not to give up against his greater strength. My damn brain had to count for something. I just needed to keep my wits about me and outsmart him.

As if he sensed my racing thoughts, he roused himself. He sat up straighter, removing his hands from over mine around the iron bars. I instantly started to lower my arms.

He raised his hand sharply in warning, but still spoke softly. "Do not take your hands off those bars."

The calmness of my assaulter's tone was so normal in contrast to the implied threat of his raised hand that I involuntarily obeyed without thinking.

I jerked my eyes up, meeting his squarely for the first time tonight. Distinctive green eyes challenged me. His mouth looked cruel. His full lips curled with a patronizing smirk, clearly getting a kick from my dilemma. So far, he hadn't hurt me, only restrained me.

'Could I push him further?'

He continued to read my mind. His voice was pleasantly conversational over the implied threat. "I'll only tell you this once. If you take your hands off the bars, I will make you regret it. You will be punished. Do you understand me?"

'Punished! Holy crap! That answers that!'

My attacker didn't even wait for my response. By my silence, he was confident I was too intimidated to think of disobeying him. He moved his total concentration to his reason for breaking into my home. It almost drove me beyond endurance this guy could dream for a minute he'd won that easily. It wasn't easy, but I made myself demurely lower my eyes in pretended submission and bide my time.

When he slowly pulled my nightgown down, I determinedly kept my eyes closed. As he must have intended, with my arms stretched over my head and from the tightness of the stretched neckline pushing up underneath; my breasts were high on display in exaggerated offering. I could feel my nipples were erect from the rough friction of the lace, his hands, and the cold air. As he touched me and looked his fill, I set aside the feelings of wishing to kick his ass into the middle of next week with every fiber of my being. I forced myself into calm, and then used what weapon I did have to create a diversion; my girly-girlness.

Hands around the bars behind me, I let out some scared, feminine squeaks. I tossed my head in agitation. I shook my shoulders to and fro, quivering in modest fright. My bed helped; it bounced and squeaked a little, too.

Is there a straight man with eyes in his head capable of resisting the vision of a bare-breasted girl shimmying practically in his face? Possibly there is somewhere on the planet, but not the predator in my bedroom.

His total attention glued where I wanted, my attacker was starting to lean forward. Without warning, I quickly brought both my knees up and then slammed into his side with both feet flat. I gave him the heave-ho,

A Date with Fate

using the strength and momentum of my legs. Holding onto the bars actually gave me greater leverage. He had been in motion, his foot wasn't planted on the floor any longer, and my comforter fabric was slippery. I finally caught the man completely off guard.

I didn't once let up my attack to allow my surprised assailant to catch his balance. I kept up the pressure of frenzied kicking and pushing until he slid right off my silky duvet.

Legs and arms flailing, he yelled, "Shit!"

He landed hard on the floor with a solid THUMP!

"Yes!" I screamed triumphantly when he went over the side. Hopping to my knees on the bed and scrambling to the edge, I was about to make a jump for the door and freedom.

My luck was short-lived. My assailant was ideally supposed to be slowed down. I was supposed to get a chance to run for the door. The only thing I managed to get was a quick tug up of my nightgown's neckline before I saw the top of his head rising up from the floor along the side of the bed. Remembering his threat of punishment, I threw myself backwards and grabbed the iron bars of the headboard. I hit with enough force the bed posts smacked against the wall just as he sprang up from the floor like some kind of warp speed jack-in-the-box.

My attacker stood looking down at me, hands on his hips. Gazing back, trying to look innocent, I was berating myself silently for not trying for the door, regardless of the consequences. My only small satisfaction was seeing him breathing heavier for the first time. My eyes kept dropping lower. I could not stop staring at the sight of his tanned, cut abs above his low riding jeans. They rippled with every breath he took.

When I am really nervous or really emotional, my mind sometimes goes AWOL and thinks bizarre thoughts as a coping tool. I'm terrible at funerals. I dare not look at anyone who knows me lest they set me off laughing. I have to constantly battle myself not to lose it when I have these whacked thoughts.

Right now, all I could think about was how did Muscle Man manage to still be so tan when it was near Thanksgiving? Did he use a tanning booth? Get sprayed? Have his abs "highlighted" to accentuate the definition? I imagined him in a hair bonnet while giving precise instructions on how to get sprayed tan before his big night out to sexually assault a woman. I had to turn my face into my shoulder to muffle my sudden choke of crazed giggles. A small snort escaped, but I hurriedly coughed to disguise the sound.

The predator staring at me solved my attention deficit problem when I heard the clinking noise of his belt buckle. Without saying one word, he made the desire to laugh curl up and die instantly. He unhooked his belt buckle and started to pull the belt from the loops on his jeans.

Heart thumping madly, I looked up to see his narrowed eyes watching my face. His black brows almost met in the middle over his fierce scowl. His mouth was a thin line.

'Oh help me; this is one pissed-off attacker!'

I am a baby when it comes to pain. Actually, a baby probably handles pain better than I do. I'm sure my eyes were opened as wide as they could go after hearing the belt buckle sound, so I didn't have to fake that. I swallowed hard over the dry lump in my throat. I moistened my lips with my tongue. I blinked and tried for sweetly reasonable; even if it was to tell a lie.

"Um...Mister, you'll notice I didn't take my hands off the bars?"

He ignored me. He paused, then let go of his belt. Instead, he undid the top button of his jeans and pulled down the zipper. Emboldened with relief at the immediate threat of pain off the table, and ignoring the zipper part, I was done with being reasonable. Sweet has never worked all that well for me, anyway.

So I jeered at him.

"I almost think you didn't have fun getting kicked to the floor by a girl. Hey, you never said I couldn't throw you off the bed like the annoying, little meat puppet you are."

Right then, as I heard myself talking smack, I swear I was having an out-of-body experience. I had a vision of the entire scene as if I was perched up in a corner of the ceiling with a birds-eye view of the room. I saw an angry, tough, and half-naked man looming over a defiant, defenseless, and half-naked woman. She looked tiny sprawled out on the big bed, holding onto the iron bars behind her, and running her big mouth like a lunatic.

Why do I feel compelled to keep taunting my assaulter against everything I have ever read or been told to do in this situation?

Maybe I was being strategic and thought I had a better chance with him mad and out of control. Maybe I wanted to prove he could restrain me physically, but he couldn't break my will. Maybe I'm such a smart ass I cannot keep my mouth shut even if it means getting beat with a belt, or worse.

So I laughed in his face.

"Why, I do believe the big man isn't used to getting his ass kicked to the floor by a 'little girl'." I drawled. Then I gave another, much more exaggerated shimmy. "Oh, Muscle Man is so very frightening and so very strong. I'm just shaking."

It felt mighty fine to smirk up at him for a change.

For about two seconds.

Until all hell broke loose.

A Date with Fate

When I had begun taunting him, he seemed to ignore my provocation. He had stood silent, arms akimbo, and no expression on his face under the beard.

Then he looked me straight in the eyes. I almost choked on my own breath when he let me see the blazing intent in his face. His dark glance swept over me, as if appraising where to get started to make me pay for my comments.

'Oh, have mercy! I'm so in trouble!'

I knew he had decided where to start when his attention fixed on the vee of my clamped together thighs and he smiled broadly. It was a nasty smile. My heckling hadn't made him lose control or deflated his intent, but had the direct opposite effect. Almost biting my tongue off in order to keep quiet and not challenge the situation any more, I unthinkingly twisted my body to get away from his blazing eyes.

That was stupid.

My predator's short laughter was as nasty as his smile. My move gave him an eyeful of my entire bare-assed backside. I couldn't do anything about that right now, but I vowed fervently I'd never go to bed without undies, or my gun, again.

Simultaneously with these thoughts, I desperately flung myself off the bars towards the opposite side of the wide bed and away from him. I kept rolling, but I felt my ankle snagged. Caught in his grip, I kicked wildly as he dragged me back parallel to the edge of the bed where he was standing. Swiftly, he pulled down his unbuttoned jeans and kicked them away.

'Oh, HELL no!'

I screamed and scooted away backwards as fast as I could go, practically crabbing it on all fours. I shouted again when he stretched over me and gripped my shoulders. His strong hands snapped both the fragile spaghetti straps of my nightgown. In one swoop, he tore it down and off of me like he was a magician whipping a tablecloth off from under a feast-laden dining table. It was done so efficiently, I didn't have time to even flinch.

I clambered up to my knees, frantically trying to cover myself. I swore hotly in his face, "You...you ASS, you are so going to pay for that!"

With that incredibly lame threat hanging in the air, I dove again towards the other side of the bed. My attacker gave a battle cry and dove onto the bed after me. When he landed, the bedsprings wailed. The end of the bed screeched crookedly sideways, scraping about a foot across the hardwood floor.

I was bounced over the mattress as I scrambled on hands and knees to get away. I shrieked when I felt him grip my naked hips. The force of his hands collapsed me face first into my comforter with a gasping "Oomph!"

My enraged curses were muffled, but his answering war whoops of victory reverberated loudly in the silent room. He squeezed my ass with both his hands before flipping me onto my back like I weighed nothing. I was lying across the width of the bed. My assailant was beside me, sitting back on his calves and waiting.

He was a naked devil grinning maniacally down at me.

I tried to move my feet on the slippery comforter under me. I wanted off this bed. It was an irrational goal. Even if I could get past him, the floor offered no better refuge. I was way past making sensible choices and reacting on instinct. My wildly bicycling feet kept sliding out in front of me.

I screamed in frustration when I saw him watching my sorry performance to get away with an unholy leer. I was a nude woman going nowhere fast and bouncing all over the place. I swung to slap that smug look off his face, but he deflected my hand. Then he pounced. I was completely enveloped from head to toe with his much larger body.

The heat, the weight, the scent, the feel of him—everything was overwhelming. I was surrounded by the man and felt like I couldn't breathe. He buried his face in my neck and nipped me. I shouted breathlessly in surprise at the bite. He breathed a harsh, satisfied growl in my ear. I knew then this predator was seriously enjoying the fight of catching me.

He reached down between us and probed between my thighs. Using his hand first to get an opening, and then using his forearm, he forcibly wedged my resisting legs apart. I tried to keep my thighs clamped and legs crossed at the ankles, but he was too strong.

The next was a blur it happened so fast. With his upper body weight pinning me down, he hooked his elbows under both my knees, and then raised both my legs up and out. My legs were spread and I was open to him. My attacker aligned his whole body tightly against mine while pressing me to the bed. He was breathing quickly and smiling. He flexed his hips in a deliberate, age-old motion.

Feeling him heavy and hard between my legs shot a final spike of adrenaline through me. I was bucking, heaving, and pushing trying to propel him off me. Muscle Man pinned my hands to the bed on either side of my face and rode me until I tired, never once losing that superior grin.

Nothing I did fazed him and it made me insane. I felt a fiery blush of heat wash over my cheeks. I closed my eyes. Not in fear or defeat, but because I was so goddamn mad I was no real match for his physical strength. I had really tried to beat him and get away tonight, any way I could. I wanted to burst with the roiling emotions churning up my insides. I hated losing. I couldn't remember the last time I had lost at anything important.

A Date with Fate

He rose up on both elbows. I slowly opened my eyes to see him looking down impassively at my scowling face. The impassive expression couldn't disguise that his green eyes were glittering with triumph. If my eyes could kill, he'd be dead meat.

My assaulter suddenly smiled. The arrogant ass had straight teeth that were startling white against his tanned skin. And he had one dimple.

He reached back with a hand and pulled open my nightstand drawer. He came back with a condom. He leaned to his side. Never taking his intense gaze from mine, he tore it open and smoothed it down over his erection with no wasted motions.

He came back over me. He ordered softly, "Enough play. Put your arms around my neck and hold me tight."

I was pinned flat on my back and in no position to negotiate. I didn't let that minor fact stop me from taking my time thinking over his words. Our faces were only inches apart. He watched me with wary, lowered eyes as I slowly ran my hands up his thickly muscled arms. I trailed my fingers along the top of his smooth-skinned shoulders. Still inherently unable to completely give in, I held him loosely about his neck with my arms crossed at the wrists.

I waited.

He gave me a sardonic look and lifted one black eyebrow.

I moaned softly at that single, arched brow and finally obeyed to the letter of his demands. I wrapped my arms tighter around his neck. With both hands, I ran my long fingernails through the back of his hair against his scalp. I pulled his face down to mine.

I whispered an inch from his lips, "You win. Tonight."

Then we were kissing—wild, endless, drugging kisses. I soon lost myself in abandon. I was in the place where conscious thought has no meaning and nothing existed beyond the touching of our entwined bodies on the bed.

Poised above me, he murmured against my mouth, "Christ, I've missed you." He kissed me deeper and continued proving it.

Much later, he gave me a little squeeze within his arms. "Seriously, a baseball bat, Anabel?"

I lay across his chest, my face nuzzled against his warm neck. I was too exquisitely exhausted to move, but I couldn't help my tiny grin at his aggrieved tone.

I murmured drowsily, "Luke, Luke. No harm, no foul balls, right?"

Hands around my waist slid lower. He positioned me on top of him while responding dryly, "Yeah, it was a real no-hitter."

Sleep is vastly overrated.

Chapter II
"Fever" by Peggy Lee

Saturday, 11/17/12
6:30 AM

    My name is Anabel Katrina Axelrod. I also answer to Bel or Junior. I'm the namesake of my maternal grandmother, Anabel Katrina MacKenzie. Hence the Junior. Hopefully, Bel is self-explanatory.
    I'd woken up groggily a few minutes ago and glanced over at my bedside clock. I suspected it would only be around 6:30 AM, and groaning softly, saw it sucked to be correct. My internal clock woke me around the same time every day. It didn't seem to care I'd only slept two hours.
    I lay on my side drowsily in the dark, pleased to remember it was Saturday. My shop was covered by my staff on weekends. Stella, one of my two store managers and also my niece, would be at the helm today.
    NanaBel, as our grandmother is affectionately called, was the original proprietress of Bel's Books and the former owner of this building. That includes this second floor apartment where I grew up and still live, but now own.
    Some of my earliest childhood memories are running tame in the store below. I was happy to play rambunctious games of Tag, Hide n Seek, and Red Light-Green Light in the aisles with my siblings, but it's always been about the books for me. More often than not, you could find me curled up in a wing chair with my nose buried deep in a book. I don't recall a time when I didn't read predominantly adult literature, except for the occasional R. L. Stine thrown in.
    I loved helping with the customers. To hear it from NanaBel, you'd think I was the most precocious kid to ever walk the earth. My grandmother claims I was a cross somewhere between the top sales person she'd ever seen and a little con artist. If you believe NanaBel's version of my childhood, after hanging with me the adult customers often left the store in a daze with a bag of books they didn't remember choosing, much less buying. You'll never convince me those people did not enjoy reading Robert Heinlein, Robert McCammon, and Georgette Heyer as much as I did.
    I had an epiphany in middle school. I decided my main goal in life was to own Bel's Books. I've never looked back. I have worked in the book store officially (meaning actually paid a real wage and not child slave labor) since I was fifteen. I became Store Manager at eighteen. Now

A Date with Fate

pushing twenty-nine, I have been sole owner of Bel's Books for the last three years while a gleefully retired NanaBel travels the globe. She's kicking up her heels and making up for lost time.

My thoughts drifted from the store to the pressing issue of the man currently spooning me. His name is Luke Drake. He is my lover, not an unknown assaulter I was freaky enough to make out with because he could pin me.

If anyone knew what I was up to last night, some may judge me a sick puppy. I think they'd be wrong. Not necessarily the sick puppy part, the jury is still out on that decision, but wrong to judge. I firmly believe what consenting adults do in the privacy of their own sex life is their own business.

Last night's shenanigans were a first for me. I'm sure people must play sex games all the time, although nobody I know has ever told me about them if they do.

That's not as strange as it sounds. My friends, family, casual acquaintances, and even complete strangers off the street have confided in me all my life. It used to stump me as to why people voluntarily tell me their personal business and deep, dark secrets. They get no prompting or encouragement from my end. I have determined it's because humans are typically contrary creatures by nature. Plus, I can keep a secret; a trait I sometimes bitterly regret. As to why complete strangers confide in me, your guess is as good as mine. I chock that one up to another mystery of the universe like black holes and dark energy.

Personally, I try very hard to keep my private life private. I rarely share specifics with anyone about my love life. Still, it doesn't stop my friends and neighbors from laying on me every agonizing detail of their own sexcapades.

I'm here to tell you it's also a myth that chicks talk about their adventures in lovemaking more than guys. When a man talks about not liking to discuss 'feelings' he sure doesn't mean in regards to how his wanger felt last Saturday night when out with so-and-so. My male friends are most gruesomely detailed oriented. Like it or not, I'd definitely have heard if any friends of mine were up to anything remotely interesting and kinky.

This morning, He-Who-Dominates has me in a similar hold he used last night to restrain me. His one arm is draped over my hips on top of the blankets with his hand resting against my stomach. His other arm is under my pillow and across my chest. Even asleep, Luke's large hand is greedily trying to cup both my breasts at once. I wasn't teasing when I said earlier this man is seriously infatuated with my bosom. I know, I know-- it's difficult, but I try to tolerate his fascination. However, I'm not sure if I like waking up this way. Not that Luke's embrace is too tight, but rather I'm not used to sleeping with any man and then waking up in his arms.

Luke is still sleeping deeply. I experimentally wriggle my butt and push a little back against him. He murmured something unintelligible and kissed my neck. His hand caressed up the curving indentation from my hip to my waist before he relaxed back into sleep.

'Huh, that was kind of interesting.'

I feel languorous and feminine, cozily surrounded by warm, hard muscles and soft, tickling hairiness. His knee is inserted between my thighs and my derrière is nestled tightly against him. How do people get out of bed and accomplish anything if this is how they wake up every morning? It makes me want to lazily stay in bed and do dirty, fun things-- not get up and get busy doing my boring chores.

Even his steady breathing near my ear is not too irritating. Instead, the rhythmic sound lulls me. My mind wanders to contemplating how I came to have Luke still in my bed after playing "Who's on Top?" last night.

Along with it being the first time I've acted out one of my sexual fantasies, allowing a man to stay overnight was also new territory for me. Don't get me wrong, I'm not being ingenuous here. I have gone out with quite a few men over the course of my twenties, but I don't do sleepovers. I kid you not; there have been no pajama parties with the men I've dated since I was nineteen.

I have an ironclad rule about sending a man on his way, or skipping out myself, when the date is over. Does anybody really like the inconvenient awkwardness of waking up together the next day with morning breath and bed hair? I sure don't. I schedule a date for an evening, not my whole, cotton pickin' weekend.

As I lay in bed with morning breath and bed hair, being a woman of sound mind who can rationalize her behavior with the best of them, I logically justified my unique transgression of allowing Luke to stay the night. It was a true statement our night practically began this morning. Then there was the tiny detail of my utter exhaustion. I guess experiencing the second best sex I've ever had in my life caused me to pass out in satiated bliss. I forgot my sleepover rule and I forgot to boot Luke out.

My all encompassing rule number one where men are concerned is quite simple and easy to remember; never forget my rules.

Even thinking of Luke brings on a sleepy smile. I admit I'm in lustful la-la land over this dude. After last night, there wasn't an iota of doubt in my mind Luke really sends me.

This doesn't change the fact my rules have evolved over time and are now cast in stone. They are based on first-hand knowledge from my experiences with the most dangerous predator known to prowl the planet; men. I live by these rules for good reasons. I like to be free to pursue the goals I've laid out for my life and not get bogged down with relationship issues. Following the rules helps me avoid a lot of problematic situations

A Date with Fate

where men were concerned. Not following my own rules allow males to have the opening into my life they are genetically predisposed to pursue, and it creates big, fat messes.

Let's face it, stereotypically men are hunters and women their prey. I have no desire to be bagged this week's trophy kill by confusing the excitement of this elemental chase with the female equivalent of romanticized "in love". I don't need to pretty it up with a pink bow.

I thrill at the chase, and for a select few hunters, throw myself in for the kill. By faithfully following my simple rule number one, I have lived to walk away, unscathed and intact, from the exhilaration of the hunt for the last decade.

Since I always manage somehow to be honest with myself, in spite of myself, my quiet introspection quickly brought me to a couple of conclusions. The first; I could try and justify it all I wanted, but I have been breaking my rules for Luke since the day I met him. The second; I was going to stop breaking my rules for Luke right this minute. I liked wanting all sorts of different men in my life for all sorts of different reasons, but actually needing one, main man in my life? Not so cool.

I officially was introduced to Luke two months ago at my younger brother's place. My brother, Reggie, gives new meaning to the word friendly and his house is like Grand Central Station at quitting time. It's a joke in our family that if you want to run into anyone from Northfield stop over at Reg's house, located twenty minutes outside of town, and you will.

Reg lives on a sweet piece of property overlooking Lake Roberds. It's outside of a small town called Faribault, located south ten miles down the road from Northfield. The house that came with the lake property is a two-story old relic that defies style classification and needs massive amounts of TLC. He decided not to bulldoze citing the old house has "good bones", and he has been busy renovating since last spring.

Reggie owns his own contracting company and has many friends in the different trades. Whenever I come to visit there is usually a guy or two helping him work on the latest project. It gives me warm fuzzies watching this anachronism of the bartering system in action. Keeping a fridge stocked with good beer and occasionally returning the favor seems to be all the payment these men require of each other. I won't even get started on the assortment of women 'just dropping by to help', and I don't mean my sisters or other female relatives. My brother's a very popular guy.

Since I am always an exemplary role model of a sister, I drive over to Reggie's once in awhile on a weekend day with sustenance. I like to check out the ongoing progress on the house. Reg and I have always been close, but with both of us being so busy lately we don't hang out as much. It was easy and convenient to do something together before he moved out from my apartment to the lake this past summer. Now it takes planning.

Sometimes, I'll pitch-in and work around his place. Having no prior experience, I'm not exactly DIY construction worker material. Honestly, I suck real bad. My little brother is being surprisingly cool with my tool-challenged ineptitude. He's an awesome teacher, and so are most of his friends. I never thought in a million years I'd get pumped being taught my latest handyman lesson, but I am really getting into it.

It makes me proud that my baby brother no longer screams like a woman and ducks when I have the nail gun in my hand. It's true what they say about men; they have no tolerance for a little pain. It was only the one time, and the nail I pulled out of Reggie's thigh was a short, tiny thing--a finishing nail is what I believe he shrieked when correcting me. Yes, okay, he did bleed. But, sweet Jesus, the way he carried on you would think I punctured his femoral artery instead of the back of his leg. It was totally unfair to blame me for the resulting infection.

I met Luke Drake on the third Saturday back in September. I'd woken up early to an idyllic, late summer Minnesota day. I hadn't seen my brother for over a week, so I decided to whip up some banana bread to bring over to his house. My plan was to soak up some sunshine for an hour on Reg's new deck overlooking the water. I had plans later with a man I'd met a couple weeks back in the store. We were going to the Renaissance Festival in Shakopee. He was a very nice guy, but you can't force the love. I knew after our first date it was friends-only on my part. Still, he was fun and a girl could always stand another friend.

After taking care of some business down in the bookstore, I arrived at the lake house around eleven in the morning. Turning my aging Jeep 4x4 into Reggie's graveled parking area, I saw a black and white SUV was pulling out. Driving was Jack Banner, Chief of Police in Northfield.

My parents died together in an airplane crash when I was six. My dad had been a cop in St. Paul. Jack was my dad's young, rookie partner and good friend. My folks were flying home from Jack's Canadian border cabin in a small plane when the engine malfunctioned and they crashed. I don't know if Jack felt some misguided guilt about orphaning my siblings and me, or if he was simply a glutton for punishment, but he's been a fixture in our lives ever since. I consider him part of the family and torment him accordingly.

He slowed alongside my Jeep. I smiled a greeting through our open windows.

"Morning, She-Devil." Jack takes great pleasure in calling me defamatory names. Although, She-Devil was pretty mild compared to some doozies he's thought up over the years.

He calls me these names as a result of my actions from when I was only six. After we'd heard the news of our parent's death, Jack found me off crying in a corner by my lonesome. He attempted to pull me onto his

A Date with Fate

lap to comfort me. I took a hunk out of his shoulder with my bite and told him to "keep his stinking hands to himself or I'd report him to my school principal".

I was a second-grader then, and fresh from learning all about sexual harassment—I knew my rights as a woman.

In my teens, and whenever he was around, dear Jack made a habit of trying to embarrass me in front of boys while intimidating them into behaving. He would take my date aside. First, he'd warn them not to even think of messing with me. Then he'd tell the boy I may look like an angel, but inside I was feral with a bite much worse than my bark. He had the scar and rabies shot to prove it.

I don't think Jack ever quite got this didn't scare off the boys, but made me more fascinating. Maybe it was fascinatingly scary. My dates were never one hundred percent sure why I bit Jack, a cop and twenty years older, in the first place. Being a laconic man, he never mentioned that part. If they asked me, I'd shrug and smile mysteriously.

"Well, good morning to you, Chief. Do you have to go and protect the unsuspecting public, or can I tempt you with some yummy banana bread?"

At forty-nine, Jack is a fit and handsome man in a tough and craggy way. To be fair, he has always been tough and craggy, so he hasn't changed much over the years. His white blonde hair is touched with a little silver now, his skin is ruddier and lined from years spent fishing on lakes in the sun and wind, but his deep-set, gray eyes are sharp as ever. They miss little.

Jack is a macho man. He's the real deal, not a poser like many men who act tough. Jack's no swaggering dude compensating for insecurities or serious woman-bashing issues. Chief Jack likes women. He's just clueless understanding anything about us.

Jack's got that cop stare down. The one that makes most people nervous and want to confess to crimes they hadn't even thought of committing. Add that to the physique of a powerful bull in his prime, speaking only when he has something to say, and wearing a default facial expression so flat it makes a shark look animated, and you have one very tough hombre. Anyone with half a brain would think twice before crossing him.

Happily, I am immune to all that. I'm not sure if that means I have more or less than half a brain, but Jack's always been a pussycat in my eyes.

"I'm heading into the office. Paperwork." His eyes were shaded by the clichéd mirrored aviators all cops seemed to wear. He made a curt motion with his left hand draped over the steering wheel. "Gimme some to go."

I tilted my head to the side and waited

"What?" he barked, after the silence dragged on.

"Please Anabel, sweetest of all women and best baker on earth. Isn't that what you were about to add?"

This earned a fleeting tightening of the lips. For Jack, that was tantamount to a belly laugh. "Damn, are you going to make me lie for food, Junior?"

I tapped my forehead. "Oh, that's right. You are getting up there in age, aren't you? I don't want you lying when you're so close to meeting your maker."

Jack gave me "the look". I chuckled and reached for a foiled wrapped loaf of bread from my wicker basket. I nodded to him, tossing the bread between our trucks. Reflexes lightening fast, Jack snatched it out of the air, cradling the loaf as gingerly as an infant in his ham-sized hand.

He nodded back and took his foot off his break. "You just made an old man very happy."

I am very conscious of my civic duty. I consider it part of my voluntary contribution to community service hours to give the bachelor Chief Jack a hard time.

"Oh dear, Jack, I'm truly sorry." Sad lips, I was mournful. "From some of the…er…females I've seen you with over time, I suspected it didn't take too much to make you happy. Seriously though, a little loaf of my bread is all it takes?"

Jack braked abruptly. He stabbed a finger at me. "Listen, Miss Thing, you couldn't handle what it takes to make a man like me happy. Not after all those pansy-assed boys you've had jumping through your hoops over the years." Seeing my grin, he shook his head and bit off something about smart-mouthed women under his breath. "See you tomorrow night."

This wasn't really a question, but I saluted sharply. It was a standing invitation that I hosted a family dinner on Sunday evenings at my place. It was my way of atoning for doing my best to avoid most of them the rest of the week

I caught the quirk of his lips again before he drove off down the bumpy driveway to the main, black top road that circled Lake Roberds.

There were three other vehicles parked at my brother's that day I met Luke. One was my brother's red truck with the white "Axelrod Contracting" logo on the door. I made a sour face at the next car; I knew who drove the light blue Honda Civic with the vanity plates. I didn't have a clue who owned the third vehicle. I let out an appreciative whistle. The owner may be unknown, but I definitely recognized the brand spanking, Mack Daddy of a new truck.

I love my jeep, Lady Liberty, but she's getting up there. I'd been circling around this identical truck for a couple of weeks now at the Apple Ford dealership. I hadn't yet decided if I was going to move in for the kill.

A Date with Fate

I was deeply in want, but trying to talk myself out of crippling truck payments. Not to mention the very real possibility of crippling myself trying to get up into the front seat. I would need to carry a stool for entry assistance into a truck this size, especially after a meal and a couple of glasses of wine made me weak.

Picking my way over the graveled area towards the house brought me closer to the truck. I adjusted the heavy basket on my hip that contained the loaves of banana bread, a pink bakery bag of cookies, and bottles of OJ and chocolate milk. A gust of warm wind off the lake swirled my dress around my thighs when I stopped to admire the truck more closely.

I held my sundress down while I toured around the vehicle. It was a 2012 Ford F-150 Harley-Davidson. The color was called Tuxedo Black. I had bonded so completely with this beauty in the last two weeks; I was half-tempted to prostrate myself on its hood to get some sun, instead of on my brother's deck.

"Very pretty. Are you Little Red Riding Hood coming to visit?"

I started at the voice, unaware I was being watched. Then I chuckled at the comparison. I guess with a stretch I could be said to resemble Ms. Hood. I carried a basketful of food, my long, blonde hair was held off my face with a black headband, and I was wearing a scarlet red dress.

I glanced in the direction of the low voice, but couldn't see him. "Let me guess--Grandma?"

The shadows were deep on the old-fashioned porch. Two, towering Red Oaks majestically spread their canopy of leafy branches over the front yard and house. I heard a low laugh. I expected to see a friend of my brother's, but a stranger walked off the porch. He came down the front steps toward me. He was carrying a mug full of steaming something.

I put a hand to my heart and breathed, "Oh no! It's the big, bad wolf!"

He flashed a grin, bright white against his tanned face. I wasn't actually kidding; he really did look like a badass wolf.

Even before I got a proper look at him, something about the confident way he carried himself made me perk right up and pay closer attention. I noticed his eyes were slowly, continuously scanning the yard around us as he walked. I peered around curiously to see what had him so vigilant.

It looked like Reggie's front yard to me. Lady Liberty's engine still ticked as she settled down. The birds were busily chirping. Crisp, autumn leaves were rustling in the trees from the breeze. Otherwise, aside from myself, there were no terrorists or snipers I could see. All was quiet on the Lake Roberd's front.

The aroma of his coffee wafted my way and had me salivating. At least, I think it was the coffee. Watching him walk, I was experiencing a strange phenomenon. Everything appeared sharper, brighter, and vividly more in focus around me. This all ready perfect day seemed to suddenly have infinite possibilities.

When he was a few steps nearer, our eyes clashed over his coffee cup. I was jarred to my toes at the impact. I held his intense stare for a beat before disengaging and looking away. I found I had to exert willpower to glance away with a semblance of composure. I was blown away by the insane desire to lean against his chest and stare up dreamily up into his eyes. This was so not like me. I don't lean, much less do dreamy.

Not looking directly at him, I still felt the touch everywhere his eyes skimmed over me. He didn't linger too long on any obvious points, but I was thoroughly, expertly checked out from the top of my black headband down to my black, seriously cute, wedge-heeled sandals.

When not looking into his eyes, my mind started functioning properly. My memory clicked into place and I mentally snapped my fingers.

'Holy Hannah!'

I knew why he looked familiar. I had glimpsed this man once before when he came into my store last spring. I think it was in April.

I was working alone that afternoon. I was sitting on a stool at the long check-out counter reading some report or another.

I had been feeling nervous flutters in my stomach for the last half hour. I was idly wondering if it was the caffeine from the espresso shot in my latte, or if I had forgotten something I had to be excited about that day.

The string of bells on the shop's door jingled and jangled. I had glanced up to see this man walk in. The sex kitten voice in my head stretched awake from her catnap and purred, *'Ah, here's the explanation for the butterflies.'*

Sounds weird I know, but this happens to me frequently enough that I've learned to listen to the different voices talking to me in my head. I end up regretting not paying attention if I don't. Besides, I look forward to the sex kitten voice. That voice is welcomed with open arms when compared to the mean mommy voice reminding me to be a responsible grown-up and do some grunt work.

The man's gaze had fixed on me. I was twenty feet away, but immediately reacted to the intensity of his look. I had no clue why, but being the focus of his concentration held me electrified on my stool like a switch had been turned on. It was horrible, bizarre, and uncomfortably exciting.

This tough-looking man staring at me across my store was certainly no male model. I hadn't heard him speak, and knew nothing about him. I know men, I really like men, and men do not make me lose

A Date with Fate

my cool and get all electrified and turned on for no reason other than a mere glance.

I've discovered a few facts about myself over the years. I don't have personal preferences what a man must look like before I will go out with him. I've come to accept the truth (by being bored to death) that often fabulous-looking men have more hair than wit. They can make me plot an early escape from a date. Conversely, an average Joe with a clever sense of humor can become irresistibly attractive upon getting to know him better.

Sure, some men are hot and can appeal right away. And some women will do a one-nighter with a man they have just met. A drive-by has never been my thing.

No, it takes a whole lot more than the excruciatingly boring pick-up scenario of a player to get me interested in getting naked. The routine of first staring at me across the room, then ignoring me, then finally talking to me by telling me a corny joke or giving a compliment, is so irritatingly lacking. I think a predator out only to get laid is such a tired cliché. I waste no time telling them not to waste their time on me. The actual sex with the drive-by man has to be described as underwhelming at best. Or so I've been repeatedly told in confidence from far too many women.

Nope, I need a dude to have real brains and lots of personality to interest me in even a first date, much less get me aroused to start with the stripping. I know this makes me sound like I think I'm all that. I cannot deny I've been told I'm conceited, arrogant, and definitely too picky--by both sexes. I've been called cold, cruel, and frigid, although never all three at once.

These kinds of comments make me smile and shake my head.

Here's the deal; arrogant me simply can't imagine deserving anything less then what I want. Why it's considered conceited because I have some self respect and standards is beyond me. The picky part; I can't help guys with brains and a personality aren't plentiful. I would love to find men so described under every stone and rock. I'm sure were that the case, women would leave none unturned across the globe. If any man thinks I am frigid or cold; they are one hundred and fifty percent accurate. If speaking up, saying no, and knowing your own mind is perceived as cruel by those on the other end of the stick, I'm okay with being cruel.

Except for one awful aberration in my late teens, I have been unapologetically playing the field, staying single, and loving it. Guys chase as they will, but never catch me for long. I didn't want to be caught then, and I don't want to be caught now.

My attitude goes as far back as pre-school days where my first devotee, Bucky Mitchell, would throw a fit and not go to school unless I picked him up on my way. It's my belief I skipped kindergarten and went directly to first grade just to avoid his possessiveness, and not because I could read and write like NanaBel claims.

So sitting in my store last April while minding my business, you can bet your bottom dollar I was confoundedly stunned to find myself aroused from receiving a mere glance sent in my direction by this man, a total stranger. My female parts didn't give a rip if the man could add two plus two, spell the word dog, or even get a basic knock-knock joke.

Was I experiencing my first attack of extreme pheromones I'd read so much about over the years? Whatever it was, it felt revoltingly exhilarating.

Heating up, and then fanning my cheeks in metamorphic agitation, I watched the man reach into his jacket pocket and check his cell. He quickly glanced back up and looked directly at me. He appeared to hesitate, but then turned around abruptly and left the book shop.

I let out a whoosh of a breath I didn't know I had been holding. I felt like I'd just dodged a bullet. If the chimes hadn't banged loudly against the glass of the door behind him, I might have believed he had been an apparition of crazy, lustful thinking on a rainy, spring day.

If they had witnessed my girly reaction to this stranger, anybody close to me could not be blamed one bit for serving me up a heaping plate of crow. Somehow, it slipped my mind and I never mentioned it to anyone back then.

Then, there I was in Reggie's yard a few months later in September. That same man I determinedly forgot was now only two feet away. I was on the fence about seeing him once again because I like my life uncomplicated. I wasn't sure if I was ecstatic or depressed to be experiencing the same horribly stunned reactions as before.

One thing I do know; turnabout is fair play. It was only natural I'd take a moment to swiftly check out the man of my pheromone-induced, nightmare of a daydream.

From the angle I was standing, I didn't even have to squint to see the left hand holding his coffee mug. There was no wedding ring or white skin line. Not that an absence of a ring proved he wasn't married. Men willing to cheat were obviously sneaky by definition and married men were the best at it, or the worst, depending on your opinion of cheaters. Married men are absolutely off limits to me, no exceptions.

I'd guess him at early to mid-thirties. His better-be-single eyes were bottle green under black, slightly arched brows. His wide mouth and full lower lip were surprisingly sensual against the harsh lines of his face. My next thought was his eyes and lips were the only pretty things about him. Everything else shouted hard-bodied, aggressive male. Exactly the kind of man I usually high-tailed it away from, as fast and far as my little legs could run.

A Date with Fate

He was dressed in a faded black T-shirt, paint-spackled jeans, and work boots. He didn't have an ounce of fat on him anywhere that I could see in my peripheral version. He glowed with strength and vitality. I would try not to hold that against him. The not an ounce of fat part, that is. The vitality was hotter than hell.

I exercise most days and watch what I eat, but there's no getting around the fact I'm more petite centerfold than runway model. From the tightly leashed energy emanating from his being, I bet my lean, broad shouldered, mystery man had to consume enormous amounts of calories to keep at a normal weight. Some people are born under a lucky star. I would eat my weight in chocolate éclairs every day if I had such a metabolism. Well, truthfully, it would be a split--fifty two pounds each--between chocolate éclairs and frosted sugar cookies.

He was bronzed a dark tan everywhere I could see in a way men seem to get when they spend a lot of time outdoors with their shirts off. His silky, thick hair was cut short to his head and mussed on top. It was deep black and shined brilliantly even in the leaf-filtered sunlight. He was lean cheeked with a high bridged, distinctively bold nose reminiscent of a swarthy Greek or Italian somewhere in his gene pool. Contributing to the badass look was black stubble covering the lower half of his face and strong, square chin. Dressed in work clothes and needing to shave, he still portrayed an aura of the sharp professional dressed down for the weekend, not a biker dude.

With his flexed arm holding his mug, I saw he had impressive pipes. Since we are objectifying here, I have to confess muscular arms absolutely do it for me. A tattoo or three could possibly send me over the edge.

This wasn't a man I'd call cute or handsome or a hottie. Fierce suited him with his air of coiled intensity and his dramatic, dark coloring. His likeness could be depicted in a mythology book when illustrating Mars, the Roman war-god.

Practice makes perfect. I am expert at keeping a poker face as these incredibly detailed impressions of the man streamed across my third eye mind. Inside, I was recoiling in disgust at my helpless fascination with everything about him.

I serenely continued admiring the most gorgeous of all trucks before finally breaking the hormonally charged silence and answering.

"Yes, it's very, very pretty. The paint job really rocks, and man, those are some sweet rims. I mean, what's not to love about a 6.2 liter V8?" I flashed him my change-my-light-bulb-pretty-please smile. "I know it's none of my business, but will you please tell me what you paid for it, down to the last penny?"

His green-eyed gaze was amused, if also warmly appraising. "Wow, impressive. So, you're a woman who knows her trucks. I think the wheels are particularly awesome, too." Pausing, he looked me in the eye. "And you're also right; it's none of your business what I paid for it."

His immediate, wide grin took the sting out of his blunt words. I flashed a sunny, sympathetic smile back in acknowledgement of his temporary rights to deny me.

'Ah, the dumb guy probably paid the dealer's "bottom price" anyway, and was too embarrassed to admit it.'

He took his time and blew across his hot coffee, did a test sip, and winced dramatically. He then focused on me, and again I felt the power of his stare hit me over the head.

'Whoa! Okay, this was some serious, force field level magnetism going on here.'

I had to practically physically brace myself not to be pulled into the tractor beam of his charisma. I wanted to beg him to go steady, or be my valentine, or take me to a homecoming dance somewhere—I was crushing like an innocent schoolgirl that hard, that fast. It was nauseating, confusing, mesmerizing, and not to be tolerated.

His black-lashed eyes were not only beautiful, but shined with a lively intelligence and, dare I pray, humor? I hoped this was true. Poor war-god, from the way I was reacting he'd need a very healthy sense of humor in his immediate future, and the smarts to understand what hit him.

After his studied pause—the pause I felt not the slightest need to rush to fill—he smiled slowly and continued, "But the pretty comment was about you."

I smiled a little sideways at him, but otherwise ignored his flirting for a moment. I sighed gustily. I put my whole body into it. I'm not too shabby at drama myself.

"Well, if that isn't a blasted shame."

War-god's eyes glinted, but didn't stray from my face during my full body sigh. "Oh yeah, what's a shame?"

"This is the exact truck I wanted to buy. I have been scoping it for the last two weeks. Now, you have it."

I gave the truck one last covetous glance, and then resignedly shrugged. I got a firm grip on the heavy basket handle and walked past him to the front porch stairs. He came after me and motioned to take the basket from my arm. He looked confused at my comment, but game.

"Here, wait a sec, let me carry that for you. I'm Luke Drake, by the way. Pardon me if I'm slow, but why is it a blasted shame if I have this truck?"

I was on the stair above him when I relinquished the basket with a smile at his good manners. I guesstimated he was about five-ten or eleven. My wedge heels and the extra stair height put us at eye level.

"Hi, I'm Anabel Axelrod." I automatically put out my right hand for a friendly shake, but Luke's were presently both occupied with the

A Date with Fate

mug of coffee and the basket. "Oh, I'm a little bummed right now. I'll never know what price I could have talked them down to at the dealership for this truck."

"Oh yeah, why's that?" Luke asked, somewhat distractedly. He was transferring the awkward basket over to his arm, preparing to politely shake my hand in return.

"Isn't it kind of creepy to go buy the same exact truck of a man I want to date?" I rushed on hopefully, "But maybe you don't think that would be too cutesy if we drove twin trucks?"

I saw when the meaning of my words hit home.

His eyes shot up to stare at me.

I smiled shyly and blinked.

My badass wolf burst out laughing.

My smile went huge.

I really love it when my instincts are spot on. I had hit the seldom seen, nearly extinct trifecta of manly muscles, intelligence, and humor.

Luke started to answer, but then the front screen door banged sharply. We both turned to look as my brother came out onto the porch.

Walking towards us, Reggie called, "Hey, if it isn't the most favorite of all my sisters! I thought I heard your Jeep." Eyeing the food, he rubbed his hands together. "So, what have you brought me?"

Reg gave me an affectionate, one-armed squeeze around the waist while checking out the basket on Luke's arm. He grabbed and opened the Northfield Bakery pink bag holding the chocolate chip cookies.

He took a deep whiff. "Either these smell almost edible or I'm hungrier than I thought."

I hadn't actually baked the cookies myself but based on general principle, I casually rubbed my cheek with my middle finger. It was a private gesture of affection for my brother. Luke glanced up from the basket just in time to catch me being sisterly.

Reggie chuckled at my blush. "Luke, meet my sister." He relieved Luke of the basket. "Junior, meet Luke Drake. Luke's my new neighbor down the road. He's inherited Ben Drake's farm." Reggie noticed my blank expression. "You know, Junior, the farm that has the toy John Deere combine mounted on the mailbox. Old Ben was your uncle, right Luke?"

"Great uncle." Luke absently answered my brother.

I wasn't listening much to Reggie, either. I ignored the questioning gleam in my brother's blue eyes as he looked from me to Luke. I also ignored his brief, knowing smirk shot my way before he waved to the screen door. "Let's head inside and go to the deck."

I went up the steps, feeling the searing intensity of Luke's gaze on my back with every step. "Thanks for the intro, but Luke and I have met." I flashed a mischievous glance at Luke over my shoulder. "He knows I want his…truck."

I didn't wait for the men, but walked ahead into the house to get supplies from the kitchen. I could hear the low rumble of Reggie's voice behind me on the porch stairs saying something that caused Luke to laugh out loud.

I rolled my eyes. He was probably being a traitor to the blood and warning Luke not to let me near his truck. I have a slight problem with curbs. One of the few side effects I live with as a result of poor vision in my left eye. That's my story and I am sticking to it.

I used the Omnipotent Sister trick and called back to him through the screen. "I heard that, Reg. Good thing you have three other 'most favorite' sisters who get their tushes out of bed and bake for you."

I snickered when the immediate response was, "Oh, peace out, Junior! You're so sensitive." I heard a low voiced, "Shit, she's got the hearing of a bat."

I passed through the sizeable living room set up with four sawhorses instead of furniture. The flooring was still at the plywood subfloor stage, but I observed it was screwed down in place since the last time I had stopped by.

There were two, ancient six panel doors laid across the sawhorses in the process of being stripped of their multi-layers of old paint. I wrinkled my nose at the noxious odor. That job I did not want to do. Thankfully, the doors and windows were wide open to let the breeze in and the toxic fumes out, but it was still a brain tumor waiting to happen.

In the spacious but outdated kitchen, I reached on pointed toes for a few of Reggie's endless supply of paper plates located up in an old cabinet. When that didn't work, I jumped up and down, boosting off the cracked Formica countertop to get leverage to reach far back into the overhead shelf.

I expertly bounced, jumped, boosted and stretched in one fluid motion. I almost managed to grip the plates.

Before my next attempt, I called out, "I'll get the napkins and plates, and then meet you guys on the deck. Do you need anything else out there, Reg?"

"He sent me to remind you to bring paper cups for the juice." Luke's quiet voice was right behind me. I whirled around in surprise. I could feel the counter's metal edge cool against the exposed, bare skin of my lower back.

He smiled slightly, his glance briefly lingering on my hands covering my racing heart over the V neckline of my halter top, sundress.

He leaned towards me.

I caught myself from puckering up just in time. Luke was only reaching beyond me into the cupboard. He placed a stack of paper plates onto the counter, and then politely stepped back. His expression remained blandly neutral, but I had seen the flare of momentary reaction passing over his face when I'd whirled around at his voice. I also saw the amusement that now glowed in his eyes.

Flustered, I automatically smiled my thanks back without a thought. I was too busy trying to figure out if I had been flashing him when expertly boosting since my sun dress was short and sassy. I usually only do that sort of thing by accident on purpose. He was definitely silent and tricky.

I wouldn't even let my mind dwell for a microsecond that I had been willing to kiss him without conscious thought. I breathed in deeply. I grabbed a firm hold of my usual sangfroid with both hands, exhaled, and settled into my normal cool.

Our smiles slowly faded. We stood a foot apart, unabashedly sizing each other up. I've never met a man before--that wasn't also a gross pervert--who made absolutely no bones he was taking his sweet time looking me up one side, and down the other. Weirder yet, I stood still and let him. Speaking of bare bones, I've never before told a man I was planning on dating him, either. Both were oddly exciting notions, even as I wondered what in the hell was happening to me.

Luke spoke first. "You are one scary sister."

I nodded. Not exactly what I expected to hear, but I'll accept any compliment thrown my way. "Why, thank you."

"I understand you hit curbs while driving." He said it as a serious statement, arms crossed at the chest and eyes narrowed.

I ducked my head and scuffed my foot, and then peeked up quickly at my interrogator. "Yes, but only the curbs on the left side. A mere nothing, I assure you. Anyone could do so, if they only covered their left eye and tried."

He kept a stoic face, but his eyes had that glint I was all ready coming to recognize. "Shooting the nail precisely into your brother's thigh? That had to take a cold, calculated aim. I believe there was the added bonus of an infection. Is that correct?"

I airily waved him off. "Yes, that's correct, but enough with the compliments. You'll make me blush."

He frowned severely down at me. "I'm to understand you bite, too?"

"Okay, that's it. I can only take so much sucking-up flattery." Laughing, I reached up and lightly shook his shoulder. "Please, snap out of it, I beg you!"

We grinned at each other for a couple of seconds.

I reluctantly remembered to drop my hand. The same hand that twitched to start smoothing across his broad shoulder.

Luke leaned forward and loosely bracketed me against the counter with an arm on either side. "Anabel, are you thinking what I am thinking?"

"It would be proof there is a god!" I answered fervently.

Faces inches apart, he quizzically cocked one black eyebrow at my happily enthusiastic answer.

'Oh, that move is no fair! Totally below the belt.'

I was enslaved with that diabolically arching eyebrow. He was so hot while looking all cool, calm, and yes, in control. Also, I couldn't cock just one eyebrow in question if my life depended on it. I had to settle for cocking my head to one side in question back at him.

A small smile hovering on his lips, Luke went on smoothly, "I'm thinking we need to go out on a date," he paused infinitesimally, "tonight."

"Oh." A little bit of a letdown in the originality department, but he made up for it in the urgency department. "I was thinking I want to have your children, but if you want to start with a date," I shrugged, "I'm up for that."

Luke gave a shout of laughter, but started shaking his head emphatically in denial when I continued speaking. "I can't accept for tonight, though." I shrugged lightly, again. "Sorry, but I have previous plans."

"Oh, no you don't. You can't do that to me. Now that we've established what we will be doing on our first date, I can't wait for another night." He stopped laughing and laser beamed me from those dark green eyes. "Seriously, cancel your plans and come out with me tonight."

I opened my mouth, firmly intending to answer with a resounding, "Seriously, dream on, buddy-boy."

Imagine my surprise when what came out instead was a breathless, "Okey-dokey."

I looked around in shock to see if it was really me who had said that peculiar answer. Luke didn't give confused me a chance to renege. He stood back and was all sharp teeth and smiles, radiating male satisfaction with closing the deal.

"Cool. Seven o'clock?"

After a pause, I grumpily replied, "I guess that's okay." I have a firm rule to never break existing plans with friends to be with a man, unless it was his funeral. I added a muttered, "Svengali."

Luke looked taken aback for a second. Then he grinned while again shaking his dark head in amusement, or maybe bemusement, I couldn't tell which. He probably couldn't, either.

He placed a few paper cups on top of the plates sitting on the counter.

He brushed my cheek with a knuckle. "So you know, my future plans include a large family." His glance traveled slowly down and stopped on my hips. He nodded. "Good. Your short and a little on the oldish side, but those look like sturdy, childbearing hips."

It was my turn to burst out laughing. "I'm so happy you like midgets and antiques. But, hmm, maybe I misjudged your brains. 'Sturdy'

A Date with Fate

is a word no woman ever wants to hear in association with any of her body parts."

I probably shouldn't set a precedent of cracking-up when teasingly insulted, but Luke was too funny and I don't have a PC bone in my body. After adding plastic utensils and napkins to the pile; I nudged him out of the way with my healthy hips.

Giving me a sly grin that brought his dimple into play, he stood aside with a slight head bow to allow me to pass.

I sashayed my loaded plates through my brother's dining area, working it with my swaying hips to get around the card table and chairs sprawled haphazardly in the path to the deck doors. I angled my left butt cheek up to open the lever door handle.

I looked to see if Luke was following. He wasn't. He was leaning against the kitchen doorway. His arms were folded and he was seemingly engrossed watching my childbearing hips in motion.

Straightening up, Luke shook his head decisively. "I stand by my choice of sturdy. Your hips are workhorses." I was smiling again as he started walking the opposite way; to the front door. He tossed back over his shoulder, "I'll pick you up at seven tonight, Anabel Axelrod of Bel's Books."

It took me a second to realize he was leaving. He had probably been on his way out when I arrived earlier. Then his words sunk in and cheered me right up. He recalled our almost meeting those months ago, as well.

When agreeing to go on a first date with a man, I always avoid being without a getaway car. I have gratefully escaped early from many brutally boring date nights with this sensible rule.

I thought of my day ahead and took a few steps back into the dining room. Luke was at the screen door in the living room, and had it opened.

"Let's make it eight. Oh, and I prefer to meet you, Luke. I may want to have your children, but I don't really know you, right? So where shall we meet?"

Luke gave another crack of laughter like I had said something hilarious. "Anabel, I'm picking you up. Eight is fine." Across the room, he gave me that appraising look again while his fist tapped out a quick, staccato beat on the wooden door frame. Brow creased, he said, "Listen, I'd really like it if you wore a dress tonight."

Seeing my surprised, wary look at his clothing specifications, a huge grin transformed his harsh face with boyish charm.

He snapped his fingers. "Oh yes, I almost forgot. Tiny, pink panties are optional."

It was extremely difficult, but except for a small moan of agony and squeezing my eyes so tightly shut I saw stars; I stifled my mortification knowing he *had* seen my bare ass within five minutes of meeting me. These weren't just tiny, pink panties I was wearing, but a butt-flossing thong.

I opened my eyes to frown very sternly at his smiling face. "Look, Luke, if I break my rule about being picked up can you promise not to dismember me on the first date or worse yet, bore me?"

Pushing the door open, Luke casually shrugged a shoulder. "I never make promises I can't keep. You may prove irritating."

I blinked in disbelief. By the time I recovered to retort, I was talking to the screen door. Stunned, I realized Luke really had left. After a moment of taking this in, I started laughing in rare enjoyment. This first date could prove very interesting indeed.

I went out on the front porch to the top of the stairs. He was almost at his truck. I called out, "You didn't even ask me where I live, Mr. Will-of-the-Wisp. You'd better show up!"

He opened the truck door and called back, "Somehow, I don't think finding you will be difficult." I could see his confident grin. "You'd better be ready when I get there."

I have to get in the last word; it's a failing and a gift. "Let it be on the record; I am very disappointed you have something against tiny, pink panties!"

War-god was laughing behind the light tint of his windshield when, with a final wave; he drove away in my shiny, new truck.

I stood on the porch staring unseeingly outside.

By my track record, I tend to go out with men who are fun and possess a sense of humor. They generally share the personality trait of being easygoing. Or to rephrase the great Chief Jack Banner, they are pansy-asses that jump through my hoops. They don't find my rules a problem and they don't try to control me.

If Luke's personality matched his persona; this was no docile, nice guy. I didn't see any voluntary hoop jumping in Luke's future. Control was his first name and probably his middle name, too.

It was puzzling I felt such an intense attraction to a man I had a sneaking suspicion fit none of my criteria. I snickered to myself; I probably fit none of his, either. I'm most definitely aware that most men thrive on the challenge of the hunt. Never before in my dating career have I skipped to the kill and offered myself up on a platter, complete with an apple in my mouth, like I did today.

I laughed out loud recalling the expression on his face. I cheerfully decided it would take more investigation, up close and personal, to unravel this mysterious behavior on my part. I highly doubted I'd prove too easy for war-god Luke, no matter what his thoughts may be right now.

I brightened a little at my next thought. Maybe Luke and I just needed to hit the sheets and I could get it out of my system. Although

A Date with Fate

honestly, I have never before felt such a sexual attraction for a man with no basis on anything but being in his presence for a few minutes. Even after I had a basis of knowing most men, I've never felt so…whatever the hell I am feeling. This was off the charts for me, but I wasn't too concerned.

You can never tell what life may bring. Anticipation of the unknown is half the fun of living. The other half is doing it. This stirring of interest for our first date was worth it, regardless of what happened down the road.

I had a hop in my step as I headed for the deck to grill my brother about his new neighbor. I also wanted to make sure my cousin Candy, of the light blue Honda Civic, was eating all the donated, and probably poisoned, bakery cookies. Not stuffing her face with my yummy banana bread.

Chapter III
"Son of a Preacher Man" by Sarah Connor

Saturday, 11/17/12
6:45 AM

In theory, I have the odd weekend free from work to enjoy my life. In practice, I pop in and out of the store frequently on these days off. It can hardly be avoided living as I do above my store. Or so I tell myself.

The life of a small business owner means there's always work to be done. I am fortunate to love what I do. I am lucky to be surrounded by an experienced, loyal staff that has become my second family. Working at the bookstore can be tons of fun.

I do have a life outside of Bel's Books; it just doesn't start until after store hours. I've developed some habits over the years that are hard to break. One of them is routinely working six or seven days a week. My family and friends know where they can find me most days from ten in the morning until eight at night.

Stella's opinion is that I'm a control freak and a workaholic. She supported her logic when pointing out I describe working seven days a week as only a habit, and not a bad one. She's encouraging me on the weekends to let go and let Stella. I have a feeling she's a wee bit right. I have been giving her more responsibility. I'm making a concerted effort to live a less vampish lifestyle by actually going out and having fun during daylight hours, not only later at night. Both ideas are a work in progress.

This Saturday morning, I silently slipped out of my warm bed and from Luke's warmer arms. It was harder than I liked to leave the bed. It was harder yet to do it quietly; my antique bed is a real springy squeaker. I did both, though, because I like my morning alone time. I have my rituals. I guard this time so zealously from friends and family, all but one don't remember I exist before ten in the morning.

My brain wakes up around the same time every morning regardless of the amount of sleep I have. Luke told me his brain was trained to sleep whenever and wherever he got the chance.

After our first date, and to explain his sudden and frequent absences, Luke told me in the vaguest terms about his current career. He's employed by a consulting firm based out of Chicago. The firm specializes in prevention security--whatever that is. I can only picture Liam Neeson beating up bad dudes all around Paris in the movie "Taken". If that's what

A Date with Fate

Luke does, I have never noticed any bloody knuckles or nasty wounds when he returns, so he must be good at preventing.

I do know his work involves travel and long hours. He is gone from town for varied lengths of time. Often, he's away for a few days, sometimes a week or more. I don't know who or what is being prevented and secured, or if it's a dangerous career. I do know I can't picture Luke placidly manning a desk without going nuts.

What Luke has told me about his recent past is also very sketchy on the details. He saw right away I was skeptical with his glossed over, surface descriptions. It was probably the raised eyebrows and scoffing noises that gave me away. He bluntly suggested I trust him in general about everything, and to specifically not ask questions about his job. The job part was non-negotiable.

Oh hello, I'm female and breathing. Of course this made me want to ask a million questions, but I honored his suggestion and haven't asked him a single one.

Generally, when a man I've known only a short time says the words 'trust me' with the implied message 'or else', it doesn't exactly inspire my confidence. It does inspire hilarity at the idea I could be manipulated by the inferred threat if I ask too many questions he'd break it off. These men think they are pulling a fast one. Typically, they are jerks hiding a girlfriend or wife. I've seen women fall for this line of BS. Most likely it's because this type of 'if you loved me you'd blindly trust me' men are pretty slick at romancing girls wanting desperately to believe in love, and to be loved.

I don't think I am delusional about Luke. I do trust Luke has legitimate reasons to be closemouthed about his professional life. He is not telling me to 'trust him' to have his evil way with me. I love letting Luke have his evil way with me. No, I believe he is in a profession where loose lips sink ships, and any knowledge can be dangerous to the unwary. I could easily see him killing someone if there was a good reason. Chances are I'd agree if I knew the reasons. Whatever his job entails, what I don't sense is a mindless, gun-for-hire mentality. Luke is no thug.

I am happy to give people their privacy, unless it doesn't coincide with my needs. So far, Luke's detailed career path wasn't on my need-to-know list.

That is trust for Luke in his career. Luke's a man. As programmed, he will try to take advantage of me not asking questions about his professional life, and carry that unquestioning trust over to his personal life. Most men balk at sharing their personal, innermost thoughts and feelings at the best of times. Telling a woman they're starting to get involved with to just 'trust them in general, no questions asked' was a nice move, if you could pull it off.

Like most rational people, I give my trust and respect as it is earned by actions to back it up. Like most rational women, I know better than to state any of the above to a man needing to be in control and keep his secrets.

Does it make me a nosy girl if I found any answers I need from other sources?

I don't think so, either.

It pays to be friends with the older generations in town. These elderly folks are an amazing and underutilized networking resource. They have everyone's bloodlines memorized. They recall family scuttlebutt going back thirty or forty years like it happened yesterday. I simply put the word out I was looking for someone who had been friends with Luke's deceased great uncle, Benjamin Drake.

The only drawback to this plan was getting these nice folks to stop telling me stories and quit talking once they'd started. I may not know exactly what Luke does on the job, but I had more scoop on his life history then a girl could ever want to know.

For example, growing up Luke had been Army mad and it was never doubted he'd have a military career. The various storytellers were all murky on which branch of the military Luke actually served. They all agreed, with a wink and a nod, he was definitely in some elite, everyone was kung-foo fighting, sharpshooting unit. According to his elderly cronies, it was a sad day for Uncle Bennie when his great nephew retired from the military. The culprit was an undisclosed injury Luke received that no longer allowed him to perform his ass-kicking duties.

Luke has actually told me a lot of these same stories of his life as our dating progressed over the last two months. I have to be careful to pretend surprise when hearing them a second time. I was nearly caught hurrying him up on one anecdote and beating him to the punch line. He had squinted and scrutinized me suspiciously after this faux pas, but I avoided detection with a failsafe diversion—I started talking about sex.

Luke speaks of any childhood memories fondly and easily. He is an only child, his growing up years took place without any angst or trauma, and he actually likes his parents. His dad is a pastor and his mom's an attorney in the Chicago area.

Any of his adult stories of the last ten years are still vague on specifics and glossed over on the details. It is true; his twenties were spent in the Army. He did opt out after an injury left him less than one hundred percent up to snuff. He alluded he was in a Special Forces unit. I have the impression he still uses those skills currently, but I've never asked a direct question of him towards further enlightenment. I think it's driving him nuts I don't seem interested in his 'special skills', but he started it.

The info important to me that was garnered from the village elders is that Luke doesn't have wives and kids tucked away in a compound in

A Date with Fate

Idaho, he did not torture small animals or set fires, and there are no known felonies. It doesn't hurt matters he turns me on like no man ever has before, and he hasn't demanded the exclusivity I'm not willing to give any guy at this point in my life.

I quietly left the bedroom, and my uninvited sleepover guest, to attend to my morning ablutions in the bathroom across the hall. Catching a glimpse of my matted, wild hair in the mirror, I burst out laughing.

'Yikes! Mental note to self; don't go to sleep with damp, tangled hair after being tossed around your bedroom.'

I twisted it up, tangles and all, and stuck in a clip. I went straight to the walk-in closet and threw on shorts, a sports bra, and running shoes.

I headed back out to the wide hallway on this side of my apartment and went left, towards the open stairs.

Before you reach the stairs to go down, and if you hang a left again, the hall widens into a foyer area. Along the left wall sits a large church pew painted white; a find at the Elko Flea Market this past Labor Day weekend. A massive, elaborately framed mirror is leaning propped against the opposite wall.

I moved on through a wide arch into the open living room. My apartment on this side is designed shotgun-style. The living room opens into the dining room, which opens into the kitchen. The kitchen leads into a back hall with a laundry room. There's a back door to a balcony off this end of the apartment. This whole space runs the length of my apartment from front to back. It's parallel to the bedrooms on the other side of the middle wall dividing the second floor in two.

Once I did my routine of opening the white shutters covering the tall windows, these three main rooms were about one hundred by forty feet of airy, light-filled space. Loft-like, the tall ceiling and open duct work was painted a soft, chocolate brown.

This apartment is my Shangri-la, my bastion of tranquility. I know it's probably silly and sentimental for a building to mean so much, but there is no place on earth I'd ultimately rather be.

Scattered with my treasures, the spacious rooms are decorated with an eclectic twist. There's a mix of valuable antiques, my flea market finds, a few modern pieces of furniture, mementos of my family life, and colorful, old Persian rugs covering the hardwood floors.

Standing at my kitchen island, I ate a handful of mixed nuts and dried fruits while downing a small glass of apple juice. I took a bottle of mineral water from the fridge and headed back the way I had come.

Eyes averted to avoid testosterone temptation; I passed my closed bedroom door. I continued down the hall to the farthest bedroom on the right.

I had converted this second largest of the apartment's original six bedrooms into an exercise room. I jumped onto my treadmill and pretended to enjoy jogging in place for the next forty-five minutes. I left the overhead TV off. Today seemed like an awesome woman singer day. I have hundreds of songs spanning four or five decades on my iPod guaranteed to get the blood pumping. I ran and sang my heart out until I was sweating like a piggy and feeling it in my legs.

I prefer to run outside, but with Luke still here I wasn't sure of the sleepover etiquette, so I'd decided to stick around. Besides, singing inside was way less embarrassing to my street cred.

Temple worshiping complete for now, I headed for the showers. I stripped off my sweaty clothes and stepped into the pounding waterfall. It felt amazingly soothing. I rotated by head and neck.

'Holy Moly, I was sore!'

I ached all over in places I didn't even know existed on my body. Not that I'm complaining, but I wasn't used to being chased, manhandled, and flipped around as part of foreplay. I felt myself relaxing as the steam and pummeling, hot water did its magic.

I took care of the labor-intensive process of shampooing and conditioning my tangled hair. I lathered my body with Spanish Gardenia shower gel, my most recent present from Stella to try out. As I did my routine of exfoliating, shaving, and washing, I thought objectively about the previous night's fun and games.

Sex can potentially be amazing under any circumstances. For me, the fantasy Luke and I played out beforehand raised the eroticism, physical and mental, to a whole new level of excitement and intensity. I was definitely budging to the head of the line to sign up for more play dates.

I decided I relished every minute of being dominated Luke Drake-style, even when I fought it the hardest. I rubbed the tender area on my poor skull where I could still feel the divots from Luke's front teeth.

I grinned ruefully. *'Well, maybe not when I fought it the hardest.'*

Role-playing as an adult is reminiscent of putting on a play like when we were kids, minus the actual sex parts, of course. As a young girl, I remember how thrilling it had been when the neighborhood boys would participate willingly in our little productions. Often in the lead girl role, it was the difference of shyly kissing a real, live boy or having to lip smack against the back of one of my sister's hands in the name of theater.

The thrill has not lost any of its shine to have a real, live man participate with enthusiastic willingness in our very own private theatrical production. Kink is way cool.

One of the reasons I have never acted on any of my sexual fantasies in the past was it requires a level of trust I am not willing to give a man without some basis in reality. Since I don't really do relationships, allowing a guy I don't know very well to have access to my home and control over my body would be incredibly stupid. Having no idea if he would physically harm me, or give me a STD, is not my idea of a sexual

A Date with Fate

thrill. Sounds more like a nightmare on Division Street to me. I am not that kind of adrenaline junkie, nor do I have a death wish.

Luke's been out of town working longer stretches than the norm lately. We've gotten together maybe five or six times in the last two months. This doesn't sound like many dates, but when he's around and I can get away, our dates often start in the morning and last until very late.

Luke also calls me several times a week when he's gone. He has a pattern of definitely calling on Friday nights if he won't be around on the weekend. I've always despised talking on the phone. Now I have epically long conversations that would rival a teenager. I'm surprised how intriguing it's been getting to know a man this way. I feel a connection to Luke on a different level because of these marathon phone sessions.

The only hint I had that Luke may surprise me with a live performance of my very own sexual fantasy was a conversation that took place on a date about three weeks ago--at the end of October.

The date had started with spending a Saturday together in Minneapolis. Luke doesn't know the city very well. I suggested we do some outdoor exploring because it was gorgeous out. I cannot tell a lie, I was a tad hung over from the previous night at Rueb's, a local bar, and almost cancelled. But it felt good that Saturday to get outside in the fresh air and clear up my slight hangover.

First, we biked across town along the creek on Minnehaha Parkway. We worked up an appetite and had a huge breakfast for lunch in Uptown at French Meadow Café. I'm a sucker for their Eggs Benedict, plus we split one of their enormously delicious cinnamon rolls. We later walked it off around the scenic, nine mile circuit of Lake of the Isles, Calhoun, and Harriet. The two levels of lake paths were busy with bikers, joggers, and walkers outside with the same idea to embrace the sunshine.

In Minnesota, everyone takes advantage of beautiful, fall days like a bunch of paranoid hoarders. We all know what's lurking around the corner to descend on us at any given moment. It's not unheard of for the temp to be fifty one day with a blizzard the next.

Speaking of hoarders, while we walked, I was munching on chocolate-dipped macaroons from a bag that had magically appeared in my hand upon leaving French Meadow. I noticed that no matter how much we were laughing and talking, Luke always kept an eye out on our immediate environs. He truly has a special talent for vigilance. I never felt like I had less than his total attention, but he also managed to admire the awe-inspiring architecture of historic homes surrounding the lakes, watch the people around us, watch me, and watch the ground where we walked.

Turns out this observation knack of his was a good thing for me. Luke steered me over an ankle-twisting pothole in the path, and around a deep puddle I would have gone swimming through. I was oblivious to these dangers to my person. I was too busy waxing on enthusiastically about a recent book I'd read and loved. He later caught me mid-air when I took a swan dive over an exposed tree root. The story he'd been telling had me laughing so much, I hadn't been paying a bit of attention to the path under my feet. That one would have really hurt, so I appreciated his save.

This would all be a mite embarrassing were I the type to actually care about such things as my own dignity and public humiliation. It was odd to receive a deep kiss for being an oblivious klutz, but I grinned and bore the punishment. I gave in gracefully to Luke's vehement insistence he hold my hand to keep me alive.

Our daytime date was a great time. We spent hours marveling at how smart we were on almost every subject under the sun—when we weren't heatedly debating about the other's idiotically wrong viewpoint. The drive home down 35W was quieter. It was laced with long looks in anticipation of what we'd be doing later when we were alone inside my apartment.

In the dusky, late afternoon light, we relaxed together. Luke was a shadowed outline of a man sprawled at the end of my comfy, leather sofa. I was idly mulling over if I should invite him to come with me to the Halloween costume bash I was invited to later that night. I was envisioning him in his Army uniform; Major Anthony "Tony" Nelson to my "I Dream of Jeannie" genie. Who cares if he wasn't Air Force, or a major? I'm not picky; a man in uniform is hot.

Luke reached over and started playing with my hand, running his thumb over my knuckles and between my fingers.

Apropos of nothing, in a voice as smooth as the velvet pillow I was leaning my cheek against, he spoke. "Tell me your secret fantasy, Anabel."

'Holy...so much for being relaxed!' After a moment, I remembered to snap closed my hanging jaw. Luke didn't chatter away in idle conversation to hear himself speak, so I knew immediately he was totally serious. His face was smoothly composed and gave away nothing of what he was thinking. Just like that, easy as you please, he asked me to tell him something I have never divulged to another living soul.

I was confused, too. First off, did he mean most people have only one secret fantasy? Because I knew immediately what my number one secret fantasies was out of about fifteen fantasies. Secondly, did this mean he was into kinky sex stuff to ask me this after dating for only a couple of months, and those dates being spread out? Was he going to get progressively weirder on me? Or, was I the weird one since I found myself really tempted to answer him? Thirdly, did he ask all the women he dated this question, or did he sense something about me that made him bring this up? Fourthly, oh forget it; I could keep up this way forever on this titillating subject.

A Date with Fate

I crawled closer to Luke. My free hand was curled around his ear so I could whisper my number one secret fantasy. I wasn't being inordinately shy. Not completely. I like to use any excuse to whisper near his ear, or kiss and suck lightly on his neck. It drives Luke crazy.

Poised to speak, I hesitated. I thought a second if I had the nerve to tell him.

Then I thought another few seconds about why I almost trusted Luke. I'd only known him a short time.

Then I thought a couple seconds more if I liked the idea of almost trusting him. That was a no-brainer.

I sat back on my heels. I released his hand. I folded my arms over my chest. I realized my nipples were standing at attention from him only asking me this question. I blew out my breath in frustration. This was not such an easy question to answer, even if my breasts disagreed.

'What to do, what to do?'

I rested my head on the back of the sofa, distractedly running both hands through my hair on either side of my head. I looked up at the ceiling for the answer.

I reasoned my dilemma out in my head. I use my hands a lot when reasoning things out in my head. Sometimes, I even hum and mumble under my breath the words that go flying through my brain like a ticker tape at the stock exchange. This helps me organize and make decisions, never mind it makes me look insane.

The left hand: Okay, on this hand I have Luke. A man I cannot deny I am totally sexually smitten with--even if I wanted to. Why? Because Luke all ready knows. Oh yes, Miss Blabbermouth here told him within five minutes into our first date. Yep, that's how aloof and hard-to-get I play. For the tenth time, I glumly reassured myself there were extenuating circumstances why I told Luke. Anyone hearing the story of our first date would agree I had grounds to react as I did. No, I was more disgruntled about how much I looked forward to being with him, no matter what we were doing. That rule-breaking concept alone was technically reason enough to never see him again, much less confess my sex fantasies.

The right hand: On this hand, I have Luke sitting here right next to me wanting to know my secret fantasy. A man I find interesting, a man who attracts me tremendously. I was relatively sure he was not a Dexter; either that or I hadn't proved too boring, yet. He has been kind enough to prove he's healthy by showing me the latest medical report after a routine testing through his secret job. The reasons of death by dismemberment or disease need not stop me. Telling him my number one fantasy could be very fun indeed.

Still indecisive, I worried my bottom lip and mulled it over.

It's not like I don't know myself. Any problems or issues I have, I know why I have them. Trust does not come easy. Was sharing a fantasy something I wanted to do? If I did want to share, was I going to be honest and tell Luke my number one fantasy? Or was I going to be a namby-pamby baby and share a white bread fantasy to get off the hook--like he is a peg leg Pirate and I'm a tied-up Princess.

After that brief pep talk with myself, I made my decision.

I gave a nod of thanks to the team of voices huddled in my head and clapped my hands. Then I turned to Luke.

His forgotten beer was arrested halfway to his parted lips.

Even in the dim lighting, I could see he was watching me with fascinated interest. I couldn't quite meet his searching eyes; I guess I was a little shyer about this subject than I realized. Also, I didn't want to see any calm, experienced amusement in his expression, or I'd smack him and lose my nerve.

I spoke in a rush before any of the above could happen. "Okay Luke, my top sexual fantasy is I want to be secretly nominated."

'WAIT! What in the hell did I just say? That came out all wrong!'

It also came out louder than I intended. In my agitation, I forgot to whisper my answer in his ear. In the stillness of the apartment, I swear the word 'nominated' bounced off the walls and was still echoing like we were in the Grand Canyon.

Over my own incredulity, I had no trouble seeing Mr. Kinky regarding me with surprised incomprehension now added to the fascinated interest. And the one, arched eyebrow I love so much.

I moaned and put a hand to my forehead. I think I felt a headache lurking.

I closed my eyes and hurriedly corrected myself. "I meant to say my SECRET fantasy is I want to be DOMinated." Even in my embarrassment, I remembered my manners. "Please."

This brought to mind another point to clarify. I rushed on while holding up my hand like a traffic cop. "This is not to be confused with actual rape—that's violence and I am not, I repeat, not into violence. Or pain. Or nipple clamps, or ping-pong balls in my mouth." I had recently seen the old movie "Pulp Fiction" for the first time. Talk about strange, yet disturbingly funny. "No drugs. Don't get any ideas about E, or anything crazy like that, okay? And needles?" I cringed and shuddered. "You come near me with a needle and I'll kill you. Absolutely no needles--no way, no how..." my voice trailed off as I finally met Luke's gleaming eyes. He was sitting perfectly still, and staring at me as if transfixed.

I then had the most alarming, lowering thought. Moaning again, I covered my mouth and felt my eyes widening in horror.

What if I had misunderstood what he meant by secret fantasy? What if he meant something normal like which wife on "The Housewives of Beverly Hills" I would most enjoy torturing slowly before delivering a death blow? Or how many castles I'd buy if I won the lottery? What if he

A Date with Fate

didn't mean anything sexual at all? What if he now thought I was a creeper, pervert girl that wanted to wear a spiked dog collar and be hung from my foyer chandelier?

In the dead silence of my living room you could hear the proverbial pin drop.

I couldn't stand the suspense. I squared my shoulders, dropped my hands down from over my mouth, and glared at the silent man staring at me.

"Well, dammit?"

Luke carefully set his beer bottle down on the table at his side.

When he reached over and pulled me onto his lap, I was somewhat mollified that maybe I hadn't misunderstood his question. When his hand smoothed back my hair and he slowly kissed my neck, I realized if I was a creeper pervert, well then, so was he. His kiss made me shiver and rub up against him. No wonder he likes being kissed right there so much.

'What was I worried about, anyway, for god's sake? I'm must be losing my touch. This was a man's lap I was wriggling on; of course he meant sexual fantasy.'

He finally spoke near my ear. "If you had said you wanted me to tie you up, I'd have worried you were lazy and looking for an excuse to get out of any work."

I giggled while he nuzzled me again.

'Christ, now the man had me giggling. What next? His name tattooed on my ass inside a heart?'

"Maybe if I don't call you some Friday night when I'm out of town, you should wonder why."

'Holy BeJoly! What had I gotten myself into?'

His cell announcing a text interrupted our heated kissing. With one last, quick peck and no explanation other than "duty calls", Luke left immediately after checking the message.

Last night was Friday night, and the first time I'd seen Luke since that day almost three weeks ago. It was a hell of a homecoming.

Chapter IV
"Call Me" by Blondie

Saturday, 11/17/12
7:40 AM

My brain seemed to have only two gears this morning. It had switched back into first. From daydreaming about Luke and fantasies, it was now thinking about work again when I stepped out of the shower.

Bel's Books inventories a select amount of new books, bestseller hardbacks and paperbacks, but mainly we are a used bookstore. We do not operate like some used bookstores that buy books from people for pennies on the dollar and then resells the book at half price.

In fact, we do not buy used books from customers at all. Instead, we give a store credit for a percentage of the book's value based on a sliding scale, dependent upon the age and condition of the book. In this sense, we could be considered a paperback exchange. Our inventory is continuously being restocked with approved trade-ins, but no cash is being paid out. Customers can then apply their store credit towards the reduced retail price of their next book purchase. They can buy new and used books at a lower price than other used bookstores or e-book prices.

Toweling off, I was toying with an idea of creating a membership club. I would charge a flat, yearly fee to customers interested in belonging. It would be similar to the subscription lending library concept popular in England during the late 1700's to mid 1800's. I set the idea, and the modern problems involved, on the back burner in my brain to simmer away.

It was time for the really important decisions of my relaxing weekend off to enjoy my life to the fullest.

I have a wide array of moisturizing lotions and potions to choose from to anoint myself. Stella is always giving me something new to try. My niece is a fervent supporter of all things organic. Not a carcinogenic chemical or a poisonous perfume was allowed to slip past her eagle eye and into my bathroom, much less soak into my skin. Should the apocalyptic need occur, I could most likely eat or drink from most jars or bottles in my bathroom. Super to know, but the lotions needed only to smell delicious to make me happy.

I relish everything ultra-feminine. I've never worried if I am cool or a hipster, I could care less. I am what I am; a female that unashamedly,

A Date with Fate

blissfully wallows in every frowned down-upon stereotype out there for being such a girly-girl in the new millennium. In my mind, there's a balanced symmetry that is very satisfying to my soul about loving everything pink while also running a business and digging guns, trucks, and power tools. I prefer sci-fi, zombie, and action movies over drama and tear jerkers. I love wearing dresses and pretty undies more than jeans and T's.

Although, after Luke owning my butt so easily last night, I needed to step it up. It may mean possibly breaking a perfect, French manicured nail, but I am going to search out a teacher and put the time into learning some solid fighting moves. Playing with Luke, the message really hit home that a weapon or a serious drop kick to the gonads wouldn't always be possible to decide a bad situation in my favor.

I was pondering the merits of gardenia oil over orange blossom lotion when I heard the buzz of my cell announcing a message. I had forgotten the phone was in the bathroom on the charger.

There was a text with the one word: *Awake?*

Let me backtrack here a second. When I introduced myself, I mentioned which nicknames I do answer to, but neglected to say which names I don't answer to. I will never answer to the name Ana.

I'm sorry Anna's of the world, but that name brings back memories of a little brat I met when I was five and starting the first grade. It was the very first day of big-girl school for me.

She called me "a baby" when I got teary-eyed before class started. I had choked up because bossy Anna informed me the fistful of yellow, daisy-like flowers I had painstakingly picked for my new teacher were dumb, icky weeds.

None of the adults heard Anna the Botanist tormenting me first. No, they only saw me swatting her with the flat side of my Troll lunch box upside her fat head. I was officially marked a troublemaker and a kid to keep an eye on from day one of my school career because of Anna Lynn Johnson.

Don't worry, I got even.

Anna Johnson and I have been fast friends ever since. We are the inseparable, dynamic duo—Anabel and Anna, still hanging and still managing somehow to get into trouble together almost twenty-five years later.

To this day, it's still perceived by many that I lure her into bad behavior with my evil ways and she is the proper, good girl. The reality is somewhere closer to this: On the outside, Anna is pretty and vivacious. She's a brown-eyed, brown-haired cutie that resembles a chipmunky cheerleader. With her trendy hairstyles and preppy, conservative clothes, she could pass for a preschool teacher or a pastor's wife. On the inside, she is a frustrated cage dancer and wildly fun.

Anna wasn't technically an orphan like me. Her Mom gave birth then dumped the baby Anna on her much older, spinster sister Lily. She took off for parts unknown and died a couple of years later in a DUI, head-on car crash with a telephone pole. Anna's father was a blank space on her birth certificate.

Unfortunately, Anna has no siblings or extended family. Her elderly Aunt Lily provided the basics; shelter, clothing, and food, but she is a rigid, morally self-righteous woman. It isn't just a shell on the outside that covers up a tender heart. Aunt Lily is through and through one uptight, battle-axe of a fundamentalist church lady.

She is a cold and unaffectionate woman, but I guess if she loves anyone it is Anna. This questionable love manifested itself by her being extremely over protective of Anna growing up, to the point of ridiculousness.

Aunt Lily believes evil lurks in the hearts of all mankind, especially women. Yep, EVIL is just waiting to prompt us female sinners to do any number of deviant deeds. I've not heard too many people referring to Jezebel in casual conversations, but Aunt Lily seems to know the woman personally. Anna's aunt is a woman who believes many women are reincarnated Jezebel's responsible for tempting and leading poor, defenseless men astray.

I discussed this with my grandmother after first hearing the name Jezebel when I was quite young. NanaBel's private opinion to me was Aunt Lily's harshness stemmed from a bad experience with love that soured her as a young woman. My private opinion to nobody but myself; describing Aunt Lily's temperament as only soured at love was like saying Hitler was merely miffed at the Jews.

Aunt Lily diligently works full-time at her church thrift store during the week. She belligerently stomps around brandishing her antique cane she was never without while bullying people into buying junk they don't need. On the weekends, she devotes her time to her church--doing God only knows what.

It wasn't Dickensian, but still sad. It was not a very fun home life for a kid as lively and loving as Anna.

Somehow, ruthlessly sly NanaBel convinced the domineering and fanatical Aunt Lily that it was her own idea that Anna spent a majority of her time on Division Street with us. Anna was growing up smack dab in a nest of bourgeoning mini-Jezzie's while being nurtured by the biggest Jezebel in the Northern Hemisphere, or quite possibly, the world. Yep, that's right, my grandmother.

Anna fit right in to our riotous household like a homing pigeon come to roost. Anna and my grandmother were a mutual adoration society. Anna was treated like another granddaughter, Chore Chart and all. My siblings probably thought she really was another sister; she'd practically

A Date with Fate

lived in the apartment since first grade. Because of Anna being my BFF, I chose bunk beds for my room instead of the Princess Pink Ruffles canopied bed I lusted after with all my little girl heart.

When the need arose, and it frequently did, I would complain in a whisper to NanaBel about the latest stunt Aunt Lily had pulled to keep Anna at home. Aunt Lily was always denying permission for Anna to come with me to a materialistic birthday party, or to the ruinous movies. NanaBel insisted it was done out of Aunt Lily's love she harbored for Anna, even if she was cold and undemonstrative. I was pretty convinced it was because Aunt Lily was a mean, old bitch, but I wisely kept my own counsel. I didn't want to be grounded for discourtesy and cursing. NanaBel was tough on those subjects, especially with seven-year-olds.

Besides, NanaBel would pick up the phone and perform her magic. Nobody can withstand NanaBel, and she'd smooth over whatever objections Aunt Lily had to allowing Anna to join me and the other kids having fun.

Anna's also my one exception to my rule of everyone forgetting my daily existence before ten in the morning.

I checked my phone. It was 7:45 AM. After her text, I called Anna and put it on speaker. I chose the gardenia oil and begun to smooth it up my legs, feeling my bliss at the slightly peppery, floral scent.

"Okay, it's opinion time." My friend announced in lieu of a greeting. "I'm deciding between mammoth, blueberry muffins with a sugar crusted topping, or vanilla frosted, raspberry scones for the feature of the day. Which sounds more scrumpdillyicious to you?"

I didn't need to think. "Size always matters. I vote massive blueberry."

I could hear pots and pans clanging noisily in the background as she worked. Whatever Anna did, she did loudly and with frenetic energy. Her home kitchen was outfitted to meet professional catering standards. She rose early six days a week and cooked in the comfort of her own kitchen for Bel's Books café, Laissez Fare.

A couple of years ago, Aunt Lily had deeded title of her house over to Anna with the caveat of life tenancy—good health prevailing. Anna was pleased with this deal while it chilled me to the very marrow. I was horrified at Anna's Stygian bargain of life tenancy with that strong-as-a-pack-mule, hellfire spouting, seventy-five-year old Debbie Downer of an auntie. It was a living nightmare worse than anything I could wish on my worst enemy. Anna had shrugged at my appalled protests on her behalf. For her, having her soul destroyed was worth the price of a free house.

Anna's laughter has a musical sound. The lucky wench can carry a tune, too. "I said mammoth, not massive. Besides, I remember you distinctly telling me size doesn't matter, Junior."

"No way did I say that. That'd be crazy talk."

"Yes way, you did say that." Anna also has a memory like a steel trap. I don't ever have to worry I'll be able to forget something from my past.

I scanned my memory banks and hit pay dirt. "Ah yes, I told you that years ago when things seemed to be getting serious between you and, what was his name...Stan, Steve? Whatever, we all knew he had a pencil dick. I didn't want you to feel bad."

Over the whirring noise of an electric mixer Anna exclaimed, "What? No way! How did everyone know he had a pencil dick? Who's everyone, anyway?"

"Yes way, and umm...let's see. Reggie told me and my sisters. Guess he must have seen Stan or Steve's little pee-pee somehow. Didn't they go to the same club around then?"

"I don't know, but that's too funny." She kept laughing, "I never did it with him. So that's why they called him 'Little Stevie'. Gosh, and here I thought it was because he was sort of short." She abruptly stopped laughing. "Oh just great, your jerk of a brother must have laughed his ass off knowing I was going out with a pencil dick. I can't believe you didn't tell me! Junior, you'd better tell me what you know about anyone's dick size I go out with. I don't want to hook up with any more baby dills! Oh my god..."

I meekly promised to keep her updated.

She demanded, only half in jest, "What about Jim? Do you know anything about him? Tell me!"

"Well, geez Anna, gossip from the bookstore's men's bathroom has his girth measuring in at...You freak, I promise I know nothing about Jim's manroot size." Now I was laughing. "I could guess, though, if it would make you happy. Hey, I know, we could start a Fantasy Package League like guys do with football."

After we ran with that idea, stopped wetting our pants, and had both settled back down Anna said, "Okay, I'll assume no news is good news where Jim is concerned."

Jim Mardsen was Anna's new flame. Her question about his penis size was interesting since they had been going out for a few weeks all ready, but I made no further comment.

During one point a couple of months ago, I thought Anna might hook up with Reggie. At first, this seemed bizarre to me, maybe even slightly incestuous. I mean, come on--Reg and Anna? Upon further reflection, I could see the attraction of like to like. I don't know what happened to stop the would-be lovers, but something went drastically wrong. One day they were flirting like mad, the next day they were giving each other the cold shoulder. If one entered the room, the other would leave with their face all screwed up like they smelled something foul.

A Date with Fate

Maybe it was just as well that a romance between Reggie and Anna was over before it began. My brother's m.o. is to go out with the same woman only a couple of times before moving on. He's upfront he's out only for a fun time, not a relationship. I'd hate to think he'd give Anna the same cavalier treatment, but I'd hate more to see her hurt by my feckless brother.

Most curious was Anna not rushing to tell me every detail. I had to respect her silence, and Reg wasn't talking, either. I was positive Reggie had done something extraordinarily dumb to make the normally forgiving Anna not want to acknowledge his existence on Earth any longer.

Anna sighed. "I'm going with the scones today. I can't think about mammoth anything right now. The visual is too disturbing."

I laughed.

Anna and I co-owned but she operated Laissez Fare, the organic bakery, deli, coffee and juice bar located within my bookstore. It was one in a series of ongoing improvements I was implementing to increase revenues when facing reality at the advent of e-books as competition for printed books. Laissez Fare was, by far, the most expensive investment I have made over the last two years.

Northfield is a river town of about twenty thousand located roughly fifty minutes south of the Minneapolis-St Paul metro area. The town has two colleges, St Olaf and Carleton. Both are highly ranked private schools. There were approximately five thousand students with money to spend coming to our thriving downtown area regularly to eat, shop, and hit the bars. I can't compete with the bars, but the shopping and eating parts were up for grabs. I knew anytime I stopped at a Barnes and Noble in the suburbs of the cities, I hit their café area. I had a ready-made hungry and thirsty clientele shopping at my store. I had a best friend with a culinary background tired of working for someone else. Anna and I brainstormed two years ago and the café Laissez Fare was our resulting creation.

I may own Bel's Books and the building free and clear, but the heating and cooling bills alone were killer. I needed to be innovative and proactive to keep growing my business and generating profits. The gambler in me didn't balk at using a portion of my nest egg capitol to make investments towards the future. The businesswoman in me knew making solid investment decisions meant having a well-defined and researched master game plan outlining the goals I wanted to achieve. Then I had to be flexible enough to be willing to sometimes toss the game plan aside. Opportunity has a way of popping up without warning or planning. Always helpful were a good banker, good advice, good credit, and good karma. Knock on wood.

Bel's Books is an institution in Northfield. Thanks in large to my grandmother, the bookstore has had a solid rep for over forty years. With the addition of Laissez Fare, we are now known also as the place to get organic, high-quality "fast food". We serve coffee drinks, juiced concoctions for an energy boost college kids always need, sandwich wraps, soups and salads, and my personal living hell on earth: fresh daily and incredibly tasty bakery treats.

Customers have always hung around the store. Since Laissez Fare opened, a significant number more stayed to eat and drink while they did homework, browsed and read, hung out with friends, or hit on my assorted staff members. As long as people spent money and didn't cause any commotion, I was cool with it all.

Anna was making a living doing something she loves, and by existing on a miniscule wage, has almost paid me back the start up costs. I leased out the space, got a percentage of the profits, and free coffee drinks for life. She cut me off cold turkey from free bakery goodies a week after opening. I loved or hated her for that, fluctuating with my blood sugar levels.

Banging away in her kitchen this morning, Anna complained, "Are you on speaker? I hate that tunnel sound. What are you doing now, anyway?"

"I'm rubbing oil on my buttocks. Gots some ground to cover, but I'll be done in a minute."

Anna's laugh ended on a groan. "Oh god, tell me about ass acreage. I have got to quit eating my product. I'm getting depressed my jeans are so frickin' tight lately." Anna's figure is small on top and bigger on the bottom. Any weight gain did go straight to her thighs and gluteus maximus, but on the bright side; she has a slender neck and thin face.

"Huh, that's never a good sign. Perhaps wearing a muzzle while cooking may help?" I suggest, helpful friend that I am. I glanced in the full length mirror and checked out my waistline. I should probably thank my friend for cutting me off the sugar gravy train.

Anna's ungrateful suggestion what I could do with a muzzle made me think she didn't find me helpful in this instance.

"Are we still on at ten for spying in St. Paul today?"

"Okay by me." Frowning, I thought of the sleeping Luke. He had to be awake and long gone before ten this morning when I needed to leave. If not, I could leave him a note. I guess since he had no problem unlocking my door somehow last night to come and get me, he could manage locking it on his way out.

"I'll be there before ten. Hey, wait. What are you wearing?"

"Umm...I'm naked."

Anna burst out laughing. "Junior! I meant tonight when we go to The Rock. Are you dressing up?"

Ana likes to know what others are wearing before we go out. I've never cared what other girls are wearing. I can get excited over clothes,

A Date with Fate

shoes have been known to cause spontaneous combustion, and jewelry—well, what happens between me and earrings is too private to describe, but I'm missing the let's-all-dress-alike gene common amongst so many of my girlfriends.

I put the gardenia oil aside, took the phone off speaker, and went into my closet once again. "Anna Lynn, I'm not even dressed for the first time today, much less thinking about tonight. You'll be the first person I'll tell when I decide. I'll post on face book and then twitter about it."

"Like that will happen, you Neanderthal!" Anna snorted loudly.

I always give her grief about her religious devotion to social networking; particularly re-tweeting. She's always got an eye on her phone or a screen. I *was* a social throwback compared to her. I find nothing redeeming about face book for social purposes. I get very sick of friends stalking friends on face book—who went out, who wasn't invited, who was in pictures, who was unfriended--the damn drama it causes seems endless.

Anna switched topics. "Are you done with that zombie book yet so I can read it? Hey, did Luke ever end up calling you last night?"

"Nope, I fell asleep while reading and Luke didn't call me." I wasn't fibbing.

"Oh, no! Isn't that weird for him to miss a Friday night phone call? Aren't you nervous?"

Anna knew Luke called me on the Friday nights when he was working—a ritual he had started after the first week we met. She's been there on a few Fridays when he's called, plus she met him three weeks ago.

When he is gone from town for his job, she now frets over him like a mother hen. I have no idea why. She knows fewer specifics about what he does on the job than I do. Anna's convinced he's a secret agent risking life and limb for the good of our country, an unknown and unsung hero.

She rushed on, a natural worrier. "You haven't heard from him this morning, either? I hope he's okay." She muttered anxiously under her breath. I heard water running and rattling noises, it sounded like silverware being tossed around. "When did he call you last?"

I felt bad for not reassuring her that Luke was fine and dandy and hogging my bed even as we spoke, but there...I'm over it. Anna knows what I think about sleepovers and boyfriends. She would be agog at my departure from the norm and want all the details. Maybe at some point I'll tell her more, if there is more to tell, but not now.

"Don't worry, Mother Hubbard. I'm sure he's fine." I hurried her off the phone. "I've got to get dressed. I am freezing standing here. See you later at ten."

I wasn't sure how I felt about my best friend and lover becoming friends, much less Anna starting to romanticize Luke into some sort of American James Bond. I guess it was slightly better than if they hated each other.

Chapter V
"Torn" by Natalie Imbruglia

Saturday, 11/17/12
8:00 AM

After ending the daily call with Anna, I quickly finished getting ready. I blew my long layers straight and put on a little make-up.

I dressed casually in a favorite pair of skinny, black jeans and a white, button-down shirt. I rolled up the cuffs neatly. I don't like long sleeves. Over this, I wore a short, fitted black vest trimmed with gunmetal buttons in a baroque flower pattern. I left it unbuttoned.

Stella and I are jewelry fiends. She has shopped with me since she was old enough to point and drool at what she liked. We love to look for treasures in places like antique and flea markets, or in tucked-away neighborhood shops.

We often use our finds to create something else, such as using old, architecturally interesting earrings to decorate a hair clip, or trimming the vest I just put on with cool, funky buttons. There's not too much we can't improve upon.

I zipped on sturdy, ankle boots with silver side buckles and only three-inch-high, square heels.

I was ready to search out my morning coffee.

Looking in the mirror, I put a hand to my ear and frowned. Make that almost ready.

Without earrings on I may as well be naked, but they are kept in my bedroom. So are my necklaces, bracelets, and rings. These I could live without for a short time, but not wearing earrings really bugged me.

Feeling a little cranky over being inconvenienced in my own home, I shrugged it off to another reason not to do sleepovers.

I planned to sneak in some work on the books before Stella arrived to open. My store office desktop is where I preferred to work.

I wasn't going to hang around the apartment and wait for Luke to wake up. I decided correct morning-after behavior didn't really matter to me, but I didn't want to text Luke and wake him.

I left an actual handwritten note taped to the one place a man would be guaranteed to see it; the toilet lid.

Dear Mr. Muscles,

I'm worried our dates are becoming ho-hum…
I'm out and about doing stuff, so please lock up on your way out.
If you're in town, you're invited for Sunday dinner @ 5pm.
Have I told you lately you are very, very impressive?

X
Anabel

p.s. Your turn?

    Purse swinging in hand, I was walking down the hall when the building's front doorbell rang. And rang, and kept on ringing. Whoever was outside my building pressing the doorbell wasn't letting up and the annoyingly shrill buzzing sound was continuing nonstop.
    I quickly dashed over to the master station intercom on the wall and checked out the view screen. I was surprised when I recognized who it was. This was out of left field.
    Smiling, I pushed the button to speak. "Crookie! Hey, easy on the buzzer. It's so nice to see you, but why am I seeing you?"
    The irritating noise stopped and a garbled voice queried, "An..el? Is ..at you?"
    I watched the screen as Bob "Crookie" Crookston bent from his considerable height to speak directly into the box attached to Bel's front entrance outside wall. He appeared to put his lips against it. I giggled, I couldn't help it--this was so like him. He was essentially a rocket scientist, but didn't get intercom systems and microphones had evolved since his ghetto, ancient apartment days at Purdue.
    "Tis I, Anabel of Northfield. What's up?" I reared back in shock when a blast of jumbled, shouted words was my answer. Bob excited and loud was one thing, but Bob angry and yelling? This was very strange behavior coming from him.
    Bob's an old friend from high school. We bonded our senior year as science partners and during our after school tutoring sessions. He was very tall even then and gangly skinny. He dressed goofy and wore ugly, thick framed glasses. He was your typical nerd; incredibly intelligent and incredibly socially awkward.
    Sitting next to me at our lab station, he was terrified of me for the first two weeks of class. He couldn't even look at me without turning beet red and breaking out into a sweat, sometimes hyperventilating.
    I had to put a stop to that nonsense immediately. I really needed his help; science gives me the worst headache. It was bad enough I had

gotten stuck in biology instead of my first choice of earth science--which sounded a whole lot friendlier to me.

My procrastination at taking the required science credit had caused me trouble; I couldn't afford a B or lower because my colossally smart partner was petrified of half the human race. NanaBel paid out a significant bonus for straight A's. I was too greedy to lose out on that primo deal for the first time ever in my school history. I'm a girl with goals.

After my first quiz result of a B minus, I waited after school for Bob. I had borrowed Mackenzie's pristine 1980 turbocharged Firebird Trans Am and drove that day. Mac, when she wasn't being too bossy, was a great oldest sister. She was usually willing to let me use her car during the day while she slept after her graveyard nursing shift at Northfield Hospital. Mac's only requirement was I keep the gas tank topped. I had a hard time seeing clearly over the bulge of the turbo hood, but it was worth the neck strain; I loved the scream of the engine as I shifted from second into third at 4000 rpm's.

Standing beside the Firebird, I picked Bob immediately out of the crowd of our fellow inmates by his towering height as he came scurrying down the sidewalk. Even with his head facing down, he was taller than everyone around him. By his hunched over posture, I could only surmise he was carrying a load of boulders in his backpack.

I reached in the driver's side open window and tooted the horn. He didn't look up. I laid on the horn until it penetrated even his genius fog. When he was looking my way, I waved to him with a big smile and motioned for him to come over to my waiting car at the curb. It was comical to see him look around and point to himself in disbelief when he realized it was his attention I was trying to grab. It was even funnier to see his expression as he checked out my ride. The decaled, turbo bird spitting out a large flame across the hood was pretty, damn awesome.

At my cajoling insistence, he reluctantly folded himself into the passenger side. He had to slide the bucket seat so far back to accommodate his thirty-eight inch inseam he was technically sitting in the back seat.

"What do you want, Ana...Anabel?"

Pulled so far forward in the driver's seat to reach the pedals I could be mistaken for a hood ornament, I took off into the busy after school traffic.

Once on our way, I answered him cheerfully. "Know what, Bob? I am so glad you asked me that question. What I want is exactly what I need to talk to you about today."

I kept my eyes on the road but could clearly see him skittishly glancing my way. Between keeping a watchful eye out for sneaky relatives and always liking boys, my peripheral vision was highly developed by the age of seventeen. I kept my face mostly forward for his comfort, but approached him straight on with my words.

I continued, "Here's the deal. I've noticed you need my help in the worst way, Bob."

His Adam's apple bobbed up and down rapidly before he croaked, "I do?"

"Yes, you do." I affirmed assuredly.

I downshifted and swerved sharply around Anna's Aunt Lily. She was in her old boat of an Oldsmobile doing ten mph on Jefferson Parkway--in a thirty mph zone! I barely resisted the urge to give her the finger when she angrily honked. It was tempting as she'd think it was my sister, but I heroically refrained. I sighed when I saw Bob close his eyes tight and give a silent scream.

"Relax, Bob. I'm a good driver." I sped up and took a left at the almost still yellow light and gunned it. I headed south on Highway 3 out of town. "Yes, you really need my help and today's your lucky day. Do you know why?"

Bob was still clutching the door handle in a death grip, but cautiously looking at me now. He was feeling safer to watch me since I hadn't taken my eyes off the road once since inviting him into my car. I smiled inside.

"No," He whispered.

I put a hand to my ear, "What, Bob? I can't hear you!"

Bob cleared his throat and spoke up a little. "No Anabel, I don't know why."

"Why what?" I asked innocently.

When I saw his distressed confusion, I relented with a chuckle.

"Sorry, Bob. I'm kind of a warped chick sometimes." I turned and flashed a grin. He flinched. I faced the road again, biting my cheek not to giggle. "It's your lucky day because I have something I am going to give you, and you have something you are going to give me."

I've never seen anyone go from beet red to pasty white that fast. I hurried on before he fainted, or worse. "Friendship! I'm only talking simple friendship here, okay?"

I laughed out loud when he quickly shook his head back and forth "No" in denial. Poor Bob was worse off than I even suspected.

"Yes." I insisted.

He wheezed, "I can't be friends with you!"

I frowned ominously at that. "The hell you say. Am I not smart enough to be your friend, or what?"

I waited patiently for his answer. Bob resembled a wise owl with glasses when his head bent to the side to consider my words. He probably had never considered whether he would choose to be friends with a girl

A Date with Fate

before. He was only sure that because of his paralyzing shyness most girls wouldn't want to be his friend. I could tell he was intrigued by the concept.

"Umm...I don't know. You make me too nervous to think straight." I saw him blush again and look desperately out the window, as if seeking an escape route.

His speaking in semi-coherent sentences encouraged me to believe I was doing the right thing for us both. I still clicked down the door locks in case he really would tuck and roll to get away from me. Really smart people can do really dumb things, we were screaming down the road at eighty mph, and a brain his size is too beautiful a thing to waste. At his look of fright at the clicking sound, I took pity and quickly filled him in on my brilliant idea.

"Straight up, my new friend, you are scared of girls and a science whiz. I am scared of science and a whiz at being a girl. See, I was thinking it's kismet we are partners this year. Or maybe it's destiny?" I shook my head. "Either way, we have the ability to help each other out here. We can work together after school for an hour or two and tutor each other. What do you say?"

He finally smiled at me a little, or it could have been a nervous tic. Either way, he was no Justin Timberlake but his smile was rather adorkable. If he now resembled an owlet with his staring, round eyes and perpetually surprised expression, it wasn't like he was a total dweeb. I had some material here to work with, given enough time.

Bob answered, sounding amazed. "You think I could help you? Sure...yes, I will help you with biology. There is no reason to be scared. Uh...maybe you can help me, too." After taking a big gulp of air and sounding so dubious I had to grin, he said, "I would like being friends. You are very... interesting." He ducked and blushed. His whole face and down the back of his neck was a deep, dark crimson again. I winced—it looked painful.

After we verbally shook hands on our deal--he adamantly refused to physically touch me on several grounds--I let him be. I was happy he had agreed without any more coercion needed; I only had a half a tank of gas and a few bucks on me.

After a few moments of companionable silence he peered out the windshield worriedly. "Um...where are we going? My mom is going to wonder when I don't show up after school and will report me missing to the police."

I laughed, until I realized he was not kidding.

Now, here he was ten years later, at eight in the morning on a Saturday. He was laying on the buzzer while swearing up an incoherent storm into my intercom like I'd taught him nothing over all these intervening years.

"Geez Louise, Crookie, hold on a blasted minute and I'll be right there."

I took the stairs down two at a time. I think I'd heard the name Reggie shouted by Crookie, but that only stumped me more because he and Reg have never been friends. Even as I wondered what could possibly be going on with Crookie, I was feeling a sneakin' admiration at my ability to run so quickly and quietly in my high-heeled boots without breaking my neck—sometimes my talents astound me.

Sighing inwardly, I remembered at the last minute to turn back and lock my apartment door behind me. I had to think for two. After all, I had my innocently slumbering guest upstairs to protect and keep safe. Good god, the ongoing sleepover complications and responsibilities of last night's fun just never ended.

Key ring in hand, I crossed the lobby and unlocked the deadbolt of the left door of the pair leading to the outside. I opened it a couple inches, but to be on the safe side, I toed the rubber headed door stop down to prevent the door from being pushed further open.

I could have buzzed open the door from upstairs, but for all I knew Crookie may be a tweaker on a rampage. I highly doubted Crookie was a druggie, but it had been a couple years since we last really talked and he was acting spooky. Of course, he had also gotten married which could help explain the spookiness.

He had chilled out. He was waiting with arms crossed and a shoulder propped against the red brick wall. His mouth was a tight line, his whole demeanor grim and exhausted, but not insane or jacked-up.

I eyed him up and down. Aside from looking like his dog died, Bob had steadily improved with age. He still had the same golden brown hair and hazel eyes, but now was sporting an expensive haircut and his glasses were rimless. He had filled out a bit from working out steadily over the years. He was a tall guy, no doubt about that, but slim now rather than beanpole skinny. He was clean shaven with clear, pale skin and no visible tattoos or piercings. He was your very tall, average-looking, professional man--until he smiled.

Crookie's smile was a little shy and a little slow, yet once it arrived it was so unbelievably sweet that any girl who caught a glimpse of it never thought of him as nondescript or average again. If he was a different type of man, he'd be getting some strange every night based on that little smile alone.

Today, his clothes were a little rumpled but actually fashionable. He wore a brown leather jacket unzipped over a tan sweater, and his jeans were a designer label that Stella would have a shitfest over if she saw them. I vaguely recalled her emoting something about sweatshops and chemicals.

A Date with Fate

Seeing me, he shoved off the wall and murmured my name. A quick glance around at the quiet street outside showed me it had stopped drizzling and the sun was semi-peeking out, but the air was brisk. Through the gap in the door, the coolness felt good on my face.

Even as obviously distressed as he was, I was still happy to see my old friend. Kicking up the door stop, I opened the door wide. "Hello, Crookie. Sorry for the delay. I was debating your sanity."

Crookie cracked a smile and bent to give me a kiss on the cheek when he came into the lobby. "Hello, Bel."

"Hey, what's wrong, why so grim? Wait, never mind. That's enough about you; let me show you how I've grown." I reached my arms around his waist and gave him a big, dramatic squeeze. Then I attempted to lift him saying, "See? I'm so strong now I can lift a head as heavy as yours!"

I hadn't been able to move him a centimeter, but I did manage to get him to laugh down at me in protest. He gripped my shoulders and held me away from him, looking me up and down. "Yes, I can see you have grown. Those heels may take you out of the dwarf tossing zone, but that is cheating."

I laughed while I locked up again. Our disparity in inches has been a running joke between us for years. At parties, he insisted the top of my head was a perfect spot for his beer. I insisted his navel was a perfect spot for parking my chewed gum.

"Let's go into the store and grab a coffee, okay? I know I need one." Not waiting for an answer, I crossed the lobby to Bel's Books doors. It is not safe to keep me too long from my first morning cup of coffee. I cannot be held accountable for my actions.

Genius that he is, Crooks agreed with a shrug. "Sure."

He stood with slumped shoulders and a glum face as I keyed in the code to open the beveled glass, double doors to Bel's Books. I moved them wide to each side, locking them in the open position.

I glanced at Crookie. Something very depressing was obviously heavy on his mind. Good money was on woman trouble. What else could have a man running the gambit of acting like a rampaging tweaker and then the walking dead, all within five minutes? I resigned myself to the fact I was going to be the lucky girl to hear all the gory details. So much for sneaking some work time in before Stella the Hun arrived.

The lifelong familiar aromas of thousands of books, lemon oil, ground coffee beans, and the spicy scents of herbs rushed out to envelope me. Closing my eyes and inhaling a deep, rejuvenating breath of this enchanted air was often all it took to right my world. I inhaled again.

Following me in with his hands shoved in his jacket pockets, Crookie paused. He pointed with an elbow at the huge refectory table a few feet in front of us. There were four cement troughs filled with lush, green herbs staggered down the center of the table. The weak, morning sunlight coming through the large display windows were spotlighting the troughs so they stood out in the otherwise darkened store.

"Those are different. The herbs smell great."

"Yeah, I saw the idea for the troughs—a smaller version—in a magazine. They fired my creative juices right up. I had been envisioning something for the table old worldish and rustic, but didn't want metal." I shrugged one shoulder and smiled up at him. "You know me, once I got the bug up my butt I had to build them that day. Cool, huh?" I bumped his elbow with mine. "You likey?"

I recognized the spark of interest lighting up his eyes. He murmured absently, "I do likey."

He wandered over and peered at the troughs. A lock of straight hair fell onto his forehead. He became absorbed lightly skimming his fingers over the planters, as if he was a city inspector looking for code violations in the footings of a new construction.

The long table was placed in the open space that ran the width of the store, about fifteen by forty feet when you first entered. The front display windows were along the right, facing out to the sidewalk and Division Street.

If you Google Northfield and check out the Wikipedia website, my building is visible in the first picture shown. It's the red brick one with the turret, taller than those around it. Bel's is located across the street from the old bank, now a museum famous for the robbery attempt by the James-Younger Gang's in 1876. During the week of Defeat of Jesse James Days in September, I have a front row seat in my apartment living room for viewing all the festive activities. Invites were coveted and I wielded much power. Heady stuff for sure.

"How did you make them? I have not seen cement look so textured before. What did you use? Did you at least make a mold first?"

At the last question, he sounded so accusatory I had to laugh. I rubbed my hand up and down an upright spike of French tarragon and breathed in the light licorice scent. "Sure, if you consider a mold two cardboard boxes from Just Food Co-op."

He winced. My offhand approach to creativity drove him so crazy that I always exaggerated the details to shake him up. Super-smart nerds need shaking up. They deserve some fun, and they need to remember being a genius isn't everything in life. I'm just the girl to do this dirty job.

He tilted his head and motioned for me to continue. "Go on. I know I am going to regret asking, but I am curious how you made the troughs, Anabel."

My brain yearned for its morning coffee, but I knew once he got all Crookie'd up on a subject he would not budge from this spot until his curiosity was satisfied.

A Date with Fate

He really was going to regret asking.

"I started by borrowing several things." Sure enough, he was all ready shaking his head at me. He hates the incorrect term 'borrowing' Minnesotans use to cover any item they get from another person, regardless if it is returnable or not. If you want to drive him insane, ask to borrow a piece of gum or a piece of tape.

I hid my smile behind my hand. "Let's see, I borrowed an empty five gallon, paint bucket from Reggie's yard, and also borrowed his cute, blue Makita drill." This last elicited a dismayed gasp. "Then I jumped a fence and borrowed a garbage bag full of baled hay from a roll in a pasture. Straw, by the way, is what gives the troughs the texture you were asking about." Crookie raised his brows and nodded. "Okay, now don't ever tell Anna, but I borrowed a tin of black tea leaves from the Fare. Next, I used Reggie's drill to mix up the whatchamacallit cement stuff…"

Crooks moaned out loud, muttering under his breath. I heard the word 'drill' and 'cement'. Then he supplied through gritted teeth, "QuikCrete?"

I snapped my fingers. "Yeah, the QuikCrete. I mixed it in the bucket with some of the water I had steeped with the tea leaves to give it that swirly, brown color. At the end, I threw in a bunch of broken up straw until I liked the looks of the cement."

Because I don't get out much, and I really do enjoying terrorizing my friends for my own private entertainment, I paused here. I held up my hand to the weak sunlight and experienced a blonde moment. I examined my manicure closely, as if checking for a broken nail or chipped polish.

He made a pushing, hurry up motion. "Go on. What next?"

I looked up. "Oh, sorry. Do you like this color of polish, Crookie, or is it too pink?"

A hunted look in his eyes, Crookie brushed his hair off his forehead impatiently and waved my hand off. "Uh, sure. It is real nice color. So, you decided on the consistency of the cement by looking at it, Anabel? You did not follow any instructions?"

"What instructions? I'd only seen a tiny picture in a magazine and a one-liner of a description mentioning the straw. I was totally winging it here, Crookie. What would you expect me to do?"

He practically pulled his hair out. "Anabel, there are instructions on the bags of QuikCrete for correctly preparing the cement."

"Gee, I never thought of that. Huh." I fluffed my hair with both hands. "Oh well, let's see. Next, I filled the largest box on the bottom with globs and globs of the cement mixture. Oh yes, I stuck in a few plastic straws I also borrowed from the Fare to use as drainage holes." Crookie had a hand under his glasses, rubbing his eyes. "I placed a smaller box on top of the globs of cement. I weighed this down with a couple of big rocks I borrowed from the border of Aunt Lily's flower garden." I leaned in confidingly and lowered my voice. "Please don't mention those rocks to anyone, okay? I guess they had insect fossils imprinted on them and it's kind of a sore subject that they went missing. Anyway, where was I? Oh yeah, then it was a matter of eyeballing and filling up the four sides until they were kinda even." I was having a hard time not losing it. His eyebrows were raised so high in disbelief at my decidedly unscientific approach to building the troughs, I felt like we were back in high school biology class. "I waited for a little bit until it looked, you know, kinda-sorta dry, then I removed the boxes. Voila! I made about ten of the troughs in one day, gave a couple to my sisters, and was spent."

He was still frowning. "You know, Anabel, you cannot 'borrow' something you cannot return."

I protested, laughter finally bubbling out of me. "Hey, no fair! I returned the drill. Reggie said it didn't take too long to chisel the dried cement off."

Revulsion dripping from every word, he asked, "You did not even wait the right amount of time for the cement to set properly, did you? Do these troughs leak?"

"Only when they get wet."

Hearing my dry tone, I saw it finally seep in I had been having a go at him. He looked completely blank for a minute, and then his whole expression brightened when he flashed his incredibly darling smile.

Undismayed, he pointed an accusing finger at me. "You are such a ....how can I still fall for your tricks after all these years?"

"Obviously you aren't getting enough teasing, that's for sure."

"Trust me, Anabel. I have never been teased by anyone like you in my life. I will have you know at work I am highly respected and revered." Crookie then sighed like he had the weight of the world on his shoulders. "I have been doing nothing but work for about eight weeks straight."

"Poor baby. It's probably a good thing the brainiac women at your lab don't tear you away from your microscope and tease you. They get one load of that super-hot little smile thing you've got going on and no more cats would get dissected that day."

"Cats dissected? Microscopes?" He shouted with laughter. "Bel, you have no clue what I do for a living, do you?"

I hooked my arm through his and led him back through the dim store. "It has to do with science, enough said. Come on, Big Brain, this is one blonde that needs her morning coffee something fierce."

Crookie patted my arm anxiously. "Does this mean you *did* follow instructions on the troughs?"

I only chuckled evilly in reply.

I motioned him into a chair at a table for two in front of Laissez Fare's counter. I plunked my purse down and went behind the service bar to begin making a Latte for myself. Looking up to see Crookie sitting

A Date with Fate

slumped at the table, once again the picture of abject depression; I added fresh beans enough to make three shots of espresso. I had a feeling I was going to need the triple whammy.

"Can I make you a coffee, too, Crooks? Or something else?"

He shrugged and muttered, "I do not care, Anabel."

I didn't care, either, but I made him one. For the next couple of minutes the loud, gurgling noises of the commercial espresso machine were the only sounds. Carrying over two large cups of frothing coffee, I sat down across from him.

Taking a slow sip of the nectar of the gods, I opened my eyes to see him cautiously doing the same.

"Is your mother enjoying living in Florida?" I asked politely, delaying the inevitable to better savor my hot drink.

Crooks snorted softly. "As you know, my mother does not enjoy anything, but she has her sister to nurse so she is at least occupied."

I grinned. "So, I guess the better question would be; are you enjoying your mother living in Florida?"

He nodded rigorously. "Yes, immensely, thank you for asking. How is NanaBel?

"My grandmother, the lucky bum, is probably punching a camel in the head as we speak. She's on her way to the Luxor region in Egypt. After that, she's off again to Germany to stay with friends. Can you believe it's a house party at a castle over the holidays?"

"I love that woman." Crookie stated. "What are your sisters up to lately? How's Jasmyn?" Crookie has always had a fascination for my sister, Jazy. I think he'd like to put her under his microscope and study her closely.

"My sisters..." I repeated, smiling a little. "Let's see; Mac married a man twelve years younger, Kenna divorced her latest, he was twenty years older, and Jazy's single and working her way through the southwestern suburbs, specifically the Prior Lake area."

Crookie grinned in spite of his depression; he knew my family well enough he'd get the subtext of all I was really saying.

We both sipped our coffees in silence for a few moments.

Scrunching his face, Crookie carefully set his full cup back on the table.

His eyes anxious but determined, he demanded, "Anabel, is your brother hiding here?"

"Hiding? No, Reggie's not hiding here. Why are you asking me such a bizarre question?" I probably looked as bewildered by the abrupt question as I sounded. Crookie visibly relaxed his shoulders at my answer.

"He is not ever home. He does not return my calls. I think he is hiding from me, the bastard." Crookie was beginning to get agitated all over again.

"Yikes, Crookie, wait a minute here. Why would Reggie be hiding from you, of all people? I didn't even know you guys spoke."

I was completely confused. Crookie hadn't lived in Northfield since he was married two years ago. At his new wife Cheryl's urging, they had moved to Edina. This is a suburb bordering Minneapolis to the immediate west and known for its over-priced real estate and snob appeal.

Crookie really is a scientist with advanced degrees in the biotechnology and chemical engineering fields, and who knew what else. Not me; science still gives me a headache. I knew he invented and patented a food industry process while still in graduate school that was making him a mint. I was proud of him and his accomplishments, but begged him not to tell me any details. With his brilliant mind, Crookie probably has invented many more things I wouldn't want to know about by now. He was courted while in college by many companies but chose Ecolab, a local company in St Paul, and has worked there since. He's correct; I have not one clue what he does there.

I hoped this didn't make me a bad friend, but I couldn't be blamed science hurt my head, right?

That's what I thought, too.

He gave a bitter laugh. "Oh, it is not me he has been 'speaking to', but my wife, Cheryl."

I took another long sip of my coffee to buy some time, my synopses finally firing from the triple hits of espresso. It was starting to become a disturbingly clearer picture once I remembered Cheryl's sister had moved to Northfield a few years ago. That was how Crookie had met Cheryl in the first place. "The Day of Infamy" was how I believed Anna and I had termed it at the time.

Cheryl's a bitch—with a capital C.

My brother has dated a multitude of women over the years. I was under the impression he didn't mess with married women. Reggie chose to take the simplest, most direct path from point A to point B in life. He followed this principle where women were concerned, too. I'd yet to see him get worked up over whether a woman wanted him. If she did, fine. If not, he'd shrug good-naturedly at the rejection and move on. He avoided the complicated. I reasoned you couldn't get much more complicated than a married woman.

I sighed at this point in my musings. What was I thinking? We are talking about a man and his penis here. Incredibly moronic destinations are often visited when the little head is doing the driving.

I thought seriously about the man I knew my brother to be. When Reggie started his own company he worked long, hard hours in all kinds of extreme weather for five years to build up his business. It's paid off; he is reputed to be a solid, dependable contractor.

A Date with Fate

This tickles my grandmother to no end. She had stressed over Reg not having the proper male influences in his life while growing up.

NanaBel has raised all five of us kids--MacKenzie, Kenna, Me, Jasmyn, and Reggie--since I was six years old and our folks died.

I suppose living with a grandmother and four older sisters since the age of three, and being the youngest and the only boy, there could be a small case made for Reggie not having enough male influences.

It's true that as a little dude, my sisters and I did doll him up a bit. We applied blue eye shadow and then mascara to his incredibly long lashes, curled his blonde hair, buttoned him up in a frilly dress, and encouraged him to dance like a ballerina. He was so adorable with hands pointed up over his head and tippy, tippy, tippy-toeing all around the room.

It also wasn't helpful Jasmyn is only a year older than Reggie and way meaner. Jazy could beat him up until they were into their teens. We take sisterly joy in reminding him that by the time he was tough enough to possibly win a fight against any of his sisters, he was too old and knew better.

My brother has actually enjoyed constant, male camaraderie his whole life. My dad's old cop buddies, particularly Jack Banner, and our Uncle Trevor--who had no sons, along with NanaBel's platoon of male friends were all constantly trying to outdo each other. They vied to teach him traditional manly pursuits and made sure he did everything boys should do. Reg was spoiled and happily soaked up all the attention.

As a result of these men, and despite his sisters, Reggie has grown up to be a halfway decent man with widely varied interests. Not a woman-hating, homicidal, cross-dresser.

He may never be ready to settle down, but with four older sisters that he loves, respects, and more importantly, fears; I give him credit to steer clear of the wife of any of our good friends. Unless trashed, then all bets were off.

I spoke quietly, "Are you sure about my brother?"

Crookie shrugged. His face twisted and I wanted to tear my eyes away from the sight of his emotional torment. I forced myself to keep a steady gaze. I've known this boy since grade school and we've been friends since high school. We were tight for several years, even when he went away to school in Indiana. I visited him at Purdue quite a few times, or saw him when he came home and brought his new college friends. I'm still in touch with a couple of them. One of his old roommates' visits me on his way to a relative's cabin up north every summer.

Yes, we were tight—until he got hitched.

Cheryl and Crookie dated for only a brief, few weeks before they went to Vegas on a weekend trip and came back married. Surprise! Since the deed was done, I could only wish the best for Crooks. I kept my true opinion of his bridezilla to myself; it would do no good to discuss it.

His new wife hated my guts. She made Crookie's life miserable until we gave up trying to stay friends in the face of her jealousy. Crookie was such an inexperienced man and no match for Cheryl's manipulations. He innocently emailed me the truth of how she threw fits if he even mentioned my name after they were married. He was so upset by this behavior in the woman he was convinced was perfect, and had been so happy to be in love, I had sincerely wished him the best. I let go of our day-to-day friendship for his sake. I had no wish to rock their marital boat.

Crookie and I hadn't seen each other much more than three times in the last two years. We talked briefly on the phone, or shot the occasional, under the radar "I'm still alive / how are you / miss you" text quickies, but that was the extent of our communications.

Cheryl didn't fool me for a second. She's a female most kindly described as a selfish user. We've all met her type. Cheryl's sure she deserves everything while doing absolutely nothing to earn it. These truly pitiable, but highly destructive soul-suckers use sex and emotional manipulation to live off some poor schmuck. The schmuck is intelligent enough to make tons of money, but inexperienced enough to fall for the machinations they initially mistake for love. Cheryl's the kind of human incapable of love for others, but she's honed her acting skills to temporarily reel in her victims throughout her life.

Crookie is a kind and gentle man who convinced himself his amoral wife was worthy of his love, saw only her positive points she was careful to show him at first, and worshipped her like she deserved it.

I reached across the table and linked my hand with his, squeezing. His eyes were glistening behind his glasses. I ignored this. "Tell me."

He did. Once the floodgates opened, Crookie couldn't stop talking. He must have been keeping all this dammed up for the last two years, miserable and alone.

Cheryl was caught cheating the first time six months into their marriage. She blamed being lonely because Crookie worked too much as the reason. It never stopped from there, and it was always somehow Crookie's fault, or somebody's fault—just never hers. His voice droned on in a monotone reciting how his lovely wife was always the wronged party in some scenario, as she continued wreaking emotional havoc while telling Crooks how much she loved him. I was so bummed listening. Seeing the shell of a man Crooks had allowed himself to turn into by not getting rid of Cheryl immediately after the first infidelity because he got caught in her web and loved her was not my idea of a fun time. It made my stomach hurt.

Love, for lack of a better word, is the strangest, most inexplicable emotion to me. I am honestly afraid of the concept of even "normal" love,

A Date with Fate

much less getting tangled up with a person suffering an extreme psychological disorder. What sane person wouldn't be?

Being a normal couple "in love" can be fantastic, but I've observed eventually most people settle in, become bored, and take it for granted. Then the strangest thing happens. A lot of them assume they are *supposed* to become bored and take it for granted, and live out the rest of their lives this way.

How could the excitement of two or three fantastic years together at the beginning ever be worth the resulting lifetime of ongoing monotony called "being in a committed relationship"? I'm not stupid or cynical, or against love or marriage. Love is exhilarating and wonderful and delicious. I would love to believe in love. It's just after years of observation, my conclusions are that being committed until death do us part would kill me. Love and commitment--they appear to be two, extremely different concepts, and not the couple we are taught to believe go hand-in-hand so naturally.

Crookie would be the first to tell me scientific research suggests falling in love is a biochemical process in the body responding to cues from your glands. In your brain, the hypothalamus signals your pituitary gland to open the free bar and pour shots of dopamine, nor epinephrine, phenyl ethylamine, estrogen and testosterone into the bloodstream. You don't stand a chance against wanting to mate over the euphoria of that chemical cocktail running amok through the body. Phenyl ethylamine's a natural amphetamine. Our sneaky bodies are getting us high, encouraging us not to eat, and telling us we don't need sleep. We can live on love.

Then, anywhere from months up to a couple of years later of this incredible euphoria, after you are good and hooked, the body begins to produce the hormones oxytocin and vasopressin to calm us down, to normalize us, and get us back in the swing of daily life. We should be content to bond in "roommate love" for the next thirty-forty-fifty years. Hey, grow up and be mature—the honeymoon can't last forever, right?

My friends say there are many benefits to being in love and part of a couple, and life can be just as monotonous or lonely when single. This is true. They say you learn to accept the boring and mundane as a way of life in exchange for the benefits. This I don't get.

These words had me envisioning lifers at a factory job. You're working your whole, adult life at a job you admit you don't particularly like anymore because the health insurance plan is hard to beat, and you've put some hard years into the company. You're scared silly to go be self-employed on a Cobra plan. Most people have never researched or compared the costs of a self-employed Cobra plan. They're content to assume it is way too expensive. They'll carry on being miserably bored, unhealthy victims in their lifer jobs and gripe to anybody who will listen, but they'll be safe and insured.

My friends assure me, as they take their separate vacations and pursue their separate friends and hobbies, they are as happy with their marriages at five, ten, or fifteen years as they were at one year. They've just grown and it's a different kind of happiness. According to our body's chemical engineering, they aren't wrong.

My friends tell me as a couple you are not alone; you have someone to share your life with—for money, sex, affection, moral support, household chores, to cook for and eat with, the bills, the kids, the vacations, and old age.

I don't tell these friends what I think of their marriages or committed relationships—what do I know what makes them happy? I get the general idea is to grow old together having shared all these small and large moments of a lifetime. I get in your forties-fifties-sixties these couples will sit outdoors in individual claw-foot tubs. They'll hold hands across the grass. They'll relax overlooking a pond on the edge of a forest; after popping a blue pill and waiting for life to kick back in.

After what I have seen with my own eyes, this old idiom seems to regularly spout off in my head like a nervous refrain, "There but for the grace of God, go I."

Unfortunately, all I have to do is hang around ninety-nine percent of people around me that are happily committed, roommate love couples to be reminded there are stereotypes out there for a reason. These are the solid marriages I'm talking about. These aren't the truly miserable ones with the extra problems of addictions, sexual or emotional infidelities, or mental and physical health issues.

Is staying together as a miserably happy couple because you followed a biological instinct, mated, and possibly had a child or three really beneficial to anyone involved, other than possibly financially?

Is smiling though gritted teeth while pretending you are not bickering, or bored as a way of life, truly how we are supposed to live out our lifetimes as a result of falling in love?

Is no longer bothering to charm or be charmed by your loved one, having to be reminded by one's soul mate to treat them with consideration and affection on special occasions, designating a night when you might actually try to spend time together with the person you love most in the world while racking your brain to figure out where to go and what you can talk about, and being routinely a hundred times more interested in your work or your computer screen--is that what it means to be half of a happy, devoted couple in a committed relationship—all in the name of love?

Or, would most humans be smarter to treat relationships like you do your cars--trade them in every few years for a newer model more suited to your evolving, individual tastes and lifestyles?

I hoped I never learned the answers to any of these questions.

A Date with Fate

I gave Crookie my full attention again at his next words. "Two months ago, I sunk to new, low depths. I decided to spy on Cheryl down here when she was coming to visit Tina, her sister." He kept his eyes on our loosely joined hands.

His free hand was nervously opening and closing the lid of the peridot ring I always wore on my left ring finger. Trust Crookie to notice the miniscule hinges off to the side of the emerald cut stone. This very old, silver ring was a gift from NanaBel after a venture to Italy. It's called a Borgia ring because the gem stone top opens to one side revealing a tiny compartment purportedly designed to secretly carry poison. I carried a breath mint in mine. Hiding my amusement, I amended that thought. I used to carry a breath mint in mine. Crookie had absently removed the mint, sniffed it suspiciously, and then popped it in his mouth.

He peered up at me and observed out of nowhere, "I am always so amazed when I see you in person and realize how petite you are compared to how I think of you. I could snap your finger like a twig, it is so delicate."

"That was such a..." I pulled my hand back and securely latched onto my coffee cup with both hands, "totally creepy, Crookston thing to say!"

He laughed with me, but sobered up quickly. "Before I left for work that Friday morning, we were fighting again. Cheryl informed me she was leaving for Northfield to stay for the weekend." He ran his hands through his brown hair, leaving it standing on end. "I have to say, things were so terrible by then it was a relief to hear she was going somewhere for a few days, you know?"

I nodded, and then took a big swallow of coffee to not say anything else. And then another. He didn't need me adding to his misery by questioning why the hell he stayed with that hooker as long as he had.

He took a small drink of his coffee, too. I fondly watched him precisely wipe off his mouth with the precisely folded napkin. "After thinking about it all day, I decided I was going to get the proof she was playing me like I suspected for months. I knew it was true that she was, but I needed to see it for myself. That was my thought process. Probably the scientist in me needed the hard data to accept the cold facts." I smiled sadly in my agreement. I'm sure that was exactly the reason. "I drove down here and arrived about ten o'clock. I went directly to Tina's street. Do you know her, Anabel?"

"I met her once at a party a year ago." I made a face. "She was really wasted on something and hanging on some dude I didn't know."

"That sounds like Tina. Listen, I will hurry to finish my story because I know I am taking up your time. This probably was not how you planned on spending your Saturday morning, right?"

He looked so morose and miserable. I got up and put my arms around him, rubbing his back.

"You will always be my friend, Crooks. You did right coming to me because I always have time for my friends. I'm glad I was home to answer your rude buzzing."

He mumbled a "sorry about that". He wrapped his long arms around my waist nearly twice and held on; burying his face against my, for this particular moment in time only, maternal bosom.

I stood there rocking us slightly and stroking his head. He was quiet for so long I was starting to worry he was silently bawling. Then he turned his head, and I was relieved when he spoke quietly with no trace of tears.

Sensitive soul that I am, I hate it when men cry. It gives me the heebie-jeebies.

"When I got near Tina's, I parked down the street and walked up to the house. There were a few lights on and a couple of parked vehicles in the driveway. One was Cheryl's BMW; the other was a red truck I suspected was your brother's. It had a white logo on the door, but it was too dark out to decipher the writing." His head rose and fell with my deep sigh and he patted me in comfort this time--on the butt. I cuffed his head, but only lightly due to the extenuating circumstances. "Ouch! I walked right up to the front bedroom window and looked in through the curtains. Cheryl was with a man on the bed." He made a choking, scoffing sound. 'I finally had my proof in the flesh, all right. I did not even have to break a sweat figuring it out. Shit." He paused a second. "Anyway, I could not be totally certain from the angle, but the man was blonde and approximately the size of your brother." Crookie looked up at me, his face anxious. "I need to know if he was the man I observed with Cheryl. He is my only clue to go on. She has not been in contact since that night, Anabel, and I am really fucking worried now."

Hearing Crookie swear so much this morning was almost as alarming as his story. He normally spoke very correctly and properly, rarely using contractions, much less curse words.

I pulled back in disbelief, my hands on Crookie's shoulders. "What do you mean 'worried now'? Didn't this happen two months ago?"

"Correct, but I left immediately after seeing her in that bedroom. I called her cell from my car on the way home and it went directly to voicemail." He choked out another bitter laugh. "She was otherwise occupied, remember? I left a message telling her not to bother coming home because I was divorcing her. From that moment on, I would not be speaking with her again except through our attorneys. I told her not to attempt to get her belongings because the locks would be changed on the doors of our house. I was finally, irrevocably done with her." His eyes were cold behind the reflection in the lens of his glasses. This was a grown-up Bob Crookston I was gazing back at; no more illusions of love clouded his vision. "I did have all the locks changed immediately that next morning. I paid a hefty premium to have the job done on a Saturday, too. I retained a divorce attorney immediately, and followed every step he outlined for my situation."

Crookie gave my waist a shake in emphasis. "Do you know what, Anabel?"

"What, Crookie?"

"It felt fucking fantastic."

We both laughed a little hysterically at that statement. Man, I couldn't blame him for any retaliation he took to nut up at that point. In fact, I cheered him on wildly for remembering he had a set of balls after being so systematically emasculated.

His next words made me stop smiling when their full import set in. I patted his shoulder and left him to go sit back down in my chair, needing to think.

"Cheryl has not called once. Neither has her attorney, if she has one. Tina finally called me back a few days after this happened. She made Cheryl leave her house that same Friday night when she got home from her job because they got into a screaming match." He snorted, saying dryly, "Apparently, Cheryl drank Tina's liquor. Tina has not spoken with Cheryl since that night around eleven. She said good riddance, as far as she was concerned." Crookie paused and started to drink his Latte, then stopped. "Could I please get some water, Bel? I am not a coffee drinker."

I chuckled, "Sure."

I went to the fridge behind the bar and brought us back two bottled waters, my brain buzzing over what Crookie had just related.

A frisson of foreboding ran through me thinking about the fact Cheryl hadn't contacted him, or been to the house to get any of her stuff for over two months.

We drank some water in contemplative silence. "Has she taken any money out of the ATM or used any credit cards during this time?"

He shook his head. "No credit cards. She withdrew several hundred dollars before going to Tina's on that Friday, but nothing since. She also has money at her disposal in the checking account I left open. I have been depositing a regular stipend on my lawyer's advice for Cheryl's living expenses, but no money has been withdrawn."

I was quiet again and Crookie sighed. "I know this seems strange that I am only now getting anxious she has not been in contact, but you have to know Cheryl. She would think nothing of stringing me along, not answering her cell and trying to heighten my worry by disappearing." Crooks abruptly stood up, then started pacing back and forth in the aisle in front of our table. "It has been great having her gone. I have thrown myself into work on a big project and have not even thought about her for a week or two at a time." He scrubbed at his face with both hands while making a growling noise. "This is so messed up. I do not have a clue where she is, I do not care where she is, yet I know I need to find her so I can move on and get the damn divorce."

I thought over what he had revealed for a few seconds. "I can tell you this, Crooks. She is not living with my brother." I frowned. "What about other friends and family? Nobody's heard from her or seen her?"

Crooks smirked. "What friends, Anabel? I used to buy her stories that other women were jealous and mean to her. Tina is the only other family." He sat back down; long legs sprawled out in the aisle while his eyes stared up at the ceiling. "You did not like Cheryl from the beginning, did you?"

"No." I made a moue of distaste at the memory. "You married her before I could talk sense into you. I doubt I could have made you see reason, but I really regret being gone on vacation right before you lost your ever-loving' mind and eloped."

He angled his head to the side and smiled at me. "I appreciate your honesty. It is refreshing, that is for sure." He smirked again. It was a look I would be happy to see erased from his repertoire of expressions. It spoke of hurt and rejection. "If anyone could have convinced me to slow down, it would have been you with your outstanding reasoning capabilities."

"Cute. When you didn't listen, O Thee of Little Faith, I would have laid a smack down on you." I shot him a sly smile. "Then I would have driven you far away and straight into the arms of a talented, pretty prostitute with a heart of gold. Yep, I would have locked you up with Goldie for a few days, or weeks, of compiling raw data for scientific comparison."

When Crookie's indignant guffaws died down, I tapped my fingernail on his upturned palm resting on the table. "Seriously listen to me, old friend. It's not your fault Cheryl is what she is. You fell in love, you had faith, and you believed her to be the woman she pretended to be." I spoke softly and soothingly stroked his arm. "It's so her loss. You are such an amazing man. Any woman would be lucky, and so honored, to be loved by you. Why, Snookie-de-Crookie, I'd scoop you up for myself if I didn't know for a fact you recite the periodic table out loud while having sexual intercourse."

"God, you are a wonderful, terrible, rotten, little girl!' exclaimed Bob "Crookie" Crookston while laughing loudly, blushing, and then groaning in despair. He began to bang his forehead against the table.

"Oh, Bel, help me here. What am I going to do?"

Alarmed with the head-banging, I got out my cell and pressed 5, holding up a gimme-a-minute finger at his look of inquiry.

"Hi, Reg. Serious question for you. Yes, I said serious, not spurious. Can you talk?"

A Date with Fate

Crookie sat up quickly and reached for my phone. "Let me talk to him!"

I shot him my special Librarian frown--reserved expressly for grabby, excitable men. I stood up and walked out of his reach zone, but close enough he could still hear my side of the conversation.

"This is important, but you are not going to like me asking. Please bear with me for a minute, alright? First, I'm going to need you to swear to God here, okay? Yes, a blanket swear to God is exactly what I am asking for, that's correct. Thank you. Yes, I do appreciate you. Now remember, don't be mad I'm asking, but have you ever... umm," I glanced at Crookie and shrugged in apology, "had sex with Cheryl Crookston?"

I winced and held the phone away from my ear so Reggie's shouted response didn't break my eardrum.

Puzzled, I answered, "No, I'm not calling for Anna. What does Anna have to do with anything?" Then I got sidetracked as he continued shouting.

When he showed no signs of winding down, I interrupted. "Geez, you said you wouldn't get mad, so enough all ready! You know I don't normally get up in your business, so can you just answer my question, please? I said it's important."

Reggie's shouted response, "No, I swear to God I haven't sonofabitchin' had sex with Cheryl Freak-Show Crookston, that fuck-any-dick-with-a-wallet, ditch digging whore!", was audible probably in the next county.

I winced again. Crookie's face was set in stone. He sat with arms crossed and was staring down at the table. He had his answer from my brother.

I know Reg was being truthful about not having sex with Cheryl. Not only because of the sacred 'swear to God' clause used in our family of mainly atheists, agnostics, and general heathens to determine the ultimate truth; but because he rarely got mad. One reason he would flare up was if he suspected his word was doubted by someone he loved, meaning one of his sisters. In his anger, he was known to string together colorful swear words. These curses often make no literal sense yet, somehow, they get his point across quite concisely.

I was taken aback by his immediate anger in this case, and the Anna reference, but I shelved that thought for another time to think about.

I rushed in to calm my brother down. "I hear you, Reg. I didn't believe you'd touch her with a ten-foot pole. Here's the problem. Bob Crookston hasn't seen Cheryl in two months. He was under the impression you may have." I nodded over at Crookie. "Yes, he mentioned he had called you. I'll tell him that, but I have one more question. When did you see or talk to Cheryl last?"

I listened to his succinct answer with raised eyebrows. Unfortunately, it was both my eyebrows. I flashed on Luke, thinking of his warmth and strength upstairs in my room.

'Was I crazy to have slipped out of bed?' I had a sudden, sharp pang to be up there cuddling with him instead of down here; dealing with the serious, fast becoming ominous threat of the missing hooker wife. Then the realist in me shook off the unprecedented yearning to be held and protected from life's little peccadilloes, and I snapped out of it.

I listened to my brother relate what he knew for a few seconds longer. My relief he hadn't been involved with a married woman was more intense than I had anticipated. I don't know why I am always surprised when people show their ethical side. It's not as if I have been constantly battered with deception or immorality to be as skeptical of human nature as I am. Maybe it's from all the reading I have done over the last twenty years. I should have watched more television.

"Yes, I agree. Jack will definitely be next on our to-do list after I talk with Crookie. Thanks for being cool about this." I laughed at my brother's pithy, one-word response to end the call.

"When did he see Cheryl?" Crookie asked, leaning forward intently. He looked tired but hopeful, eager for some definitive answers at long last.

"Reggie saw her later that night."

Crookie shook his fists high in the air. His grin stretched from ear to ear. "Yes! You do not know how relieved I am to hear someone actually has seen her since Tina's. What happened? And who is Jack?"

I drank some water, thinking I wasn't as sanguine. I grasped the more far-reaching consequences of Reg's story, but I understood Crookie's elation. I filled in the gaps by repeating Reggie's story of that night.

"Okay, first of all, Reggie says sorry for not getting back to you, but he's been super-busy with work and forgot. Secondly, it wasn't Reggie with Cheryl in the bedroom at Tina's with the candlestick. Maybe it was Colonel Mustard, but it wasn't my brother."

Crookie shrugged acceptingly. "Okay."

"Cheryl, however, did stop over at my brother's that night after Tina kicked her out. He was putzing around in his kitchen when he heard the knock. Reggie remembered the time since it was late and he'd glanced at the microwave clock." I paused to recall accurately what Reggie had said. "It was Friday, the fourteenth of September, at 11:33 PM. I'm sorry, Crooks, but she hit on him the minute he opened the front door. Reg told her 'Thanks, but no thanks', and tried to send her politely on her way."

Crookie blew out a breath, "I am fine. I have had a long time to get used to the idea. Go on, please."

"Cheryl went off on him in a rage about Tina throwing her out. Then she screamed at Reggie about liking the sex he had with her the

A Date with Fate

previous weekend after the bars closed, so why was he turning her away that night?

"Reg said she was nuts because he's never touched her. The most personal contact he's ever had with Cheryl was to reluctantly buy her a drink over at the Contented Cow the week before this happened. He made her leave that night, and she drove off. End of story. That was the last time he has seen or heard from her." I took another long, satisfying drink from my bottle of cold water. "In answer to your second question, Jack Banner's a friend of my family. He's a cop. You've met him over the years. Don't you remember him?"

"Oh yes, that Jack. I did not connect the first name when you mentioned it. He is the tough guy that always had his eye on you."

"Yeah, he's watched out for all of us since I was a kid."

He smiled at a memory. "I recall very well. For a period of time, I was somewhat concerned he may take advantage of you. When we were seniors, I asked you if older dudes around forty attracted you, remember?" He smiled again. "When you answered that I was trying to make you hurl and it was not going to work; I did not worry about him any longer."

I let out a peal of laughter. "That's why you asked me that? I thought you were asking because of Mr. Brock, that sub we had in Biology for two weeks. He was such a douche. So many of the girls thought he was hot, too. Major icky!" Crookie laughed while I shuddered at the memory of Mr. Brock's fixed, creepy stare on my chest or rear, depending on if I was coming or going. "Jack's the Chief of Police now in Northfield. Reggie and I both think you need to report Cheryl missing to the cops. If you agree, Jack will tell us the way to go about it."

Crookie sat forward enthusiastically. "Absolutely, I agree. Something is not right about Cheryl being missing this long."

"Gee, you think?" I didn't try to conceal my snarkiness.

Crookie may be relieved to have all this off his chest, but I didn't have a good feeling about any of this situation. It wasn't my Law and Order SUV voice talking in my head; it was more like my Law and Order SUV voice screaming in my head. This was not the end of the mess, but only the beginning.

I know women, I like most women, and I know how women think.

Cheryl is too much of a troublemaking bitch to drive off quietly into the sunset without a word of farewell.

It appeared my baby brother was the last man to see a woman now known to be missing for over two months. He had just reacted in uncharacteristic fury at the mention of her name.

I needed another coffee.

Chapter VI
"Call Me When You're Sober" by Evanescence

Saturday, 11/17/2012
9:15 AM

Sitting on my faux leather chair in my office tucked under the stairs, I was swiveling idly back and forth while staring blankly at the November's sales numbers displayed on the monitor in front of me.

I only had a short window of time to get in some work, but I was finding it hard to concentrate on the open Excel spreadsheet. I usually get so absorbed poring over reports that I have to tear myself away from the computer, but today I couldn't focus worth a damn.

Crookie had left about fifteen minutes ago to meet Jack Banner over at the police station. When I had called Jack, he had listened impassively to my explanation of events without much more than a grunted question here and there. When I was finished, he had ordered Crookie to the station immediately.

Jack had also been explicit Crookie come alone. I reluctantly agreed, but only once Jack reassured me my friend didn't need me to hold his hand. At least for today, Jack had bitingly added, he'd probably hold off beating Crookie with a police baton.

I guess it was my day to torque off the males in my family circle.

That still didn't stop me from cautioning Crookie to be careful what he said, and to query whether he was positive he wanted to go to the station without legal representation.

He had given me an incredulous look. "Why do I need a lawyer to report Cheryl missing, Bel?"

"Let's suppose the worst here for a minute. Say something bad has happened to Cheryl." I could get into this idea and rubbed my hands together. "Suppose someone has butchered her into manageable Cheryl pieces and then put her through a wood chipper, ala Fargo. Then the killer throws the mulch, formerly known as Cheryl, up in the air like confetti all over a plowed up corn field." I smiled brightly up at Crookie's horrified expression. "Can you account for every moment of your time over the last two months without knowing what time you may have to account for?"

Crookie appeared so struck by this idea it was my turn to be incredulous. Had he never once thought of foul play as a reason Cheryl hadn't shown her face in two months? I wanted to kill her myself and I hadn't set eyes on her in over two years.

A Date with Fate

I gave up trying to talk sense. Crookie was too happy knowing Reggie had seen Cheryl later that night. I hoped I wasn't sending a big-brained lamb off to slaughter.

Before I locked the lobby door behind him, an exuberant Crookie turned and swept me up in a boot dangling, bear hug. He nearly squeezed the life out of me. "I have missed you, Anabel." He squeezed me again. I think I felt a rib cracking. "Thank you so much for your help."

When he started to squeeze me a third time, I started smacking him about the head and shoulders in muffled protest. My face was mashed against his chest. Being hugged as a five-footer is often not pleasant.

He set me down and lifted his hands in mock surrender. "Okay, okay. I will see you tomorrow night for sure. I will contact you later today with an update--if that meets with your approval?"

At my regal nod as I fluffed my messed up hair, Crooks went smiling on his way, a much more optimistic man then when he arrived.

I glanced over at the door leading to my apartment.

I bit my lip and clenched my fists. I was so incredibly tempted to run up those stairs. I forced myself to turn right and keep walking back into the store. I checked the time on my cell. 9:20 AM. I touched a finger to my naked earlobe.

'When would Luke wake the hell up and leave, and quit harassing me?'

My cell vibrated in my hand. It was before ten in the morning but I saw it was a text from my sister, Jazy, so I read it.

R we on 4 2nite @ Macs?

I thumbed, *Yep 7 Pick me up?*

Almost instantly, Jazy's response buzzed back. *K Ciao*

I put my phone away appreciating Jazy's no-frills approach to plan making. It was her basic approach to life, as well. She wanted something, she went after it. She didn't want to do something, she didn't do it. No fuss, no muss. It would never cross her tomboy mind to ask me what I was wearing before we went out. Sometimes, she was called cold; but that was usually by a frustrated, horned up guy disappointed to realize he wasn't getting lucky. I call her refreshing.

I headed to my office where I still sat minutes later, staring off into space in a fugue state. I kept thinking over what my brother had said about Cheryl Crookston.

Things weren't adding up and it was nagging the bejesus out of me. What had he meant when he initially asked if Anna had put me up to asking about Cheryl? That was so high school. I hadn't even done that sort of thing when I was in high school, so it rankled. It also made me speculate what Anna could know about Cheryl's disappearance.

I had to wait to talk with Reggie until later sometime today. He was out on a job. I was impatient for answers and waiting isn't my style, but interrogating him on a job site isn't cool. Not with power tools to be considered. It was a relief when this train of thought was interrupted by my cell.

It was a text from Anna again.

Do not worry. Am sure Luke OK.

I leaned back in my desk chair and stretched, then snickered and shook my head. Luke really had an admirer in my old friend.

Anna had met Luke, and fell in love with him, on what was supposed to be our sixth date at the end of October. This was a little over three weeks ago, on yet again, another Friday night.

Luke showed up to the store earlier than expected that night. His flight landed ahead of schedule and he came straight from the airport in Minneapolis to Bel's Books, about a forty-five minute drive with no traffic.

Before he arrived, I was closing out the last till and preparing cash drawers for Saturday. Anna was still doing her own work over at the Fare. We were alone in the closed store. Anna's laptop was open on her service counter and softly playing some Andrew Byrd. We talked sporadically of inconsequential things as we plugged away.

I was privately amused Anna was still here because I knew she was dragging her feet. She was dying to get a chance to check Luke out. I had inadvertently whipped up her curiosity to a fever pitch. Not by saying so little about our first few dates—that was the norm—but by the very existence of a sixth date.

Anna had clapped her hands together earlier today and stated she had to meet this paragon of perfection. If Luke still had me interested after the fifth date, instead of ditching him or turning him into only a friend after the second, then she wanted to meet the man.

I didn't think I was *that* bad with the men I went out with, but Anna assured me that I was even worse.

If I had my way, I'd keep my time with Luke a secret between ourselves and not let the real world intrude. Unfortunately, I have to live in the real world.

It's my choice to live in a smaller town. I'm highly visible as an owner of an established store; a big fish in a little pond. For the most part, I'm very satisfied with my choices. This is one of those rare situations when I regretted never leaving Northfield. I know what a fish swimming in an aquarium feels like, and I long for the anonymity of the open ocean found in big city life.

My personal life seems to be of acute interest to many people. I know most of these people care about me, so fair enough. If Luke and I were going to continue seeing each other, it was probably necessary for Luke to meet my friends and family before the speculation grew too rampant and our dating was made into some big deal. Secrets appear juicy, but reality often proves duller than the fertile, dirty imagination. Dull is exactly the image I like to present where my personal life is concerned. To keep everyone out of my business; I was going to have to let them in it a little first.

Luke had been gone for work and we hadn't been out in over three weeks. I had missed his last two phone calls because I was out on other dates. When I've missed his calls in the past, I don't call him back unless he leaves a voicemail requesting I do.

Luke did ask me to call him back on Wednesday. My date was at a Euchre tournament with Rob. He's a guy I consider more as a fun friend who likes playing cards as much as I do. It ran late. I was wiped and fell into bed when I got home. I meant to call Luke back, but crashed before I did.

Thursday's date was with my octogenarian banker. Mr. Barkley is an old school charmer whom I adore and respect. He's one of the last of a dying breed of gentlemen from a different era, and this is a great pity.

I have a vastly entertaining time sharing a late Thursday dinner at his bachelor pad at least once a month. My banker's forgotten more on most subjects than most people will ever know in their lifetime, and he's a fascinating conversationalist. Mr. Barkley is very droll and debonair.

Last night, after a simple dinner of perfectly prepared oven roasted chicken with tarragon buttered root vegetables, I was relaxing back on a plush loveseat.

Sipping on my Chardonnay and nibbling a piece of dark chocolate, I teased my host. "Mr. Barkley, with all due respect, if you were even fifteen years younger and didn't manage my business affairs so expertly, I'd cave to temptation and give you a run for your money."

Eyes twinkling roguishly, his patrician silver eyebrows were as waggish as his response. "My dear Miss Axelrod, were I even five years younger, it would be to your greatest pleasure to fire me."

The Thursday night missed call from Luke had no voicemail. I had only been able to text Luke a quick hello in reply to his missed calls during the hectically busy last two days. This week had been hellish at the store. Getting with Luke over dinner and drinks after not seeing him for such a stretch was a plan I could totally get into.

My smile of welcome was enormous that evening when I looked up and saw him silently entering through the unlocked, back entrance of the store. Seeing him dressed all in black with a matching black expression on his swarthy face, it hit me how much I'd missed him.

I could see his eyes glittering from several feet away.

Bel's had been closed for awhile and Luke had no idea Anna was over at the Fare finishing her own work. She must have been down behind the service bar and I'm sure he thought I was alone.

With no return smile, he pinned me with a look. It was rife with sexual intent. My body responded by shooting pings of tingling awareness down to my very favorite vacation spot in the universe. I didn't say a word, finding myself fascinated and unable to look away from Luke's mesmerizing eyes. I wondered vaguely if this was how a staked goat felt being stalked by a ravenous lion; happy to be the sacrificial offering and eaten alive. He strode up behind the counter and then my back was up against my closed office door, his mouth on mine with demanding hunger.

His kisses seemed almost harsh or angry, but I was too busy loving the touch of his lips and tongue to care too much right then what his problem was. When I moaned my desire softly into his mouth and pressed closely up against him, Luke paused in his sensual assault on my senses.

Straightening up, he slid his hands down from encircling my waist to cup my bottom. He was staring down at me, broodingly silent and unmoving, while he held my ass in his hands. Then I felt his fingers slowly gathering up the hem of the back of my short, sweater dress. Feeling the thin fabric moving up higher, inch by inch, I was glad I'd chosen not to wear tights tonight. There was nothing but smooth thighs above my boots. His long fingers were absently stroking high on my thighs. Soon they were outlining the lower curves of my ass they'd found left exposed along the bottom edge of my boy shorts. Those fingers would come close, but never quite touch, the wetness his caresses and kisses were causing between my legs. His eyes were veiled beneath the lowered fan of his dark lashes and his mouth was serious, but I caught a flicker of satisfaction pass over his face at my unconcealed pleasure.

He slowly raised his eyes. I didn't try to hide the aroused smile of happiness I wore as a result of his greeting. I didn't even know if I could hide my desire should I want to for some reason; it felt like it would shine through. This man could bring me from zero to creaming my bikinis with only his knowing stare. His passionate kissing and intimate touches set me on fire in a way I've never experienced. I burned for him and let him know it.

I sensed something in Luke relax at my candid look. He smiled slowly, and heat flared openly in his eyes before I closed mine to his softer, slower kisses. He was expert and thorough, not missing touching on any area of my parted lips.

My hands flat on the door, I tilted my head back offering my exposed throat to his mouth. He leisurely kissed and sucked on me while his hands trailed up my sides, and teasingly skimmed over my breasts. At the feel of his teeth gently biting and then his tongue licking against my neck, my nipples hardened to tight, distended points obvious through even my bra and sweater dress. Luke continued to ignore them, except for brief, feather light touches with his fingers as he traced the curving fullness of my breasts with his hands.

A Date with Fate

I ran my fingers up the back of his thighs and squeezed his ass, digging into the rounded, taut muscles. Pulling him against me, I rubbed his heavy arousal against my lower stomach. I brought my hands between us, and ran my nails and palms up the front of each thigh. Lightly tracing over his balls, I cupped and softly squeezed him. Using both hands, I stroked up the length of his erection straining against the zipper of his pants. I allowed my roving fingers to apply harder pressure around the head of his dick for a moment, moving up and down. Luke murmured encouragement in my ear and pushed against my hands.

It was his turn to groan faintly when I sent my hands moving slowly up under his open jacket and along his hard stomach muscles. I caressed across his chest. I lingered over his flat nipples. I lightly pinched on the tips until they hardened into points I could feel through the cotton fabric of his shirt.

Luke pulled my hands away and held them down against my sides. He whispered compliments while placing slow, open-mouthed kisses down my neck and across the tops of my breasts. I smiled dreamily.

Earlier this evening, I had dashed upstairs to get ready before my crew clocked out. Black is my color, and I was all about it tonight except for the sparkle of my silver jewelry. My mid-thigh length sweater dress was incredibly soft cashmere. A wide belt cinched in my waist, and I wore suede, high-heeled boots that zipped up the back. A multi-strand necklace of delicate, silver chains graduated down from my throat and over my cleavage partially revealed by the scoop of the sweater's wide neckline. My streaky blonde hair was twisted and piled up on my head in a tousled look. I wore diamond studs in my ears.

Squeezing his hands, I arched against him like a purring feline under his kisses. Luke murmured against my skin, "You look pretty tonight and smell so good." He kissed the top curve of my right breast. I felt his tongue lightly lick my skin. "When you didn't answer my calls..."

"I'm finished!" Anna popped up from behind the Deli case, shutting the sliding door with a thud while wiping her hands on a towel. "I am going to have to...."

Anna's voice trailed off as she saw us. Luke had instantly spun around at the sound of her voice while keeping his left arm protectively around me. Even plastered boneless against the door and still in a sensual daze from Luke's ministrations, I had to snicker at the identical shocked surprise on both their faces. Luke had made me forget we weren't alone.

Anna recovered quickly. She made a beeline over to where we were standing. She glanced at me, and I groaned silently. I knew that innocent, quivering lips from trying-not-to-smile look. She gave in and grinned broadly.

"Hey, I'm Anna Johnson, Junior's friend and partner. You must be Luke." She dragged her gaze from Luke's face and looked at me again with bright, inquisitive eyes that didn't miss a detail of my unfocused state against the door. Her grin got bigger, if that was humanly possible. "I'm so happy to meet you."

Luke bumped Anna's fist with his own, losing his dark glare and smiling back easily. "Thanks, Anna. It's great to meet you, too. You two have been friends a long time, since grade school, right?"

"Yes, first grade. Did she also happen to mention when we met she smacked me with her lunch box?"

I found my legs and pushed off the closed door to stand next to Luke while shaking my head and muttering, 'And they're off....'"

Luke grinned, his dimple creasing his cheek. "No, she didn't mention that part. She did that to you? Anabel seems to have violence issues. She smacks, she bites," he squeezed my waist and slanted me a sly look, "she pushes. As her best friend, should I be worried, Anna?"

I rolled my eyes as Anna trilled with laughter. "Knowing her, I'd say you should worry most when Junior is quiet for too long. All the rest is just her way of showing affection."

Luke chuckled, but I observed a calculating look fleetingly pass over his face as he spoke with Anna. If I hadn't been watching him closely, I'd never have seen it flash by. It made me straighten to alertness, curious what he was up to.

"I think we'll need to talk more about Anabel's bad habits. This would be only for my future protection, of course." Luke gave me a quick smile. He ran his hand lightly up my arm and settled his arm around my shoulder.

Laughing, Anna instantly agreed. "Oh, but of course!"

Protesting, I yanked on the zipper of his leather jacket. "You're both crazy. I haven't heard even one bad habit mentioned here yet. What are you two talking about, anyway?"

They both groaned. Luke hugged me close while saying to Anna over my head, "Add delusional to the list, Anna."

Anna was laughing, but I saw her fascination with Luke's easy affection towards me. Moving away from his arms to walk a few steps to the checkout counter, I groaned again silently. I was really in for the third degree soon.

"Since Anabel has no bad habits," Luke coughed into his fist and cleared his throat, "then what should you warn me about, Anna?" He leaned in and joked conspiratorially, "It must be all her dirty secrets only a best friend knows you want to tell me about."

I relaxed. My earlier suspicions from seeing that look pass over his face melted away. Surely he wouldn't announce his intentions to pump Anna for intel about me, not with me right there?

Luke and I have talked about anything and everything as we explore getting to know one another. Anything and everything except our

A Date with Fate

personal pasts, if we were currently seeing anyone else, or our wants and needs in a relationship. We are carefully dancing around those touchy subjects.

I was happy never to go there. Those types of conversations got out of hand too easy. Talks like that invariably brought up issues. Issues caused misunderstandings and problems. Problems meant explanations, discussions, and more discussions. Enter next the resolutions, and then the ultimatums. Ultimatums brought on head-aches. Who in their right mind actively seeks a head-ache? One minute you are happily dating and thinking everything is groovy, and nothing needs fixing. The next you are depressed and contemplating lifelong self-pleasuring as the only answer.

I had no idea how Luke would react to finding out I was dating other men. Men can be so contrary. Too often in the past, it seems to drive a man nuts when they really get I'm not looking for a shout-it-to-the-world, sexually monogamous boyfriend scene. They see it as an insult or a challenge. It seems simple to me. If I care about one man enough, I will be monogamous to him because I want to be with no other man. You can't force loyalty with words. It's a gift you give with actions. Relationships don't really come with an automatic, thirty-year guarantee regardless of the wear and tear of daily life.

I didn't know what Luke intended to say to me about missing his recent calls before Anna interrupted moments ago. All these thoughts made me unsettled and slightly nervous, so I excused myself to finish closing up.

Walking into my office, I heard Anna giggling to Luke, "Junior is so full of dirty secrets; I wouldn't even know where to begin. It doesn't matter though, since I can't tell you a single thing."

'*Crap!*' With a man like Luke, that was the same as waving the red flag in a bull ring.

"Anna, was that a challenge I heard?" was Luke's teasing response.

'*Crap and more crap! Anna, use your brain here….*'

"God, no!" was Anna's cheerful answer.

'*Thank you, I love you Anna!*'

"There's no challenge, Luke. Best friends are vaults. Period. The end. It's a girl thing."

"So, vaults and best friends are only a girl thing?" was the silken reply.

"Oh, I don't know about that. I'm sure there are many gay guys out there that know what I mean, but most straight guys don't have a clue how a woman really thinks."

"Yes, men are basically clueless idiots, aren't we?" Luke easily agreed.

Anna and Luke laughed happily together.

'Reminder to self: kick Anna's ass later.'

I didn't know where Luke was going with this, but somehow it didn't sound good for Team Anabel.

I quickly took care of the rest of my closing business. All the while, I was very aware of Luke's eyes tracking me around the store from where he stood chatting with Anna. I didn't glance over at them, but I was aware of his every movement, as well. It gave me a feeling of heightened excitement for the night ahead. Maybe Anna was right; this was not normal behavior coming from me about a man near our sixth date. Since I rarely had a sixth date, I couldn't be sure what normal was.

Grabbing my purse, I was ready to go. As I approached the pair, I was momentarily surprised to hear Luke casually invite Anna to join us for dinner. She was pleased as punch but demurred, not wanting to horn in on our date.

I thought it was a great idea and seconded the invite, pleased Luke suggested it. Anna knows I wouldn't ask if I didn't want her, or if I thought Luke was asking only to be polite, so she cheerfully accepted.

I figured I had all night to be with Luke. A couple of hours of him getting to know my best friend was a good transition into a letting people know we were dating, and that it was no big secret.

Luke led the way out as I locked up. Behind his back, Anna kept giving me big eyes while grinning and nodding her approval of Luke.

Mouthing the word "Wow!" she motioned towards him ahead of us and silently clicked her fingers like pincers. Okay, she was specifically pretending to pinch his ass. Even as I elbowed her to behave, I had to agree his back side looked very fine from where I was standing.

On that note, the three of us walked our merry way down a block to Rueb's to have a drink and some food. Anna and I were both starving since neither of us had time for lunch that day. Inside Rueb's, it was not too crowded. We'd arrived between happy hours. Luke got us settled at a table, ordered a round of drinks, and proceeded to get to know Anna.

When I introduced them, I had a vague thought Anna's giddy bossiness could put Luke off, or his supreme confidence would repel Anna. Not so. He encouraged her to talk about growing up with me in Northfield. He listened attentively and soon had her forgetting any self-consciousness around him.

I was supplied with drinks and then, for all practical purposes, ignored.

Anna gets very excited and animated when telling stories. She jumps and bounces all over the place, or up and down in her chair if restrained by locale or seat belts. She laughs often and she's also a toucher. The girl is always grabbing someone, or something, or herself. When telling stories, she could go on endlessly with minute details. She easily gets sidetracked and digresses into other stories, forgetting her original train of thought until reminded.

It's the way a lot of girls talk when getting together and doesn't faze me. Women have so much to say. Although, I think Anna does take the prize for going off the beaten path during a conversation. I was used to prompting her to go back and finish a story if I ever wanted to know an ending.

It didn't seem to faze Luke, either. He sat back and nursed his beer, kept the drinks coming for us, and smiled often at Anna's antics. She told him many adventures of our growing up years that had Luke chuckling even while he sent me appraising looks. This was probably due to the fact I was usually getting us in and out of trouble. He most likely was reconsidering my offer of having his children. If I'm a scary sister, imagine what I'd be like as a mother.

Typically, I don't drink much when I am out. My norm is to sip on one cocktail forever. I don't have anything against drinking per se, I just don't seem to need alcohol to let loose and party. I often forget to drink. I have fun talking with friends and dancing without getting drunk, even though people often think I am drunk.

Tonight, Anna and I were totally wasted within an hour.

I understood much later it was all part of a diabolical Luke Drake plot to infiltrate, divide and conquer, then interrogate. I think I have a firmer grasp where his detailed career path may lead. Something like Lead Man in the neo-Spanish Inquisition sounds about right. It may be time to find out exactly what this man is up to when he's out of town.

After plying Anna with several drinks, no food, and his smiling regard, I was astonished to see my male-savvy friend was drunkenly lulled into putting her guard down completely with Luke.

I unconsciously finished off my third vodka tonic. It was one of those nights when it felt good to kick back and the drinks were going down easy. I shook the cubes in my glass while Anna giggles ran up and down the scales as Luke entertained her with sexist, blonde jokes and politically incorrect, tiny person one-liners.

I snorted into my empty glass. *'Yeah, go ahead and giggle, Anna; you're a five-foot-five brunette, and not a short, little Blondie like me.'*

I caught Luke's small smile at hearing my snort.

Our server, a woman I didn't know named Cindy, quietly delivered a shot to me. She nodded towards a man I didn't know sitting alone at the bar.

Raising the shot glass in a toast, I threw it back in one motion and sputtering, I nearly threw it right back up.

'Woo-wee!' I slammed the shot glass down on the table and shook my head in revulsion as the unknown, clear liquor burned down my throat.

Once I was sure I wasn't going to die, I became aware Anna was laughing uproariously at Luke's dry retelling of how we first met. Instead of taking my female side like a proper best friend, she kept telling him it was "so funny". She thought the part when he attempted to leave me standing there talking to myself while he exited Reggie's house was "flipping awesome".

I snorted again. *'Ha-ha. Too bad she didn't know the story of our first date that same night. Then she'd REALLY have something to laugh about at my expense.'*

The faithful Cindy arrived a few minutes later with a tray. She set down a fourth vodka tonic for me and a rum and coke for Anna--courtesy of Mr. Funny Man himself. She then put a second complimentary shot at my elbow.

Cindy sang softly out of the side of her mouth, "Somebody loves you...." and nodded towards the same guy at the bar. He raised his glass, smiling, when I glanced over.

I turned my head to Cindy and smiled wryly. "You mean somebody's trying to kill me." Resolutely, I cheered myself on. "Okay, man up, Anabel!"

As Cindy giggled, I took a deep breath and bravely threw this shot back after the first. It went down smoother. My body involuntarily shook for a minute like I was having a seizure, but it didn't burn as bad as the first shot.

'I was getting good at this!'

In victory, I held up the shot glass and grinned with numbed lips at my two new friends, Server Cindy and Guy at the Bar. They clapped in praise, and then a laughing Server Cindy whisked the shot glass away.

Luke had paused in his current story to Anna to watch me take the shot. I saw him watch my new friend, Guy at the Bar, who was talking with the bartender and unaware of Luke's once-over. He watched my finger as I rubbed it slowly over my lips to restore feeling. He watched as I propped up my suddenly buzzing head with palms on my hot cheeks and elbows plopped on the table.

I couldn't help smiling happily at Luke's watchful, unsmiling face. I think he's the hottest man I've ever seen in my life.

"Thank you, Anabel."

"Sure. For what?" I grinned.

"For what you just said to me." He answered, brows raised.

"I didn't say anything." I scoffed, laughing. I amended emphatically, "I was *thinking* something."

Luke tipped back in his chair and crossed his arms over his chest, grinning and shaking his head at the same time. He started to reply, then stopped and laughed out loud.

A Date with Fate

Tipsily, I can't turn off my delighted grin as he laughs. Luke has an excellent sense of humor, but I would never call him happy-go-lucky. As we've gotten closer, I know under his amiable, calm surface he's often on the more serious side and can sometimes be dark.

His voice is naturally low and gruff, but when he laughs the sound comes from far down inside him, popping out almost against his will and he appears slightly surprised. I think Luke grins dryly at irony, snorts wryly in his own secret amusement at people, and sarcastically chuckles at life's little foibles, but he doesn't often genuinely laugh for the sheer, wonderful fun of it. I always feel like I have won a prize, or done something special when I surprise his happy laughter this way.

Anna was noisily sucking down the last of one drink and waving enthusiastically across the room to someone she knew. Hearing Luke's deep laughter she said, "What's going on? What did I miss?" She took a big swig of her new drink. "Wuke, finish telling me about that westaurant in Chicago where your friend works."

I giggled at Anna's use of w's in place of other letters. This always happens when she's getting wasted and never fails to tear me up. Luke righted his chair. He shrugged helplessly at me like he had no choice but to entertain, and then resumed his conversation with Anna.

I snorted in my glass for the third time. *'Yeah, dude's about as helpless as a King Cobra.'*

Abandoned, as well as neglected, I was feeling warm. I picked up my drink and put the cold glass against each rosy cheek to cool off, and then I took a long swallow to cool me off inside. When I focused in on their conversation awhile later, my mouth dropped open in shock to hear Anna seconding Luke's every opinion like Polly the Parrot starving for a cracker.

This made me woozily realize I was hungry and that I needed to go to the bathroom.

I interrupted Luke to excuse myself. He was explaining to a bewitched, befuddled Anna either a punch line of a joke or his political viewpoint—I couldn't be sure which--that in a perfect world we would be better off led by a triumvirate of Republican businessmen with absolute power.

Luke stood up and gallantly pulled out my chair. This caused the adoring Anna to clap and extravagantly compliment his wonderful manners.

I muttered, "Thanks should go to his mother."

I got up without making eye contact with Luke. This was to hold myself back from delivering a sucker punch to his helpless, eight-pack. He would have only added the blow to the list of my imaginary bad habits. I carefully made my lonely way to the Ladies room sans best friend; an event seldom seen in my lifetime.

I did my thing, washed my hands, and swayed and grooved to a man named Marvin singing about getting it on. The music was bouncing off the tiled walls at a high volume through an unseen speaker. I patted at my hair, and made sure my clothes were still on after that song was finished. I reapplied my lips gloss, not really able to see my face too clearly in the wavy mirror. They should really do something about that.

On the way back to our table, I made a detour to thank Guy at the Bar for sending me those god awful shots. Grabbing a handful of nuts from a bowl, I munched hungrily while leaning my back against the bar next to his stool. He looked like a nice guy, so I told him that. I also let him know he shouldn't waste his money on me, that I was there with my date.

"You are?" Guy asked, confused.

"Yep, I am here with that man." Guy at the Bar turned and followed my pointing finger towards the empty pool table. I closed one eye, my left, and corrected my aim to my table.

We both watched Anna take a big slug of her drink. She continued talking and making strange motions like she was sawing a piece of particularly difficult wood in half. Luke was nodding, but his eyes kept coming back to me and my friend at the bar. He was not smiling again. His face looked hard and a little cruel when he wasn't smiling.

Guy said, "Sorry, my mistake. It didn't look like you were with him. What do you think your girlfriend is doing?"

I nodded my agreement on his first comments. "He's a very tricky date." I peered at Anna. "I cannot tell a lie. I have no clue what she's doing. Is it just me, or does it looks weird?"

Guy at the Bar, after some consideration, agreed. "It looks weird."

He tapped my hand that was beating time to the music on the bar. "Your date doesn't look very happy right now. Do I need to worry?"

I looked over at Luke. "Huh. I can't see real well since the lights are so dim in here," I smiled brightly at Guy, "but, hey, I was just thinking myself he looks kind of cruel. I think it's his mouth. What do you think? Don't worry though, okay? I won't let him beat up a nice guy like you."

"Good, thanks. I don't know about his mouth. I think he just looks pissed off."

In considering silence, we both glanced over at Luke.

Luke raised his right brow. For some reason, I had no problem seeing that motion. Similar to the Patellar reflex, this gesture made me want to straddle his lap every time it occurred. I snorted a giggle at the thought. Luke frowned and nodded his head slightly towards my empty chair.

I shoved off the bar. "Ah, he had me at the eyebrow move. Bye-bye, Guy, and thanks again." I patted Guy at the Bar on the shoulder.

"You're welcome. You're nice, too." He smiled. "If you decide you don't like his tricks...."

A Date with Fate

I laughed and waved, saying over my shoulder, "Thanks, but so far, I like his tricks just fine."

As I sat back down, Luke reached for my hand and linked it with his. I leaned over and kissed his cheek, then slowly wiped off my lip gloss with my thumb. He smiled, but it didn't erase all the hardness from his face. He turned back to Anna's story.

I leaned over and kissed his cheek again, smiling big when he turned to give me a stern look for interrupting, but squeezing my hand in his. Anna also mimicked his stern look, but since she was swaying in her chair it was impossible not to giggle. I leaned her way and gave her a kiss on the cheek, too.

"That's for being such a cute chipmunk."

She grabbed onto my right arm and started shaking it while laughing in excitement. Anna announced loudly, "You are dwunk. Oh my god, Wuke, Junior's dwunk. She never gets dwunk!"

"Hey, maybe you're drunk.' I countered, pulling my arm back before she wrenched it from its socket. "Did you ever once think of that, Miss Chippie?"

Luke laughed out loud.

I grinned at him. "I'm not drunk. I just think I need glasses. Really, I swear."

Anna bounced in her chair. "Wait! Everyone be qwiet! I have to finish telling you, Wuke. Listen, now, okay? Junior, be qwiet for a minute. You don't need glasses, okay, you are just shit-faced. Let me finish my story."

I nodded, relieved to be assured I didn't need glasses. I looked at Luke and saw he was giving me one of his intense stares while Anna chattered away. She was doing that peculiar sawing motion again while speaking of tree forts.

I gestured helplessly and mouthed, "I'm shit-faced."

I brought a finger to my lips, shushing him. He grinned, and swiftly kissed our joined hands. I glanced over at the talking Anna and scootched my chair closer to Luke's.

I whispered, "Don't let me drive home."

He whispered back, "We walked."

I whispered back again, 'Yeah, but I may want to drive our truck."

"There's no way in hell you are driving a tricycle, so don't worry."

"I *wasn't* worried about driving a tricycle! What the…"

Server Cindy interrupted my snorting giggles to bring me a fifth vodka tonic, a double. I swore to her I didn't order it. Laughing, she pointed to a nearby table of four men playing cards I hadn't noticed. The bar had been steadily getting busier and more crowded as we drank.

These guys I knew, or at least I thought I recognized them from working over at Reggie's place. They were sort of blurry, so it was hard to be sure. I waved my arm in their general direction with a big smile—in case they had a hard time seeing, too. They called back greetings. I spun around in my chair and chatted with them all for a few minutes; turns out they didn't know my brother.

I turned back to Luke and Anna. I was sucking my fifth drink down through the little straw like it was water. I swallowed vodka down the wrong pipe at hearing what was going on right beneath my nose.

Anna was most distressingly, without caution or forethought, drunkenly answering any questions Luke idly put to her about any subject of our past. My past.

I had been dimly aware of hearing her speaking in the background, but now caught the end of her saying, "...and this was the wast guy Junior went out wiff. He bored her, too. I hope you don't bore her, Wuke."

I narrowed my crossing eyes suspiciously at this little development. Luke and his double gazed back at me with an amused expression on their faces and a dangerous glint in their four eyes.

We had been at Rueb's for one hour.

I was completely trashed and Anna was firmly Luke's new best friend. I had no idea what she had been singing to Maestro Luke this past hour, but the vault door was definitely ajar.

Anna's head now rested on the table, she was near to passing out. I absently pulled the straw out from between her lips, needing to exert some force to get it out from her clenched teeth.

I knew dazedly, on some level, I should be disgusted with myself for underestimating how deviously good Luke really is, but it seems I'm too happy of a drunk to care.

Luke smilingly suggested we get Anna home and then we could continue on with our date. Even in my drunken state, I felt a moment of satisfaction seeing the blank expression on Luke's face when I told him, most regrettably, our date was over. We'd be taking Anna back to my apartment for the night. She was way too drunk to be by herself. If I brought her home this trashed, Aunt Lily would blame me and chase me with her antique, sword cane—set on slice and dice.

Back at my place, Luke led us like a Sherpa up the Mount Everest of a steep staircase to my apartment.

The outside air had braced me a little, but I still had problems focusing my eyesight and Anna's legs weren't working so well. Luckily, that didn't stop us from singing various duets for Luke's listening pleasure all the way home, into my building, and up the stairs. I thought our rendition of "Coming 'Round the Mountain" was particularly fine. I did the 'When She Comes!" and "Yee-Ha!" parts with bump and grind gusto.

At the summit of the stairs, a swaying Anna abruptly covered her mouth with her hand. Letting out a dreadful moan a zombie would be

A Date with Fate

proud of, she ran stumbling towards the bathroom. Since she left the door open, violent retching was soon heard.

Luke winced at the gagging sounds, shooting me a quick, guilty look.

I spread my arms wide in answer and shrugged, laughing. "Hey, Torquemada, don't feel too bad. You can lead the girls to the bar, but even you can't force them drink."

Luke's grin was wide as he repeated incredulously under his breath, "Torquemada..?" while shaking his head.

He was reaching for me, and damned if I wasn't eager, when Anna's pitiful voice could be heard beseeching my name from the bathroom.

"Hold your horses, little doggie, I'm a comin'!" I called down the hallway.

I turned back and smiled a cheery, boozy good night. "Well then, Luke Drake, thank you so much for the dinner."

Rubbing his forehead, he laughed and gracefully admitted defeat.

After quickly making plans with me for the next day to explore Minneapolis, Luke stopped his descent to leave with one foot on the stairs. He was looking on in amazement as I painstakingly made a note to myself of our date. It was on my foyer mirror with a tube of lipstick from my purse.

"Sweetheart, why don't you let me put the time in your cell, instead of these," he waved toward my note. Doubled over with laughter, he was barely able to get the next word out, "hieroglyphics on the mirror?"

I called down the hall I'd be there in a second. I walked over to Luke.

He waited for me, still chuckling. I reached up and planted a chaste kiss somewhere near the region of his dimple. "You'll not trick me into giving you my cell phone so you can plant a bug in it. Don't be too surprised if I wear an aluminum foil headband tomorrow to block your micromindwaves. Now, good night My Pharaoh, unless you'd like to help with Anna in...?"

Luke made a face of mock horror and beat a hasty retreat down the stairs. He ordered up from the last stair. "Anabel, buzz me out the front and lock up right away."

All ready at the master station, I rolled my eyes at his orders. I called back down over the ledge. "You called me my first nickname. Don't think I didn't notice how cutesy you really are!"

Smiling over the sound of his loud snort of male disgust as he left, I waited to see him leave the building. I verified those doors were locked and the alarm reset, and then went to see if Anna was still among the living.

Once I got Benedict Anna alone, she got a friendly reminder on the merits of remembering to keep her mouth shut, the definition of the word vault, and who was truly her best friend. She was a captive audience. She was draped over the toilet in my bathroom and still puking her guts out from all the liquor Luke poured down her unsuspecting throat.

As I held back her hair off her face, I softly brought up the pinky swears from grade school. I gently reminded her of the painful, penknife slices of Indian Blood Brother oaths in eighth grade. Did she really forget the five beers each, tearful declarations of best friend love in high school, as we vomited in tandem? I even dredged up the sincere, if paranoid, swear to Gods to be friends forever the time that we smoked weed at eighteen and got so high. We laughed and ate until we passed out like beached whales on my bedroom floor. The deal clincher that made her beg for me to take pity; I'd tell my brother everything she's always said about him if she opened her trap to Luke ever again about my personal business—wasted or no wasted.

After her next bout of dry heaves was completed, and I had soothingly wiped a cold, wet cloth over her face—poking her in the eye only once--and then gave her mouthwash to rinse, she totally agreed Luke was very tricky and promised she was onto him.

A couple of hours later, I tucked her into the guest bedroom. I set a glass of ginger ale on the bedside table and a big soup pan for any further emergencies on the floor. Anna asked in a small voice if I was mad she'd ruined our date.

"Please, and miss the sight of you barfing? While trying desperately to not toss my cookies, too? Nothing compares." I waved a negligent hand. "Don't worry about it. I'm seeing Mr. Tricky tomorrow. Besides, you may have actually saved me tonight."

Anna stopped punching her pillow into submission and frowned blearily up at me. "How did I save you?"

"Holy Hannah, I was so blasted earlier! If you weren't here, I cringe to think what I may have said to him if we were alone." I smiled wickedly. "Or what I may have done to him."

Sighing, Anna snuggled under her covers. "Great, now I really feel crummy. Luke probably hates me knowing he missed a wild night of a trashed Anabel. You hardly ever drink like that. What if you would have started drunk crying, or blacked out after dancing nude on the dining room table? That would have been so sweet! You should call him and tell him to come over. I probably wouldn't hear anything."

"Huh. Appealing as that sounds, I think I'll pass. Pass out, too. Sweet dreams, you little lightweight."

"Thanks for keeping your toilet clean, June."

I was at the door when Anna called softly, "Hey..."

"Yes?"

A Date with Fate

"I liked him. You need a man like him to keep you on your toes." Anna paused. "Or do I mean on your knees?"

She was still chuckling delightedly at her own joke when I closed the guest bedroom door behind me without answering.

Anna is my best friend. We are soul sisters until the end. Even though I have three blood sisters of my own, there is a universal truth known by the kind of females I like best; a woman can never have too many sisters.

Chapter VII
"Love Shack" by The B-52'S

Saturday, 11/17/12
9:40 AM

    I heard the front door unlock and recognized the rhythm of the heels tapping across the lobby floor. I went to the door of my office. The store woke up, becoming bright and cheerful as the overhead light fixtures hanging from the soaring, tin stamped ceiling were switched on by Stella.
    She walked her way towards me down the wide aisle of the huge, open room that is the main floor space in Bel's Books. This central aisle flowed straight down the length of the room and ended at the Laissez Fare café. Continuous, short bookcases lined either sides of the aisle, and created wide rows much like in a school library.
    These wide rows of bookcases were organized to create different "room" areas on each side of the main aisle. There were various kinds of seating in each of the rooms where a person could page through a book, or sit and schmooze with a friend.
    Narrower aisles ran along the length of the outside walls of the room. These exterior walls were lined with tall, built-in bookcases, and interspersed with an occasional doorway leading to other rooms.
    The long, wooden checkout counter where I was standing is located along the side aisle when you first entered Bel's Books front doors and took an immediate left. It was basically under the hallway of the bedroom side of the layout upstairs. My office was reached by a door behind this counter. The office is an odd room that was built under the stairs leading up to my apartment. I like the slanted walls and various ceiling heights. It's a cozy place from which to rule my little empire.
    Further down this side aisle, and past the checkout counter, is an entrance to a short hallway leading to restrooms, a staff break room and sizeable kitchen, a storage closet, and the entrance door to the basement of the building.
    Completing this northern side of the building were two rooms used for gatherings; The Hearth Room and The Garden Room. When the pocket doors between the two rooms were slid into the walls, they became one common space large enough to hold a big party, reception, or meeting.
    I rented out both rooms to various clubs, businesses, and private citizens to accommodate whatever the occasion. Laissez Fare catered, or

the renters could bring in their own licensed caterers. This practice allowed for the serving of alcohol if the correct state liquor licensing was in place.

Once, a group of Wiccans held an impromptu Litha celebration here. The weather outside was too stormy and dangerous on the night of the summer solstice for the group to attempt meeting outside. I don't know where I got the idea, but I had a hazy thought they might get down performing wild, pagan dance moves. I was mildly disappointed to observe they stayed sedately dressed in your average, summer clothes, many wore flowers in their hair, and they mingled around while eating lots of fruits and veggies.

It was probably just as well I was way off base. The actuality of a bunch of people dancing wildly while in their birthday suits is very similar to a nude beach; it sounds sexy, but the reality is pretty scary and can put you off your dinner.

With her head down and digging for something in her purse, I only got an intermittent glimpse of Stella as she came forward. I did manage to notice a sparkly, yellow bag was hanging from her elbow. She was dressed in the uniform of the store; jeans and a T-shirt with BEL'S BOOKS spelled out across the front in bold lettering.

I saw she was wearing high-heeled, platform pumps that explained the clunky sound of her heels. They were two-toned in the colors blue and green that appeared to be patent leather, but I knew had to be man-made. Being Stella, she tried to live by her ideals and convictions. At the forefront of her beliefs was the concept to harm no animals in the choices of clothes she bought, or the food she ate. She bought nothing made of leather and ate vegetarian.

Stella was trying to be vegan, but was totally depressed with her progress. Try as she may, she can't stay away from the cheese. As she struggles with her inner dairy demons, she compromises and eats her cheese from dairy farms where the cows are treated gently. Thanks to my niece, I knew way more than I ever wanted of the standard processes used in the production of dairy products. My oldest sister, Mac has a lot to answer for in the raising of Stella. I figure she has to be the one to blame since it never crossed my mind to wonder about the status of cow's teats and the levels of blood and pus acceptable in the milk we buy at the grocery store. These kinds of facts really disgusted me, and maybe Stella was having a hard time being vegan, but she'd grossed me out for life.

My only niece initially made the decision to be vegetarian at age fourteen, and got flak from a lot of the adults in her life. Pushing the great age of twenty-nine, I've observed the older some people get, the less they seem to remember what it was like to be a teen full of zest and purpose. They thought it was just a phase and humored her. Four years later, when the phase didn't go away but became a way of life, it made some people uncomfortable. Beats me why.

Stella is often patronized for her beliefs and asked really stupid questions. She normally handles these people and their intrusive, arrogant questions with a patient grace.

My personal favorite was from Marge Clausen, an overweight, sedentary busybody in her forties that has been coming to Bel's Books since I was a kid. I overheard Marge asking the lithe, athletic, glowing-with-health Stella, "Are you sure you are getting enough protein, dear?"

Aside from the obvious, the question brought home to me that when you are vegetarian people take an uncommon interest in whether or not you are getting all your protein and vitamins. I don't recall ever hearing an adult ask a flesh-eating teenager those types of questions, regardless if their physical condition was bulimic skinny from barfing up their vitamins, or morbidly obese from a steady diet of junk food and no exercise.

Eating organic was not as trendy four years ago. To be a vegetarian, paired up with insisting on organic whenever possible, was to some people downright un-American and threatening. I got a good chuckle out of this attitude, as if slaughtering cows and chomping down steaks built character, good health, and a powerful nation.

Personally, I am a chomper, but I buy organic and local wherever possible. I take an interest in knowing where my meat comes from—especially beef--what it is fed, and how it is processed for two piggybacking reasons.

One, can you say Creuetz-Jakob disease? This is the disease named for the human related result of eating cattle infected with Bovine Spongiform Encephalopathy, more commonly known as mad-cow disease. The idea of contracting this disease scares the-you-know-what out of me. I have not completely eliminated beef from my menu, but I consider eating it an extreme sport.

Two, having your fourteen-year-old niece sadly shake her head at you when seeing the burger in your hand and saying, "Auntie, you know you are eating sad, sick meat that had a face."

Good god, I'm only human and have a heart, even if on the shriveled side, and a brain, hopefully not spongy. Stella masterfully played me like a violin. Now, I try to make sure the animals I eat have a happy life on a nearby farm. I like knowing they're running around frolicking and eating grass free of pesticides or organic, vegetarian feed. I like thinking their teats are not abused. I like imagining they don't know what hit them when they are butchered locally for my eating pleasure.

I've always steadfastly supported Stella all the way in her convictions--just because. More and more, I was coming to believe she has the right way of it with many of her practices; they were sensible and realistic. My niece is full of true grit and determination, two traits I admire greatly in women when used in the pursuit of self discovery and personal goals.

I had to give her kudos for being able to pull off the shoes, too. They looked like a throwback to old pictures I'd seen of the seventies fashions. The saying, "Keep on Truckin" flashed across my brain. The girl was stylin'. This was a good thing since she's majoring in fashion design.

Stella is eighteen and a freshman at St Catherine's College. She also works at Bel's as my right hand woman. Mac is footing the tuition bill for this private school and it is not trivial. Stella is a hardworking kid. She is earning her own money to help contribute to the cause, and otherwise supports herself. She also has a serious addiction for clothes to feed.

When Stella chose St Catherine's in St Paul, I think we were all a little stunned. The only thing she seemed to have in common with the private, all-girl, catholic St Kate's is the fact she's female. We are a heathenish lot when it comes to organized religion. Most of my siblings went to state schools and majored in partying for their first couple of years.

I'm the only one without a degree. I considered it a waste of time and money for me since owning Bel's has always been my focus. NanaBel, surprisingly, didn't try to dissuade me, but said I could always go to school should the urge arise. I haven't regretted the decision to not pursue a traditional college career, but initially I did miss the continual learning a structured school setting had given me. I hadn't understood how much I loved soaking up knowledge until I was done with high school and putting in long hours at the store. For the first couple of years, Bel's Books consumed my every waking hour. It was exciting. I kept taking on more and more responsibilities. I had tons to learn, but as I became more familiar with all aspects of managing the store, I knew it was not enough.

Loving the business I own and run doesn't mean it is continual fun and games. Mainly, it is routine tasks; a lot of the same old, same old. Once I determined what my restless problem was, I solved it.

I came up with a life action plan I refer to, please forgive me, as the Bel Curve. Continued education is the overall goal, and having fun while achieving this broadening of my horizons is the overall focus. The subheadings BRAIN, BODY, and SOUL organize my pursuits of a well-rounded education. This system works well for me. I've always devoured books, but sometimes I will take a class on a specific subject. Sometimes I will learn an active skill, try a new hobby, or take on a sport. My only rule of operations; I gotta love what I am learning or doing. It's fine to continue on one subject and delve as deep as my interest lies, but if I don't love it, I move on to the next challenge.

At our gentle teasing and questioning, Stella stubbornly insisted St. Kate's has the program she wanted. She proved once again she knows her own mind, and has thrived in her first quarter in the diverse, small class environment. It's a great school.

My heart swells with love for my niece as I watch her today unawares. She is extremely pretty in a vibrant palette with her lustrous, dark chocolate-brown hair and aquamarine eyes under slashing, dark brows. She is rosy cheeked with the MacKenzie dimples, and has a beautiful smile with white, slightly crooked teeth. She insisted she didn't want braces in the interests of perfection once the dentist admitted her bite was fine. She thought her one or two, slightly crooked teeth were interesting. Such confidence from a sixth-grade girl boggles the mind.

Mac had Stella at seventeen. She got pregnant by her longtime, high school sweetheart, Freddy DeVere. I recall vividly the drama at the time. From my nine-year-old prospective, I was repulsed at the idea of Mac having a baby. NanaBel supported Mac in whatever choice they made about the pregnancy; keeping, adoption, or abortion. Her only requirement was that Mac discussed what she was thinking, feeling, and reasoning with her family as she made her decision with Freddy.

I kept my lips zipped so I could listen, round-eyed and big ears, to all the discussions around the dining room table without being sent out of the room. Years later, I grasped how NanaBel turned a difficult situation that often rips families apart into a time of family unity and excitement. She showed us all the stepping stones to making sound decisions while incorporating our very human strengths and weaknesses into the equation.

One of NanaBel's favorite axioms has always been, "Your actions should bear scrutiny--your own." All my life, I've watched her in action practicing what she preaches. I have come to greatly admire her philosophies.

She doesn't give much credence to public opinion other than as a tool to weigh the lay of the land, and then manipulate to her own ends. She also doesn't consider "manipulate" a four-letter word. My grandmother is quite Machiavellian in her thinking. You've got to love that trait in a woman, especially a woman solely in charge of your family's future.

What NanaBel does believe is that it's very important to be able to sleep at night after deciding on the path you'll take, so don't ever lie to yourself in the privacy of your own mind.

Self-delusion is major no-no. Even if it's admitting you're selfish, unfair, unethical, immoral, twisted, or just plain wrong. Vigorous self-honesty, self-examination, and self- acceptance promotes the eventual best choices.

Liking yourself and striving to be the person you want to be; along with plenty of exercise, regular meals, and a good night's sleep, gives you the energy to have a fun, hardworking, and productive life. NanaBel's formula is all about life being hard work and a good time. After twenty some cognizant years of my own empirical observation, it's my conclusion my grandmother is the coolest woman in the world.

A Date with Fate

Mac and Freddy chose to have the baby. Freddy was a year older and going to school at the U of M. They waited until after Mac had graduated high school, and baby Stella was born in July, before getting married. After the wedding, they lived in a tiny apartment in Dinkytown near the University. They were a happy, little family—deliriously in love and flowing with plans for a bright future.

Seven months later, Freddy was T-boned on an icy, February day by a delivery truck running a red light while doing fifty. Poor Freddy was hit on the driver's side and killed instantly.

A devastated Mac and baby Stella moved home to their Division Street family. Eventually, Mac used the resulting insurance settlement to pay for schooling to become a nurse. She socked away the rest. We all chipped in our time and it was a group effort raising baby Stella. For the first few months, Mac was sleepwalking through the days while dealing with the reality and grief of being a new mother, a bride, and a widow--all at the age eighteen.

I was just eleven when they moved back into the apartment with us in Northfield. It was a sad time; Freddy had been dear to us all. My sadness was eased a little since it took about one nanosecond for me to fall irrevocably in love with having the baby Stella around 24/7. Time went on, Mac slowly dealt with her loss, and eventually she moved back into the sunlight of the living. She had to tackle me to wrest baby Stella out of my grubby, little arms. We agreed to share.

I now think about how hard Stella works going to school and holding down a full-time job. I think about how friendly and kindhearted she is---the girl takes a spider outside rather than kill it, (which in the winter I find an interesting choice), and I press my hands against my chest. I almost feel my heart swelling; I'm so proud of her. Stella's probably the closest I'm going to get to a daughter of my own, even though she's only ten years my junior.

Stella glances up at that moment, her pretty face inquisitive. "Why are you standing there holding onto your boobs like that, Auntie Bel?"

She grins at me as I drop my hands, laughing at her valid question. "Oh, just enjoying feeling myself up this fine, Saturday morning. These are the things I get up to if left to my own devices for too long."

Stella burst out laughing, shoving me playfully in the shoulder. She unlocked the big drawer under the checkout counter near where I was standing. She stowed away her Big Buddha purse.

"Nifty shoes, hippy chick."

Stella pointed her foot, the better for me to admire. "Thanks. I ordered them online through a website on Etsy. Only thirty bucks!"

I point nonchalantly to the yellow, gift bag tantalizing me on her arm. "What's that little morsel?"

Stella holds the bag up in surprise, as if just noticing it. "This gift bag, you mean?"

"Yes, that gift bag. Is it a present for someone….like me, for instance?" I ask without shame.

"Now, why would I have a present for you?" Stella teased, pursing her lips in thought. "What have you done for me lately?"

I clapped my hands. I love presents. "Hmm…let's see. What have I done for you lately? Good question. Does it have to be something I have actually done, or does what I *intend* to do count?"

Stella giggled. She handed the bag over to my greedy, clapping hands. "I believe you would do anything for a present, wouldn't you?"

Distractedly, I pushed my long hair behind my shoulder while murmuring, "You ask that like its wrong. Have I taught you nothing, Stell?"

I opened the sparkly bag and pulled off the decorative, tissue paper that serves no purpose other than to keep me from the loot underneath. Inside were two wrapped items. I took both out and laid them gently on the wooden counter. Savoring the gifts was as fun as opening them. Well, not really, but a close second.

I carefully folded the gift bag and handed it back to Stella. "You really shouldn't have, Stella sweetness, but here you go. Recycle this for next time."

She stuck the yellow bag under the counter while dramatically snorting and rolling her eyes. I don't know where she gets some of her facial tics from; must be my sister, Mac.

I opened the gift on the left first. "Thank you so much! What is it, exactly?"

Stella took it out of my hands. Using scissors, she sliced off the tab wrapping covering up the white, slim tube. She popped off the lid. Her bright blue eyes were intent and serious, little frown lines of earnestness on her forehead. "It's called lip stain. You are going to love how it feels and looks. Jane Iredale's line may not be certified organic, but I have checked out the ingredients. There is no propylene glycol in her stains. Or sodium lauryl sulfate. It is safe and nontoxic for you to use."

Oh, man, I could just squeeze her endlessly for being so incredibly cute when she's so serious, but I settle for a quick hug and warm praise. "I appreciate your research. Thanks for being so smart. I cringe at the poisons I'd consume without you policing the profit-hungry, corner-cutting bastards of the cosmetic industry."

Eyes sparkling, she nodded, pleased. "Put some on and try it. Then hurry and open the next one."

I live to obey. Stella was right; the lip stain felt great and tasted even better. Jane and I had a future. "Mmm…delish."

A Date with Fate

Stella handed me the second wrapped package. I laughed in delight when I opened it and saw the earrings. They were shiny, delicate silver in the shape of an elongated sphere with a blue topaz stone dangling in the center.

"Stella, they're perfect! I love them. Thank you!"

"You're welcome. They reminded me of your eyes. Sammy made them. Isn't she good at jewelry design?"

"She *is* good." Without thinking, I put on the earrings. I went over to a mirror hanging on the wall right inside my office door to check them out. I curled my hair behind my ears and turned my head, this way and that, to catch the sparkle in the light.

"We should talk with Sammy about selling her jewelry here." I idly mused, thinking about Stella's talented best friend. "What do you think, Stell?"

Stella came to lean against the door frame "Sure, we could do that. Those look totally cute." She got a perplexed look on her face. "I just noticed something. This is probably the first time in my life I've ever seen you without earrings on all ready. What are you, psychic or something?"

I watched my blue topaz eyes widen in the mirror, and saw my Pretty Pink Just Kissed lip stained mouth stay closed. I felt tongue-tied, although Stella had no way of knowing why I had no earrings on. I had no facile answer for such an easy, simple question. I felt like a complete idiot standing there saying nothing.

Stella's straight eyebrows drew together. "Why are you looking so strange? What's wrong?"

A voice behind her at the door inquired, "Who's looking strange?"

It was Anna. Stella and I both turned to her. I was relieved at the interruption until Stella said, "Can you believe Bel had no earrings on this morning and won't tell me why?"

"Wait a minute..." I protested, but Anna overrode me.

"What do you mean? She's got earrings on, Stell."

Stella's arms were folded and her platform shoe was tapping. Her eyes narrowed. She was on the scent, but still confused.

"These are earrings I just gave her as a gift, Anna. She didn't have any of her own on to begin with, and she keeps staring at me like she's guilty of something when I asked her why."

Anna peered at me suspiciously. I shrugged and went for clueless. Without hesitation, I threw Stella under the bus. I did a circular motion with my finger near my head, signaling Stella was a kook.

This is what I get for shaking up my routine, and for having a nosy niece that keeps an eagle eye on me and knows all my ways. No wonder I have no children of my own if this is the peppering you get for not wearing a pair of earrings one damned day. All because I had a lousy sleepover, I have resorted to lying to my niece and best friend.

"I saw that!" exclaimed Stella, laughing. "I'm not nuts, and you'd better tell us what's going on, or I will drive you crazy until you do. You know I can do this…"

I did indeed. Relentlessly single-minded as a rat terrier was another trait she, no doubt, got from one of my sisters. I learned a long time ago, Stella was not a female you could depend on to take a hint and shut up in public when you didn't want her to pursue a delicate subject. Nuance and subtleness were not words in her vocabulary. You had to drag her off to the side and threaten her with bodily harm to get her to be quiet if there was something she had sunk her teeth into and wanted an answer on. I either had to come up with a quick explanation after screwing up my timing so bad, or spill the beans I had Luke upstairs. Then I'd really be in for a waterboarding session.

"Okay, then. I will tell you why I have no earrings on today." I pulled my hair back with one hand, blowing out a heavy breath in defeat. Both Anna and Stella watched me suspiciously from the doorway of my office.

I bent my head in shame. I confessed in a quiet, dignified voice. "I have a prescription drug problem that I have been trying to kick. My hands were shaking too much to fit any earrings through the holes in my ears this morning. See?"

I lifted my head and held a hand up, letting it quiver and tremble in the air between us all. "Are you two happy now?"

Anna and Stella looked at each other, then at me, and then back at each other. They went hysterical at the same time. They held onto each other. They screamed with laughter and made mean-girl comments about my acting skills. I sat in my office chair, swiveling gently and smiling contentedly, while they were busily whoopin' it up at my expense. I cast a quick look at the clock. 9:59 AM and counting.

"Ah, Stella love, I hate to interrupt your bonding moment with Anna here, but I do believe it's time to open the store?"

"Damn!" Stella cried as she ran out of the office. She called back over her shoulder, "I haven't forgotten this, Auntie."

"Thanks again for the lovely presents!' I called after her.

Anna plopped down on the moss green, velvet loveseat near my desk. "Okay. What are you holding out on, Junior?"

"Forget the earrings. I think some serious stuff is going down. I'm very worried, actually. Bob Crookston was here earlier, and you will not believe what has been going on with his wife, Cheryl."

Anna's cocoa-brown eyes were shaped round, but now they got huge. Her eyebrows rose high under her long bangs. She sat forward expectantly. "Why? What's going on?"

I stood up, needing to stretch. The only two hours of sleep was catching up with me. I also wanted to get out of Dodge before Luke sauntered in. His untimely appearance would ruin my clean getaway after all my hard work not telling on myself that he was upstairs.

'Geez Louise. How late would the lazy man sleep on a Saturday, anyway?'

"How about I fill you in as we drive? Are you ready to go now, or do you need a few minutes?"

Anna jumped up again. "Give me a couple to make sure everything's in order with Trent. Did you know the Ladies of the Lanes bowling league are meeting here today at one o'clock in the Garden Room?" Stretching my arms towards the ceiling, I paused to give her a look. She laughed. "Of course you did." She snapped her fingers. "Oh, and do not let me forget to tell you my news, too. It's the main thing I wanted to tell you this morning when we talked, but you got me flustered with the puny penis thing. Thanks again for that, by the way."

I smiled, reaching over and shutting down my PC. "My pleasure. Okay, hurry up and we'll talk in the jeep."

"The catering is no biggie. Trent's got it covered for today. It's coffee in urns, bottled waters, wraps, and a variety of cookies. They're good to go."

I perked up at the mention of cookies, my stomach growling. That handful of walnuts seemed like years ago and the lip stain wasn't very filling. "What kind of cookies are we talking?"

"The kind that makes your ass big, Junior. You can't have any for free."

Laughing, I followed Anna out into the store. She took off to Laissez Fare to talk with Trent. I could see the big guy was already at work making drinks for a couple of younger girls.

Trent looked my way. He did an exaggerated double take, grinned widely, and held both hands to his heart. In return, I drew a heart in the air with my two forefingers, and pointed at him with a small smile. The two girls, they were barely in high school, followed his glance over to me and scowled.

Trent Christensen is twenty-three-years old, grew up in Northfield, and has worked with Anna at the Fare since it opened two years ago. He's currently training to be a Pastry Chef at the Minnesota Institute of Arts Culinary School in South Minneapolis. I wouldn't be surprised if he and Anna partnered up in the future and expanded the business. I'd be interested in backing them to start branding and packaging their own recipes for sale locally—maybe wholesale and retail distribution. I put aside the idea for further consideration to discuss with Anna.

Trent's very attractive; like a giant Teddy bear. He stands a solid six-five. He has a curly mop of black hair, and dark blue eyes that have a way of twinkling slyly at you even when his mouth wasn't smiling. He's a large boy, but you want to cuddle him. Women of all ages love him. Men find him harmless. Like the two girls glaring over at me from the Fare, both ideas make me laugh. Trent has the greatest, if the weirdest, customer service skills. I like working with him just to hear what may come out of his mouth next. The customers get a kick out of his conversational gambits, too.

Stella was over helping a customer in the Sci-fi section. I recognized the younger guy since he's been in the store often lately, but haven't met him yet myself. Stella seems to help him whenever he's browsing. I chuckled to see her talking and smiling animatedly while gesturing emphatically with her arms like she's a full-blooded Italian, instead of predominantly Scots and German.

I looked to my left. I saw Larissa Butler down at the end of the checkout counter ringing up a single book purchase. That was some fast shopping, but I knew from experience there were certain people that weren't bookstore browsers. Sacrilegious, I know, but there you go. They entered the store, went directly to the new book section, grabbed their book of choice, and vamoosed.

Larissa's a part-time employee and a friend of Jazy's from back in high school days. I've known her casually forever, but not really known her well until she started working for me last summer.

She had married young and moved out of state. I hadn't seen much of her for several years. She came back to Northfield after a particularly nasty divorce about eighteen months ago.

The older man who'd swept her off her feet and married her turned out to be a monster, not Prince Charming. He'd been terrorizing Larissa by beating the crap out of her for years because he was insanely jealous and possessive. Larissa's a knock-out. She's tall and slender, has a heart-shaped face, big, crystal blue eyes, and perfectly straight, thin blonde hair. She's also so sweet-natured and harmless you can't even hate her for being beautiful. It would be like hating rainbows or white, fluffy clouds.

As for smarts, Larissa's not the sharpest knife in the drawer. While a sweetheart, most of her limited conversation and interests revolve around cute, baby animals. Since my sister Jazy is horse crazy, I can only guess that was the reason for their teen friendship.

Larissa is a woman whose life took a horrifyingly wrong turn by hooking up with the wrong man. If life was fair, she would have an adoring husband who doesn't blink an eye she's a boring dimwit because she's so sweet and beautiful. They'd have three shy children she'd dote on with all the baby love in her heart, and a house full of kittens.

Instead, she'd been living a nightmare for years with a man who beat her up regularly for her every supposed infraction. Thankfully, her parents finally figured out what was going on, helped get her out of that life, and got her some professional help. She left her crazy ex, took back her maiden name, and has moved back home to get her life on track. The

A Date with Fate

ex has been serving time for assault. Not for beating Larissa, but from going nuts on some poor trucker at the MacStop gas station off 35W in Lakeville when stalking Larissa last year after the divorce.

I hired Larissa when Jazy told me her story and asked for my help. I was appalled when I realized the extent of the damage this girl has suffered. I didn't even know her that well, yet I could see the dramatic difference in her personality and confidence.

Months after being home with her folks, when Larissa first came to talk with me about a possible job, she was still a shell of her former self. Skeletal thin and dull-eyed, submissive and subdued, she was broken and pitiful.

During the interview, I took one look at her and every fiercely protective, maternal instinct I didn't know I possessed came roaring to life. I spoke to her softly and gently about our shared past, a light banter to put her at her ease. After several minutes of this, I was rewarded with quick, furtive glances of eye contact. After I spent a half an hour telling her cute, g-rated stories about the store and our lives with NanaBel, she was able to watch me talk, sat up straighter, and actually smiled cautiously once or twice. When the hour interview was over, she was softly talking with me. The tiny, spark of hope I saw in her gentle eyes made me want to lay my head down on my desk and weep like a baby for all she'd endured. The scars I caught a glimpse of on her thin arms under the cuffs of her blouse, some faint white lines, others angry red circles, made me want to repeatedly punch a wall.

Maybe not a perfect choice for an employee in sales, but I was determined she was going to succeed at Bel's. She could have a place here for as long as she needed or wanted. Once I worked through the process of getting her trained and comfortable, Larissa's turned out to be a good, dependable employee and part of the Bel's Books family.

It appeared routine and steadiness were key for her, so I made sure she did the same duties every shift. I pushed her to learn new things, but slowly and surely with no pressure. Working a Saturday shift was new for her. Her normal schedule was during the week days, usually when I was working. I think she felt safest with me around.

She's looking much healthier these days. Larissa's on the timid, quiet side by nature. Gradually, she's gaining back some confidence and some much needed weight. She's no longer rigid with internal fear when a man comes near her in the store, or jumps in terror if a book is dropped with a loud smack. She seems content working at Bel's Books. I believe the upbeat, fun atmosphere is having a soothing, beneficial effect on her battered spirit. The older ladies and young mothers love her. They probably feel like they're being assisted by a shy Cinderella, you can almost hear the cartoon chirping birds and talking mice.

After her customer left, I walked down to her. "Howdy, Ms. Butler, what's shakin' today?"

Larissa doesn't like being hugged, and I can relate to that. For some reason, she loves double high-fiving. It makes her giggle. Her giggle sounds like a squeaky, little mouse, and that makes me giggle. She said my giggle sounds like I just did something naughty, which makes her giggle more. I have no clue what she means by naughty, but when you look into her eyes and see the child-like innocence shining back despite what she's gone through; I don't think our concepts of naughty are remotely the same.

"Hello, Anabel." Gigglefest over, she motioned grandly to the store at large. "I'm keeping it real today."

Larissa was proudly smiling when I burst out in delighted laughter to hear her quoting Billy Carlson, my other store manager. He's a great guy with a great, big heart. It seems simple enough on the surface, but it's a leap of fantastic progress for Larissa if she's comfortable enough with Billy to be intentionally joking about his sayings.

A few minutes later, I was sitting and drooling at the Fare counter while waiting for Anna to be done with her work. My eyes were reluctantly drawn away from the bakery case when I noticed the water level in the bottle sitting in front of me shake, and a second later, shake again.

This will always remind me of the build-up scene in the first Jurassic Park movie when something was coming and the puddle did the tremor. I feel the same dread now. I turned on my stool to observe Aunt Lily thumping her way down the main aisle towards us. Her head was swiveling side to side as she glared around Bel's Books. You'd swear she had entered a den of iniquity instead of what most sane people refer to as a used bookstore. I've heard her dogmatic opinion ad nauseam of the dark sin that lurks in any books not of a non-fiction, Christian genre. I've got nothing against believers, but Aunt Lily's not a woman you want as your poster girl. Any organization she reps gets a bad rap just by being associated with her fanatic, mean self.

Her sparse, gray hair is worn scraped back in a wincingly tight bun. Her black brows resemble furry centipedes in motion across her broad forehead. They shade the beady, unblinking eyes of a carrion predator. She has a beefy nose with wide, flaring nostrils. Her mouth is perpetually twisted, as if sucking nonstop on a lemon. If that wasn't scary enough, she has a massive body an aspiring lumberjack would be proud of, even at her age. Aunt Lily is the stuff of nightmares. Not quite as terrifying as a T-Rex, but pretty damn close.

On the crook of one meaty arm hung her purse she's carried forever. It's a huge, black monstrosity circa 1900. It's shiny and furry looking. It's possibly constructed out of an animal she killed and tanned herself for fun as a child. Hanging daintily from the other elbow, and incongruously out of place, is a familiar pink bakery bag. Firmly clenched in her right hand is the black cane that resembled a long chunk of basalt. She certainly doesn't need the cane for walking, but uses it purely for intimidation purposes.

It worked.

To keep current with food trends in her café, Anna likes to do what we term 'spying'. Spying involves periodically visiting different surrounding towns and checking out the competition to see what's cookin'.

Our spying adventures began, in part, because of Aunt Lily. Since the opening of Laissez Fare, Aunt Lily takes perverse pleasure stopping by Bel's with food from other eateries about every second month.

After watching her depress Anna once too many times, I always try to wander unobtrusively over to the Fare's counter when she stomps down the main aisle trailing her miasma of malevolence. Aunt Lily's main goal seems to be driving home to Anna how her cooking doesn't measure up to whatever's in the bag. Yeah, she's a real sweetheart of an Auntie.

I am positioned perfectly for the interception today. Aunt Lily's big on proper posture, so I slump lazily on my stool. My back and elbows rest slovenly on the counter behind me. My legs are sprawled apart while I wait to make my move.

"Oh my, onward Christian soldier." murmured Trent in my ear, leaning down right behind me. The high school girls had wandered off, and except for the oblivious Anna banging trays around behind us in the sink, we were alone watching Aunt Lily's forward progress up the aisle. "Didn't she bring a bag from the Northfield Bakery last time she graced us with her charity? On the subject of charity, what would you say if I told you I was signing up for ChristianSingle.com?"

I answered out of the corner of my mouth. "I'd say, "What did the Christians ever do to you?" that's what I'd say."

"God, Anabel!" Trent exclaimed in a fervent undertone. "I love your sassy mouth. Are you sure you won't reconsider and go out with a younger man with the soul of an old degenerate?"

I stifled my giggles with difficulty. "Quit it! Don't make me laugh."

Trent straightened up to his full, impressive height and said with exaggerated courtesy, "Why hello, Ms. Johnson." He leaned forward, one arm resting on the top of the cash register. "Are you having the best day of your life today?"

Ignoring Trent like he was invisible, Lily Johnson placed the pink bakery bag on the counter. After looking me up and down, Aunt Lily pinned me with the glare of virulence she keeps reserved for Liberals, Infidels, and Jezebels. She snorted angrily at my wide smile of greeting, and at my thighs swaying indecently opened and closed.

She turned her attention to Trent and continued her pleasantries.

Her cane hit the edge of the counter with a loud crack a scant inch from Trent's hand. He jumped back in stumbling haste at the unexpected attack. He sidestepped behind me. I felt his hand clutching the back of my vest like a talisman to ward off evil.

Aunt Lily started thundering. "Young deviant, the best day in the life for the devout will be the day they meet the One True God and His Son, Jesus Christ, our Lord and Savior. Renounce your ways and fight the devil inside you before it is too late!" Oh yes, did I forget to mention Aunt Lily is convinced Trent's a despicable homosexual? "Be saved or beware! You do not want to face Our Father come Judgment Day as the sinner that stands before me." She paused and ordered menacingly, "Now, boy, be useful and inform my niece I'm here."

Anna turned off the water at the sink, saw her Aunt, and came hopping over to join us at the counter. Aunt Lily spread her lips in a scary grimace that was supposed to pass for a smile.

The Behemoth cooed. "Anna, come taste these divine Cruellers from the Northfield Bakery. Chef Leonard received his training at the International Culinary Center in New York City."

She said the words with a malicious reverence, as if the school was located in the Garden of Eden and not just NYC, and the training received guaranteed a quality of baked goods comparable to that of manna from heaven, and not a basic recipe anyone could follow.

Anna blinked once, her happy smile of welcome wobbling. It disappeared at the sight of the Northfield Bakery bag.

Before Aunt Lily could stop me, I snatched the pink bag off the counter. I glanced inside.

Disdainfully, I wrinkled my nose. "Don't you mean Crullers?"

The crull in Crullers rhymes with skull. Not to be confused with Cruellers. That is pronounced like the word cruel. As in the cruel and unusual punishment Anna's aunt was attempting to deliver right along with the pastries. Anna had plans to attend that school in New York, but cancelled and went local when Aunt Lily had a "heart attack" and desperately needed her niece by her side.

Aunt Lily's eyes were slits of hard obsidian. She reached for the bag. "No, Anabel Axelrod. Chef Leonard said these are Persian Cruellers."

I held the bag back. I shook my head decisively in the negative. "They most certainly are not. Cruellers are twisted and shaped round. They're also generally thought to be of French origin. What's with Chef Leonard and the pretentious Persian name? What a poser. Persia's isn't even a country anymore. He may as well have called them Prussian Cruellers or Rhodesian Cruellers." I snorted derisively. "No, these are crude donut sticks that are knock-offs of the more elegant, delicate Cruellers. New Yorkers call them Crullers. They sell them on the street out of those icky carts."

A Date with Fate

I tilted my head while I took in the sight of the angry, red-faced woman standing in front of me. "Do you have any idea why this Cruller is shaped like a rectangular stick, Aunt Lily?"

After getting an eyeful of Aunt Lily's working mouth and clenched fists, Anna broke in tentatively. "Umm, maybe we should try one and…"

Trent interrupted Anna. He was feeling braver a few feet out of thrashing range, and was my obliging straight man.

"Tell us, Anabel! I'm very interested to know why these Crullers are shaped like a stick."

I met Aunt Lily's basilisk glare with a relaxed, cool smile. I was totally at my ease with certain people wishing me dead after they've had the pleasure of beating me bloody with their cane. Using a napkin, I reached into the bag and pulled out a sugar glazed pastry.

The Cruller glistened under the light from the pendants hanging over the counter.

I held the pastry aloft with two fingers like it was dog poop. "I've been told on good authority, this Cruller shape came about because New Yorkers found it too difficult to fit the original, circular Crueller into their coffee cups for dipping." I smiled angelically at Aunt Lily. "It never crossed their minds to break them in half."

Trent guffawed loudly and Anna let loose a giggle before hurriedly covering her mouth. Aunt Lily continued to stare at me with a flat expression somehow more ominous then if she was enraged and swinging.

I made a face at the Cruller in my hand, and continued to pour gasoline on the blaze of my eternal hell-fire. I took my time inspecting the pastry while making soft, negative noises in the back of my throat.

I finally finished my careful exam and looked up at the trio watching me.

Thighs still lazily swaying to and fro, I sighed. "Okay, not real thrilled here with the weight or looks of this thing, but time for the ultimate test. How does it taste?"

I pinched the tiniest, most miniscule sample bite humanly possible. After barely allowing it to touch my tongue, I sat up straight and promptly spit it out into the napkin with a loud, disgusted exclamation.

Gagging, I shuddered. "If you think these fat-filled disasters are divine, Aunt Lily, you've been sampling your soup kitchen food too often. Ugh! Majorly greasy grossness!" I spit again for good measure.

If I have my way, Aunt Lily the Unloving doesn't leave any happier then when she arrived. Today, she furiously did an abrupt about-face and thumped out of the store without another word to anyone. Not to be immodest, but I have to pat myself on the back here. I think it was my personal best ever Interception of The Behemoth.

Trent leaned across the counter and twirled me around to face him. His grin was wicked. "I want you for my bride. Think about it. In the meantime, don't hog the bag. Man, I love these things!"

I had stuffed half a Creuller in my mouth the minute Aunt Lily was out of sight. Chewing while rolling my eyes in heavenly agreement, I passed over the pink bag. Trent and Anna dived in.

Anna aimed a swat at me. Over a mouthful, she garbled, "Way to go, Junior. I have to live with that woman!"

I protested around my own mouthful. "Don't call "it" a woman. You choose to live with it and will get no pity here, Miss Martyr."

Stella came over and grabbed the bag from an unsuspecting Trent. She looked inside and scoffed. "No more cancer Cruellers for any of you. I can pour some poison down your throats if you're still hungry. It's the same thing as eating all this leaf lard, refined sugar and bleached flour."

Trent put his hands around his head, as if hugging his bursting brain. "My GOD, I love the women in your family. You are all so mean! Stella, please, you can pour anything down my throat—even leaf lard, whatever the hell that is. I promise I'll swallow and die a happy man. I'm waiting for you to hit legal drinking age, and then I am moving in, girl."

My niece folded her arms and snickered. "Trent, aren't you in school learning to be a Pastry Chef? Leaf lard is pig fat found deposited around the kidneys and loin of the poor pig. It's used in baking because it doesn't have much pork flavor and gives pastry crusts that flaky texture."

On a dirty laugh, he repeated the only word a man would hear. "The loin, eh?"

Stella threw up her hands and walked away. The brat took the pink bag with her. Trent hopped the counter and followed, protesting loudly.

Anna regularly insists on fairly evaluating the treats Aunt Lily drops off. Normally, I wouldn't eat them if Anna paid me considering who delivered them. In fact, Trent was right and Aunt Lily must be slipping. The bag of chocolate chip cookies I'd brought over to Reggie's the day I met Luke were the last offering Aunt Lily had delivered to Bel's, and had also been from the Northfield Bakery. Chocolate chip cookies were easy for me to resist. Plus, I figured if the Behemoth sprinkled them with poison my brother's cast iron stomach could handle it. It was an added bonus that Cousin Candy was there that day and ate several.

Even my fear of being poisoned by Aunt Lily, or refined sugar and bleached flour, couldn't hold out against a bag of fresh Persian Cruellers. They are finger-licking fabulous. Although, the whole leaf lard thing was now ricocheting around in my cranial cavity; right up there with those poor cow teats.

'Damn, I hated when Stella ruined another one of my life's little pleasures.'

Chapter VIII
"Would I Lie To You?" by The Eurythmics

Saturday, 11/17/12
10:23 AM

Anna and I were finally heading out the back door to the double garage on the southeast edge of my property in the parking lot. I let out a long sigh of relief to finally escape the building for the next few hours.

We hopped in Lady Liberty. I drove the couple of blocks through town, crossed the Water Street bridge over the Cannon River, and then we were headed north on Highway 3.

Farmington's a small town a straight shot north about twelve miles. This was our first stop on today's agenda before heading to the Grand Avenue neighborhood in St. Paul. I didn't waste any time. Verbatim, I started filling Anna in on my conversation with Crookie from earlier this morning.

Anna got to know Crookie pretty well our senior year in high school. It was usually a package deal back then—if either Anna or I made a new friend, so did the other. Anna was even starting to like him-like him a few years back, but couldn't be convinced to tell Crookie. It was frustrating for me because the giant nerd was completely oblivious of her interest. Anna always thought he was a hottie with a body. I thought they'd make a cute couple, but then there was "The Day of Infamy" and here we are today; cursing his soon-to-be ex-wife to hell and back.

Anna is furious at Cheryl's slutting it up during their marriage, never dreaming it was that bad since the beginning. Every time she interrupted my narrative to call Cheryl a splendidly foul name, I'd agree with an, "Amen, girlfriend!"

It was immensely satisfying talking with someone who was as irate over Cheryl's behavior on Crookie's behalf as I was. This is why best friends are so terrific. Maybe when Cheryl resurfaced Anna and I would beat her up.

When I arrived at the point of my total recall recital when I called Reggie to get the low down, I could see she was listening intently to every word. Anna wasn't bouncing around in her seat any longer while throwing jabs and pretending to be a boxer beating the daylights out of Cheryl. She was biting the inside of her cheek and casting quick glances at me as I drove.

This is a sure tell with Anna that she has information. She sometimes looks so guilty and furtive when she knows something I don't; it takes all I have not to bust a gut.

When I repeated Reggie's inventive swearing answer about not screwing around with Cheryl, Anna's face went hard and her lip curled in contempt.

"I suppose you believed him?" She demanded, sniffing haughtily and tossing her head.

"Sure, I guess so. Why would he tell me a lie about boinking Cheryl Crookston?" I asked casually.

Anna snorted. "Oh, I don't know, Junior. Let's see, maybe because he can? Or he doesn't know the meaning of the word truth? Or because your brother's a total buttwipe?" Anna shrugged in disgust. "Take your pick."

"He's that bad? Huh."

We were both quiet as I accelerated into the oncoming lane and passed a slow pickup truck. Anna was white-knuckling the dash, but I was thinking about my brother while looking at the countryside around me.

Heading north to the suburbs of the Twin Cities, Highway 3 is two lanes traveling through the rural lands of harvested fields, pastures, and the occasional farmstead with windbreaks of evergreens. The landscape was drab and brown this time of year. Despite this, it still had its own kind of sepia, picturesque beauty. It had stopped drizzling again and was a partly cloudy morning of about forty degrees. Depressing to some, but considered balmy weather in November by us. We could just as easily be up to our privates in snowdrifts.

Anna relaxed when we were back in our lane in one piece. "I know what that 'huh' sounds means. I didn't want to drag you into the middle of this because I know how close you and Reg are, but with Cheryl missing everything is different."

"I agree. I have that "something is rotten in the state of Denmark" feeling about the hooker. I don't want any trouble for Reg since we know he saw Cheryl that night."

Anna snorted again, louder. "Oh, you don't have to worry about your darling Reggie having trouble over that detail."

I snorted back. "Good, but enough pussyfooting around. Tell me what you know, please."

Anna angled in her seat to face me. She got comfy. "Okay. I was baking a cake in the kitchen that night when Cheryl came over to Reggie's." Anna pretended not to notice my surprised glance. "Slut Cheryl started humping on your stupid brother the minute she was through the door. I shit you not, Junior. She jumped on him and he almost fell down! I never came out of the kitchen," Anna lowered her voice and mumbled quickly, "because my shirt and bra were in the other room."

A Date with Fate

She hurriedly resumed in her regular voice, this time ignoring my open mouthed, surprised glance. "I peeked around the corner and saw everything; but Cheryl had no idea I was there. Your brother got her off him, she yelled some crap at him, he kicked her out, and she drove off just exactly like he said." Anna reached over and smacked me on the leg. "Quit laughing, Anabel! It wasn't funny."

"Ow! Hey, I'm driving here." I couldn't help it. I was laughing in relief Reg hadn't been alone with Cheryl. Okay, I was cracking up even more at the thought of Anna topless in Reggie's kitchen while Cheryl was in the living room putting the moves on my brother. This sure explained why he remembered the exact date and time.

I brought myself under control. "Oh Anna, I'm sorry. I bet it sucked big-time." I broke down giggling again and slapped the steering wheel. "But come on, you gots to admit it sounds like a French farce!"

Anna crossed her arms and smiled smugly. "Sure I do, Junior. Just as soon as you admit what Luke's truck was doing parked down the street from your parking lot very early this morning. Where was he, hmm? Playing with his cucumber in an alley?"

'Ah, man. Have I said lately what a pain in the butt best friends can be?'

Growing up the middle child with four siblings, you learn real fast there are two ways to deal with sticky situations. Go on the offense with no holds barred, or avoid, avoid, avoid. Both of these choices involve creating more confusion or interest in something more important than the issue causing you to be on the hot seat.

Some might see a third alternative. Admit when you're wrong. Take whatever punishment was coming to you like a man, get it over with, and move on.

Fortunately, I realized real young I was not a man. My take, after plenty of experience, is that the third alternative of copping to your crime was rarely a good idea. This third alternative guaranteed you were most definitely getting a whipping in some respect. By acting on the choices of going on the offense or avoiding the issue altogether; there was still a hope in hell you could get off scot-free.

We were in Farmington and I slowed down, putting on my left turn signal for the red light at Hwy 50.

I glanced at my smirking friend. I chose to ignore what she said about Luke's cuke and divert. "Okay, Betty Crocker, keep your secrets to baking the perfect pound cake. Please answer these questions, though. Did you drive over in your own car to Reggie's that night or get dropped off? And where, pray tell, did you leave your shirt and brassiere?"

"Yes, I drove over. I came from Rueb's after having a late drink with Jazy and Tre J. As for my shirt..." She closed her eyes to recall the night while I grinned in amusement at the revealing booty call nature of her answer. "I left my shirt and bra, I think, on the card table in the dining room."

I sighed. It wasn't too hard now to figure out what caused their nasty attitudes towards each other these past months. This next was not going to be pretty.

"Reggie swore to God today he never had sex with Cheryl Crookston."

The light changed to the green arrow and I accelerated through the intersection. Anna audibly sucked in a breath, her face gone stark white. Her sprinkling of freckles across her nose stood out against the pale relief of her skin.

"Are you freaking kidding me?" she moaned incredulously.

I knew that was a rhetorical moan, but still answered. "No, I am not kidding you. He swore he's never touched her, and I believe him one hundred percent. You messed up, didn't you?"

"Oh, crap, I really think I messed up in the worst way, Junior." Anna agreed, still moaning. Then she smacked the dash. "Why wouldn't he swear to God when I asked him? He only stared back at me and wouldn't answer. I went nuts thinking he had been with Cheryl! I thought the big dickhead went silent rather than swear."

Then she went quiet, biting her lip and staring out her window. I didn't say anything, but waited for her to tell me the rest. I drove west to the main drag of Farmington's small business district.

"After Cheryl left that night, we had a knock-down about all this." Angrily, she threw out her arm and almost nailed me, but I swerved. "I can't get over he let me think he had lied! Junior, our fight went ballistic. I really went off on him and left pretty hysterical. It killed me to hear he had sex with Cheryl the night after our first, real date." She added for clarification, "Our first date was that Friday night before she claimed he did her in the parking lot."

I nodded, keeping my eyes on the road. "I'm following so far."

Anna gave a scoffing laugh. "Reg said he only bought her a drink at the bar on that Saturday night because she cornered him. Yeah, right. I blew him off and didn't believe him." Her voice escalated. "My god, Cheryl's exact words were 'they fucked in his truck when the bar closed'. She didn't even know I was there listening in the kitchen, so why would I believe she was lying?"

Anna wailed those last few words. I saw her wipe her eyes with her hand. She reached down blindly for her purse, rooting for a tissue.

She sniffed. "Our week together was so amazing. I wanted to tell you so bad, but didn't want to jinx anything. It was all too new." Anna sniffed again and laughed bitterly. "I know Reggie's history better than anyone. The last thing I wanted was to be another dumb chick he nailed that thought she could change him. How sickening would that be? Oh Bel,

A Date with Fate

I really believed him when he said it wasn't that way with us....but he let me go that night and he hasn't tried to get me back." Anna covered her face with her hands, losing the battle to keep her composure. Her narrow shoulders were shaking with her sobs.

In the course of normal events, Anna didn't cry over guys. True, she was a romantic, but more apt to tear up out of happiness over a sappy movie or a newborn baby. Men she got mad with got a piece of her mind—not sobbed over two months later. I was feeling her misery. My brother had really gotten to her.

I turned right and spotted a diagonal parking spot across from Ye Old Downtown Bake Shop. I zoomed in and turned off the engine.

I reached over and rubbed Anna's shaking back lightly, making comforting noises while she cried it out. I agreed with her that boys suck in general. I agreed with her their purpose for existing is to make our lives miserable, when they weren't making us delirious. While I privately thought castration fell under the category off cutting off one's nose to spite one's face, I agreed with her when, hiccupping, Anna cursed it was the solution to all her problems.

Along with pissing off the males in my life, it was my day to take care of my sad and freaking out friends.

Rubbing and soothing, I thought Anna was right to believe in Reggie's words to her that he was serious, even if they tentatively dated only one week. I know my brother. If he told Anna he had feelings, he meant it. This certainly explained his crappy, snarky attitude these last couple of months. He must be going insane watching her start dating Jim Mardsen while not knowing how to stop it and still save face.

At that idea, I chuckled inside. Reggie's always had it too easy where women were concerned since he normally didn't give a damn. If he was into Anna, he was like a babe in the woods stumbling around with emotions he didn't know what to do with, probably didn't want, and choking on his manly pride. I also understand why he wouldn't swear to God to Anna.

As I absently comforted the crying Anna, now thankfully winding it down, my mind was busy thinking how I could help them both out. It was a shame their fragile relationship had been busted to smithereens by Cheryl appearing on the scene. What are the odds you have to deal with a mental chick like her the first week you are going out with someone?

I decided it would do no harm to share some of my theories on what went down that night with Cheryl. I hated seeing my friend so down and it might help. Anna has a mind of her own. She'd decide on the course to take with Reggie after I told her. Hopefully, her choice would involve mega amounts of torment.

I love my brother, but due to an accident of birth I've had to listen to many sob stories from many women that have tried and failed to capture him. It's one of the drawbacks of being a store owner and available to the public ten hours a day. I can run from these cast-off beauties, but I cannot hide. It's no wonder I have so many rules about men. I'm sometimes amazed I don't bat for the other side. I guess it just goes to support the nature versus nurture part of that debate.

I squeezed Anna's shoulder. "If you are done being a little crybaby, I want to tell you something that could cheer you right up. It's why I asked you those questions about your car and bra."

Anna snorted and gave me the evil eye while blowing her nose loudly into a tissue. She motioned for me to continue, but I was spooked. For a second there at Anna's expressive glance, I had actually caught a glimpse of a terrifying resemblance to her Aunt Lily. I shook it off.

"I think Cheryl absolutely knew you were there, or that some girl was there. That's why she tried to kiss Reggie right away and claimed to have sex with him. Hell, she had just come from being in bed with some man we know for sure wasn't Reg. It's possible she's a nymph-o, but I doubt she was coming over for more good lovin' right then from my brother.

"No, what Cheryl probably wanted was a place to stay for the night. It was late, and he was someone that popped in her head. Reggie's known as an easygoing guy, he'd bought her a drink, and he lives down here. She'd think she could get what she wanted from him, right?"

Anna was nodding cautiously, curious to see where I was going. I had been thinking about this for awhile and it fit.

"The skank knew she couldn't go home to Crookie because of his voicemail saying he was divorcing her. It's not that far to drive to the lake. I do remember Reg saying she and Tina hung around last summer a few times, don't you? Wasn't Tina's boyfriend at the time helping Reg with the pontoon boat's broken engine?"

Anna looked thoughtful. "Yeah, I do remember that, now that you mention it. Why would Cheryl lie, though?"

I raised my brows at Anna. "Good god, all that woman does is lie. It could be as simple as Cheryl being mad Reggie wasn't home alone for her convenience, so she started talking smack for the sheer, mean hell of it."

Anna stared at me in stupefaction for a second. "Junior, I think you are so right! Oh boy, she did seem out of control. I was so pissed off at what she was saying; the crazy way she acted didn't register so much. She could have seen my car. I didn't hide it, and then the bra, too. It's a hot pink, push-up. You know, one of the super-duper padded on the sides and underneath for that extra lift bra?" She gave me a disgusted look. "Wait, you don't own one of those, do you?"

On the off chance I didn't get it, she made cupping motions with her hands. This move pushed her breasts up close to her chin. The type of padded bra she was so enthusiastically describing is a lethal weapon. Not only for the miracles it performed, but it's also incredibly heavy and stiff.

I shook my head at the image. "Right, a little hard to miss those bras. Here, look in the mirror."

I flipped down the visor above Anna so she could spiff up. I summarized while she vigorously rubbed mascara off from under her eyes.

"Okay, my brother never nailed Cheryl Crookston, you wouldn't believe him, and he refused to swear to God. Why, you ask? Because, dear Anna, he wasn't thinking of you as a sister anymore." I grinned. "Hear him roar, you were his potential mate, his woman. He thought you should believe in him with no safety net or water wings. It was a test, perhaps subconsciously on his part, but nevertheless a test."

Seeing Anna's astonished start at this statement, I smiled and reassured her. "That's right. So what did you do? You forced his manly pride and backed him into a corner. You saw his refusal to swear to God as him lying. Then you took off all mad, but only after you guys fought like wolverines about it first. You were feeling crushed and played, and why not? Poor baby, that was too bad of Reg to expect blind trust from you after Eve of Destruction took off. Since then, the two of you have done nothing but snarl and snap every time you see each other. Did I miss anything?"

I snapped my fingers. "Oh yeah, and you hooked up with a new man." I laughed in wicked delight thinking about it now. "Reggie is really all up in his manly pride now. He's picturing you in his porno imagination doing circus sex acts with poor Jim of the undetermined package size. Now did I forget anything?"

Anna was giggling hysterically while dabbing at her running eyes and nose. I could only hope it was with a different tissue. After a bit, she calmed down enough to peer in the little mirror to poof up her hair.

"Great, I look like crap." She turned a hopeful gaze my way. "You really think that's why he wouldn't swear to me? I'm mate material now, not a sister?"

"Yep, I really think you could be Playmate of the Year."

Anna's horribly red-splotched face broke out in a beatific smile. "The truth is I've got a boyfriend I don't like more than a friend. I've barely kissed Jim. I definitely haven't done circus sex acts with him, you dirty girl." She grinned and hugged herself. "But I really, really, REALLY love the idea of Reggie not knowing this and being as miserable as I've been." Anna paused to savor this thought of my brother's jealous agony, her gaze far off and the grin turned gloating. This is why I love supporting my friends. I twiddled my thumbs patiently. "I've fallen half in love with your numb nuts of a brother. He probably hates me about now. Even Aunt Lily suspects how much I like him. Did I tell you she caught me blubbering in my hysteria over him that night when I got home? Talk about a lowering moment! Can you imagine the friggin' lecture on chasteness and jezebels I had to suffer through at one in the morning?"

"No, and if you try to tell me, I'll punch you in the mouth."

Anna started laughing. She was all smiles now. "Yet strangely enough, I am happier than I have been in weeks. So yeah, I think that about covers it."

I grabbed my purse. "Perfect. Can we go spying now? I'm weak with hunger. I could possibly eat a small pony--should a slow one cross my path anytime soon."

Anna snapped the visor up, still grinning. "I'm buying. How does a Shetland sound?"

"Hairy, but I'll take it."

She giggled. "Deal, but one more thing first."

I whined pathetically, "What now?"

Anna, leaning my way across the jeep, presented her face to me sideways. I gave a beleaguered sigh and leaned her way. I pressed the side of my face to hers.

"Cheek!" we said in unison.

Chapter IX
"Zombie" by The Cranberries

Saturday, 11/17/12
3:00 PM

After several more conversations concerning the mystery of the missing Cheryl, several more one-sided conversations about the wonder that is my brother, and several hours of walking around in St Paul, we drove home to Northfield.

Turning into Bel's parking lot, I cruised by an older model, white Dodge Caravan that had its motor running. It was idling in a space near the entrance to the street. I caught a glimpse of a big man seated behind the wheel. I didn't know the van or the man, but I absently reasoned he was waiting for someone in Bel's, perhaps his wife.

The lot actually only had two parked cars besides those I recognized as belonging to our various employees. Even on a Saturday, late afternoon could be a slow time in the store. There was still another two weeks before the holiday season officially began after Thanksgiving.

I parked Lady Liberty in the garage. I glanced at my phone and saw a voicemail message from Crookie. After listening, I updated Anna.

"Crookie reported Cheryl missing with Jack in Northfield. After that, he went to the Edina police, too. Turns out he knows one of the cops there; he's the husband of a co-worker. Oh, and he's coming over tomorrow night for dinner."

"Awesome," Anna beamed, "it will be so nice to see Crooks! I'm relieved there's an official search now for Cheryl, aren't you? I can't stand her, but I'm really curious to find out where she's been all this time."

I absently nodded my agreement. I was checking out a text message I had missed from Luke earlier in the afternoon.

Yes. My turn

The meaning of the words 'my turn' washed over me. For a few moments, I was adrift in the seductive world of wondering what Luke may choose for his turn at a fantasy. Pornographic imaginations must run in my family. Greedy, impatient girl that I am, the next thought was how long he'd make me wait to find out. Then I laughed softly at the brevity of his text.

Anna smiled in inquiry at my laughter. "What?"

I slipped my phone in my purse and shook my head. "Men. You gotta love 'em."

Anna looked dubious. "You do?"

Chuckling together, Anna and I toddled towards the back entrance door of the store, agonizing over who felt the most bloated from all we'd eaten. We each carried a handled bag stacked with takeout boxes from our ventures on Grand Avenue to share with our staffs.

Anna bumped me with a shoulder and a knowing grin. "I noticed Luke's truck is no longer parked down the street."

"Huh. Guess he must have finished his business in that alley."

Anna griped, "Oh, come on! Maybe one of these days you'll tell me something about your love life for a change, Anabel."

"Sure, that could happen." I agreed easily. "I'm telling you upfront, you'll be bored to tears. It's not like I do nudie extreme-baking like some people I know."

Laughing, I darted out of the way of her swinging purse and ran for the back door. I happened to glance in through the glass before pulling the door open. What I saw caused me to gape in stunned shock. I stood rooted in place, unable to look away for a few, frozen seconds.

I slammed myself against the wall on the side of the door and hissed at Anna, "Quick, come over here. Don't go in front of the door."

Anna ran up and backed against the wall next to me. Her eyes were huge as she took in my shocked face.

I opened my purse and fumbled for my cell. I held up my hand before Anna could speak.

I punched 9, saying to her, "Listen, some guy is in there and he's got Larissa. I saw him shaking and hitting her. Stella's up front. Everyone else I could see is okay, but the guy is screaming." I paused to talk into my phone. "Jack, 911 at Bel's. I think it's a domestic. He has my employee and he's hurting her. Stella's in there, Jack. I saw it through the back door...really? Where? Well, then fucking HURRY!" I threw my cell into my purse and dropped it to the ground.

Jack was a few minutes away. There was a frat house fire by St Olaf's. I knew my eyes were huge, too. I couldn't seem to blink. I was speaking way too fast; the words pouring out of my mouth at the same time I was thinking furiously. I was imagining the fear and pain poor Larissa was feeling. I was filled with terror he may hurt my Stella, or our employees and customers. If he hadn't all ready.

Thinking of him hurting one of my people in my bookstore brought on a wave of protective rage that shook and consumed me. I was blind with the raw power of it and couldn't breathe. My throat felt like I had swallowed a rock and it physically hurt. This had happened to me once before in my life when an older bully was pounding on a much younger Reggie on the playground after school. The kid was years older than me and a foot taller. It hadn't mattered then; all I saw was Reg getting creamed. I waded in, jumped on the bully's back and started punching his head and face. I got my ass kicked.

It didn't matter now, either. Like I remembered from long ago, the rage ebbed and while not gone, was banked and glowing red. I could breathe again. I wasn't a kid this time. I was dead calm and able to think clearly. I knew what I had to do.

I unbuttoned my shirt halfway down and pulled it apart. I ran my hands through my hair, twisting it up in a loose knot and pulling down a few strands.

"Give me your cheaters, hurry." I ordered Anna.

"My cheaters?" Anna repeated, dazed but automatically opening her purse. Anna wears contacts but always carries a pair of glasses. She handed them over, and I put on the black frames. I could see perfectly.

She asked in confusion, "What are you doing, Anabel?"

"Stay out here, okay? I promise it will be fine and you can't get hurt. Wait for Jack. He had two 911 texts and is on his way."

Anna held onto me, protesting, but I shook off her arm. Hurrying over, I took a deep breath, and then threw open the back door.

I didn't hesitate, but walked boldly, loudly into the store. I slammed the back door behind me. I threw the full bag of food I had brought in with me to the side. With a noisy clatter, it landed in the direction of the Fare.

I started yelling at the top of my lungs and bitching out the employees.

I saw Trent and Brenda Blackman, a part-timer working for Anna; shoot me identical, terrified glances. They'd been watching the scene unfolding in front of them at the checkout counter where Larissa was working. Trent was huddled protectively over the crying Brenda as they stood together behind the Fare's service bar.

In the first seconds, I swiftly took in the three customers in the store while my eyes sought Stella. I registered relief in the back of my mind seeing her still standing near the front of the store in the Romance section. Her arms were around two elderly ladies that were leaning on her, bug-eyed with fright. Even from this far, I could see Stella was scared to death, too.

I quickly scanned the whole floor while continuing my screaming tirade. I strode up the side aisle in a loud, heel-clomping walk with my revealed breasts thrust out, my hips swaying, and my hair tumbling down around my face. I strode towards where I knew Larissa and the man were. I hadn't looked at them directly yet, but I could plainly hear Larissa's soft, pained cries. The enormous wall of cold rage inside me was demanding to be let loose and kill something.

Since the minute I had thrown the bag of food towards Trent, and at the same I was sizing up the store, I was screaming nonstop like a drill sergeant in the loudest voice I have ever used.

"WHAT ARE YOU DOING ALL STANDING AROUND NOT WORKING? I LEAVE THE STORE FOR AN HOUR AND THIS IS WHAT YOU SLACKERS GET UP TO? HOW DARE YOU NOT WORK HARD WHILE I AM OUT TRYING TO DRUM UP BUSINESS SO YOU CAN KEEP YOUR JOBS AND GET PAID!"

Everyone's attention was now on me in horrified bewilderment. I noticed Billy with a petrified, elderly woman on the opposite side of the store in Sci-Fi.

I made my eyes pass over Larissa and the man next to her for only a brief second without stopping. They were on my side of the aisle. I continued my blistering, tyrannical raving directed at the staff's ungrateful lack of work ethics and brains.

I was only three yards away now from Larissa. The man who had been holding her in a tight, punishing grip by her upper arm was not tall. He was wide, but not muscled; carrying an extra thirty pounds in a gut. He was much older than Larissa, easily in his forties. He had the red-veined nose of a drinker and his dark hair was oily and thinning. If he was ever attractive in his youth, those days were long past. His eyes were close-set, and he looked rat-faced mean and vicious; just like you'd expect a wife beater to look.

I had his full attention, too. He had turned to face me, now only loosely holding onto Larissa's right arm. I saw the slack-jawed surprise on his face at my yelling like a Nazi boss on steroids. Then he zeroed in on my unbuttoned blouse showing off considerable cleavage. I did not need a padded bra. Only a few seconds had passed since I burst shouting into the store, and he still appeared too confused to even form a sentence. He was as stupid as I'd counted on.

I saw Larissa's swollen, vacant eyes and a puffy redness swelling around her mouth. I saw blood smeared on her lip and chin. Then I saw everything glaringly outlined in a red film of indescribable fury in front of my eyes. I didn't stop as I strode forward the last couple of yards, quickening my step to almost a trot.

I ignored the man and yelled, pointing at Larissa. "I KNEW IT WAS A MISTAKE TO HIRE YOU! YOU ARE WORTHLESS! LOOK AT YOU, JUST STANDING THERE WHEN THIS MAN NEEDS YOUR HELP. GET BACK TO WORK, YOU IDIOT, OR YOU ARE FIRED! DO YOU HEAR ME? I WILL MAKE SURE YOU NEVER WORK IN THIS TOWN AGAIN!"

With my peripheral vision, I was aware of the spread of a dawning smile on the man's face at my screaming words to Larissa.

I was two feet away.

A Date with Fate

I moved forward while looking up and pointing at the ceiling. "LOOK UP THERE! OH MY GOD, LOOK, LOOK!"

I positively shrieked the last 'LOOK' and I knew with an unquestioning certainty everyone in my store was anxiously looking up to where I was pointing to on the ceiling. All of them full of confusion.

Without hesitation, I took full advantage of this confusion my abusive, screaming tirade had caused. With all the momentum of my skipping trot behind my left leg, and with many years of playing soccer and kick ball rising to the surface, I kicked the distracted fucker square up in his scrotum with my steel-toed, booted foot.

When Larissa's abuser dropped to the floor, cupping himself while rolling, retching, and screaming in agony, I heard myself screaming, too. I hopped on my right leg, arms out straight for balance, and I kicked him again as hard as I could. Then I kicked him again and again, over and over.

Everything happened fast after that, and seemingly all at once.

I vaguely was aware of cop cars pulling up in front of Bel's, lights flashing and sirens wailing and doors slamming.

I was aware of Stella running towards me, tears streaming down her face.

I was aware of the freed Larissa lurching away, sobbing and falling to her knees on the floor behind the checkout counter.

I was aware of Anna's piercing voice screaming my name somewhere behind me.

I was aware my hair had tumbled completely down in my face and Anna's cheaters had gone flying off somewhere.

I was aware of Trent and Billy gently, inexorably pulling me away from the screaming, heaving man on the floor. I had been kicking furiously at him, shrieking the word "BASTARD!" repeatedly with supreme satisfaction in time with my kicks.

Once they pulled me a couple of feet away, I shook the guys off. I held out my hands to let them know I was calming down.

They were shaking like I was in the throes of a severe bout of malaria.

Trent and Billy stood protectively between me and the man on the floor; never taking their eyes away from him for long. The bastard was in a fetal position, crying and blubbering.

Billy was bouncing nervously and started talking fast, nonstop. "Anabel, that was some serious fucking shit! Are you okay? Man, he caught us all by surprise. He came out of nowhere, suddenly shaking and hitting Larissa!" Billy appealed to Trent. "Right, man? He said if any of us tried anything he'd break her neck. He was trying to drag her out of the store. Is this her ex, or what? The crazy fucker warned us not to touch our phones, but I texted the cops from my pocket. Then you come flying in the back door like...like, hell, some sort of librarian gone wild. What was that;

it was so fuckin' unreal! I can't believe I saw you do that!" Billy voice had an edge of hysteria underlined with admiration.

I patted his shoulder. It took a lot of effort to lift my arm and I was absently surprised by its heaviness. "It's cool now, Billy. We're okay, right? Right, Trent?"

Billy and Trent looked at each other, and they both nodded quickly. Trent tentatively cupped my shoulder and peered down at me.

His voice was cautious and his face was white. "Yeah, we're okay, Anabel. Are you okay? Do you need some water or something?" He motioned towards my shirt. "Not that I mind, but do you want to button up your shirt, or maybe sit down over there?"

I didn't answer and my hands were clumsy. I gave up after one button. I noticed the cops were coming our way led by Jack. He took in the scene, gave me a cursory once over—pausing at my chest. Then he turned away and started giving orders.

Stella grabbed me in a fierce hug then, and I hugged her tightly back. I pulled away to look her in the eye. "You're fine, right?"

She nodded, wiping her tears away. Unable to talk, she nodded quickly again.

"Go help Larissa, okay? Ask Jack if you can take her into my office, and close the door until the EMT's get here. Call her parents." My words felt sluggish and slow, but Stella nodded a third time and took off without another word.

I should go to Larissa, but I didn't know if seeing me would traumatize her further after yelling the way I had. I could hear her continued sobbing even over the ex's mewling cries and curses from the floor.

I turned as Anna ran up. She enveloped me in another hard hug. "You crazy...God, you kicked the CRAP out of him! If you EVER do anything like that again ..."

I whispered, "I don't feel so good."

She didn't seem to hear me. She released me and turned to Trent and Billy. From far away, I could hear her voice talking urgently to them. She hurriedly left to go tend to her crying employee, Brenda.

I felt adrift, not knowing what to do with myself. *'Where was I needed?'*

The few customers in the store gathered around closer to Trent, Billy and me. They kept a wide berth from the police and the man on the floor a few feet away. They were all chattering at once, and exclaiming over what I had done. Two of the elderly ladies I now recognized as the sisters, Millie and Ethel. They played bridge here every Thursday afternoon.

Millie was saying, "Anabel, my dear girl, are you..."

I lifted my hand, mumbling, "Sorry...excuse me."

A Date with Fate

I then rudely walked away from them all--my customers, my staff, and the police. On increasingly wobbly legs, I headed towards the back door. I needed air desperately.

A couple of uniformed cops were coming up the aisle from that direction. They gave me a curious look, but rushed past me to join in the excited confusion of action behind me. I kept heading for the back door and freedom. It seemed like I was wading through water. I kept my head down, watching my shaky legs move slowly like they didn't belong to me.

Sounding like he was yelling down a tunnel, I heard Jack's official voice directing his men to secure the man on the floor. The wife beater screamed and cried, incoherently bellowing curses, and tried to fight them off. I heard a crackling sound and then silence. I ought to be interested as I've never seen anyone tasered before, but I felt strangely tingly and numb.

Some instinct had me looking up. Luke stood framed in the back door entrance a few feet to the right of me. His searching gaze swept right past me without pausing as he scanned all the activity happening in the store.

His head snapped back to me. His eyes briefly closed tight while he murmured something under his breath. I saw he was frowning and his mouth shaped my name, but I didn't hear a sound over the roaring in my ears.

When I felt Luke's strong arms, a feeling of safety washed over me that I've only experienced before in my life when held by my grandmother as a child. My whole body was quivering with the shakes now and my head hurt. The tingly feeling was worse. I felt outside myself looking on from far away. Before I could rest my forehead against his wide shoulder for just a minute, I knew there was something important I needed to tell him.

'Oh, yeah.'

I whispered, "Sometimes a kick in the gonads does decide things in my favor."

Chapter X
"King of Anything" by Sara Barilles

Saturday, 11/17/12
4:45 PM

Anna was patting my hand and peering down at me worriedly. Even when she's worried, her face looks like it's trying to stop itself from breaking out into a smile of knowing a secret you don't. This isn't on purpose, but a nervous reaction to stress. Anna can't help she looks guilty when she's anxious, but you can imagine the trouble it's caused us.

It took me a second to realize I was lying on the sofa in my apartment. I stared around bemusedly for a moment and then it all came rushing back.

I pulled my hand back and sat up hurriedly, and then swayed with the rush. I pushed aside the afghan. "Whew! What happened, how did I get up here? How's Larissa?"

Anna handed me a small glass of orange juice. I accepted gratefully and started chug-a-lugging.

"You fainted."

I started coughing on the orange juice at her flat words. She thumped my back.

"No way in hell I fainted!"

Anna's worried visage disappeared and she glared at me. "Yes, you did faint. Luke came in the back door and swept you in his arms. You dropped like a girl in a Harlequin book." She mocked nastily, "Even your hair swung perfectly over his arm to the floor in a cascade of shimmering blondeness." Anna finally stopped whacking my back. "Overall, Larissa's okay. Her parents took her home right after they all talked to Jack. Everybody's doing just peachy once the shock wore off. Her ex, Ron Hansen, showed up only a couple minutes before we did. The bad news is, he hit Larissa in the mouth and shook her around, that poor girl, but luckily he didn't have time to do anything else besides threaten the other people." She added an afterthought. "Oh yeah, I got your purse, and Stella closed the store."

A Date with Fate

"Thanks."

I didn't dare laugh. It was weird seeing Anna upset at me. It's unnatural for cute, chipmunky types to be mad. I plunked the empty juice glass down on the coffee table and lay back, crossing an elbow over my eyes. I was relieved all was handled downstairs, but wondered how long I had been out on the sofa.

Besides, I didn't really feel much like laughing. I'm sure passing out is a normal reaction when dealing with the aftermath of adrenaline and shock in an average person. I hated knowing I reacted like an average girl. I had to face the truth. I wasn't some tough chick that could kick a man in the balls a few times, then walk away and get ready for a night out with the girls. Apparently, I needed a nap first.

Anna wasn't done with me. She went on mercilessly. "Then Luke carried you up here." Over my loud groan, she carried on. "You came to out of your faint and said," Her voice went falsetto, "'Oh, Luke, you are so strong, please be my man and take care of me'."

I peeked over my arm at Anna. "Yeah, right. How can you say the words 'Harlequin book' to me with a straight face, you mean, little vermin."

"Listen, Junior, if you hadn't just *fainted for over an hour*," Anna loudly emphasized the words, "I'd be tempted to smack the stupid out of you for running into the store the way you did!"

I sat up again and regarded the pissed off Anna standing above me. My head still had a lingering trace of the pounding headache I'd felt earlier, and it felt tender to the touch. I was slightly nauseous, and even though I was no longer shaking, I felt weak as a kitten. I was in no mood for taking any shit.

"Are you mad I went into the store, or just mad I did it without you?"

"Both!" Anna yelled, shaking her fists at me. "My god, Junior, that crazy madman could have had a gun or…or…a knife! You could have been seriously fucked up. I could have helped, but no, you ran off. You left me out there not knowing what the hell was going on! That really blows!"

"Well, excuse me for not stopping to draw a play action in the dirt." I shot back, and regretted it instantly. My head was thumping again and I rubbed my forehead in agitation. I went on more reasonably. "Come on, Anna, I couldn't drag you in there with me. What if I got you hurt?"

Anna did a little jig of frustration in front of me. "That's my point exactly! You left ME behind to watch something bad possibly happen to YOU, you moron woman!"

I reached for her arm and pulled her down beside me on the sofa. I wasn't quite yelling, but my voice was still raised. "Fine. Next time I plan to go kick the crap out of some wife beating ex-con, I'll send you an engraved invitation, okay? We'll attack him together singing a duet. Will that make you happy, you bloodthirsty badger?"

Anna snorted and frowned, fussing with NanaBel's knit afghan until it covered over both of our legs and laps. "Okay, fine. Just don't leave me behind ever again."

"Gotcha. No behinds will be left." I pushed her knee with mine and teased her. "Come on, you know you love me like I'm your best friend, so don't be mad at me." I nudged her again. "How's about next time we'll do a bunny hop together to lure whoever we're attacking into a false sense of security before we jump him? Do you like that plan?"

Anna relented and smiled a little, pushing my knee away with hers. "That sounds like it would work. Just don't forget about the singing part before we let loose a flurry of blows on their unsuspecting head."

"Oh, please, like I would ever forget the need to sing with you right before commencing some serious flurrying. Good god, next you'll be questioning my head blowing abilities."

Laying her head on my shoulder, Anna chuckled. "I would never question your head blowing abilities, but I think…"

"I think you two are completely, bat-shit crazy, that's what I think."

At the sound of the caustic voice booming across the space like a cannon salvo, we both jumped sky high. Anna squealed and threw the entire afghan over her head. I sprang to my feet, turned to face the foyer, lost my balance, and nearly fell backwards over the coffee table. Only by windmilling my arms frantically was I able to stay upright.

"You scared us sneaking up like that!"

Jack stood surveying me with legs slightly spread, hands on his hips, and his ever present aviators pushed up on his head. He shrugged off his POLICE jacket and tossed it back on the bench in the foyer. "Three people come stomping up your stairs and you two were so loud you didn't hear us? Not my problem you were scared, Sheila Shit-kicker."

A Date with Fate

That was a gentle reminder I was doomed for eternity with a slew of new names to live down after today. Head throbbing like a bass drum, I massaged my temples.

Next to him, a grinning Stella held a tray with a trio of oversized mugs; steaming curlicues rising enticingly up from their depths. Her eyes were pink around the edges, but she was no longer crying or upset. Behind her was my hero. Luke had no expression whatsoever on his face as he steadily regarded me.

If I had thought I might be shy facing Luke after I had passed out in his arms like a pussy, it paled in comparison to the embarrassment I now was feeling. Realizing he had been listening to Anna and I acting like the immature weirdino's we so often are was cringe-worthy. I wished I had an afghan over my head.

I took in that his short, black hair wasn't mussed just so, and his unbuttoned shirt over his T was wrinkled. I saw faint, dark shadows under his eyes. I'd never seen Luke looking so rumpled and unkempt. Usually, he looked sharp and put together, even when wearing his five o'clock shadow.

My blush of embarrassment was quickly turning into confusion at being observed so coolly by this detached, expressionless Luke. Stella walked around the sofa. She carefully set the tray on the low table. I was distracted when she handed me a cup of hot chocolate piled high with mounds of whipped cream and chocolate sprinkles. I could now sit down and ignore Luke's strange behavior with some semblance of dignity. I also ignored Stella's giggles and Jack's disgusted expression. Jack came into the room and sat down heavily on the roomy, club chair he always preferred across from me.

Anna popped out of her blanket burrow and eagerly accepted a mug of chocolate. Stella served herself and then perched on the sofa on my other side. With spoons in hand, the three of us dug into the rich, cold cream atop the hot chocolate, oohing and aahing as we slurped contentedly.

Still not looking in Luke's direction, I moaned in gratitude. "Thanks, Stell. This is just what the doctor ordered."

"You're welcome, but it was your boyfriend's idea." Stella winked with a broad smile at my startled glance. "Dr. Luke said you'd need something 'hot and sweet' after you woke up." She wiggled her eyebrows and said under her breath, "That's what she said...."

Anna snorted into her hot chocolate, almost spilling the towering spoonful being navigated to her mouth.

I snorted, too. But only due to the fact that Stella looked so lascivious when winking and being suggestive it was quite creepy.

Jack, smacking the arms of his chair, stood up. "Fun time's over, girls. Anabel, since you are feeling better let's get down to business."

Anna set her cup on the tray and raised her hand tentatively. "May I go to the bathroom, Chief?"

Jack threw her an annoyed look and didn't bother with an answer. In his shirtsleeves and shoulder holster, crossed arms bulging with muscles, and chewing rhythmically on a piece of gum, Jack was the embodiment of impatient, masculine authority. Knowing Anna had seriously been asking for a hall pass, I nudged her it was okay. She took off in grateful relief for the guest bath. Chief Jack terrifies her.

Stella worriedly asked Jack, "That man won't be able to get out of jail and come back, will he?"

The law is one subject Chief Jack is happy to expound on at length. I lost track of their conversation when Luke sat on the sofa next to me in Anna's vacated spot.

I finally made myself meet his hard, dark green gaze when he leaned in, not touching me, but with an arm behind me along the back of the sofa. Up close, his serious expression wasn't looking so detached. I could see he was extremely unhappy. I sighed inside, wishing I was wrong and that he wasn't mad at me, too.

Luke spoke softly. "I was relieved Anna was giving you a hard time, until the end. Then I was disappointed in you both. Instead of admitting the correct choice was waiting in safety and letting the professionals handle things; you promise your friend she can help next time. How asinine can you be?"

When he paused, I was so dismayed at his unexpected words I sat frozen. He was completely composed on the surface, yet I've never seen his eyes look so coldly furious. Mine felt huge with surprise as I stared into his face. The random thought crossed my mind that this was the Luke people saw on the job—whatever that was. He looked so ferocious; I'd want him covering my six any time. I just didn't want him on my ass and disappointed in me.

"I'm a very strong man, Anabel. If we were alone right now, I would love to put you over my lap and spank some sense into your hard

A Date with Fate

head via your ass until my arm was very, very tired. That's how pissed I am at your lack of care for your own safety."

At my sharp intake of breath, he pulled back and met my narrowing eyes with a serious, yet slightly mocking look of his own.

Now I was pissed. I couldn't believe he was casually mentioning spanking me after what I had just done to a man who was hurting a woman. I couldn't believe he thought I was so stupid I didn't care about my own safety. I was here, wasn't I? I couldn't believe he called me asinine for joking around with my friend! That really hurt. Most of all, I couldn't believe everyone seemed to want a piece of me for kicking down that low-life wife beater.

He ignored my cold gaze. Taking his time, Luke's glittering eyes traveled over my face before settling on my mouth. He gave an odd, half-smile then, as if the joke were on him.

I faced forward and sat stiff.

'The ass should worry over his lack of care for his own safety with me. He obviously didn't get me.'

Luke leaned back in close to my ear. "Or should I kiss you instead, and then make love to you until you can't walk for a week?" I felt the whisper of his lips on my neck. "I wonder if you even know which you'd prefer."

'What the hell?' Could Luke seriously think I'd choose to be spanked over being made love to? Until I couldn't walk for a week, no less?

His use of the words 'make love' made it through the mad. I hesitated a second in my offended thoughts. In getting to know Luke these last months, I've come to respect his perspectives on life. His observations on the world around him are sharp and concise. He is a logical thinker and a man of action. He expected a lot out of himself, and probably has similar high standards for those people involved in his personal life.

My shoulders relaxed as the defensive anger drained out of me. Luke didn't want to physically hurt me. With his broader experiences of fighting to draw from, he was upset at what I had done and scared at what could have happened. He cared about me. I shouldn't repay him with anger because he said incredibly dumb, male things to express himself in the aftermath of relief.

I stifled my shiver his mention of spankings and his light caress on my neck caused inside me. I decided in this instance he was way off-base, but I understood why he was frustrated enough to need to say such things.

I sensed the day we met I didn't fit the description of the type of female he normally dated. I think he was hit over the head and stunned with the same feelings of unexplainable, inexplicable attraction that I experienced. My independent ways would always taunt and challenge him. I bet any women Luke previously dated didn't cause him any trouble or worry. They'd have a set role he gave them in his life. He'd feel secure in the knowledge they'd be waiting for him in their quietly calm, dependably mature worlds while he went out and lived dangerously.

In case nobody noticed, I am not that kind of woman. Also, weird stuff happens to me all the time. I don't understand why, but it's like I'm some sort of magnet for the bizarre and freaky.

I fear Luke is destined to be disappointed in me if that means I must sit back and never take risks to prevent his worry. I appreciated his shoulder, but I didn't need a constant hero, or a daddy, or a control freak. A man that considers me his equal, not in the sense of physical strength, but in the mind and spirit; was what I was cautiously hoping to find in Luke. It was why I dated so few, perfectly nice men more than once or twice without getting bored. I knew what I didn't want in a man. What suited the real me has always been a different story.

Jack and Stella were still talking, but I noticed Jack's cop eyes strayed often to Luke beside me.

'What the hell again! Did I actually see a glimmer of approbation there, and not his usual instant dismissal? Didn't that just figure!'

This was turning out to be one humdinger of a weekend.

"Anabel, look at me."

I did look at Luke, but I kept my face politely inquiring, determined to not let him see how he affected me.

His expression had softened. "Bravery is being able to act even when you're scared. You are a brave woman, Anabel. Your friends are lucky to have someone care about them like you do." His lips tightened. "You were also an idiot. The situation could have gone south and gotten real ugly; fast. You need training to do what you did." He patted my thigh and made to get up.

His blunt words had reaffirmed all I thought and gave me some hope we could find our middle ground. Except for the idiot part, but I was willing to work with him on his stupidity.

I put a hand on his arm and stayed him. "You are almost absolutely right."

Luke was surprised. I had caught him off-guard. "What, specifically, am I almost right about?"

Palms up, I shrugged. "Pretty much everything you've said."

He smiled a little then, and some of his tense grimness eased. "I am, huh? Everything?"

I ignored his innuendo and lightly stroked his forearm. "I definitely need some self-defense training. If you could help by pointing me in the right direction, that would be great. I did do something stupid on the face of it, and I was lucky the good guys won." I kissed him softly on his cheek. I sat back and smiled up at his still face. With sincere gratitude I added, "Thank you for catching me when I passed out."

Luke surprised me by abruptly getting up, walking over to Jack, and putting out his hand. The big cop stood back up and they shook. "Jack, I'll get out of your way."

"Luke, we'll talk again soon." Jack let go of Luke's hand and thumped him lightly on the shoulder. I gawked in amazement.

'Had there been an alien abduction while I napped?'

Body snatching was the only explanation for Jack's easygoing acceptance of Luke.

Luke nodded. "I'll get Anabel back to you in a minute; I want her to walk me out. Maybe you could talk to Anna first?"

At Jack's nod, Luke turned back to me. He raised his brow and put a hand out. Feeling dazed, I automatically clasped his hand. He tugged me to my feet and led me around the coffee table.

Luke then grinned at my niece, his dimple flashing. "Stella, I'm sorry for the circumstances, but it was great meeting you. You were amazing down in the store today. I know you'll keep Anabel on the straight and narrow."

I huffed in disbelief as Stella laughed, blushing. She dimpled back at Luke as they bumped fists.

'Okay, did Anna say I napped for one hour, or one week?'

We passed Anna on our way to the stairs. Luke paused to say good-bye. Anna gave him a huge hug with many exclamations of thanks. Luke squeezed her back with one arm, smiling broadly at her laughing promise of free cookies for life. I stood numbly upright, tethered to reality by Luke's hand clasped tightly around my own. I didn't even wonder too much why Luke deserved free cookies for life while I, as part owner, had been eighty-sixed from any bakery freebies forever.

I felt like I was caught up in a waking dream where nothing was as it seemed or supposed to be. I was half daydreaming myself how I'd like to demonstrate to Luke my appreciation of his being there for me downstairs.

'Didn't I hear a blow job is the male version of a bouquet?' It was an interesting daydream, until reality slapped me awake. What I wanted didn't matter; there was no way I was going to start anything with three sets of big ears and eyes straining from the living room.

The responsible, mean mommy voice in my head scolded me. I had to give my statement to Jack, get an update from Stella and Anna on the store and the welfare of my staff, and then get everyone out of here so I could be alone. I needed to contact my family and friends soon or they'd come charging over. Luckily, the customers witnessing the events were all elderly, so there probably were no pictures or video posted on the internet. The staff I could trust. I thought about the news, what was being reported on the incident, and how it would impact business. Later on, I was still planning to go over to Mac's for dinner at seven.

It was 4:40 PM according to the Breitling on Luke's wrist. This day felt like it had lasted a week and it was only half over. I covered a small yawn behind my free hand. I was still a little groggy from my nap.

When Luke and I reached the top of the stairs, he surprised me again by not leaving but turning to the right. He led me down the hallway. He pulled me into the first open doorway which happened to be the bathroom. He shut the door behind us.

There was a charged silence in the darkness.

I reached up and touched his hard shoulder with my free hand. I smoothed down his rigid arm. "Luke, nobody has ever been there for me..."

Luke cut in, "Don't you mean you've never had a man be there for you before?"

Struck by his words, I shrugged and touched my forehead against his chest. "I guess I do mean that."

There are men who have wanted to be there for me in my life, but I don't make it easy for them. I don't know how to be anything less than self-reliant and independent. Putting it bluntly, there's never been a man that's impressed me enough to make me want to lean on him in my personal life.

A Date with Fate

Luke still held my one hand, so I reached and clasped his other hand. I found it easier to speak of these things in the dark. I wondered fleetingly if that is why Luke left the light off.

"Listen, it means a lot you came to check on me." I laughed ruefully. "I absolutely can't stand the thought of passing out and being carried anywhere, but if it had to be done, well, I'm glad it was you. I'm sorry I scared you."

Luke was silent. I was starting to get uncomfortable, wondering why he wasn't answering when he spoke. "Quit being so hard on yourself; it's not like you fainted from seeing a mouse. You took on a man, Anabel." He added softly, "I didn't mind carrying you."

"Hey, I didn't faint." Recalling Anna's obnoxious description, I frowned. "If you say I was 'as light as a feather' I swear I'll wallop you."

I could hear the smile in his voice. "Why the hell would I say that? You were dead weight in my arms. It felt like I was carrying two hundred pounds of flopping female." He squeezed my hands. "I probably should apologize here for accidentally banging your head kind of hard against the wall."

"Oh, My Hero!" I was laughing quietly. "That explains why I have such a sore head and headache. I was worried about stroking from high blood pressure. Here, close your eyes, I'm turning on the light."

I reached past Luke and hit the switch. The main bathroom in my apartment is divided into two, with a pocket door in between. Luke and I were standing close in the smaller room that is used by guests, and fitted with a toilet and vanity. Through the sliding door was my larger, personal bathroom that included the mirrored vanity area, the shower and tub room, and then a huge, walk-in closet—formerly a small bedroom I had redesigned with Reggie's help.

"Here we go." I straightened up with the bottle of Advil. Tossing back a couple, I turned on the cold faucet. Leaning over the tap, I took a gulp of the streaming water. It tasted so refreshing; I kept lapping thirstily for a few seconds. Finally replete, I stood up and wiped my mouth with the back of my hand. I looked into the mirror and saw Luke behind me, his face amused.

"What?" I smiled back at his image, patting at the water droplets spilling down the front of my black vest and white blouse.

Luke put his hands on my hips, pulling me back closer to him. "You and Reggie hung out a lot together growing up, didn't you?"

"Yes, but it was probably from Jazy where I learned the useful habit of drinking from a faucet like a dog."

Luke's dark eyebrows flew up in surprise and I grinned.

I couldn't be around Luke for long and not be aware of his maleness. Actually, I couldn't be around him for even a second without my feminine instincts responding. It didn't matter how much I enjoyed talking with him, I was always conscious on a deeper level of the hum of desire his presence aroused in me. Now was no different. I went with the pull of his hands, relaxing back fully against him.

Luke's hands slid from my hips and he hugged me from behind. I rested my hands on his locked forearms. He rested his chin on my head, a perfect spot for him. I didn't mind, despite the tenderness from my various head contusions from the last couple of days. We were silent, staring at each other's faces reflected back in the mirror two feet in front of us.

The contrasting images of his black hair and dark tan against my blondeness and fair skin were vividly erotic. I watched him bend his head and move my tangled hair aside with his chin, kissing my neck with his dark eyes still on mine. He kissed my cheek next, as if he was unable to resist the pink, flushed target.

Luke's glance came back to my face in the mirror. His smile started slowly and built to blatantly lecherous. I had no doubt what he was thinking about to give me such a leering look.

He didn't make me wait. "I was right about everything?"

I turned and slid my hands up his arms to his shoulders. "Well, sir, I was so wrong to say you were almost absolutely right about *all* the things you said."

"I like it when you are polite and respectful. Yes, go on. Keep telling me how absolutely wrong you were." Luke lifted me so I was sitting on the vanity. He used his knee to spread my legs and stepped between my thighs. His hands splayed on my lower back urged me forward on the vanity until we were touching.

His expression was much lighter now, no longer so black and grim. The glint of desire in his hooded eyes and the small smile playing on his mouth were an aphrodisiac for me.

Is there any sight more tantalizing than the man you want waiting with obvious heat for your response?

I can't think of one, either.

A Date with Fate

I brought my hand up to cup his cheek. Eyes on my thumb, I rubbed it lightly over his lower lip and then rasped over the black whiskers surrounding his mouth. They were much softer than they looked.

"I think I'm sure which I prefer." I leaned back and smiled flirtatiously. "Most respectfully, I request the choice of being fucked for a week until you cannot walk."

Luke groaned softly, placing a hard kiss on my lips. "That was *not* one of your choices."

I traced the outline of his mouth with the tip of my tongue and then sucked gently on his full, bottom lip. "Oh Luke, help me. I have such a bad time with details. Does that mean no?"

"I'm still deciding if I can make an exception in your case." His hands were at the buttons of my shirt, swiftly working his way down until the shirt parted. He spread the cotton fabric apart, taking my black vest with it, and pulling my arms down from his shoulders. Leaning back and smiling up at him, I braced myself with a hand on either side of my hips on the vanity. He pulled my shirt and vest halfway down my arms, and then stopped.

I was wearing a T-back style underwire bra that clasped in the front. The bra was not frilly or fancy, but the fabric was sheer. My round, full breasts and nipples were clearly visible.

Luke leaned forward and kissed a dark pink tip. He drew my nipple into his mouth through the shimmering nylon of the bra, biting gently and then sucking. With his hand, he cupped my other breast and his thumb rubbed slow circles over that stiffening point. Loving it, I tilted my head back; offering myself up to the arousing pleasure Luke's rhythmic kissing and sucking were drawing from my responsive, sensitive nipples.

At the press of his hand on my upper thigh, I opened my legs even wider and felt him move in against me. Through his jeans, Luke slowly stroked his erection over the thick middle seam bisecting the crotch of my jeans. He was putting pressure against the exact spot where I needed to be touched.

I leaned back farther, resting on my elbows. The back of my head touched against the mirror behind the vanity. I said his name on a low moan.

"Please let me know when you decide on my case."

Luke straightened up, eyes lowered and intently watching his hands on my breasts cupping and squeezing. My hands were trapped at my sides from my shirt and vest pulled tight over on my arms, but I couldn't care less right then.

Moving to hold my cheeks with both hands, Luke stared down at me with serious eyes. I smiled a little in uneasy question, not really knowing what his look meant, or what he wanted to see in return.

Right at that moment, I only wanted to see and feel his hard cock with no jeans between us. I wanted him filling me up and satisfying the craving building up inside from his sucking and biting on my nipples and stroking between my thighs. I wanted to straddle him and ride him, our bodies touching and rubbing everywhere. I wanted to stare into his beautiful, green eyes while we did this, and I wanted to watch him come.

"Take down your jeans."

Luke ignored my whisper.

"Please?"

He leaned over and kissed my mouth, but held his lower body away from mine.

"I want to touch you."

He started with slow kisses; only barely touching our lips together.

"Pretty please?"

Each time Luke kissed me, the kiss was fuller and longer; making me want more.

"With sugar…"

He kept denying me until I slowly sucked his tongue into my mouth. The soft suction triggered Luke, and the tempo of his kissing leapt from slow and languorous to fast and intense. He gripped my ass tightly, lifting me against him. His tongue was stroking deep into my mouth, matching the motions of his hips as he moved up against me. I rubbed myself back against the length of him in answer.

He turned his head and broke our kiss. Breathing heavy, his voice was rough. "I am still pissed at you, Anabel."

I rained his face with small kisses, answering tenderly, "Oh, I know, Luke. Never stop taking your anger out on me."

I kissed his wide grin and knew we were good.

Abruptly, Luke backed off. He latched my bra together so quickly I didn't have time to marvel at his expertise of covertly unsnapping it during our passionate kissing. He pulled my shirt up off my arms, and started buttoning me up even faster then he undid the buttons a few minutes ago. He straightened my vest with a sharp tug and hopped me off the vanity.

A Date with Fate

He smiled at my agape expression, putting a finger to his lips as he pointed to the door. He glanced in the mirror, adjusted his jeans, and pulled the tails of his shirt smartly into place to cover the evidence.

There was a loud knock on the door. "Whatcha doing in there, June? Are you almost done? Jack's done with me and the natives are getting restless out here."

"Yes, I'm coming!" I pushed Luke and mouthed with a huffy, mock pout. "Not."

He covered his eyes with one hand, shoulders shaking.

"Anna, would you please get me a water from the fridge, and I'll be right there, okay?"

"Sure thing." I heard Anna walking away, and turned anxiously back to Luke.

He kissed me good-bye before I could say anything. "Go on, I'll slip out after you. What's the code for the back door in the store?"

I smiled my relief we weren't caught. I gave him the code, making a mental note to ask later exactly how he *had* entered my locked building last night.

I flushed the toilet to be convincing, combed my hair quickly, and then checked over my appearance in the mirror for any telltale signs of lingering lust. Luke opened the door enough to make sure the coast was clear.

I spoke low to him. "Sneak out real quietly and watch out for the second stair down." His frowning disapproval over his shoulder at my orders made me grin. "Hey, it's how I heard you coming up the stairs last night, so I thought you may want to know. The code works for Bel's entrance doors and back door. Oh, and thanks again, Luke."

I started to edge by him to leave. He smoothed a hand down the back of my hair to my hip. He closed the door in front of me.

Green eyes glinted. "Don't thank me too soon. I'm still not sure what I am going to do with you. Can we get together later?"

I flashed on my vow to follow my rules. With a chair and a whip, I held back the sex kitten voice roaring in my mind. "I've got a thing with the girls tonight and it will go real late. Tomorrow?"

"Yeah, that's right, the Sunday dinner at five." He did not sound like a happy camper. Clearly, by the look on his frowning face, Luke was not a man used to waiting around for what he wanted.

He smiled invitingly. "You're sure we can't make it sooner than that? Dr. Luke thinks you are making a big mistake going out tonight with the girls. You need a quiet night at home. Dinner in bed, temperature taken--that sort of thing."

I hid my smile at how appealing he looked. He was making this hard. "Oh, well, Mac is feeding me dinner and she's a nurse. I promise I'll take it easy tonight and make no sudden, sharp moves." Although, thinking of the way I danced this could be a falsehood. I patted his cheek, some devil prompting me to add insult to injury. "Dr. Luke doesn't have to worry his pretty, little head over me."

I opened the door and scooted past a frowning, frustrated Luke. I went to join the others in the living room and take my licks from Chief Jack.

I was doubly glad I was sticking to my rules. Being the target of Luke's determined charm, which probably worked for him more often than not, caused me to laugh softly at the difference in the sexes.

When a woman wheedles at a man to break his plans with his friends to spend the whole night home with her instead, she's dismissed as clingy or needy. A man doesn't think twice to ask since his needs come first. The fact Luke hadn't asked me previously on a date for tonight didn't cross his mind, or deter him if it had.

There was only one redeeming factor in Luke's favor for trying to coerce me into breaking my plans. My understanding I was to blame that a couple pints of his blood needed for normal brain functionality was currently coagulating in a more southerly spot in his body.

Except for catching considering looks from the three in my living room, I was not questioned about Luke. He slipped out undetected and we got away with our bathroom interlude unscathed. That was the only thing I got away with unscathed for the next hour.

Before Jack started in on me about the ex, Ron Hansen, I'd taken him aside to ask for the low down on Crookie's missing wife. Jack was closemouthed about police business, but he grudgingly verified he'd spoken with Reggie and knew of his involvement on that night. He relented enough to tell me he was coordinating efforts with the Edina police to find Cheryl. He counseled patience, and I backed off. Jack wasn't much in the mood to share his cop intuitions with me right then. I even rose above it when Jack said the word 'patience' with a definite snarl.

I told the facts concerning my involvement in the assault on Larissa into a tape recorder and signed my statement. I suspected Jack was doing us all a huge favor conducting his interviews here in the apartment.

A Date with Fate

There has to be some benefits for having the Chief of Police as an honorary family member. Especially considering what followed.

I dutifully sat through Jack's censorious tongue-lashing of the perils involved when a female civilian plays hero. I got through this with my good mood intact only because I was gleeful inside knowing Anna and Stella also had to sit through Chief Jack's pacing diatribe.

I didn't dream of sneaking a glimpse at their faces. Jack probably *would* spank me on the spot if he detected the tiniest glimmer of amusement in my demeanor, he was really worked up. I deserved to be commended for keeping it together knowing the girls sat on either side of me staring at Jack with round-eyed astonishment.

Neither of them ever saw this spitting nails, disciplinarian side of Jack. I'd seen it somewhat regularly over the years with my propensity to jump in where angels fear to tread. (His words, not mine.) Why he compares me to an angel quite regularly is beyond me. You'd think him dealing with the criminal element; Chief Jack would have gotten past the baby face and big, blue eyes years ago.

I pondered this anomaly as I gazed up at him with a rapt expression while he spewed fired and brimstone. I also pondered why as men aged they did not notice their eyebrows needed trimming. Every time Jack passed by the light, I saw several eyebrow hairs sticking straight out. Yes, they were white blonde, but they were a good inch long. How he could miss these when shaving or brushing his teeth was beyond me.

Jack finally calmed down from a frothing-mouthed dictator into lecturer mode, and I focused. I shifted my eyes for a quick glance at the clock on the wall. Ten minutes was shorter than most of Jack's tyrannical raves. I think the poor man was tired. With a final warning glare at my upturned face, Jack crabbily advised I may need to be questioned again depending on what legal action arose from Larissa's ex-husband's assault.

Jack had some concerns an attempt could be made by the ex to sue me for causing him a long term disability. After the taser affects wore off, Ron Hansen was heard screaming, "My balls, my back!" repeatedly.

Jack thought with Trent's and Billy's eye witness statements that type of case would not hold up for long. I was curious what he meant by this, but didn't ask him to clarify. I was in no mood to ask Chief Jack any questions and get him wound up again.

He did let slip Ron Hansen was only released late this morning from Dakota County Jail after serving close to a year for third degree assault charges. It crossed my mind to wonder how Ron had arrived at

Bel's Books. It was logical to presume he'd need transportation to get from the jail in Hastings to Northfield, thirty two miles to the southwest. This detail spurred me to tell Jack about the van I'd observed in the parking lot when Anna and I returned from spying. I had automatically assumed the man in the van was waiting for a customer in Bel's, but he could have been waiting for Ron to kidnap Larissa out of the store.

Unfortunately, I didn't get the plate number and could only tell Jack the make and model. Anna vaguely remembered seeing the van, but had nothing else to offer.

My description of the man driving was more detailed. He was pale white, and while sitting in a van made it harder to be sure, he looked very large and heavy. He appeared to be stuffed uncomfortably behind the wheel of the van. I'd place his age in his late thirties. He was wearing a light colored jacket, had a completely bald head, no facial hair, and a big schnoz.

Jack stepped into the foyer and called it in immediately for follow up. While he was on his phone, Stella overheard him verifying no first responding cops to the back store entrance had seen the van when they arrived in the parking lot at Bel's.

We reasoned the driver was a fellow parolee, or friend of Ron Hansen's. If this was true, the cops would easily track him down by the physical description. If he was an accomplice, I knew Jack would find him. We all agreed it was too suspicious the van was not seen by any of the first responding police.

Anna thought it would be a smart idea to find out more details from Larissa. Maybe her ex had mentioned where he was taking her and if he had help. Stella verified the man had been yelling his head off at Larissa, so it was distinctly possible he told her things that could be of use.

Jack overheard us and looking alarmed, issued a stern warning. "Do not start playing at amateur detectives or certain heads will roll."

I promptly promised with Anna and Stella quickly following my lead and seconding their agreement.

Jack eyed the three of us for a long moment, and then surveyed me with his cop stare.

"Swear to God, Anabel."

"What am I swearing to here, Chief?"

Jack thought it over. "Swear you will not play detective on your own. Swear if you find out any information by sheer chance, you will report it immediately to me."

A Date with Fate

I took my time, no need for Jack to be suspicious if I agreed too fast again. "Deal. I swear to God. But that was two swears, so you owe me."

Jack grunted. He eyed me carefully while searching for visual clues how he may have been hoodwinked. I smiled placidly back under his suspicious regard. Concluding he had covered his bases, he turned to Anna next.

"You!" He pointed a finger and demanded, "Swear to God!"

Anna immediately put a hand to heart and fervently swore.

Then she promptly smiled nervously and looked guilty as hell.

Jack scowled.

Anna kept swearing to God repeatedly and then kept smiling repeatedly.

Jack shook his head slightly to clear it. With a last warning glare at my anxiously grinning friend, he appeared satisfied Anna was sufficiently cowed. He moved on.

When his scowling face moved Stella's way, she held up a hand and stopped him before he spoke.

Stella, the daughter of my heart, was shakily courteous but firm. "Sorry, Uncle Jack, but I don't do swear to Gods."

Jack's mouth dropped at this statement. After a stunned moment, his brows lowered and he mocked her in a girly voice. "'I don't do swear to Gods, Uncle Jack'." Face like a thundercloud, he shouted, "You're an Axelrod, of course you do swear to Gods!"

Stella shrank back against the sofa and visibly swallowed, but held her ground in the face of his temper. "Umm…I am a DeVere, remember? I am the only kid in this entire family. I stopped doing swear to Gods before I was ten just on general principle."

Jack looked at me, an accusatory glower on his face.

"What?" I crossed my arms and smiled evilly. "Surely you don't blame me our Stella's chock full of principles? Maybe you could trust her," I glared back at Jack, "if you asked her nice."

Jack threw his arms in the air with an oath. He settled them on his hips. He locked eyes with Stella. "Do you promise, Stella *DeVere*, to stay out of police business like a good girl?"

Stella lifted her chin at his tone. She replied coolly, "Sorry, Uncle Jack, I don't do promises, either."

Jack's stoic, cop face was a contortion of frustration.

In his everyday existence, he was The Chief. In his world, if Jack even casually glanced at someone in his employ they quivered and asked, "How high today, Sir Chief?"

He dealt with high-powered, muckety-mucks on a regular basis. He carried big guns, he captured dangerous criminals, and he dealt with life or death situations as a norm. To not be able to control a couple of girls with his formidable force of will alone had to be unendurably tormenting.

Jack, probably longing for the simplicity of a rookie cop needing a new asshole ripped for some minor infraction, stabbed a finger at each of us and enunciated in an awful voice, "Stay. Out. Of. Trouble."

The cursing Jack departed down the stairs, thankfully taking his cranky mood with him. I got down to business with Stella and Anna.

Stella said, "Larissa really wants to speak with you."

I sighed; this was a load off my mind. "Good. Under the circumstances, I was worried Larissa would hate me for screaming and yelling abuse at her. She knows it was a distraction and not meant to be real?"

Stella rushed to reassure me. "Oh, she knows! It's the opposite, Aunt Bel. Larissa worships you for saving her. She was terrified because Ron was trying to force her to come with him. He threatened to rain down all sorts of nasty shit on her head for divorcing him." Stella continued, furious. "Can you believe in his fucked up mind the jerk blames Larissa for him being jailed for assault?"

I shook my head. "I see only two choices for a violently abusive man like him. Put him down, or a total lobotomy. Men like him are wired wrong; plain and simple." I paused, stomach sinking thinking about it. "He's always going to be a serious threat to Larissa's life."

"You need to worry about him now, too, Junior." Anna softly reminded.

My eyes got big at that distinctly unhappy realization.

I also wasn't so happy hearing Stella and Anna change the topic and start singing Luke's praises for taking charge downstairs while I was passed out. I had let my people down by collapsing. After I'd zonked out and was napping in the comfort of my apartment, Luke had smoothly stepped in and organized the chaos downstairs.

I heard how he encouraged Stella to close and lock the store to keep away the gawkers. At his advice, she recorded a brief statement on Bel's Books voicemail greeting stating the shortened hours for today. It was essentially the same brief statement he coached her to give the woman reporter from the Northfield News.

Luke counseled the nervous Stella it was important we control the information being officially stated from the outset, and that I would want her to do so. He was absolutely correct. Stella was anxious for my approval she did everything kosher. I smiled brightly and thanked her profusely for her correct, quick actions.

I was grateful, but inside I was having a bitch of a time knowing I hadn't been there doing my job as owner and fearless leader.

Anna couldn't praise Luke's handling of the three lady customers highly enough. "You wouldn't believe how great he was with them. He encouraged them to tell him their part in what happened. He really listened, and then complimented them until they blushed." She laughed. "My god, after talking with the cops those ladies marched right out of the store feeling like super heroes, and not victims in the wrong place, at the wrong time. Luke's such a good guy, Junior."

I nodded in agreement with her opinion, but for different reasons. He was a good guy. Good at manipulation. Knowing they were all women, even if over the age of retirement, I'm sure it took him only seconds to have them eating out of his hand. It was masterfully done. It neutralized the negative comments these same customers could justifiably spread about their "shopping experience" at Bel's Books. I stewed broodingly over the fact I should be ecstatic for Luke's strategic thinking, not simmering with aggravation they were needed on my behalf.

Anna went on blithely. "He also talked with Trent and Billy before they gave their statements. They both felt bad they hadn't done more to try to save Larissa. Luke told them," Anna lowered her voice in a creepily accurate parody of his low voice, "'Boys, you did the smart thing. Had you men interfered, it could have resulted in Larissa being seriously hurt like the ex-husband had threatened'."

Anna smiled at my expression while Stella was making noises on my other side. "When the guys sang your praises to Luke about witnessing the royal ass whipping, he just smiled and shook his head. You're gonna love this, Junior, because he told them," Her voice lowered dramatically again, "'Remember, dynamite often comes in small packages and the same applies to a little woman'."

My friend and niece snickered together at my distinctly unloving look. Anna continued on. "According to Luke, it was his experienced opinion you were only successful because no man expects a super-hot, little boss lady, even if she was screaming like a lunatic, to stroll up and kick him in the balls!'

Stella chimed in. "Yeah, Luke really got Trent and Billy laughing their butts off and no longer questioning their manhood. So, I guess that part was good, right?"

I sniffed. "Sure. I'd hate to have demasculinized employees running around loose and causing havoc in the store."

Stella fell back giggling on the sofa while Anna laughingly said, "But wait! That's not all!"

They both laughed harder when I said a choice word.

"Trent and Billy totally agreed with Luke that the man was a serious threat to you." Anna snickered and made a face. "Even while he was on the floor screaming in agony and even as you repeatedly kicked him. They definitely heard him yelling death threats if he got his hands on you. They definitely stood guard over you to make sure the ex couldn't attack you from the floor."

That sure cleared up Jack's reference earlier about Trent's and Billy's statements to the cops verifying I had the right to protect myself from Ron Hansen. Based on his earlier comments, I could tell Jack had approved of Luke's assistance in "clarifying their thoughts" before the guys gave their statements. Problem was; I did as well. I am Grandmother Machiavelli's handmaiden and can pay homage when someone deserves credit. Luke, damn his diabolical brain, really deserved credit.

Misunderstanding my silence, Stella frowned. "We do think Luke is a butthead to talk to Trent and Billy about you like a sex object, Aunt Bel."

I thanked the loyal feminists before me, amused that they supported me despite their adoration of all things Luke Drake.

To be fair, I then explained Luke's strategy to them both so they would understand his good intentions towards me, and see how truly sneaky he was capable of being.

To Anna, I raised my brows. "You haven't forgotten our one hour lesson at Rueb's with Mr. Tricky?"

She shuddered and laughed. "Ugh, I'll never forget that lesson with Mr. Tricky! How was I supposed to know this was the same thing? You're right, he's truly sneaky."

I also confessed that I had used similar tactics on Ron Hansen. I explained it was my understanding of how a misogynistic, abusive man would think that made me approach Ron Hansen as I did. "He'd see me as harmless eye-candy if my shirt was undone. It allowed me to get close enough to get my kicks in." I nodded in remembered satisfaction. "His reaction was what I'd calculated on. I had no intentions of coming out of that encounter anything but the winner against that little bastard."

I told the girls it wasn't worth trying to convince the men that swiftly calculating odds and taking action was anything but an idiotic move for a woman with no weapons and no training in fighting. Mainly, I didn't bother because it *was* idiotic when you looked at it that way. For me, it boiled down to a simple choice. I'd rather regret attempting an action that I thought could be successful over agonizing later that I did nothing to help.

Stella and Anna were both nodding in thoughtful agreement when I finished.

There was a crease of worry between Stella's eyes when she asked, "I don't get something, though. Where did you learn to understand what an abusive, misogynistic man would be thinking?"

"The Oxygen channel, Oprah's book picks, and observing politicians." I promptly answered.

Anna's musical, deep laughter echoed off the high ceiling. "Hey, is Chief Jack an elected official?"

We held our sides laughing.

Catching my breath, I narrowed my eyes at Stella. "Don't even think of doing anything like I did today if you value our lives. Your mom would pulverize me and ground you for life, or vice versa."

Blue eyes sparkling, my cheeky niece vowed, "I swear to God and promise I won't."

The three of us cracked up for a solid minute at that one.

Locking up behind them a little later, I wasn't smiling any longer when I thought over the last few hours. Hopefully, none of this would ever be an issue again. It wasn't like I had plans to romp on men's ding-dongs as a way of life. Well, there was one man's ding-dong I currently wanted to romp on. In my brooding, dangerous mood when thinking about Luke's involvement all over my life, I wasn't quite sure whether it was to inflict pleasure or pain. Cruel of me, I know, but I never denied I was a control freak. I definitely needed a fun night out with my girls.

Chapter XI
"Girls Just Wanna Have Fun" by Cyndi Lauper

Saturday, 11/17/12
7:00 PM

Somehow, everything got accomplished on my mental check list by seven o'clock. The quick shower I took had me raring to go. I was ready to put this day behind me and party.

Outside of Bel's Books, I was waiting to be picked up by Jazy. The November night skies were clear and the cold air was refreshing; I could see my breath. The temperature had steadily dropped over the day and now hovered in the high twenties. There was a big snow in the forecast for early tomorrow and I thought about sledding in the afternoon.

Pacing and rubbing my chilled arms, it was easy to conclude I came close to smothering in the birth canal as I arrived in this world. It's the only explanation for my irrational dislike of being bundled up in coats, or constricted, in any way. I'd reluctantly brought a light jacket tonight with mittens stuffed in the pockets, in case of an emergency. Not that I had any plans to wear it. It still took wind chill factors of around thirty below to get me to admit winter had arrived in all its frigid glory and dress appropriately. I was proud of myself that I'd brought a jacket along for the ride. This was a positive sign. Maybe by the age forty I'd bring a hat, too.

When I was young, it was a common winter theme in my life to endure endless trudges home from impromptu, fun sledding wearing only wet shoes and sopping jeans. In my own miserable world, I'd chant a mantra of negotiations with that higher power to "Please, oh please just get me home before amputation is necessary, and I'll be a good girl forever."

I regularly suffered through the pins and needles pain of frozen feet and ears thawing out. I often had chapped inner thighs that burned like a son of a gun. I worshiped the manufacturers of petroleum jelly. I am super-depressed Stella found my hidden cache of Vaseline during her most recent "search and destroy" sortie into my apartment.

I slowed my pacing to admire the street before me. Like Bel's Books, many of the buildings lining Division Street were built in the late

A Date with Fate

1800's and stood only two or three stories tall. Up and down the blocks, the buildings shared common walls in the thrifty, expeditious mode of construction popular during frontier times. Their storefront facades were designed to be unique from their attached neighbors by the different materials used, such as painted wood, brick, stone, and decorative awnings. It made for a quaint, charming downtown, even allowing for the occasional modern building thrown into the mix.

Division Street was fancied up for the holidays. The streets lamps were swirled with evergreens, red satin ribbons and bows, and aglow with white lights in the shapes of large snowflakes. Many buildings were similarly adorned; it reminded me of a village on an old-fashioned Christmas card dusted with glitter.

I love this time of year. Bel's staff had a party and decorated the outside of my red brick building last week. Spruce treetops and red holly berries were in the display window boxes, lacey garlands of evergreens draped around the entrance doors, and an enormous wreath hung outside on the turret that capped the corner of my building. All of these were intertwined with hundreds of tiny lights. When snow dusted the greenery, the teal blue lights twinkling at night through the sparkling white stuff is magical.

Interrupting my sightseeing, a Chrysler Town and Country minivan honked softly and pulled up to the curb. I recognized our friend, Tre J driving with Jazy riding shotgun. The side door slid open, and an old Led Zeppelin tune poured out. I climbed into the beckoning warmth, agreeing silently it had been way too long a time since this woman had rock 'n rolled.

I had earlier whipped off a mass text to my siblings and friends that all was fine, details to follow. NanaBel was out of touch in the desert for the next couple of days, so I'd email her in a day or two. I returned Reggie's calls and left a quick, comprehensive voice mail message with details on Cheryl Crookston and Larissa's ex since I wasn't seeing him tonight like I would be my sisters. I'd spoken briefly with Larissa's parents; she was doing well, but sleeping. I made plans to visit her on Monday morning. The mean mommy voice should be happy with me and leave me the hell alone for the rest of the night.

With the dome light still on overhead, my youngest sister turned in her seat to do a swift eye-balling of my person. I felt like a horse at a sale barn being appraised by an expert for soundness.

Jazy, satisfied I was not physically altered in any way, still wore a quizzical expression. This was for the mental check up portion of the exam. If I was one of her horses, she'd probably make a clicking sound to observe how I responded.

I grinned crookedly in reassurance, at the same time I lifted one shoulder in a "What's a girl to do?" unrepentant shrug.

Jazy returned a wickedly devilish smile--complete with two dimples and an emphatic power fist for a job well-done.

Enough said. Sister Whisperer gets me.

Jazy and I are two years apart in age. We are instantly known as sisters by anyone seeing us for the first time, or hearing us talk and laugh. We share the same sapphire shade of blue eyes we've been told matched our mother's. The resemblances are marked between Jazy and me, but her features are all slightly larger, her body type less curvy. She's an auburn brunette to my blonde, and tops out at an impressive five-four. Jazy wears straight bangs, but her hair waves and curls loosely atop her shoulders with no help from a curling iron. Good thing because Jaz is a wash and go kind of outdoor girl. She's passionate about three things in her life—horses, Harleys, and heavy petting.

Tre J turned down the volume on the music, and then reached back and pulled me up into a huge hug.

I hung awkwardly on my knees between the seats while she enthusiastically gushed while patting my back. "Bel, we are so relieved everything ended well. Jaz and I were just saying how we wished we could have been there to see you in action." She pulled back, a wide smile making her eyes crinkle. "Did you really unbutton your shirt, take off your bra, and show some nip to distract him? Awesome smart move! Girl, you are so my hero! Poor Larissa, how did she ever marry that skeevy mother?" Her face darkened. "He'd better pray I never meet his ass in a dark alley."

Laughing to myself in rueful weariness, I realized this was the kind of rumor humor I'd be dealing with all night. I patted her shoulder fondly in return, as I detached out of her smothering hug.

"Thanks for the vote of confidence. You smell good tonight, by the way." I climbed into my seat and buckled in. "If it's all the same to you both, I'm not saying another word until we get over to Mac's. When Jazy mans the blender and I have one of her special Margaritas in hand, then we'll talk."

A Date with Fate

"I hear you!" Jazy did a little drum roll on the dash in front of her. "See, told you she wouldn't want to talk about it until Mac's. Let's hit it, Tre. My ass-kicking sister needs a drink"

"I'm hittin' it, I'm hittin' it!" The side door slid shut next to me with a click. Tre J was laughing as she sped off around the corner onto Fourth.

Tre's a Norwegian Valkyrie built like a brick shithouse with an easy belly laugh as generous as her personality. She's a friend of both mine and Jazy's since we were little. They are roommates and work together on Jazy's farm at the Lazy j Stables. They board, train, and sell horses, plus give riding lessons. Tre J is also in school training to be a Physical Therapist.

"What up with the van?" I could feel the maternal hormones oozing from the leather seats around me. I took in the requisite DVD player screens necessary for a child's entertainment while being driven somewhere for five blocks. I shuddered. I did not want to become infected with the highly contagious BiologicalClockTicking disease. Last I knew, Tre J drove a monster truck capable of pulling a multi-horse trailer.

They laughed at my bewildered tone. Jazy answered, "It's Tre's turn for sober cabbie. She borrowed it from her sister thinking we may want to get in some serious partying tonight. We can easily all ride together in this van."

I leaned forward. "Way to be thinking, Tre. Oh, and just to be clear; I've never believed Jazy's trash talking behind your back. This proves you haven't taken one too many hockey sticks to the head."

Even playing around, Jazy packs a mean punch. I've seen her take on a misbehaving, twelve hundred pound horse. I successfully dodged her until Tre's long arm blocked off my sister's frustrated, laughing attempts to get me.

Although a year behind me, and for reasons still known only to her, Tre J appointed herself my personal bodyguard when we were still in grade school. My budding career as a little smarty-mouth without a care to the recipient's age, gender, size, or disposition was already blossoming, but I'm still appreciative. I probably have Tre J's threatening stare to thank for my smooth transition into a full-bloomed, adult smart-ass with all my own teeth intact. She is an amazing six-feet-tall, weighs a glorious two hundred pounds, and was famous for playing defense in college women's hockey. You do not want to piss off a woman acclaimed for wielding a hockey stick in comparison to that of a Norwegian war axe.

Tre J stands for January Jolene Jivers. In grade school, she despised her first name with a passion second only to the disgust she felt for her middle and last names. I believe the phrase "trailer trash and porn star" was gritted out between her clenched teeth when asked for the explanation why she felt such enmity for her name.

Feeling her pain and learning to count in Norwegian at this time, I suggested we change her alliterative, three banger of a name to Tre J. She was thrilled. Much to her mother's chagrin, the name Tre J was officially adopted. We even presented her with a commemorative birth certificate, complete with my inked footprints representing her newborn feet. The dreaded January Jolene Jivers never crossed our lips again.

Laughing and chatting, we detoured a couple of streets over to pick up Anna. Then it was back a few blocks up Fourth to Mac's yellow Victorian. Elaborately trimmed out in white gingerbread; the house is a showstopper. The detached garage is as cute as the house. Above the garage is a studio apartment where Stella resides in solitary splendor.

The arrangement of Stella living in the garage studio works well for Mac and my niece. Stella has the relative privacy she needs as a commuting, college freshman. Mac has the relative privacy she needs to enjoy her new husband of less than six months. They both can keep one eye on each other.

For eighteen years, Mac had remained single after Freddy's death. Six years ago, she purchased this house and moved out of the Division Street apartment with Stella.

Last May, on her thirty-sixth birthday, Mac met twenty-four-year old Diego Dos Santos at the grocery store he owns in Faribault. She was shopping his wide selection of peppers. He assisted her with her choice. Sparks flew from their first glance. The flame grew as conflagrant as a forest fire after their first date. One month later, Diego hot-footed Mac down the aisle.

I compare my eldest sister to a locust. She lies low and leads your normal, somewhat staid life--then bursts out with lollapalooza drama every eighteen years. Her fifties should be interesting.

Diego is Puerto Rican by ancestry, but was born in upstate New York. His family moved to Faribault when he was a little boy and opened the grocery store. He's been the head of his family for several years since his father died of a heart attack when Diego was twenty. He stepped up to take over the reins of that store, and has recently purchased another small grocery market in Northfield. He's an intelligent man, an entrepreneur, and extremely pretty. Not that his sizzling Latin looks had anything to do with Diego being able to convince my sister he was the man for her. Really.

Does it make me bad I snicker behind my hand seeing my bossiest, prissiest, gearhead of a sister dueling her macho, movie-star handsome, youngster of an el esposo for supremacy on all fronts? And, often as not, losing?

I don't think so, either.

Diego and Mac openly bicker and banter over the seesawing role of Alpha in their marriage. He's used to running the show, and so is my big sis. They could sell tickets; their power struggle is that fun to watch.

It's my guess the newlyweds quite often, and quite sensibly, take the issue to the mat in the bedroom where they wrestle over the matter to their hearts content. I give them until New Year's. They'll figure it out, or kill each other by exhaustion. Either way's a win.

The four of us piled out of the van. We were joined by Stella coming down from her studio and, amidst greetings and chatter; we started trooping up to Mac's back porch.

I couldn't miss the "SWEETAZ" vanity plate on the light blue, Honda Civic parked in the driveway. I thought Candy's gun safety seminar in Duluth went through Sunday. I'm never pleased to see Candy, but tonight was the rare exception.

Since birth, my cousin Candy has been spoiled shamelessly by her father, my Uncle Trevor. She runs roughshod over her fluttering, ineffectual mother, my Aunt Carol. The only issue I have ever seen my gentle Aunt Carol take an unswerving stand on was not allowing Candy to have any pets. I'm glad I don't know why. The general family consensus would have it that being spoiled is responsible for the ruination of whatever character potential Candy once had. Personally, I believe she was born a sociopathic personality; there was no character potential to be had, or lost. What was lost by her unfortunate parenting was the chance to become well-adjusted and perhaps develop her differences for good instead of evil.

Candy hates she can't manipulate me and use her superficial charm to blind me to her real nature. I don't know why, but I have always seen her for what she is. Had she not tried to tangle with me because of this from the time I was five, maybe things would have been different.

Anna and I dubbed Candy's lying, conniving, cheating, and tantrum throwing ways being "Candy Coated". It's like getting slimed, only much worse.

NanaBel feels sorry for this granddaughter. Even though Candy is three years my senior and has tried her damnedest to make my life a living hell; NanaBel has asked me repeatedly to go easy on Candy since we were kids. It proved impossible to like her, but for years I have avoided her, ignored her, and reluctantly turned the other cheek and kept quiet rather than destroy her--all in honor of respecting my grandmother's wishes.

NanaBel wants me to have pity for Candy because she's an unhappy, empty soul and vastly needy. I say pity is a wasted emotion that benefits no one involved in the long run. The person being pitied learns nothing of value as a result from their actions, and the people doing the pitying get the dubious satisfaction of being condescending and feeling morally superior. Big whoop.

In this particular instance, I have disagreed with my grandmother's judgment since day one. Throughout our childhoods and into adulthood, NanaBel doesn't know half the shady shit Candy's pulled. Candy grabs anything she wants as her due and knows no boundaries in her pursuit of this belief.

I'm a girl who believes more in the motto of her forbearers from Scotland, *Nemo Me Impune Lacessit.* This is the Latin that translates roughly, "None shall provoke/injure me with impunity". Combine that sensible motto with the proverb, "Revenge is a dish best served cold" and I'm good to go.

Candy and I are long, long overdue for a cousinly chat, and NanaBel is far, far away in Egypt. You see, Candy has pushed me to my wall. She didn't ask to borrow my gun, but stole it out of my apartment last Wednesday. Leaving a "Got your gun" note on my kitchen island hardly constituted asking my permission. Using the word stole is not too harsh or inaccurate. She knows I would not extend her a helping hand if she were drowning; much less lend her my gun.

Tonight Anna, looking very cute and cozy in a purple wool jacket complete with matching plum colored mittens, hat and a scarf, gave the Honda a scowling glance, as if reading my thoughts.

She touched my arm and held me back as the others continued up the sidewalk.

"I've been meaning to tell you something all damn day, but keep forgetting and getting sidetracked." Anna didn't wait for my response but rushed on. "I wanted you to hear this before Candy or Kenna tells you. I ran into Mike last night at the Contented Cow. He's joining his Uncle's law firm in Minneapolis and is back living here. In Northfield, I mean."

A Date with Fate

She hesitated briefly. "He asked all about you. He wanted me to give you a message."

I stood frozen for a moment, processing what she said. My brain felt as cold as my hands. I'd drawn a blank for a second when she said the name Mike, but at the mention of my cousin and my sister her meaning became crystal clear.

Mike McClain was my one awful aberration of a boyfriend and long term relationship. When we'd broken up, I'd talked about it only with Anna, and only once, so she'd understand why he was out of my life forever. My family was extremely surprised initially when we parted ways, but soon forgot about it when I appeared disinterested and never spoke of him. The name Mike McClain was rarely brought up again in my presence since I was nineteen. It helped that his parents moved out of state due to a job transfer his second year in college. He'd never come back to Northfield. Until now.

This was officially the day from hell. Could it get any more unreal? It only made a terrible kind of sense that ten years later, this would be the one day the name Mike McClain waltzed back into my life. My life was turning into a "Final Destination" movie. Fate was trying its damnedest to kick my ass.

"Okay."

Anna anxiously peered at me in the moonlight. "Okay? What does 'okay' mean?"

I linked my arm through Anna's and started steering her up the sidewalk, snuggling against her for warmth. "Okay means okay. Now I know. Thanks."

Anna dug in her feet to stop me. "Wait, Junior. Don't you want to know what questions he asked? Do you want to hear his message? Do you want to know if he's fat or bald, or married to a heifer and has ten brats?"

"Nope." I pulled her forward again, and this time she walked with me up to the house.

Anna was grumbling. "I didn't tell him anything about you or answer any of his questions, if you were wondering."

I may be cursed and doomed, but I couldn't resist smiling at these grumpy words. "Never crossed my mind you would."

Anna grinned back while shaking her head. "Sometimes, I don't understand you. It would drive me crazy to not ask questions if I hadn't seen Reg in ten years. I want to know, June, how can you not be curious what he looks like now, if nothing else?"

Standing under the porch light with a hand on the back door knob, I stared at my friend in silent deliberation. I relaxed and softly blew out a long puff of white, cold air.

'What the hell, it was a long time ago and this was my best friend asking.'

"You remember, right, how it was for Mike McClain and me for over two years?"

I don't know what she saw written on my face or heard in my voice, but Anna nodded solemnly, eyes serious.

I spoke matter-of-factly to get it over with. "I really loved Mike with every fiber of my being. It wasn't naively; I knew every one of his faults and I loved them, too. Yes, I was young and innocent, blah, blah, but I was never *that* young. It wasn't some high school crush for me. I would have joyfully loved him forever, that's how sure and deep and right it was for me." I smiled wistfully at Anna, letting myself recall for a moment how it felt to be so completely in love. "I never doubted he felt the same way."

I saw her face soften, but she stayed quiet other than to nod in encouragement.

"I believed back then our bond, our connection, was something undeniably special. After all the men I have met since then, I know now how true that was." I shrugged lightly. "At least, for me it was. I could live to be a million years old and I will still never get why Mike did what he did. Why he threw me away. Of course, I never bothered to talk to him about it, but you know the really strange thing about it all, Anna? I've always suspected somewhere deep down Mike didn't know why, either."

This was the hard part. I hated to even think about this period in my life, and rarely did anymore. I forced myself to push the words out. "At the time, I told you how he betrayed me. What I didn't tell anybody was how rough it was dealing. I had to cut Mike out of my heart so missing him didn't eat me up like a cancer and kill me; it was that bad. I was sick to my soul not having him in my life. My pride insisted I hide it from everyone." I shrugged. "So I did. I hid it every minute, of every hour, of every day, week after miserable week.

"Finally, after a few years, and I do mean years, I cut off my feelings deep enough that it was actually true. I no longer needed him to feel whole and right. I thought about him less and less. I didn't have dreams about him at night that made me hate waking up and facing the morning. Sounds dramatic, right? Yeah, well, how I wish I was being a drama queen." I smiled softly, reaching out to wipe a tear overflowing from Anna's welling eyes. "You are such a little crybaby today." She whipped off her mitten to give me the finger and I smiled again. "I say it's okay because he's nothing to me now, Anna, less than nothing. All right?"

Anna nodded quickly, wiping under her eyes with her bared hand. "I did know how in love you two were. Whenever I've thought about it over the years, I still can't believe he did it." She smiled a sad, little grimace. "I gotta hand it to you, though, Junior. You succeeded in fooling everybody, me included. I thought you got over him so quickly it was weird, but I was so pissed off at him I was relieved for your sake. I'm really blown away to hear how bad off you were inside. I tell you what; I wish you didn't have to be so freakin' strong all the time. Sometimes, it makes me feel like a whiny bitch always blabbing about my problems when you don't, but I guess it's just who you are." She sighed and squeezed my arm. "Okay, I see what a dumbass I was to bring him up. Let's go in and get that Margarita. What do you say?"

"I say you, Miss Softie, are a gentleman and a scholar." Grateful she changed topics; I pushed open the door and entered the toasty heat of Mac's spacious back hall. "And don't ever call yourself a dumbass. I reserved that right, remember?"

Anna's laughter trilled. "I thought you reserved the right to call me an ass pants?"

"Well, duh dumbass, that too."

I was called a mean name and pushed from behind by an indignant Anna, only to be enveloped in a tight hug by my oldest sibling. I then got cheek kisses between getting harped at for wearing no coat. All this hugging today was wearing me down. I heard Anna close the back door. I also heard the sound of a car starting nearby.

I took my head off Mac's big sister shoulder. "Did we scare off Diego?"

Mac held me away and gave me a mock incredulous look. "You're kidding, right? Diego Esteban Tomas Dos Santos trying to escape from a house full of women?" She chuckled at the absurdity. "We'd have to force him out. No, he's working at the new market. That would be Candy you hear taking off. She stopped by to drop off that duffle bag for you on the bench, but didn't stay. She has," Mac raised her hand in quotes, "a mysterious 'man meet' tonight. Didn't you see her out back?"

"She must have left by the front door." I laughed shortly, briefly feeling sorry for the man. I reached for the duffle bag.

Mac slanted me an odd look, but turned to give Anna a hug. "Hi, heard you guys had an exciting day, huh?"

Anna, still wiping her feet on the door mat, held her finger and thumb up in a little bit gesture. They laughed together. Annie started in excitedly catching Mac up on the news about Cheryl Crookston's disappearance.

I checked out the contents of the duffle while Anna was talking. The Glock appeared to have been recently cleaned. I could smell the solvent and oil. The two clips Candy had snatched along with the gun were in the bag. One ten round magazine was still full of cartridges; the other had only five bullets left. Unless she had brought her own bullets, she hadn't shot the gun much. I idly wondered what her real motivation was for going on the Duluth getaway. Had to be man related, Candy was always chasing some unsuspecting sucker.

I took out the gun, and verified there was no bullet left in the chamber. I couldn't take chances with Candy that it was unloaded properly. I inspected the Glock to verify no deposits were left in the chamber from earlier firing. I don't know why I even bothered checking, I planned to thoroughly clean the gun later again no matter what I found. I placed the handgun back in the duffle and zipped it up.

I looked up just as Mac swung her attention back to me. Dressed simply in a light blue wrap shirt and black leggings, my sister didn't look much older than Stella tonight. Every time she moved her left hand, sparkling color dazzled the eye from the four-karat diamond knob she called a wedding ring. Eyes and cheeks shining, Mac's lovely face reflected the same light. She glowed with contented happiness.

I smiled, teasingly. "So, what's on the dinner menu tonight?"

"I made Nachos." Mac laughingly rolled her eyes when Anna and I each shouted out "Nachos" at the same time she said the word. "Jazy's in the kitchen right now making Margarita's."

Mac doesn't cook your average, normal meals; her idea of dinner is appetizers. Her most frequent top choice is Nachos, but sometimes she messes with our heads and it's a layered Taco Dip or Quesadillas. We play a guessing game which of the three it will be. It's similar to Rock, Paper, Scissors. It's all in good fun, but she's gently discouraged by all the family from hosting Thanksgiving.

Anna headed for the sound of the blender. I started to follow; I could hear the tequila calling my name. The minute Anna cleared the back hall doorway, Mac had other ideas. She cupped my shoulders. We were eye to eye because she was in flats and I had on high heels.

"Thank you from the bottom of my heart for watching over Stella! I know you'd take a bullet for her, but on Freddy's grave, I swear to God if you ever do, Bel, that bullet better kill you or I will."

We touched foreheads lightly even as I snickered. I love convoluted woman logic that makes such perfect sense. "Sure, Spook, whatever you say."

Mac snickered back. "What, Freak? You don't think I'll kill you? Try me."

She pulled back. "Enough mush. Now, how come I haven't met this Superman Luke, and what's up with the Candy Coater?"

Seeing Mac's sly, humorous smile, it struck me how much Mac and Stella look alike with their expressive, aqua-blue eyes and their matching noses; elegant with a slight bump near the bridge. Mac recently started coloring her dark hair a pale, golden blonde. She said it was to cover the gray. Since NanaBel was white by age forty, I'm not surprised. It still took me a minute to recognize her in public. I have walked right by her on the street more than once. It looks good on her. I don't know why she's pissed Reg has taken to calling her Malibu Barbie. I think it's a cute name.

My oldest sister is persnickety. She's immaculate, from her personal grooming and stylish clothing, to her overall spotless house. Nothing falls out of her kitchen cupboards in surprise when you open a random door, and you could eat off the floorboards of her vehicles. I didn't let these flaws stop me from adoring her. I knew it was that responsibility-driven, overachieving, first kid birth order issue she couldn't help. Not everyone can be the well-adjusted middle child.

What Stella didn't inherit from her mother was Mac's clever ability to size up a situation in a glance, and her innate understanding of the words subtle and nuance. Mac took in my outfit of choice for tonight and added, "Oh yeah, and I like the innocent, cupcake look. Doing a little damage control, are we?"

Smiling broadly, I held my arms out and curtsied in obsequious response to her mental acuity. I was a sweet, feminine confection in a high pony tail, pink silk top and tight, winter white slacks. I was even wearing brown heels. No all black for me tonight; looking like a dominatrix was no way to help the cause.

I was sure the grapevine drums were beating loud along the Mohican; I'd be getting all sorts of crap from friends and acquaintances tonight. Waiting around to go out in public wasn't going to do me any good. Mac was spot on; I was planning on showing John Q Public things couldn't have possibly been as bad as they'd heard at Bel's Books just a few hours before.

I skimmed over the Luke part of her question by telling her she'd meet him at dinner the next night and could decide herself if he was Superman or Jimmy. I pointed at the duffle and indignantly told her what Candy had done.

"That shit's so weak! She's out of control. You never mess with someone's gun." Mac shook her head in disbelief.

"I know, right." I agreed, smiling tightly.

From the doorway, Jazy spoke. "Candy needs her ass kicked up between her shoulder blades. Margaritas are served, my sisters. Now, Bel can start talking."

I moaned while following them into the kitchen. "Ah man, can't we do a mind meld instead? I just want to eat, drink, and be happy. Then go dance and not say a word for hours."

Jazy patted my shoulder. "Embrace the suck, Anabel. Embrace the suck."

Mac and Jazy laughed merrily at my expression.

Kenna wasn't joining us and I was relieved. I like my second oldest sister, but there was a constraint between us due to old history and bad blood that prevented me from fully relaxing when she was around. It may have something to do with the fact she was pals with Candy. It may have something to do with the fact that she's changeable and unreliable. She and Mac get along like oil and water, so there's tension there. Mac's pretty straight and Kenna carries around her own pharmacy. You could take your pick of reasons; I was simply glad she wasn't around tonight.

The six of us were a lively group sitting around Mac's kitchen island on bar stools eating Nachos and drinking Margaritas. Stella and Anna took turns filling the others in on the blow-by-blow recounting of the day, so I didn't have to talk much. I was able to kick back and mostly listen while my five favorite females excitedly dissected the mystery of the missing Cheryl Crookston and the horror story of Larissa's ex.

I smiled in the right places, and occasionally commented, but I found myself still feeling like I was outside my own skin looking in. I wanted to relax, but I pushed away my drink. The tequila wasn't calling my name, after all. My right foot was jiggling my leg up and down like it was motorized.

I took a deep breath and tried to center in on what was causing my unrest. It was hard to determine if I was still experiencing an aftermath from today, or if I was anxious over something else. I concentrated on breathing slowly in and out, the girl's conversation a pleasant buzzing in the background. I emptied my mind of any conscious thoughts of Luke, or any of the other people bugging me from today.

I didn't come up with any answers, but I was ready to go when the dishes were stacked neatly in the dishwasher and Mac announced we should hit the road. I felt like a live-wire strumming with energy.

Our group walked Stella out to her studio door and said our goodnights. She was having a friend over to watch a movie. We had to tease her when she confessed it was a male friend, who was not really just a friend, yet nothing more than a friend, at this moment in time. After that clear answer, the most she would say was his name was Eric George Jasnik and he was totally cute.

Everyone climbed into the van, leaving me the front seat. I guess it was my special night.

Before I opened my door, I whispered to the waiting Stella, "Hey, is this the dude you've been helping so much lately in the Sci-fi section?"

She grinned, putting her hand up above her head. "He's about so tall with blondish-brownish hair and a butt courtesy of lacrosse?"

I grinned back. "Ah, male sports are a wonderful thing. Don't do anything I would do, you hear?"

"When am I going to be old enough to do what you would do?" Stella laughingly demanded.

Squeezing her shoulders, I gave her a smacking kiss on the cheek. I opened the van door. "Silly girl, when you're my age, of course."

Stella sputtered. "You have been saying that for years, Auntie Bel, you damn brat!"

I laughingly waved and Tre J honked lightly as we left. Stella waved back before climbing the stairs to her studio. By habit, like a well rehearsed dance move, all five of us craned our heads to watch until we saw her door close and Stella was safely in her apartment.

Chapter XII
"Smackwater Jack" by Carole King

Saturday 11/17/12
8:40 PM

We were on our way to the Castle Rock N' Roll Bar and Grill, or The Rock as it's called by us locals. It's about ten minutes north of Northfield. The bar sits at the lonely junction of two county roads miles from nowhere. It's a hot spot well known for hiring local bands great to dance to on the weekends. The Rock packed the house nuts to butts, but not until closer to ten o'clock most Friday or Saturday nights.

With all the pent-up energy I was feeling, I didn't care if we were unfashionably early. We'd get a table and I could lose myself in dancing for a couple of hours on a less crowded dance floor.

A Colbie Caillat song came on and Anna started us off "I do, I do, I doing" from the back. Soon the van was swaying on its axles as Tre J whizzed us out of town and up Highway 3 towards Castle Rock.

It was fun to cut loose and act wild, singing to the loud music and dancing in our seats from the waist up. It didn't take long for Mac and Jazy to start changing the words of the song to something nasty. Anna was screaming with laughter from the very back seat while Tre J pounded the steering wheel. Tre's belly laugh is so contagious; soon we were all screaming our laughter as hard as Anna.

I don't think any of us knew what was happening when our van was first rammed abruptly off the road, tilting us dangerously and changing our laughter into real screams of confused terror.

It was the front and back wheels on my passenger side that hit the sloping, asphalt shoulder at sixty miles per hour, causing the van to violently rock and sway at the difference in the surfaces and angle of the tires.

"Hold on!" Tre J bellowed. She did not use the brakes, but took her foot off the gas to slow us down to a safe speed to cross back up. At the same time, she fought the steering to keep the van steady and not roll or flip us as we sailed half on and half off the road. The shoulder was paved here, and not the deeper gravel that would have almost guaranteed the van rolling at this sloping grade.

Glancing in her side view mirror she shouted in enraged disbelief, "That van rammed us!"

At the word "van", I whipped my head around. It was dark. I couldn't see past everyone's heads in the back, or through the tinted van windows. I could only see headlights racing up behind us again.

"He's coming after us! Hold tight everyone!" I shouted. Tre J was scowling with concentration. "Can you get us back up on the road and go faster?"

"Oh, hell yeah!" She instantly wrenched the wheel to the left.

The passenger side of the Chrysler followed and shot up over the ledge of the blacktop shoulder.

We were level on all four wheels again, but we were soon shrieking and yelling in terror because the van barreled across the middle line and into the headlights of oncoming traffic. Tre J immediately compensated by punching it while sharply yanking the steering wheel back to the right. Fishtailing wildly at first, the van straightened out. We'd made it back into our own lane right before a semi truck bearing down on us sailed past in a whoosh of rushing air. The semi's blasting horn sounded off angrily. The truck narrowly missed creaming us by a split second.

Swiveling to look behind, I snapped off my seatbelt while cheering on a white-faced but determined Tre J. "You're doing great! Go, you wild woman! He's right on our tail—GO!"

Jazy screamed a rebel yell while Mac shouted over her, "What's going on, why is this guy after us?"

Anna screamed frantically from the back, "It's the man in the van from today! He's trying to kill us!"

I had the duffle bag in my lap, but had to fall on it to keep it from flying when another smack hit us from behind as the killer van crashed into us again. The hit was hard on the back, left bumper and caused us to swerve sharply, but not hard enough to knock us off the road this time. Thankfully, Tre J has experience driving big rigs. Now that she knew what was happening, there wasn't a better person to have behind the wheel. She didn't panic. She held the van steady and we were pulling ahead while flying at over ninety.

Jazy yelled out a warning. "Curve's coming up soon!"

Tre J nodded grimly. She reluctantly eased her foot off the gas pedal. "Damn! He's catching up again!"

There were no headlights in sight coming towards us, so Tre J kept to the middle of the road.

The three girls in back cried out. "Hold on!"

The van was rocked violently from the left side, rear bumper once more. The back end tires were hopping and stuttering as they slid out to the right. Tre didn't hit the brakes, but again took her foot off the gas and went with the slide, only lightly steering. I thought we were going off the road and would flip this time for sure, but then the tires gripped and shot us out forward in the right direction.

We all held on for dear life, and then cheered in noisy relief while screaming encouragement to Tre. She kept ahead of the van behind us, swerving back and forth in a random pattern to not be such an easy target. There were no oncoming headlights, but the curve was fast approaching. We couldn't take it going this speed without serious problems.

Tre was chanting furiously, "Shit, Shit, Shit!"

I had the duffle opened, and my Glock out. I slapped in the full magazine, racked the slide to chamber a bullet, and flipped off the safety. I hit the button to lower my window.

At the sudden blast of cold wind, Tre J dared a quick glance over at me. A beaming grin the size of the Mississippi broke across her tense face at the sight of the gun in my left hand.

Jazy saw it and pounded her seat. "Yes! Shoot the crazy fucker, Bel!"

Mac sat forward to see around my chair. "Get him, Sister!"

Yelling to be heard over the sound of the air screaming in through my open window and the even louder screaming coming from behind me, I instructed Tre. "Go ahead and slow down. Keep to our right to lure him. Let him almost catch up, and then I'm going to hang out the window and shoot back at him. When he gets close you have to swerve to the middle of the road so I have a better shot at him. Got it?"

Eyes on the road, Tre J let loose a war cry. "Got it!"

Jazy unbuckled in a flash and knelt between the seats and faced back. "Don't worry, I'll tell you when to shoot!"

Anna and Mac yelled they'd tell me, too. I quickly turned to the open window and sat on my right knee, angling myself to face backwards. I put my left leg straight out and down, tucking it into the space between the seat and the door, planting myself. I held the gun tightly in my left hand, resting the barrel on the window ledge. I held onto the top of my seat with my right, hugging the headrest.

A Date with Fate

Tre slowed down abruptly. The wind had whipped stray strands of my long hair into my face. It was a good thing it was up in a pony tail tonight or I'd be blinded.

Anna was shouting prayers and giving play action from her lookout seat in the back. "Let her get him, let us be okay, here he comes, let her get him…here he comes! Oh man alive, Junior, HERE HE COMES!"

Pulse racing, I was amazingly not scared or nervous. I visualized how I was going to shoot back at the van and where I was aiming. Then I was AWOL'ing, wondering whether it was possible a person could use up all the adrenaline in their adrenal glands before the body could produce more. I focused abruptly when I felt the van veer over to the left. Bracing myself, and holding tight onto the headrest to prevent falling over between the front seats, I heard three yells of "NOW!"

I leaned out with the gun. Aiming behind us and to the left, I started pulling the trigger with no hesitation. When shooting, my gun makes the expected booming sound. The noise was deafening without ear protection. That was the last thing I heard for awhile.

The gun jerked in my left hand with the small recoil from each shot, but I knew what to expect. I religiously practiced shooting my weapon on the range at the Dakota County Rifle Club. I held on steady as possible with just one hand and fired behind us until the ten shooter clip was empty. I saw tracers from bullets meeting metal or pavement. I couldn't tell where they were hitting in the blinding mix of glaring headlights and black darkness of the night.

I leaned back in and ejected the empty clip. I snatched the half-full magazine off the seat under my knee, and prepared to keep shooting.

That's when I realized our van had slowed to a stop on the side of the road. We were parked under the pool of light cast from one of the infrequent lamp poles along this lonely stretch of highway, about twenty yards past the curve.

When first starting to shoot, I'd felt a hand slip down the back waistband of my slacks and firmly clutch a bunch of fabric to hold me steady. I don't believe I was in danger of falling out of the window, but I now had one hell of a wedgie.

Squirming on my knees in discomfort, I felt a tap on my right arm. Mac's face was relieved and smiling. She was motioning behind us.

I read her exaggeratedly enunciating lips. "He's gone! He turned and left!"

I nodded, grinning widely. I thumbed on the safety of my gun, but still kept in it my clenched grip. I wasn't ready to trust he wouldn't come back. After a few moments, my hearing was returning a little. Everyone was exclaiming over what had happened and talking at once.

I raised my voice. "Did I hit him?"

Anna was jumping with excitement. "I saw sparks bouncing off the van, so you hit that. I don't know if he got hit, but the maniac slammed on the brakes and turned around. He drove off like a bat out of hell right as we came out of the curve."

I grinned over at Tre resting across the steering wheel. "Guess who now has to be sober cabbie all the time? You were unbelievable, girl!"

Tre J blushed while we all extravagantly complimented her driving skills.

Jazy smacked my shoulder, laughing. "Speaking of sober; good thing you didn't drink your tequila tonight or this could have ended much differently." She shook her head in wonder. "To think we have Candy to thank for stealing your gun in the first place!"

I swore so fluently, Reggie would be proud. They all burst out in hysterical laughter.

Tre J calmed down enough to say, "My sister isn't going to be happy."

That set us all off again, and we let out our relief with laughter and jokes about what we'd tell her sister. Seriously, I reassured Tre J that I would take care of her sister's deductible and rental car if need be. That set off another round of debates, but I held firm. Since I was probably responsible for the man in the van trying to smash us to pieces, I'd pay for any resulting out-of-pocket costs. Tre J was a struggling student without a pot to piss in until she finished her schooling and started work in her field.

Not knowing when the man in the van had started following us, Mac called and checked in with Stella. She told her an abbreviated version of what happened. Her friend, Eric George was over, and she promised the door was deadbolt locked. She'd put a chair under the knob for insurance.

We all then climbed out shakily to inspect the damage to the van. I still clutched the Glock tightly in my left hand, but with the barrel pointing down along my thigh.

Circling the vehicle, we were pleasantly surprised to see only minor damage; a broken left taillight reflector, a few small dents, and white paint scrapes on the back bumper. It had felt much worse.

A Date with Fate

In the silence, we all stared at the white paint scrapes. It brought home how close we came tonight to becoming roadkill. Strangely, no cars had passed us since the semi that almost crushed us, and it was eerie standing out in the cold night on the deserted county road. We were all crammed together, so close our arms were touching.

Tre asked, "Did anyone call 911?"

We all looked at each other, nobody saying a word.

Groaning, I laughed. "Ah, we are SO in trouble!"

Again, everyone started speaking at once. Mac finally had the loudest, definitive last word. "It happened so fast and we had to save ourselves. It wasn't safe to try to call the police! What would they have done? Talk us through it?"

"Good, then you can call Jack and tell him exactly what happened." I suggested magnanimously. "He might think a call to the police may have nabbed this guy before he could drive away in his killer van and disappear."

In the hushed quiet of the night, we stood contemplating our close call and the call we knew we needed to make to Chief Jack. The loud ring tone of a phone made everyone jump. By habit; I'd slung my purse over my shoulder when we exited the van.

I saw who it was and answered, "Good God, it's only been two minutes and I was going to call!"

Jack Banner's reply was brusque. "What are you talking about? Never mind, where are you, Anabel? I'm calling to advise you to stay home and locked in tonight, preferably not alone. Make sure your gun is nearby and loaded."

He hadn't heard my news yet, but his did not sound so good, either. "Why, what's going on?"

"We think we've identified the man from today in the van. I have a mug shot for you to check out. If it's this man, I don't want to take any chances you might become a target after he saw you in the parking lot today." Jack's voice was deadly quiet, a clear indicator how serious he considered the situation. "He's a very bad actor, Anabel. He's a known homicidal-serial rapist."

"Holy Crap! Okay Jack, listen to all I have to say before you freak out. First off, we are all fine. I am on the side of Highway 3 a few minutes from Castle Rock's. I'm with the girls in Tre's sister's minivan. We were going out dancing. On the way, this van came out of nowhere and tried to run us off the road. To make a long story short, I think I'm a target." Jack was no longer calm. He was swearing loud and long under his breath. "Wait, let me finish. I had my gun in the van because Candy had dropped it off over at Mac's after she …uh… borrowed it from me, so I shot at him after he rammed us. I shot a full clip. He drove off. We're alive and the van is okay. What should we do now?"

"Hold on a minute." I thought Jack was going to be irate I was in trouble again, but I heard only concern in his voice. This psycho must be really, really bad. I heard the sound of a door closing in the background. Jack spoke again. "It was lucky for you girls that you had the gun tonight. Christ almighty, why did Candy have your gun in the first place? Have you lost your mind? You know what, never mind. I don't want to know right now." I rolled my eyes at Jack's impatient, unflattering assumptions. "Are you out of ammunition? I assume you didn't kill him?"

"I have five bullets left, but he seems to be gone. Like I said, he took off, so he probably wasn't dead."

Jack sounded irritable. "Let me rephrase. Did you hit him?"

"No way of knowing." I was feeling equally irritable.

"Okay, okay, you did right." He sighed. "Note where you are for my team, and then go to Castle Rock's. I want you all safe off the road. Stay in the van double parked near the entrance. I'm sure the man is long gone and you'll be fine, but keep your eyes out and your gun handy. I'll be there in five minutes."

"Police are on the way." I told everyone. They had all silently listened to the phone call from my end. I cleared my throat. "Jack said the man is a majorly bad dude, a killer-rapist."

We all scurried into the van and locked the doors.

Tre started the engine and turned on the heater.

"Jack's crime fighters will probably need to do whatever they do to the van. I bet we can't drive it tonight."

Tre groaned at my comment while pulling onto the road and heading north once again. I held my loaded gun in my lap. My gun permit is for Concealed Carry, but I don't think anyone minded the reassurance of seeing the weapon.

"Should we keep a look-out in all directions to be sure he doesn't sneak back? Until the cops come?" Mac suggested.

"YES!" was the unanimous answer. Everyone was happy to have something to do, even if it was to watch a dark road and the darker fields around us.

A Date with Fate

Mac brought up a point I was silently mulling over. "He had to know forcing us off the road while going that fast could kill us all." She caustically added, "Not that I am complaining he didn't try to rape us first, but I wonder why he wanted us dead?"

Anna's voice was raised and angry. "If he's partners with that Ron Hansen butthole, I think he wanted to get Anabel for saving Larissa today."

"He's a fucking insane individual, that's why." Jazy stated.

"In a nutshell!" I agreed wholeheartedly, shivering. I peered down the black road behind us, in case talking about the killer conjured him up again like in a Jeepers Creepers flick. Nothing would surprise me tonight.

There were no further sightings of the van the last couple of miles to the bar. We followed Jack's instructions and stayed in the van without parking, although we stopped down a few car lengths from the entrance.

Mac was on the phone with Diego. Jazy was also talking to someone. Tre J and Anna were staring diligently out their opposite windows, scanning the lot and people around us.

I kept watch out on my side while I was silently debating if I should call Luke. Jack had said I shouldn't stay alone, and I sure agreed with him. I was seriously freaked out by all that happened. The idea of being stalked by a killer serial rapist is terrifying, even with a loaded Glock 9mm in my hand.

As if reading my mind, Jazy ended her call and spoke from the back. "Reggie's insisting we go to his house after we're done here. I don't feel like dancing anymore, even if Jack says we can. What do you think? Reg's having a poker party tonight." She grinned. "The idea of being surrounded by lots of men sounds appealing."

Tre J chuckled. "When doesn't it? I'm spooked as all hell right now. I vote for your brother's house."

Mac had ended her call and been listening to us. "Diego is picking me up. He's offered to have one of his employees drive my car here if they are keeping the van. You girls can have wheels or," Her big sister gene won out and she went on, "maybe you all should come home with me? It's too bad our night out is cut short, but I agree with Jazy. I want to feel safe at home with my man."

Jazy coughed into her fist. "Your boy."

Mac stared her down. "What did you say?"

"I didn't say anything."

"I know you said something."

I piped in, helpful middle sister that I am. "She said 'your boy'."

Mac glared at Jazy with slitted eyes.

Jazy grinned in return. "Oh, don't give me that look. You call me your baby sister, right? Is Diego not younger than me?" Jazy continued triumphantly, "Ipso Fatso--he is 'your boy'!"

I helped again. "Now she's talking fancy-smack. She's calling your boy toy a 'fatty' in Jazy Latin."

Anna burst out laughing while Mac and Jazy turned on me.

I held up my hands in defense. "Just translatin'…"

Tre turned in her seat and growled a scary "back off" warning at my sisters.

We all laughed. It lightened the tense atmosphere in the van. Jazy told Mac she'd love to borrow her car for the night, but was heading for Reg's. She loves poker. Mac agreed and texted Diego our plans.

Anna spoke up. "Mac, if you could drop me off, I want to go home."

Tre J peered at her worriedly through the rearview mirror. "Anna, what's up with that? You don't want to go to Reg's and be surrounded by seven or eight dudes with bulging muscles?"

"Not when I can have Aunt Lily and her cane." Anna deadpanned.

We were still snorting when Jack pulled up in his SUV, a uniformed cop riding shotgun. I was relieved to see his craggy, grumpy face. With this psycho on the loose and gunning for me, I was more worried about my sisters and friends then I realized. I don't know why this man was after me, but I'd never forgive myself if they were hurt because of something I did. I unloaded my gun and zipped it away in the duffle.

Jack opened the side door, leaning in. "Girls, tell your statements to the nice Officer Nelson. I have drawings to show Anabel."

Climbing out into the chilled air in the well-lit parking lot, I chuckled seeing the young, dark haired cop swallow manfully. He was trying not to look overwhelmed in front of his chief when four talking women bombarded him before he even got near.

With my back to the girls, I paused long enough to say in a voice only the young rookie could hear, "Tell them oldest first, and all will be well." He gave me a surprised, grateful look of relief and I nodded solemnly in return.

Jack grabbed my elbow and escorted me into the passenger seat of his truck. He climbed in behind the wheel, and immediately shoved a single paper under my nose. There were six pictures of different men on the paper. I instantly recognized the man in the van from my parking lot this afternoon and tapped that photo. In this picture, his eyes looked deadly malignant staring out at me. I don't know if it was because I knew what a monster he was, or if he really looked that heinous. I sent up a silent plea to never be close enough again to find out, and pushed the paper away.

I concisely described to Jack what happened from the beginning. None of us had seen the driver tonight, or gotten the van's license number. Anna said she tried to see the front plate from her perch in the very back, but had no luck.

Tentatively, I asked, "Am I in trouble for shooting my gun?"

Jack squeezed my knee. "Not on my watch, Anabel. You have four eye witnesses stating the van was deliberately hit with intent to harm you." His next works erased any relief I was feeling. "Listen, I know that's your only handgun and you have it all legal, right and tight. I really don't want you without a weapon while this joker is out there, but I have to confiscate your gun as evidence. It may become necessary for ballistic tests." He squeezed my knee again. "We need to follow the rules so that when we catch this guy it sticks, understand?"

I gulped and nodded. I don't know why I wasn't expecting this and felt a moment of panic. I hit the button to roll down the passenger window halfway. The cold air helped calm the anxiety of being left defenseless. I know many people with guns. I would not be defenseless for a second longer than it took to borrow one. It wouldn't be registered in my name, but if it came to me defending myself or being killed, I guess I'd worry about the fine print later. For tonight, there were seven or eight guys with bulging muscles at my brother's.

Or there was Luke across the road.

Jack was watching my face. His lips twisted in a knowing way. "We'll get you a legal replacement immediately. Until then, what has Uncle Jack always told his little angel?"

"How would I know what you've told this creepy, little angel you refer to so often? You've always told *me* to get them coming, not going." I must be feeling more myself because I was a tiny bit happy to see the smirking look on the Chief's face replaced with his usual snarl. "Since you are absconding with my gun, are you having us tailed to Reggie's to make sure we aren't killed on the way?"

Jack turned his face upward, contemplating his choices.

I waved a nonchalant hand. "Hey, it's no problem. I can take care of myself. I'll walk into that bar and borrow a gun from someone I know in two minutes."

"I should have horsewhipped some respect into you when you were young." Jack's shark grin was a scary, rare sight.

I smiled sweetly. "Oh, excuse me. Let me rephrase. I can walk into that bar, borrow a gun from someone I know, and take care of myself, Sir Chief!"

Jack reached over the center console and patted my cheek. "That's better, Nancy Sinatra."

I suffered the pat and cocked my head. "Nancy Sinatra, hmm?"

"Aha! Will wonders never cease…I got you! Miss Know-it-all doesn't know everything!" Chief Jack crowed so loudly that the girls and Officer Nelson looked over our way in surprise.

He waved them off in scowling irritation.

I saw Mac fold her arms and give him a slow stare. I laughed to myself. Jack Banner was in trouble now. Nobody waves off MacKenzie Angelica Axelrod DeVere Dos Santos in irritation. Pain and suffering were sure to follow.

I got out of the SUV and went over to the van, reaching in to grab the duffle bag with my gun. Walking back to Jack's driver side, I handed it over with a sad, little shake of my head at his gloating expression and quirking lips.

Keeping eye contact and backing up, I started humming. Then I started snapping my fingers, shaking my shoulders slowly, and singing in a low voice to a few bars of, "These Boots Are Made for Walkin".

I flipped my long pony tail behind my shoulder in farewell and wheeled around to join the group around Officer Nelson.

With my back to him as I walked away, it felt great to let loose a huge grin when I heard Jack's deep voice threaten, "Why, you little…One of these days, Anabel, one of these days."

Chapter XIII
"Don't Speak" by No Doubt

Saturday, 11/17/2012
9:45 PM

I was finished talking with Chief Jack and Officer Nelson about police business. Other cops were around doing their police work, but our parts were done as witnesses or victims, or whatever we were this go around.

The third time better be the charm. I was fed up with everything I wanted to do being interrupted by potential crimes and criminals. It was supposed to be my weekend off; not a never ending episode of Reno 911, Northfield-style.

Mac, Anna, and Officer Nelson had been whisked off by Diego, but not before Mac's husband shot me an accusing glare for putting his precious in danger.

I was also really fed up with the men in my life being pissed at me. It's not like counseling a friend over his missing slut wife, kicking an abusive ex-husband for attempting to kidnap my employee, and shooting at a serial rapist intending vehicular homicide was my idea of a fun Saturday.

I'd held out my arms to Diego, palms up in supplication. "Hey, I didn't PLAN for this to happen! Mac, don't let your husband look at me like that!"

While Mac scolded Diego in my defense, Anna and I hugged. "Ah, June, don't let Diego get you down. What does he know?" Her smile was still a little shaky. "I will say you sure keep your promises. We were singing before we broke out flurrying."

I squeezed her and stood back, shivering as a cold gust of wind swirled around us. "Yes, we were. I'm sorry about missing the bunny hop part. I feel crappy about that."

She sniggered, straightening her purple scarf around her neck. "Next time, we'll get the dancing in." She patted my shoulder consolingly when I groaned dramatically at the thought of a next time. "I'll call you tomorrow."

It wasn't hard to conclude why she'd rather go home versus hanging at Reggie's. Poker party night probably wasn't her idea of the perfect venue for a State of the Union relationship talk with my brother.

Tre J, Jazy, and I took off in Mac's family sedan, a Honda Accord. We were being shadowed by Jack in his SUV on our way to my brother's.

We were getting close to the turn off for Lake Roberd's. I still hadn't made up my mind if I was going to ask Tre J to stop by Luke's first to see if he was home, or go with them to the poker party.

Seeing Diego so lovingly concerned over my sister made me wonder how Luke would react to tonight's fiasco. This unusual thought made me next wonder how I was hoping he'd react. Due to the overactive, filthy imagination I was blessed with, I couldn't help but picture Luke's image in the mirror in my bathroom when he had his arms around me with such bold hunger on his face. Still feeling a bit queasy over the rapist's attempt to end our existence; it played over again in my mind how warm and safe I'd felt with My Hero's arms around me before I'd passed out downstairs in Bel's.

Both emotions were extremes; one all about driving, sexual desire and the other about blissful, sweet comfort. I couldn't deny tonight I wanted to be wrapped around Luke and receiving a combination of both reactions.

I didn't need him, but I wanted him.

Guess I had made my decision where I wanted to go. Now I only had to figure out how to accomplish this without Jack, currently attached to our rear bumper like a barnacle, knowing what I was up to. I didn't have much of a choice whether Tre and Jaz knew where I was staying tonight, but if I could manage it, they'd be the only people knowing. After tossing around ideas in my head and mumbling to myself, I came up with a plan.

The music was on low in the car because the three of us were back to hashing over what the man in the van's ongoing connection was to Larissa's ex.

Despite my curiosity, it was par for the course that earlier Chief Jack hadn't divulged much info on the dude to some pesky, female civilian. I was told his name was Gustav Hammerschmidt. I was warned 'not to run my mouth with my friends too much and keep my eyes open' since I seemed to have caught his eye."

'Where was Luke when somebody really needed to be called asinine?'

From his viewpoint, I understood Just-the-Facts Jack reasoned what more did I need to know once the words 'very bad actor and homicidal serial rapist' were spat past his tightlipped mouth?

From my viewpoint, why do men find it so hard to comprehend us girls like any scrap of detail we can get to gnaw over as we build a big, fat case of anxiety driven what-ifs to uselessly stress about in the short term?

Like, for instance, even Gustav's name was scary. We all heartily agreed due to his violent sexual propensities, he probably had a prison nickname of The Hammer. How would your average man, if he was a woman, like knowing he was being stalked and attacked by a female-hater known fondly by his slammer companions as The Hammer, for God's sake? Girls like all the details. Details allow us to make intuitive leaps to conclusions that sometimes make no logical sense whatsoever, but are often unerringly accurate.

Jack was right about one thing. Officer Nelson was a very nice man. After I gave my statement, and when Jack had his back turned, Mac and I double teamed the blushing cutie. We quickly persuaded him to tell us every fact and opinion he knew about this Gustav Hammerschmidt.

Officer Nelson, Brad, had some good stuff to share. Gustav Hammerschmidt had a long history of being in and out of state mental hospitals and jails. He and Ron Hansen had been cell mates in Dakota County Jail for the last year. They had also participated in jail inmate programs together. Anger Management was the latest program. (We were all silent a beat after Brad told us that fact.) This meant they had spent a heck of a lot of jail time together. The Hammer had been in Dakota County for almost two years. He was doing time for a third degree assault charge resulting from a fight in a strip joint off Highway 52. In the meantime, Wisconsin tried to get their case together to prosecute him for nine rapes occurring around the Madison area in 2010. The last rape resulted in the girl dying from the beating he inflicted. They knew without a doubt he was their man, but the chain of evidence was compromised on the DNA samples. Careers were ruined, and the prosecution refused to charge him if they couldn't make their case. Having him off the streets in a Minnesota jail was better than nothing.

Driving through the night to Reggie's lake house, we talked over these details. Jazy tried to get some more dirt on The Hammer's background, but her cell didn't get internet service in the car. It seemed improbable to me this man would feel the need to hang around town and terrorize me because he gave a fellow inmate a friendly lift. He should have beat cheeks to avoid police interest. Of course, this is a man who has chosen to be a serial rapist and murderer as his major hobby. What seems probable to me might not apply here.

Jazy suggested The Hammer could want to date me and this was how he got a girl's attention. Tre J's opinion was he was in the Aryan Brotherhood. Ron was his butt buddy and fellow brother, and so now he was out for revenge. Both of their comments had me thinking, analyzing, and leaping.

So I called Jack's cell.

"Wait, Quickdraw, don't tell me. Somehow, even as I follow your vehicle, you've got another crime against mankind to report."

I nobly ignored his flesh ripping. Secretly, I always appreciate some good, old-fashioned sarcasm to lighten up my night. It makes me feel better to know Jack started it when I inevitably retaliate.

"Have any of your minions checked on Larissa tonight?"

There was dead silence and I thought I'd lost the call. Then Jack exploded. "Did you swear to God to me not five hours ago to not get involved in police business?"

"Mmm...sort of, but yet, not exactly. So moving on, I did swear I'd tell you anything I found out." I spoke to him nicely without stooping to his level of sarcasm. "Can you go with me here, Jack? Would that be so hard? You're just driving along singing to the oldies on KQ and reliving your glory day, anyway." That's right, I stooped even lower.

I heard his grunt and decided that meant yes. "Ron Hansen was intending to kidnap Larissa out of Bel's today while threatening he was going to make her very sorry. Meanwhile, out in the parking lot, Gustav was waiting. Do you think Ron promised Gustav a poke at Larissa for his help? Could that be why he is after me now; I ruined his fun and must die? Have you verified Larissa is safe?"

Jack swears quite loudly, but nowhere near as inventively as my brother. "I meant you should report FACTS to me, if you learned any. Not call to trade theories, or check if I am doing my job!"

"Here's a fact. You are acting very rude tonight. Why shouldn't you listen to my theories for two seconds?" I was part amused--part offended at his obtuse hard-headedness. "Have you conveniently forgotten it was me that noticed his van in the parking lot today, Chief Yellsalot? If I hadn't theorized we'd be clueless who attacked us."

I heard Jack's cell beep and a faint background squawking from his police radio in his truck. He sounded distracted when he ended our call.

"Listen, Larissa's fine. Stand by."

My phone buzzed a moment later.

Jack spoke without preamble. "Something's come up. Eyes open, Anabel. Call Reg and let him know you're turning onto the lake road. Text me you're safe within ten minutes."

Fun and Games aside, I reassured him instantly. "Roger that. Thank you, Jack."

"I've notified the locals of the situation. They'll be keeping an eye out around Reggie's place throughout the night."

"Great, I'll warn the drinking poker players."

Jack slowed, flashed his lights, and did a U turn. We all watched his fast retreating taillights disappear down the dark county road behind us. The clock on the dash read 10:09 PM.

"I wonder what's happening that would make Jack leave us before we get to Reggie's. For all his grouching, I know Jack thinks of us girls like we're his special needs kids." Jazy hurried on, "Not that I'm worried about Hammerschmidt."

Turning onto the road circling the lake, Tre J located the switch for the car's brights and lit up the narrow road ahead of us.

She was chuckling at my sister's comment. "Anabel's lucky she's not his kid. She'd probably walk with a permanent limp."

There was a snigger from the back seat. "I bet Jack dreams of spanking her."

"You twisted sister!" I exclaimed in disgust at my deviant sibling over Tre's laughter.

I had no idea what police business had Jack peeling off, but I was keeping my fingers crossed they had picked up Gustav Hammerschmidt. My life was going to suck until this dude was caught somehow and put back in a cage.

Sinning and moral debates aside, was it terrible of me to wish it would be a coffin and not a cell?

I don't think it was, either.

However, Jack's leaving did make my life simpler right now.

"Before we go to Reggie's, do you chickies want to see where Luke lives?"

Jazy leaned forward between the bucket seats. Tre J stopped the car. She turned on the dome light. Both women were staring at me in astonishment.

"What?"

I could see the shock plain on Jazy's face. I think it was the wide-open mouth and round eyes that clued me in.

She finally spoke. "You realize we've never met Luke, and only heard about him for the first time…"

Tre J interrupted excitedly, "I *never* heard you even mention a man's name you're dating! Now that I think about it, I don't remember you even going out with the same man more than a couple of times since what's his name…"

I interjected to avoid, avoid, avoid. "Give me a break, I only asked if you wanted to see where he lives. I never said anything about going out with anyone. Luke's become a friend of mine." I diverted. "Hey, just what the heck do you mean by I've never gone out with a man more than twice?"

The girls started guffawing at my righteous protests.

Jazy answered first. "Oh, Bel, puh-lease. It's been your pattern to stop going out with men after one or two dates for years." Her voice turned musing. "I'm envious of your talent for keeping them as friends. I haven't mastered that feat and I'm feeling the hate lately." Her voice got brisk again. "Not that it's a bad thing, but it seems like you're always in control. We've never seen you fall for anyone, have we, Tre J?"

Tre agreed with a smiling shrug at me and took her foot off the brake. "She's right, we haven't."

Jazy poked me in the arm. "Who do you think you're talking to here, huh? You think we're brainless and couldn't figure out why you want us to see his house?" She impatiently shook her head. "It's a classic move, Sister. It's the smart way to check out if a man's home without having to call him. Also, you don't have to tell your friends what you're really up to, or how much you like him." She paused and it was so pregnant, birth was eminent. "What exactly are you up to, Anabel?"

Tre J nodded again in agreement. "It is a classic move, Bel."

"It is? Huh."

Jazy's blunt statements certainly put to rest any question in my mind where Stella inherited her lack of subtleness and her rat terrier tendencies.

I leaned my head against my window, covering my eyes with my hand. It was my turn to laugh at me. I may not like hearing what my sister said, but that didn't make her wrong. I was performing a classic move and checking out a man.

I had never checked out a man before in this way. I mean, I do criminal background checks, sometimes credit checks, and even mental health checks, but doesn't everyone?

This house checking was a new concept for me. I was a novice at the classic moves since I never cared what a man was doing when I wasn't with him. Nor did I worry about losing face when stopping over; probably because I never did stop over. It was an unsettling feeling.

I didn't think performing a classic move of checking the situation out signified I was falling for Luke. It only meant I was going to take him up on his earlier offer to hang together tonight due to my own plans falling apart. I didn't want to interrupt by calling him if he had plans with someone else. That could be awkward. That's all I was up to.

No, the thing that floored me most was realizing I must be seriously losing it to have come up with this unworthy plan to put one over on these two worldly, talented fiends. There was no excuse for it. I know perfectly well what these two girls are like.

Everywhere we go, Goddess Tre fights off men throwing themselves at her size eleven feet for the fruitless chance to worship at the altar of her voluptuous magnificence. I say fruitless because Tre J is a twenty-seven-year old virgin saving herself for Mr. Right and marriage.

No shit.

Tre just may be the oldest voluntary virgin, next to Aunt Lily, in Northfield, or perhaps even Rice County. Not that I think any man would voluntarily put it to Aunt Lily unless under the threat of death. But to give the Behemoth her due, she has been the most zealously faithful bride of Christ outside of a Carmelite convent a woman could ever claim to be.

On that note; is it wrong to be sorry as hell for poor Jesus Christ?

I don't think it's so wrong, either.

My little sister approaches life a little differently. Jazy treats her men like she works her horses. She expertly culls a prime piece of flesh out the herd. She saddles him up and rides him relentlessly until he's broke to the bridle to her satisfaction. Then she cheerfully gives him back to his owner, a more submissive, well-trained mount that can even perform a showy trick or two.

The glass of the window feels cool against my cheek. I am feeling sleep deprived, yet full of strange, manic energy—a disturbing combination. My fun weekend off keeps throwing me curves. Feeling punchy with relief at surviving the latest near-miss; it was no wonder that all my filters and fences are down. This was the only explanation for me so clumsily messing up my need-to-know rule like an amateur with Jaz and Tre.

When life throws me curves, it's only logical to bend and acknowledge what my choices are to achieve my goals. In this instance, I may have to flex my beloved, control freak rules just a smidgen and not go it alone. I may have to take on partners and form a temporary triad.

'Okay, I can do this. This was my sister and good friend, after all. Not a couple of enemies at the gate.'

I dropped my hand and smiled. "So, was there a 'Yes, you do want to see his house' somewhere in all that?"

Tre J whooped and Jazy laughed, punching my shoulder in camaraderie before sitting back. The Dome Light of Truth was turned off. We passed my brother's driveway on the right and kept going. Absently rubbing my sore arm, I cautioned Tre J to be on the lookout on the left for the unique mailbox of a John Deere miniature tractor identifying Luke's turn off.

I had been to Luke's house once before when he needed to pick up his wallet. I had waited in the car that time. I was curious to see the inside of his house tonight. It was odd to know him so intimately, yet not know such basic things about his everyday life. My stomach was fluttering in anticipation of seeing him so soon again.

Jazy was the resident expert on classic moves. "Let's kill the headlights and coast quietly up the driveway."

I didn't comment on Jazy's directive to go in dark, this was their bailiwick, but I flicked off the radio. I knew Luke was hyper-aware of his surroundings. If he was home; I was counting on him to ask questions first and attack second. Hopefully, he believed in taking prisoners.

I had a suggestion for my new partners. "Let's wait a second here in the dark just to be doubly sure we weren't followed. Then I'll text Jack we're okay, so he doesn't freak and call Reggie."

Jazy whistled. "Crap--I'd already forgotten. Good idea. I'll text Reggie to expect us in ten. I'll text Mac we're safe, too, or else she'll be all over our ass."

I whistled back my admiration. What a team of competent connivers we made.

We waited a few anxious minutes in silence. Not seeing any vans lunging out of the darkness, we decided the coast was clear around us. I texted Jack as he'd instructed.

Tre, guided only by the light from the moon and stars overhead, slowly drove the bouncing Honda up the open, rutted lane. The tree shrouded farmyard was fifty yards ahead of us.

As we crept closer, I turned and grinned at Jazy in the backseat. This was fun being sneaky. I couldn't believe I've never tried this before. She grinned back, a flash of white teeth in the dark interior of the car.

We entered the inky darkness under the canopy of dense trees, and Tre J slowed to a stop until her night vision further adjusted.

Here the road did a loop into a big, circular driveway. I recalled in the grassy center of the circle were massive groupings of huge lilac bushes. It was late autumn and they were bare of their leaves, but the tangle of thick branches still created a barrier preventing us from seeing the other side of the driveway and the whole house.

From where we were stopped, it was possible to see a front porch light was on outside. It spotlighted the cement stoop and iron railing of the mid-century style rambler. The bushes blocked a clear glimpse of the whole house, but enough lights could be seen twinkling through the branches that it appeared Luke was home.

After a moment's thought, Jazy directed Tre J to go slowly to the right. Tre J turned the wheel and crept towards the house.

Clicking open her seatbelt again, Jazy scooted forward and softly explained her logic to me. "We need to be able to see what's going on without committing you. It's a rambler, so there's probably a picture window in front, right?" She must have sensed my nod in the dark car. "We can't get out of the car here and go surveil. It's too far away. It would be uncouth if we were caught looking in his windows." I giggled at the term and the image. "If we can get the car close enough, then maybe we can verify Luke's home alone without getting out. If we can't, having the car close makes it acceptable to be out walking near his front window like we were going to the front door."

"Hot diggety, Jaz, you really know your stuff! I had no idea classic moves would need so much devious strategy." I was in awe at the unforeseen depths of my baby sister's ninja stealth knowledge. I teased her. "Here I thought I'd just go blundering up to the door and ring the bell if he's home."

Jazy and Tre J let out similar oaths of whispered surprise. "Don't be such a stupid ass!" and "Oh, that wouldn't be smart, Anabel!"

Not offended by their words, I found myself smiling to be creeping up on Luke's house. I was holding my bated breath while Tre J inched us closer to the dwelling and it became more visible.

A Date with Fate

Tre buzzed down her window partway, head cocked and listening. We could all hear it then, the sound of loud music playing.

"He must have a window cracked somewhere."

Jazy murmured, "This makes life easier. You hear that song? It's Radiohead, good choice."

Tre fervently agreed in a quiet undertone. "I love Radiohead."

She inched the car to the end of this leg of the driveway, right before it jogged left within a few feet of the foundation of the house. Tre J had hugged the left side of the lane. We were quietly idling, a dark car shadowed by the giant, looming lilac bushes.

I was dutifully peering ahead, trying to see inside the living room through Luke's picture window. It was lit up like a small theatre stage. From this angle, I couldn't see too much. Only the back of an empty chair, a lamp, and an arched doorway leading into darkness were visible.

My cell phone buzzed loudly in the quiet car. I quickly grabbed it. Using my purse as a covering, I saw a text from an unknown number. Curious, I read it quickly and blew out a surprised breath.

I have important news. Please allow me to tell you. All I ask is 5 min. Mike McClain

Glancing up at the sudden tenseness in the air, I heard Tre's cautiously murmured, "Well, well, what do we have here?"

"Tre."

Shoving my phone in my purse, I forgot Mike's text to concentrate on what was happening. At my sister's one word instruction, Tre smoothly put the Honda in reverse and we were backing up.

The car stopped. Jazy then made her move. She slipped out, and shut the car door with a soft click. Poised for Jazy's action, Tre J was on it. She had reached up and covered the dome light with her gloves. When I glanced back in the direction my sister had gone, there was no sight of her in the dark night around us.

I didn't know yet what had them curious, but I was impressed with their tandem movements. They worked together like a well-oiled machine. I speculated on what these two were up to in their spare time. Did training horses together and being roommates explain why they'd be so in sync, or could Jazy and Tre be a couple of Peeping Thomasina's?

"What's going on, Tre?"

"Look over my way at about ten o'clock. It's through the bushes on the side of the house. Can you see it?"

I sat forward and strained to see where she pointed. It didn't take me long to see it, too. Staring fixedly, I couldn't look away from the sight of Candy's light blue, Honda Civic parked in Luke's driveway.

My mind was scrambling to comprehend. I thought back quickly over the past two months for clues to understand why I was seeing Candy's car at Luke's. My cousin had been over at Reggie's on the

Saturday morning I'd first met Luke last September. I had to assume he'd met her at least that once. I would definitely have remembered being sick if Luke had mentioned hanging out with Candy in any of our ensuing conversations. I don't vomit frequently enough to not distinctly remember the experience when I do.

As if to prove my thoughts, nausea now replaced the excited butterflies in my gut. Staring at her car, I had to conclude this meant one of two things; Luke was dating Candy, or he was friends with her. Either way, he hadn't mentioned her name to me. I never told him anything about my past with Candy, so he didn't know I despised her.

'Holy hell! Luke Drake was the "mysterious man meet" Candy had bragged to Mac about earlier tonight?'

Luke and I had no agreement of exclusivity, but would he be so crass as to be with my cousin? I also realized, exclusivity clause or not, these had to be jealousy pangs twisting up my innards at the idea of Luke being with another woman. Mixed with the pangs of horror that the woman could be my cousin Candy, and I was fighting the need to hurl.

I guess there was a third, remote possibility that could not be overlooked. Candy had shown up out of the blue at Luke's house. He wasn't seeing her, or friends with her. Maybe he'd let her in because she was selling Girl Scout cookies at ten o'clock at night and he was a good citizen.

Did I say earlier Fate was trying to kick my ass? Obviously, I misspoke. Fate was trying to kick my ass, my gut, my head, my ankle—you name it. This was a total body slaughterama of a weekend. I am stuck here watching my past comingle with my future. It's like having to sit through the repeated telling of a cosmic bad joke.

I fell back in my seat while muttering darkly, "Why does everybody think Radiohead's so frickin' great, anyway? Nothing but a bunch of New Age Pink Floyders."

Chapter XIV
"Rolling In The Deep" by Adele

Saturday, 11/17/12
10:37 PM

With gentle tolerance, Tre reprimanded me over my Radiohead comment, as if I was a cranky preschooler who knew not what she said.

I sat waiting with outward calm for Jazy's return. Inside, I was a snake pit of seething emotions and barely hanging onto my temper. Not racing to the door and finding out for myself what was going on took every ounce of self control I possessed. I really despise waiting around.

I practiced my yoga breathing. I came to a decision. Luke would get the benefit of my doubt unless proven untrustworthy, but not Candy. She knows exactly who she's messing with tonight.

Candy and Reggie were aware I had a first date with Luke minutes after it was arranged last September. I hadn't been very subtle grilling Reggie about Luke when he'd left. Reg had teased me unmercifully in front of Candy about Luke and me sniffing after each other like dogs in heat. There was no way Candy didn't know I was dating Luke.

Candy Anne MacKenzie has been living on borrowed time for the past nine years, and now she needs to die.

Candy takes after her mother's side of the family in looks. You would never guess we are first cousins, or even related. She is fond of informing people she resembles the celebrity, Tori Spelling. It is true Candy has bulbous, brown eyes.

During our teens, she acted possessed over the fact that I had a larger bra cup size then she did. Candy threw tantrums and made my uncle's life miserable over this issue. It goes without saying; Daddy soon bought her a new set of boobs. It also goes without saying; once she got her way she went big--as in ginormous. A porn star would be envious. Paired up against her thin, slight frame, Candy's melon-sized breasts appear painfully huge in proportion.

At first glance, my cousin is an attractively packaged woman complete with factory warrantee. Candy's skin is tanned mahogany, the hair's bleached white blonde and long with extensions, the teeth are whitened to that weird purplish-white hue, the make-up is piled on, the eyebrows are plucked to a thin, black half circle, and the eyelashes are false. She dresses and accessorizes expensively with Uncle Trevor's credit cards, but her taste continues to be questionable. This is from years of

Anna and I indirectly influencing her fashion choices, but more on that later.

I'm sure she sees herself as a desirable, hoochie mama that every man lusts after.

I see her as a walking toxic dumpsite.

Satisfying as it would be to pull Candy out of Luke's house by the roots of her Chernobyl blonde hair to give her a dermabrasion treatment she'd never forget on the gravel drive tonight, it wasn't going down that way. My beef with her was of long standing duration. It is not going to be about Luke.

As far back as I can remember, Candy has gone to extreme lengths to get whatever I have. If she can take it from me while doing so, even better.

She's three years older, so this caused some problems for me when we were kids. It was no fun having my G.I. Joe go disappearing from my room, only to later show up at her house, in her room. She vehemently denied taking it, of course. Since her parents bought her anything she even remotely desired; Candy had some wiggle room to smugly squirm out of trouble with the adults.

Not with me, though. I knew every inch of that G.I. Joe. I'd paid for that man doll out of my hard earned Chore Chart money. He was mine.

After seeing her smile of evil satisfaction at the look on my face when first seeing her completely redecorated bedroom, I had Candy's measure. It was crammed with the entire collection of the Princess Pink Ruffles canopied bedroom set I'd drooled over endlessly.

When I woke up from a kitten nap in my room after a big, Sunday dinner to the sight of my nuttier-than-a-fruitcake cousin about to snip off my waist-length braid, it was all out warfare.

My age, or size, has never stopped me from scrapping when necessary. Jumping up with a shout that day, I'd tripped her to the floor and sat on her. I was planning on shearing her like a sheep in retribution. The scissors were a hairsbreadth away from taking the first hunk off her scalp when NanaBel burst into my room in response to Candy's hysterical screams of terror. Biting her lip, our Grandmother coaxed me down from my heights of nap-groggy furor. It was later that same day NanaBel exacted my first begrudging, disgruntled promise to go easy on Candy.

Since I gave my word not to physically take her down, Anna and I spent many constructive hours on the serviceable bunk beds in my room devising ways to watch Candy dance on our strings like a Tasmanian Devil puppet.

The formula was laughably simple and almost always worked. I'd allow Candy to eavesdrop on Anna's and mine private conversations. I would profess to desire something like a certain person, or a really cool sweatshirt with bejeweled cat eyes. Then we'd sit back and watch the fun.

A Date with Fate

My kook of a cousin moved heaven and earth to obtain any objects of my supposed affection.

Were Anna and I wrong to believe Candy had a moral choice? If she didn't spy, then she wouldn't know what I wanted. It wouldn't work for us to be puppet masters extraordinaire.

That's what we thought, as well.

Candy dressed very strangely for years. We felt kind of bad for siccing the seventeen-year-old Candy on the thirteen-year-old boy with the terrible acne problem. But he actually dumped her first and moved on to become quite the stud.

As we got older, I learned to virtually ignore Candy. I was busy with my own life and friends. We hung with different people, and our paths crossed only occasionally at family functions. There were enough people at these gatherings to easily avoid her, and I grew unconsciously adept at being wherever Candy wasn't. I almost forgot she was demonic.

Until I was nineteen.

I was working long hours at Bel's while my one and only boyfriend, Mike McClain, was going to school his sophomore year at the U of M. Mike and I'd been hot and heavy for over two years, wildly in love. I visited him on campus as much as I could get away, and he drove the hour commute to be with me several times a week. As far as I knew, we had no issues. Our relationship together was as close to perfection as I could imagine, and we've all ready established the status of my imagination.

Mike and I were spending the upcoming weekend at a friend's cabin up north. Our friend was leaving to spend the year in Europe. This was his big blowout of a send off. I was excited to spend three full days with Mike and really looking forward to partying with our friends.

The day we were due to leave, NanaBel and several others of the bookstore staff came down violently ill with a nasty stomach virus. It was impossible for me to take off the time to go to the cabin. Totally bumming, I encouraged Mike to go ahead and have fun with his friends. I knew I'd now be working all the time that weekend.

I was only amused on Sunday at the reports starting to trickle in from concerned friends before Bel's closed late that afternoon. Nobody knew details, but several people I knew called or came into the store to exclaim over my break-up with Mike. Candy was boasting she had been with Mike up north for the weekend. The grapevine was working at top speed. Casual friends assumed we'd broken up and they hadn't heard.

It was news to me, too. Mike and I had talked briefly on Saturday afternoon and there was no talk of breaking up. It was the opposite. I had to laughingly beg him to hang up and let me get back to work while he continued to say very sweet things to me. He hadn't even mentioned Candy and my sister Kenna were up at the cabin party.

I checked my cell repeatedly and had no calls from Mike, but I still blew off what I was hearing. I was sure he'd come over the minute he got back in town. He'd tell me what was up, if anything, in regards to Candy's gossip. There was no way Mike would ever be seduced by Candy.

Not too long after I closed the shop and was up in the apartment, my sister Kenna came over.

"Yes, it is true." Kenna uncomfortably confirmed for the second time. She was miserably sticking to her guns. I accused her of bullshitting me; despite the swear to God I'd hotly demanded from her at the start of the conversation.

I'll always give her credit for facing me and telling me what she knew to be true regarding that weekend. She understood I'd be hearing stories, and came immediately to the apartment after the store closed. I was sure Kenna wasn't lying. There were no circumstances I could come up with that could mitigate what my sister saw with her own two eyes. Believe me, I tried.

Yes, it was true. Mike McClain, the love of my life, screwed my cousin. The moment Kenna appeared at the top of the stairs and I saw her guilty, evasive expression, my brain knew Mike McClain was not worth another moment of my time.

It just took a couple of years for my broken heart to catch up to my brain.

Other than briefly telling Anna what Kenna divulged to me that night, and telling my family we broke up, I never said his name again. I never spoke to him again. What was done could never be undone.

I learned I was not a forgiving soul that bleak, Sunday evening.

Maybe some people can truly forgive, or forget, such a personal smackdown. I'm not one of them. I'm not forgiving, but I will forget you until you cease to exist. Not like I never knew you or what you did. More like you are now a nothing to me. When Mike called several times, or came to the apartment and the store. I ignored him and walked away. He was dead to me.

There's a whole world out there of people willing to treat you decently, so why stay with anyone willing to betray you?

Stay out of love? Love yourself enough to deserve better. People that love you do not betray you the first time. Unfortunately, if you stick with them the odds are they will do it again.

Stay out of friendship? Adults that are your true friends do not betray you, or throw you under the bus. Your true friends like, even love, you enough to never want to bash you around with words or actions.

Stay out of fear of being alone? Accept it and get over it. We are all ultimately alone.

Stay out of pity? Don't get me going on pity again.

A Date with Fate

I look at the people I love in my inner circle as beautiful gifts on loan while I trek through my life. I want to treat them with affection, respect, humor, interest and understanding. They need to return the honor, or else why are they in my inner circle?

Sure, nobody's perfect and you don't dump someone for quirks or minor faults if you care about them. You want to be understanding of their issues, too. The level of betrayal I was dealt from Mike McClain went far beyond a minor flaw or quirk. I proved I could forget over time he ever existed, but I'd never forgive him for having to learn that terrible lesson of personal betrayal.

When push came to shove, Kenna came to the apartment to tell me what she knew out of loyalty as my sister, and to clear herself of any wrongdoing or involvement in my eyes. She may be buds with Candy, but she has no problems always looking out for number one.

According to her, this is what went down. Kenna sheepishly admitted she'd noticed Candy was flirting quite a lot with Mike, but he didn't seem interested. She didn't think anything; it was just Candy being Candy. She observed Mike spent his days boating on the lake and his nights hanging with a group of boys.

Everyone spent Saturday night drinking around a bonfire. After her second beer, Kenna started feeling really wasted and tired, probably from all the exercise and sunshine. She went to the tent she was sharing with Candy and passed out.

When Kenna woke up early the next morning to go pee, she was shocked speechless to see a nude Candy atop an obviously naked Mike. They were going at it. She realized then it was his disgusting moaning and groaning that woke her up. She said it was like he was being tortured.

Not knowing what to do, she'd crept out of the tent. She ended up in their car. She slept in the backseat until Candy found her a few hours later. Candy assured my pissed sister on their drive home that Mike had come on strong after Kenna took off for bed. He had informed Candy he was planning on breaking up with me and had always wanted her.

After my initial burst of enraged disbelief, I never said a word during this recital. Once I knew Mike had fucked Candy, the rest of the story didn't register past my numb misery. Except maybe the bizarrely odd detail of Mike's tortuous moaning and groaning. I never knew him to be a such a moaner but if I was a dude; I'd find it tortuous to screw Candy, too. They'd have to draw and quarter me first.

My unpleasant jaunt down memory lane was cut short when a light tap sounded on the back window of the car. It was Tre J's signal to cover the dome light. Jazy slipped into the back seat.

I couldn't see her shadowed face in the darkness, but her voice said it all. "It's not platonic. You want details?"

"No." I turned and faced the front. "Let's go."

I sensed Tre J's concerned glance, but she put the car in reverse without commenting.

"Wait!" I whispered, fiercely. Tre took her foot off the gas immediately. I swung around to Jazy. "One."

Jazy didn't hesitate. "She was bare-assed on his lap with his face buried in her tits."

Tre J whispered in abhorrence, "That is fucked-up."

I didn't say anything, but sat forward again and made a curt motion for Tre J to drive.

We were slowly bouncing back down the rutted lane. The headlights were still off. Tre J wasn't using the brake so no indicators of our presence would be visible out in the open as we were. Keeping my mind a blank, I flipped back on the radio to fill the silence until we pulled into Reggie's a few minutes later.

There were several cars and big trucks in his lot. He has an outdoor light mounted high on a pole overlooking the parking area, so the side closest to the house was well-lit. Tre J parked near the porch and turned off the engine. None of us made any immediate moves to open our doors.

From their expectant air, it must be customary to say something in closing to your classic move, triad partners. After all, they couldn't help but notice you were still in the car due to your target having his face buried in your almost dead cousin's balloon breasts.

I felt cold with rage. Not a very pleasant emotion I particularly wanted to share with anyone. Luckily, I'm an old expert at hiding these types of feelings.

Reflected in the yellow light shining down from the pole above, I smiled ruefully at their serious expressions. "I don't think classic moves are such a good idea for me; they are stressful."

While Jazy and Tre J were laughing in relief at my quip, I reached for my purse and opened the car door. "Come on, ladies. Don't we have something like nine men with incredible biceps waiting for us a few feet away?"

They climbed out on their side. Jaz called over the Honda's roof, "Nine? Are you including our brother in the total? Gross!"

"I'm gross? Au contraire, Miss Lucrezia, you are the one with the incestuous thoughts tonight. First it was Jack, and now Reg. Where does your sick mind dwell?"

Tre hooted, slapping Jaz on the back and sending her forward a few steps. "Her mind's in the gutter, like always."

"We can't all be Vested Virgins like some woman I could name." Jaz sniped back. "Tell me again, how is it fun holding back from the buffet of life?"

A Date with Fate

Meeting them at the front of the car, I teased my word-challenged sister. "Try Vestal Virgin, not vested. Unless you meant Tre's a western-style, cowgirl virgin?"

Tre shouted with laughter and Jazy grinned, taking my correction in stride after years of such abuse.

"Jazy, do you really think Tre holds back at the buffet of life? I'm thinking she may not partake in a full plate of happiness, but she sure gobbles up the appetizers and desserts!"

Our guilty, blushing friend Tre commanded us to stop. "It's not fair being Axelrod tag teamed!"

Ignoring Tre's cry for fairness, Jazy kept laughing. "I know, right? If I hadn't known Tre J since we wore pull-ups, I'd believe she was one of those females that's raised very strictly to be a virgin until they are safely pawned off and married. You know, the girls pretending to be goodie two-shoes, but they're actually slut monsters? They perform every sex act known to man, except vag penetration." Jazy posed angelically, her hands together in prayer. "Then they get married a pure, innocent virgin."

"What! You bitch!" Tre J shouted in outraged laughter.

"Do you remember Lydia Lee in my class?" Jazy asked us. She was wiping her eyes and barely able to speak over her laughter.

I nodded vigorously up and down. "Who could forget Lydia Chlamydia? She was famous for having anal sex with any boy who had a car in our high school. That crazy chick was something else."

"Ahhh, but was she still a pure virgin, my sister?" Jazy asked archly.

"How dare you girls talk about anal sex while on your brother's property!" Reggie's deep voice calling from his front porch interrupted our huddled laughter. "Now, who is this Lydia Lee and where can I reach her?"

Tre J was groaning and shaking her head as she strode up the front steps. "Not another Axelrod to gang up on me. Besides, you probably 'reached her' back in middle school and have long forgotten, Reggie."

"Well, I know I've never reached you before, honey. When are you going to admit you want me bad?"

I watched Reg get knocked off kilter a couple of steps by Tre's playful punch. As we joined them on the porch, Jaz cheered her on to take our brother down.

I was getting chilly without my jacket on. Under the laughing and joking front, I was feeling a heavy sense of miserable loss. I was livid with anger every time my mind touched on knowing Luke was across the road with my cousin.

I tried to shake off the depression, reaching instead for the fury. At least that kept me stronger. I hated knowing I was wrong about my understanding of Luke's character. I gave him credit for having more depth than the typical player using any woman that came his way.

Upon first meeting him, I knew he was driven and highly-sexed; the testosterone rolled off him in waves. My mistake was underestimating his level of control of his appetites if he didn't get what he wanted, when he wanted it. I gave him credit for a level of maturity and discrimination he didn't possess. Even in my disgust, it wasn't like I thought he wanted a "relationship" with Candy, unless it was with her humungous mammaries.

'My god, this sucked!' I shuddered in repugnance at the thought of him being with me and then going to be with Candy a few hours later. I took solace in the thought that since this was the kind of man Luke was, better to face it now and move on. It justified my inner voices telling me to stick to my rules and walk away intact, like always.

Jazy squeezed my arm, and I glanced over to see her watching me. I dredged up a smile. "Let's go raid Reggie's kitchen."

Reggie stepped over and enveloped us in a group hug. "I thought you were scared, little chickens after tonight. Instead, you three are out here laughing it up without a care in the world. Don't I finally get to be the tough, protective brother?"

Jazy snorted. "Did hell freeze over tonight when I wasn't looking?"

Tre J and Jaz were giggling at Reggie's offended expression as they entered the house.

"She's so fresh. I try hard, but you can't be nice to that girl." Reggie sighed sadly, and then peered closely at me. "So, Shooter, how are you?"

I made a face. "Why don't you distract me and tell me how much money you've won with your cheating ways. Let's do it in the house, though. I'm really freezing my butt off out here."

"Cheating?" Reg scoffed. "I see you're still bitter I took your money last month." His voice turned cajoling. "Come on, Junior, tell me what happened tonight. Hell, it's not every Saturday night a dude nearly loses all his nemeses, I mean his sisters, at once." He grinned and opened the storm door for me. "It wasn't like I paid the idiot to miss."

I sniggered a little, and obligingly filled him in. Sticking to the bare facts, it took only a minute. The house was not overly warm, but definitely better than standing outside in a thin, flouncy shirt and no coat.

Absently listening to Reg rant and rave on the ways he was going to inflict damage on The Hammer's sorry ass if he found him first, I gazed distractedly around my brother's place. The entire first floor, except for the tiled bathroom, was now installed with gleaming, oak hardwood flooring. The living room was furnished with two leather sofas, a big recliner, and two end tables with lamps. Reggie had a super-sized, flat screen TV

A Date with Fate

where, lo and behold, a cable sports channel was on with the volume turned low.

Winding down on the butt-kicking scenarios, Reggie headed to the kitchen for a beer. I stood back in the shadows of the doorway between the living and dining rooms, unnoticed by the boisterous group in the next room. Leaning a shoulder against the wall, I smiled faintly at the scene I observed.

A pedestal dining table and chairs had replaced the temporary card table and chairs. The table was extended open tonight to a large oval. Several men sat talking and laughing, sprawled out comfortably in their chairs. Richly fragrant cigar smoke curled lazily up through the air to be disbursed in the slowly rotating ceiling fan. Full ashtrays, beer bottles, and short glasses of hooch were scattered around the table. Bowls of chips and pretzels were at their elbows. Cards were laying face down in front of each man, and piles of chips in staggered heights and colors were stacked near their drinks.

It was the quintessential setting of a group of men having a good time together with no fussy female interference. The traditional male normalcy of it all made me glad I'd come over here after the last few hours of craziness. I wouldn't dream of emptying their overflowing, smelly ashtrays.

I idly noticed the patio door was ajar to let in some fresh air, which accounted for the cool temperatures. Two chairs at the table were currently unoccupied. One had to be Reggie's since it had the TV remote planted front and center, and the chair faced the living room. As I skimmed the room with a quick glance, I saw a few of the guys looking my way. I waved my hellos in return to their various greetings.

Jazy and Tre J were in the thick of things in the dining room, entertaining the men with our Death Race 2012 adventure. From the looks on their faces, nobody seemed to mind the break in the poker action.

Jazy seemed unusually animated. Her arms were gesturing in emphasis with her words. It reminded me of Stella a zillion years ago this morning talking to Eric George Jasnik in Bel's. From my post of leaning against the doorway, I soon figured out the reason why she was so energized. Jaz was chatting primarily with a man I'd never seen before, a very attractive American Indian. The man wore his hair pulled back in a long, thick braid. On him, the braid did not seem one bit feminine. Instead, it only emphasized his chiseled profile and high, broad cheekbones.

Reggie came from the kitchen carrying three bottles of beer, handing two off to the girls. He toggled the third in my direction, but I shook my head no. Beer's not a favorite of mine. I motioned I'd get something in a minute.

Reg slid into his chair. My eyes went to the empty chair where a larger pile of chips was stacked. I pantomimed a sad face at Reg, pointing out how he wasn't in the lead. He rubbed his cheek with his middle finger in a brotherly gesture.

It reminded me of the last time I had given him the finger that way, and I sighed in disgust with myself. I wasn't doing such a bang-up job of coldly putting Luke out of my mind. The problem was life had been really fun these last couple of months. Luke gave brightness to my days that I hadn't known I'd been missing for a long time. I felt depressed knowing Luke was an asshole and not going to be part of my inner circle. I was starting to get ticked again thinking about Luke turning out to be a dickhead.

'What a jerkface, buttwad, tailchasing...'

Sam Sheedy, a friend of Reg's from school, stood to unfold a card chair from the pile leaning against the wall. Sam faltered when he got a glimpse of my dark scowl, but then he recovered.

He spoke with bluff heartiness. "Why, it's the beautiful Anabel. Don't be shy and hide back there. Here, sit down next to me. Heard you girls got yourselves into a spot of trouble tonight?"

His attitude set my teeth on edge. I always expected Sam to be wearing a bow tie and suspenders to match his projected air of pompous superiority. He was three years younger than me, but by his jocular tone you'd think he was my grandpa. He was the last asswipe I wanted to be around tonight.

"Well, Sam Sheedy, we girls didn't "get" ourselves into anything. If you're referring to the attempt at vehicular homicide by a murdering serial rapist attacking us for insane reasons we may never understand, then the answer is yes—that did happen tonight." I smiled grimly and politely excused myself. "I'm going to make something to drink in the kitchen."

I turned around and decided to go use the facilities first. My pony tail could probably use a redo, as well. I was back to fiercely calling Luke names. I timed them to my footsteps down the short hallway off the living room leading to the first floor bathroom.

'Idiothole, assclown, bitchtard, fuckblossom...No, that one was too nice...duckfucker, dicklicker. Oh yeah, Mr. Manly would hate that one!'

I said it out loud for my own cheering-up entertainment. "Luke Drake is a duckfucking dicklicker." Happy with the result, I said it again louder. "Yes, it is true. Secret Agent Luke Drake is a big, fat, lying DICKLICKER."

The bathroom door abruptly swung inward at the same time I was knocking to see if it was occupied. I stumbled into the room and threw my hands out to keep from falling. They landed against a hard chest. I looked up. The word DICKLICKER died on my lips as I stared into puzzled, but amused bottle-green eyes.

Chapter XV
"Brighter Than the Sun" by Colbie Caillat

Saturday, 11/17/12
11:07 PM

I know the least I can about quantum physics and theories, but even I can't help knowing a body can't be in two places at one time in the Northfield area. To be absolutely sure Luke could not accomplish this feat, I'd verify with Crookie tomorrow what the advances were in this field. In the meantime, my heart was singing and I was doing back flips down the hallway--in my head, of course.

My life was again blazing in Technicolor brightness. I needed sunglasses to keep staring at Luke and not be blinded by my reflected exuberance he wasn't The Betrayer 2.0.

Luke had stepped back into the bathroom. He was leaning against the vanity with his arms crossed on his chest and his legs crossed at the ankles. He no longer looked tired or rumpled, or amused. He lounged back with a glint in his eye. He reminded me of a sleek panther ready to pounce, but in his own good time after he played with his prey. I could easily imagine his tail snapping lazily back and forth as he contemplated me. He had changed clothes from earlier today and was wearing a long-sleeved, black shirt and jeans. The T shirt was pushed up his forearms and fit close on his chest. With his arms and legs crossed over pulling his clothes taut, I was admiring his ripped body. Maybe he wouldn't wait too long to attack.

He was giving me the dark once-over I was becoming used to that signaled he was not happy with me. The one where his black eyebrows meet, and there is a crease in his forehead, and his eyes glitter, and his sensuous mouth gets that slightly cruel twist. The fingers on his right hand were drumming where they rested on his upper arm, a sure sign he was in think mode. I love it when he goes into think mode.

In an idly musing tone, Luke spoke first. "I have not the remotest clue why you're calling me a…duckplucking dicklicker, was it?" He glared down at me. "Aside from that, I didn't think it could be possible, but I'm even unhappier with you now then I was this afternoon."

His last comment broke the spell of my lustful meanderings. I nodded in fervent agreement. "Ha! You're telling me! Why, I positively hated you until one second ago, you disgusting creep. It was duckFUcking, not plucking. Now, come with me."

I took hold of Luke's hand. I forcibly pulled him with me, waving off his glowering "What the hell!" expletive.

Instead, I laughed at his irritated expression. He wasn't done reaming me for not calling him about The Hammer. Well, he would just have to wait before he got to exact his pound of flesh, and I got the fun job of soothing his savage beast.

"Quit bellyaching and come with me. There are a couple of people you absolutely have to meet." I skipped down the hallway with him in tow, urging him to hurry.

"Bellyaching?" Luke repeated ominously. Curious, he allowed me to pull him along, but squeezed my hand in warning that I was pushing it.

Squeezing his hand right back, I grinned at him over my shoulder. Then I couldn't resist stopping to reach up and kiss those delicious lips of his. I pulled back, and lightly stroked my fingertips up and down his lean, bearded cheek. I took in his black scowl.

"You, my big, pissed-off, tail snapping, black panther of a sweet, little kitty cat, are so unbelievably cute!"

Taking advantage of Luke's stunned silence as he processed my latest endearments; I peeked around the corner into the dining area.

I called an urgent "come here" to Jaz and Tre J.

All the men turned to watch as the girls hurriedly worked their way towards me around the crowded table. Their two faces were wearing similar questioning looks at my excited, laughing tone. I was grinning from ear to ear and probably looked looney, but I didn't care.

'This was going to be so good!'

I waved to the room at large. "We'll be right back." I then whispered, "Female stuff."

Predictably, six of the men immediately put their heads down at those words. They all suddenly felt the pressing need to carefully study their cards. Except for my brother, but he was used to female stuff and weird behavior from his sisters. He only cared the girls didn't block his view of the TV for too long.

The other exception was Jazy's friend with the long braid. I was surprised to notice he was slowly scrutinizing me over his cards. When he caught my eye, the man lazily leaned back in his chair and lit a thin cigar. Each slow draw hollowed out his cheeks and accented his strong, prominent bone structure. As he puffed, eyes black as midnight met mine with an inscrutable stare. He didn't do anything overt, yet I felt as if I was being measured or evaluated. He looked down at his cards, but I had the impression he was smiling slightly even though his face hadn't changed expression. Not that his face had an expression to be with.

'Okay then--strike very attractive. He was gorgeous. Jazy better watch her step with this one or she'll be the filly learning new tricks for a change.'

A Date with Fate

Luke was standing impatiently behind me out of sight in the dim hallway. When he went to move, I forgot all about Jazy's potential problems to give his arm another yank.

I hissed on a laugh, "Please, will you stay put for just one blasted minute?"

Luke was literally growling when my sister and friend rounded the doorway.

Tre was first in the hallway. "What's up, Bel?"

I didn't answer immediately, but switched on the overhead hall light.

I stepped aside with a flourish. "Jazy and Tre J, meet Luke Drake!"

I chuckled at Jazy's immediate frown and Tre J's tentative glance of puzzled confusion. I turned to Luke and saw his polite, wary confusion.

"Luke, meet my little sister, Jazy and our good friend, Tre J."

They did the "Hey's" and "Hi's" while I rubbed my hands together.

"So Jazy, does Luke look familiar to you? Have you seen him around town before? Perhaps sitting around somewhere, hmm?"

My sister started chuckling. "No, Anabel. I can honestly say that I have never seen this man before in my life."

Tre J threw me a questioning widening of the eyes. At my smiling nod of affirmation, her confusion cleared. She was soon laughing as hard as Jazy.

Luke stood silently. He coolly observed the women introduced to him laughing like hyenas for no discernable reason. It wasn't very courteous they were laughing at him, but he'd understand why soon enough. It was minor suffering compared to the amount of misery he had caused me for twenty-three minutes and forty-two seconds.

Jazy got control and casually said, "Nice to meet you. I feel like I know you all ready."

Beside her, Tre J choked on her breath. Luke shot her a concerned glance before looking back at Jazy and nodding a curt greeting.

All business now, my sister gave him a quick appraisal. "So, have you boys been playing poker long tonight? Or did you just get here after slipping in through the patio door, and you can't really say what time they started?"

I had no trouble deciphering Luke's glance my way. He thought my sister and her questions were odd. He knew something was overall odd. I couldn't wipe the grin from my face.

He was leery of answering the openly skeptical Jazy. His all ready creased brow lowered more when Tre J took a protective step nearer to me at his hesitation in answering.

"I've been here since about seven tonight." With a smile that didn't reach his eyes, he added dryly, "Through the front door."

The girls visibly relaxed. Jazy disappeared back around the corner without another word. I had no doubt she was off to corroborate his story.

I patted Luke's arm. "Of course you used the front door. Do you have a gun on you, Luke?"

At this non sequitur, Luke was finished cooperating. He put his arm around my waist and spoke to my friend. "Tre J, was it?"

At Tre's wide, brilliant smile Luke paused, struck. He was taking in her Junoesque stature and Mount Olympus beauty. Being one determined and focused man, he resolutely shook it off. "It was…nice meeting you, but would you excuse Anabel and me?"

Without waiting for her answer, he led me back down the hallway the way we'd come.

Over my shoulder I called to Tre. "Goodbye, I'll be with Luke Drake!'

Before returning to join the others, my tall guardian suspiciously watched Luke marching me away. "You scream if you need me."

I laughed as Luke muttered, "Christ."

He opened the door across from the bathroom. He swore when it proved to be a small room impossibly jammed full of boxes and tools.

He pulled me over to the last door and impatiently threw it open. Before this door bounced back off an obstruction and slammed shut in his face; we caught a glimpse of another disorganized room. It was full of random exercise equipment and more boxes. All the boxes were wedged tightly around a pool table heaped high with sporting equipment.

Luke blinked twice at the closed door two inches in front of his face. He had caught a tantalizing vision of a treasure trove. Then he was right back on point and demanding irritably, "What is wrong with your brother? Does he have any rooms that aren't stuffed with crap?"

He was heading for the bathroom door again, and I protested through my laughter. "Wait! Please, not the bathroom again! Not in my brother's house."

Without a word, Luke suddenly turned and kissed me.

There was no soft, leading up kisses and no tenderness. This was explosive and white-hot, and exactly what I needed.

In response to his powerful onslaught, I threw my arms around him. I met his hungry mouth with all the tempestuous emotions I'd kept inside all evening. Somewhere in our impassioned kissing, I was aware of his hands grasping my ass and hiking my body up higher against him. I wrapped my legs around his waist and held on tight for the ride. This was a dangerous, pushed out of control Luke letting go. He didn't give a damn about anything but showing me a thing or two. I thrilled at this side of him, and then I went up in flames and let him consume me.

A Date with Fate

I don't know how many minutes he kissed me, and swore at me in a fierce undertone for driving him crazy. Then he roughly caressed me, all while threatening me with extreme punishments for being in danger. Then he rocked against me with such raw aggression that our wildness caused my head to bang back loudly against the hallway wall.

The thumping sound of my head smacking the wall caused a millisecond of clarity. I remembered we were in an open hallway with ten, noisy people around the corner.

The pain in the back of my head reminded me that I'd lost my mind. Unless I wanted ten, curious people seeing me with my pink, flouncy top twisted up around my neck and my pink, lace bra cups pulled down fully exposing my breasts, I'd better stop Luke before I was stripped naked and done against the wall. I was regretful only my head was getting banged, but I'm not into extreme exhibitionism; or at least not when I'm lucid.

I'm also not into denial, and I wanted to be horizontal. I softly kissed the top of Luke's bent head.

"I asked if you had a gun so we can go somewhere for privacy, but we can get The Hammer if he pops up."

Luke's mouth was on my shoulder and working his way down. It wasn't easy to stop his determined hands while being pinned on the wall like a butterfly with his body as the large, hard push pin.

I felt his tenseness when he slowly returned to reality at my words. He reluctantly let his hands slide off my breasts to hold my hips. He watched my hands with heavy-lidded eyes as I wiggled into my bra and pulled my shirt back down.

His eyes closed briefly while he rubbed his jaw with one hand. After a moment, his eyes opened and he smiled wryly. "Okay, I'm listening. I understood some of what you said, except the hammer popping part."

Unwrapping myself slowly from around his waist, I let my legs slide to the floor. I nudged him slightly away from me, so I could stand on my own two, shaky legs.

"The Hammer is the rapist who tried to kill us tonight. Since I shot at him, Jack took my gun as evidence."

Luke's fingers smoothed escaped strands of my hair back behind my ears. I sighed as one curling length sprang right back again into my eyes. I had to be a mess after the last couple of hours.

His touch was gentle, but I had reminded him of my evening's adventures. He laughed shortly. "Yeah, I've been waiting to hear from you about this guy since Reg told me earlier tonight. The Hammer, huh?" He shook his head and repeated, "Christ."

Curious how he'd respond, I was breezy. "Let's go to your house right now and get your gun. I can tell you there all about what happened tonight."

"Oh, we don't need to go to my house. I always carry my weapon with me. The job, you know." Luke shrugged insouciantly. His voice didn't betray one flicker of hesitation in answering, the little devil.

"Do you have two guns with you?"

"No, but I can get you a weapon tomorrow." He put his hands on my waist and pulled me closer. "Don't you think I can protect you tonight?"

Okay, he was a big devil. "Hmm, weren't you telling me it's better to be prepared?" I gave him my best beguiling smile and ran my hand up his arm. I softly traced and massaged his bicep. I'm fascinated by this man's muscles, so this was no hardship. "You only live right across the road," I lowered my voice, "and we want to be alone, right? I do need a gun, too. Doesn't it seem like a perfect idea to go to your house?" I caressed his other arm. "You don't want me defenseless, do you?"

Restlessly tapping a finger against the wall above me, Luke wouldn't meet my eyes. He was looking down the hallway with a harried air. "Of course, I don't want you defenseless, but I think…"

The look of intense relief on his face when his cell phone buzzed was so damn funny, I had to cover my smile.

Luke took a step away to talk, but I could hear the sound of a deep, strident voice that reminded me of Jack Banner's. I didn't even bother pretending I wasn't all ears, not that it was worth it. The one-sided conversation lasted a few minutes, but Luke was mostly silent on his end.

Luke mainly listened for the first minute and then quietly said, "Yeah, it's covered for tonight. By early morning it will be full on."

He listened again, this time for much longer. He glanced my way and met my eyes, but his expression was closed and revealed nothing.

Into the phone he snorted a humorless laugh. "You have got to be shitting me? No, this is the first I've heard of that." He listened even longer, and then ended the call with, "Not a problem, I should be thanking you. I totally agree. I'll be in touch tomorrow."

After the call, Luke was staring off and scowling, deep in his own thoughts.

I tried for nonchalance when I asked, "Everything okay? Do you have to leave tonight?"

It was obvious he wasn't thrilled with the news he'd just heard. It was also obvious he was choosing his words when he focused on me and answered only the second question.

"I'm not going anywhere tonight."

I only cared he'd be around. It didn't matter right now about his ongoing secrecy concerning anything job related. Normally, I'd figure out the details of a person's job that seemed so top secret, hush-hush long before now. Something strange is happening to me. As our relationship grows deeper, it is now a matter of pride I don't do an end run to know Luke's private business. I certainly don't want unsolicited interference in my business. Sometimes, I get cranky over my stupidly inconvenient sense of fair play, but I have to offer him the same respect. The strange part for me is that I want him to tell me what he can, when he can because he believes I can be trusted. Not due to me playing Sherlock Holmes. Perhaps I needed Dr. Watson to examine my sore head.

I smiled slowly. "I'm so happy to hear that. I'll get my purse and we can go over to your house."

'*Hey, I never said I have a sense of fair play about everything!*'

I started walking up the hallway after this gauntlet. I wanted Luke to voluntarily tell me about the man at his house with Candy, and not be so evasive about absolutely everything. He had done a great job of avoiding, but I was still feeling somewhat battered from the surge of earlier negative emotions from my past, and from believing Luke was a total, cousin-humping loser.

Is it too much to ask for reassurance he valued honesty between us when confronted directly?

I don't think so, either.

I heard his impatient sigh behind me. "Wait a second, Anabel."

I faced him and waited.

He ran a hand through his hair as he came towards me. "It's not cool to go to my house tonight. I have an out-of-town friend staying there and he's not expecting me back until late."

I remained silent and waited.

He threw his hands out. "Do you have to drag every word out of me? He's got a woman over and I don't want to take you there, okay?"

I cocked my head inquisitively to the side, and still I waited.

Luke fixed me with a glare. "You wanted to know, so don't blame the messenger. It's your cousin, Candy MacKenzie."

I nodded encouragingly. "So?"

He sighed in resignation. "When I was at your store this afternoon, my friend was waiting at Rueb's. He met your cousin there. He informed me later he'd made plans to hook up tonight and was staying back at my place." He paused, weighing his next words. "My friend's not a very nice guy to women. He relentlessly goes after anything on two legs for sex, and most girls end up hating his guts."

I chuckled at his wary look, as if I may haul off and slap him for Candy's sake at his friend's predatory sexual practices.

Relaxing, Luke smiled a little. "I don't claim to know your cousin, but she probably doesn't deserve John. I love the guy and he's got my back. I can trust him with my life, but then again," he made a rueful face, "he doesn't want to fuck me and run."

Laughing at the man-whore description of his friend, I took the last two steps to Luke and wrapped my arms around his middle. I snuggled close and ran my hands up and down his strong back. I'm blissfully contented at this moment in time, even withstanding the fact I'm really tired of enduring interrupted make-out sessions.

I grinned up at him. "Oh, believe me; your friend John deserves her. I won't let Candy near my back. It's been her life's work to fuck me and run, any chance she gets."

Luke cupped my shoulders and held me away from him. "I thought your family meant everything to you. That's why I didn't want to tell you Candy was with John."

My smile was huge. "I can't stand her! He can do anything he wants to her with my blessings."

Luke seemed a little unnerved by my cheerful declaration. Then he gave me the squint eye. "Which reminds me, what's with saying you hated me earlier?" He added dryly, "And calling me a dicklicking whatever?"

"I did say something like that, didn't I?"

"Yes, you did." He raised his brows. "Do I want to know why?"

"Since you are definitely a man, normally you would not. Tonight is an exception. You will be incredibly pleased why I took your name in vain for a solid twenty-three minutes when I hated on you."

Luke laughed softly, rubbing his warm hands up and down my bare arms. "Anabel, trust me, I will never be pleased if you hate on me, but go on and tell me why the hell you did."

"I didn't call you earlier tonight because I'd asked Tre to drop me off at your house after playing bumper cars with the rapist." I nodded knowingly at his surprised expression and spreading grin. "Uh huh, see what I meant about you being pleased? Guess what else I did?"

"What?" Luke pulled me close again, his face as lighthearted as I've ever seen. For once, there was not a dark look, or severe frown, or cruel mouth in sight.

I stood on tiptoes within his arms and kissed his smiling lips, savoring the moment. Knowing me, it won't be too long before he's 'disappointed' again. I'm shamelessly taking full advantage of the lull and basking in his affection.

Even though it's against the rules of womanhood to reveal our secrets, I couldn't resist bragging a little. "I did a classic move tonight. We ninja'd your house. It was so much fun! Up until we saw Candy's stupid car, that is." I gave him a stern look when he started laughing at me. "Pay attention here. This is the start of the me-hating-on-you part. Jazy snuck out and investigated. She peeped in your windows and then reported back to us."

A Date with Fate

I shook his arms. "Stop laughing. Now, this is why I also called you a disgusting creep. She peeped on some gross sexual action going down in your living room. Jazy told me you were not platonic friends with my cousin. I hated you, but it wasn't you, and so here we are."

Luke shook his head while openly smirking. "I'm worried about my manhood. Not only did I follow everything you said with no problems; I'm shaking in my boots thinking what you may have done in revenge to poor, innocent me. I'm relieved the mix-up got cleared up so fast," his sparkling green eyes narrowed at me, "and that I passed your little test just now." He snorted. "It had all the makings of a farce."

I momentarily set aside his bashing of my storytelling abilities. I also set aside his foolish disrespect for the scary depths of my revenge capabilities. The "little test" reference I would wisely disregard permanently. Instead, I looked up at him in amazement.

"Hey, I just said that to Anna this afternoon!"

"Now I feel better. I'm confused again." Luke murmured with heavy sarcasm.

'Okay, that was it. Game on. You know me and sarcasm.'

I put on a dreamy smile and patiently explained. "You and I both used the word "farce" today, Luke. How often is that word even used in the world, much less by two people that are dating?" I gushed on, "It must mean we are metaphysically linked and thinking on the same wavelength. Do you suppose we knew each other in a previous life?" I put my hands to my heart. "I've always been convinced I was a princess. What do you think you were? Wait a sec--don't tell me. Hmm, I could see you as a dark prince. You'd be wearing black tights and one of those teeny-tiny codpieces covering your privates. How cute would that be? What's your sign, anyway?" I gazed at him adoringly, even as I implored, "Whatever you do, please don't tell me you are a boring Virgo. I hope you are a Leo. Leo men are so dramatically hot. I'm meant to be with a Leo man, or an Aries man. A Gemini could work. Have you ever told me your birthday?" Not waiting for an answer, I asked in a hushed voice brimming with portent, "Luke, do you think you are my spiritual destiny, my soul mate?"

I saw the initial wince of horror flash over Luke's face that I could be one of those alternative, horoscope-reading females—and this on top of a risk-taking, shit-kicking loose cannon. I barely kept my worshipful expression in place. Then his flash of horror was instantly replaced by a donned mask of careful interest to humor my cute, if nutty, beliefs. I bit my tongue--hard.

"My birthday is August 6th. I haven't thought about it much, but I guess I believe in spiritual destiny."

I couldn't hold back. At my peal of wicked laughter, Luke's whole body stilled. Then his eyebrows lowered. "Clearly you don't have a soul, Anabel, so that's a pointless question."

"A valid point, Dark Prince, but I couldn't resist! Hey, now where are you taking me?"

"Horoscopes aside, we need to talk." Luke expressionless voice was calm and serious.

Not liking the sound of that, I reluctantly followed as he led me down the hallway by the hand. This time it was back towards the living room. Luke didn't take me to join the crowd in the smoky dining area, but turned right.

At the front door, he stopped. His face had that detached look again. I didn't like that look.

"I know how you value keeping your personal life private. I respect you. I wasn't going to take you openly out to my truck to the only place it seems we can be uninterrupted."

Opening the door, he checked out the porch and then turned back to me. "But clearly we need to talk about a few things. These issues are too important to ignore. One of them is a deal-breaker. Your privacy and my respect will have to take a back seat because it needs to be addressed immediately."

"What issues do you mean?" I asked cautiously, nervous at his serious, cool tone. I wondered if he was still mad at me not calling about The Hammer incident tonight.

Luke held my shoulders and looked deep into my eyes. "I won't put up with any crap from you about this." I gasped up at him in surprise. He gave a sharp nod. "You heard me right, Anabel, so listen very carefully. You've got me completely confused with some other Prince if you think my codpiece would be 'teeny-tiny'."

After a shocked second, I bubbled over with surprised laughter, pushing with both hands at the chest of the devilishly grinning man in front of me.

He shrugged a shoulder, still smiling. "I couldn't resist, either."

We didn't get a chance to take another step before several voices called to us, halting us in our tracks on the threshold of the front door. Startled at our audience of ten, I quickly turned out of Luke's hands to face them.

"Where are you two going? Anabel, shouldn't you stay here under our protection?" Tre yelled the loudest.

A few of the other men sang this chorus, catcalling and giving Luke good-natured crap to get back to the poker game instead of chasing after me.

Sam Sheedy's distinctive voice was starting to slur from too many beers. "Drake, come on, we've been waiting. Get your ass in here so I can win my money back."

Luke and I shared a quick smirk over those ridiculous words. I didn't feel like smirking any longer when Jazy, with Reg a step behind her,

A Date with Fate

walked into the living room. Their bodies blocked us from view of the rowdy, shouting bunch in the dining room.

Luke's mouth twitched at hearing my little sigh of frustrated exasperation at being denied our escape when we were so close. His hand behind me privately soothed over the curve of my ass and squeezed lightly. This did not help.

"Tre's right." After shooting Luke a dismissive glance, Jazy ignored him and spoke directly to me. "It's the smart choice to stay here tonight with us to be safe, not off with one man. We've all decided the best operating plan is for us to know where you are at all times. No more taking off on your own, okay? We're not leaving you alone and unprotected until this killer is caught."

Luke face was expressionless at Jazy's attitude. His lack of reaction spoke loudly to me. In defense of my sister's plain speaking; she knew nothing about him. She didn't assume he could protect me like my own family would. Although, I must admit, even if she knew more about Luke's abilities she still wouldn't trust him with my life.

Jasmyn goes through men like tissues. She has no concerns if they are single or married. She doesn't let the minor detail men are involved in committed relationships get in her way when she sets her sights on them. If she can sway them to cheat; that is their lack of character problem, and not hers. It was understandable Jaz doesn't have the highest opinion of a man's reasoning and reliability capabilities. She causes them too regularly to lose their heads and make poor decisions. It was one of those vicious circle scenarios.

Plus, we Axelrod's have a slight tendency to stick together and depend only on ourselves at crunch times.

I don't know if Luke planned on responding to Jazy's implication he was some random idiot that couldn't find his ass with two hands, or protect me if I was alone with him, but Reggie hurriedly jumped in.

He looked curiously from me to Luke. "Where were you two going?"

I glanced quickly at Luke. His eyes were glowing with malicious amusement against the bronzed skin of his face. His slight arch of an eyebrow told me he was leaving it up to me to tell my family members what I wanted them to know. As an only child, and a grown man in his thirties, it had probably been a long time since Luke had to answer to anybody over his actions. The wicked man was enjoying my predicament.

I sighed again, this time in defeat. The habit was too ingrained in me to keep my private life private. Besides, I shouldn't take stupid risks. I'd be endangering Luke, too, and not just myself. The measurements needed to settle the dispute of the princely codpiece dimensions would have to wait.

I answered my brother truthfully. "We were not leaving. We were just going out to Luke's truck to check out a little something." Luke snorted, and I quickly changed the subject. "I haven't even had a chance to tell him what happened earlier tonight."

Reggie cast Luke a quizzical look, as if he was also starting to question Luke's smarts. "Why don't you wait for Luke inside and let him go check his truck by himself? You probably don't even have a coat, do you?" He shook his blonde head in exasperation and held out an arm. "Come into the kitchen and I'll fix you a drink. Then we can get back to the game." He brought out the big guns. "I have brownies, Junior. Frosted brownies."

"What color frosting?" I asked, taking a small step towards my brother.

"Hell, they're brownies--black, of course."

Jazy's relief at my easy capitulation was evident. "See Bel, doesn't that sound good? You love chocolate frosted brownies. Do you want to play poker, too?" She added snidely, "I know all the boys are waiting for Luke to remember why he came over here tonight."

Hearing Luke's low snigger at our well-intentioned, interfering gatekeepers, I hoped his dark amusement meant he wasn't too offended at my sibling's aspersions on his lack of character and choices. Actually, I was plenty offended enough for the both of us. They were treating me like I needed to be talked down from the ledge.

Giving her a warning nudge, Reggie interrupted Jaz again. "Yeah, they do want Luke to come back and play. He's got all their cash." He snapped his fingers. "I know, the guys will get started playing cards again, and I'll tell Luke all about what happened earlier tonight. You and Jazy can get everyone drinks."

"Why would you be the one to tell Luke about what happened tonight when you weren't even there?" Seeing Jazy's elaborate eye roll, the truth dawned. I glared at my brother. "You don't care if I go off anywhere and get killed by a crazy rapist. You only want Luke to get back to playing poker!"

Reggie held up his hands in denial and laughed, dimples flashing. "Now, Junior, that's just not true! You did tell me the pertinent facts, and I wouldn't be an Axelrod if I couldn't easily make up the rest."

Feeling like a crabby preschooler for the second time in an hour, I irritably suggested to the grinning Luke that he go play freaking cards. I informed them all I needed to use the bathroom—alone. I snatched my purse up. I started walking back past the trio of grinning baboons, but not before I used my gift and had the last word.

I stopped and opened a door in the living room near the hall. "Luke didn't know this door led upstairs to your big, uncluttered bedroom area. He really wants a tour to see how much privacy you get up there, Reg."

Walking away down the hall, my bat-like hearing caught my confused brother saying dubiously, "Okay…umm…do you want a tour of my bedroom right now, Luke?"

Chuckling soullessly while using the bathroom with the utmost relief, one voice was still doing back flips and high kicks like a deranged cheerleader in my mind.

'Yippee! Hooray! Luke hadn't betrayed me! I hadn't misjudged him!'

There was much cheering and rejoicing in this vein until the measured voice of the practical accountant piped in to put a stop to any more emotional nonsense.

This calm voice was saying that while all of the above was accurate, I needed to slow down, add things up, and study the bottom line. Was the farce with Candy a wakeup call I needed to answer?

On the left hand, was I ready for the first time in a decade to make a decision to keep going forward with a man at this level of intensity?

On the right hand, should I use tonight's misery as a lesson and protect myself by backing up a giant step and ending things between Luke and me on a good note? Before one of us does hurt the other?

Somewhat disheartened I was having a dreaded relationship discussion, if only with myself, I finished my business. Washing my hands, I had a brilliant thought that had me grinning at my messy, windblown image in the mirror.

While I teased my hair and fixed my pony tail, and then reapplied my lip gloss, I mulled over an amazingly simple concept. I could do all my thinking with that favorite area between my legs. I could keep my interaction with Prince Muscles all about the S-E-X.

After all, this was an area where our compatibility together required no calculation and was as combustible as a Fourth of July fireworks finale.

When Fate didn't constantly cock block us, that is.

Chapter XVI
"Giving Him Something He Can Feel" by En Vogue

Sunday, 11/18/12
6:00 AM

Somebody had left on the lamp all night that sat on the end table in the corner between the two sofas. Except for this soft glow above me, the living room was draped in shadows when I opened my eyes. It was still dark outside. Sunrise wasn't for another hour.

I'd definitely woken up on the wrong side of the couch. I felt testy and not my usual sunny self. I was finally horizontal with Luke. Too bad it was in my brother's living room. Tre and Jazy were snoozing away on the other sofa. Their heads were at opposite ends, and Jazy appeared to have commandeered their shared blankets. She had them clutched up possessively to her chin. She lay on her side, perched precariously close to the edge to accommodate Tre's larger bulk. It seemed like a fair trade in discomfort.

I was half lying on my back, partially on top of Luke behind me. His arms were loosely around my waist. My legs were stretched out between both of his, and my head rested on a small pillow nestled in the crook of his neck and shoulder. It was very comfortable. I still felt snappish.

I peered over the edge of the cushion to figure out what the loud racket was coming from that direction. It was that blasted Sam Sheedy. He was zipped to the neck in a sleeping bag directly along the sofa below me, and snoring up a storm. The noises he was making sounded like a wild animal caught in a trap. His wide-open, slack mouth was not the most attractive sight to see at any time, but definitely not before my first cup of coffee. If I had any change on me, it'd be tempting to drop a penny down the well of his gaping maw and wish him to shut the hell up. I laid my head back down in annoyance.

I'd gone from never having sleepovers in years to waking up two days in a row next to the same man--this second time appearing to be a veritable pajama party.

Last I remembered was listening to the girls debating the perfect crime disposal method of a butchered body (namely Cheryl Crookston) while I was industriously licking chocolate frosting off my fingers. We were sprawled on the sofas after getting smoked out of the dining room. I had no desire to play poker last night and, after sitting restlessly for a few

A Date with Fate

minutes with the boys, forced the girls to come with me into the living room. They wanted to protect me and keep me indoors; they could damn well follow where I lead.

We'd raided Reggie's closet for T shirts to sleep in. The girls also borrowed boxers that I hoped were jokey gifts Reg had received. I didn't want to think my brother would seriously wear a pair of undies that said, "Here pussy, pussy" across the front. My borrowed shirt hit my knees, so I skipped the boxers. We'd arranged pillows and blankets on the sofas. We found a fan to drown out the poker playing noise and cracked a window to get some fresh air. After arming ourselves with beers for Tre and Jazz, a hard cider for me, filling a bowl full of potato chips, and snagging the whole pan of black frosted brownies--we were ready for a slumber party.

I must have been more exhausted from all the fun events of the day than I realized. I didn't move a muscle when Luke joined me on my makeshift bed. I missed knowing I was horizontal with him all night. I couldn't believe he didn't wake me up. Also, several people had to know he thought he had the right to sleep with me. That was part of the reason I wasn't my usual chipper self.

Another reason was thinking over the text I'd received last night from Mike McClain. I had no idea what could be so important that he needed five minutes of my time. We've had no contact for years, so what could possibly be of any significance between us at this point? I wasn't happy with the cryptic drama of his message, but I figured I'd hear him out if it didn't inconvenience me. I didn't want the man in my life, but I was way over any feelings for him other than indifference.

I was also ornery knowing I had to deal with Candy on my weekend off. I don't go looking for confrontations, but I won't back down from one either. She wasn't getting away with stealing the gun from my apartment, fortuitous or not. She'd probably continue trying to avoid seeing me, yellow-bellied coward that she was, but I didn't want to put it off. Since I wasn't chasing her down; I had to orchestrate a meet. It made sense it would need to be at the family dinner tonight. She'd smugly think there was safety in such numbers, and that I'd be too busy being hostess with the mostest to get her.

This made me think about her hook-up at Luke's last night. Again, not an enticing image anytime, but especially bad before the morning caffeine. Maybe I'd ask Luke to bring his weekend guest, John the Fuck-and-Runner, to liven things up tonight. I'd sic Jaz and Tre on him.

That thought alleviated a little of my crabbiness.

Then thinking about The Hammer possibly hunting me even as I lay here spiked the cranky levels back up again.

I carefully turned around in Luke's arms and faced my sneaky prince. I propped up my head with my left arm and studied his sleeping form in the soft light from the lamp. Our blanket was pulled partially up to his waist, but one muscular leg stuck out over both of mine. He had on a T shirt and undecorated boxers. The white shirt was in stark contrast to his dark skin and the light trail of silky black chest hair revealed by the V neckline. I could see the brown, flat discs of his nipples clearly through the thin fabric. Even in repose, his biceps were cut with muscle. I clutched the bottom hem of my shirt to stop myself from reaching my free hand up to trace their outline.

I know being infatuated can be explained as an actual biochemical reaction occurring in the body. But if I found out I also suffered from the ongoing, extreme reactions the psycho-babblers termed Limerence; it would be the last straw. I'd commit the Hokey-Pokey, Hari-Kari hands down versus mooning endlessly over Luke the way I was right now. Even his short beard was a turn on to me, and I hate beards.

"What are you looking at, Princess?" Luke asked softly without opening his eyes. I smiled at his use of my royal title, so in tune with my own thoughts of him a moment ago.

"Please, it's Princess Ruffles." I whispered in correction.

On the floor behind me were wild thrashing noises. Sam Sheedy gasped, choked, and snorted like a huge pig at the trough before groaning and falling back asleep.

Eyes still closed, Luke swore succinctly. "That prick kept me up all night."

I smiled and leaned back. I gave in and trailed my hand up his arm. "So, you can see with your eyes closed? What else do you have? X-ray vision?"

Luke opened one eye and squinted down the length of my body. His hands tightened on my hips, squeezing. "Yes, Princess Muffles, I can see through your shirt. It's useless as cover. Take it off."

I didn't take it off, but I did slowly lift the thin material up high in the front so that I wasn't the only one doing some endless, infatuated mooning.

"It's Ruffles, Princess Pink Ruffles, to be precise." I then answered his original question. "I was just looking at you. I like you in a beard and longer hair."

I left my shirt hiked up while I trailed my fingers lazily down from his arm and over my exposed bare breasts. My thumb lightly brushed over a soft nipple and I felt the tip hardening. "I've been wondering why you are looking so…drug dealerish since I saw you last."

Luke's focus was concentrated solely on watching my wandering, plucking fingers when he murmured absently, "I needed to look like a dirtbag for a couple of weeks." He took his left hand off my hip and rested it on his thigh. "Have I told you lately how much I love how you mind me, Princess Fink Ruffles?"

A Date with Fate

"Mmm...Dirtbag, it's Pink, not Fink. Is this what you had in mind for me?" My fingers continued playing over my skin. They strolled unimpeded down my side, and spread across my stomach before moving lower. I lingered along the top of the narrow strip of tight silk barely deserving the name panty. I stroked one finger leisurely up and down the middle of my lips. I allowed my long fingernail to slip under the edge, and then paused.

My voice was low. "Of course you got the bad guys."

"Don't stop. I want to see you touch yourself."

I waited. A few beats of silence later he answered. "Yes. Of course I got the bad guys."

I smiled a little at his arrogant, impatient murmur. I dipped my finger all the way under my panty and lightly petted myself.

I wiggled my hips a fraction.

Luke moved his heavy leg off mine, stretching out full length on his side and facing me with his back against the sofa. Freed, I lifted my right leg slightly, sliding my foot up the sheet covered cushion towards my left knee. Luke decided I needed to move my leg higher. He put a hand around my ankle and brought my foot up, planting it flat above his slightly bent knee. The draping blanket covered me completely along my backside and raised leg. It created our own little world. As long as we were quiet and moved slowly, nobody would know what we were doing.

Luke's other arm under me glided down. His hand started caressing and kneading my ass with strong fingers. Then I felt those long fingers reaching. They slipped under my panties and touched me from behind. He began rubbing my wetness over my own finger stroking deeper between my parted legs. I moved the tiny swatch of silk to the side so Luke could see how well I was minding him.

Luke glanced up from staring between my thighs and smiled lazily. "You're right. It is Princess Pink Ruffles."

I had to close my eyes and suck on my bottom lip to keep my answering, moaning laugh contained. My left hand clutched onto Luke's arm. It was maddening having to hold my hips perfectly still to avoid detection. Every instinct was clamoring to rock and writhe against the fingers rubbing and flickering over Queen Victoria. Like good managers everywhere, I believe firmly in immediate feedback. I have been known to tell Luke if I like his performance on the job by screaming and cursing his name to the heavens, or threatening horrific consequences if he stops.

I stayed quiet even when Luke started doing my third, or maybe fourth, most favorite thing in the world; he began toying with my breasts with his other hand not busy between my legs. Without haste, he ran the back of his hand over my stiffened nipples. He languidly teased, and then captured one distended point between two fingers. I somehow remained silent, but I couldn't help arching my back for more when those fingers tightened their grip. His clever fingers pinched and pulled one erect peak and then moved to the other, each time squeezing a little harder and tugging a little farther. I swear the man has magic fingers; he seems to touch me precisely how I desperately need it, even before I know I do.

Call me weak, but when Luke's finger down below started dipping and circling, and then slowly penetrated from behind in my tied-for-third-place favorite move; I did moan softly in the back of my throat. It was torturous ecstasy. I went AWOL'ing. I thought hazily if there truly was a God; men would have been given three hands.

I don't think my low moan was noticeable over the noisy snores from the floor behind us. When Luke added a second, large finger while his wonderfully intuitive thumb stayed busy, my louder moan was in sync with some loud choking and gasping from Sam.

I slipped my hand out from inside my panties and into Luke's tented boxers. My hand could only form a C around his hard on instead of an O, but I could live with this problem.

When I pulled his eager penis out to play through the front panel of his boxers, I smiled with empathy into his eyes at his tense expression. He was having a great time, too, trying not to move against my firm grip and slow wrist action.

Looking down, the creamy drop glistening on the tip of his cock beckoned. I massaged it all over while pulling on the thick head. I stroked around the rim, and under. I loved how Luke's penis felt like hot, silky velvet sheathed over the hardness of steel.

Luke's hand left off fondling my breasts and glided under the covers to join the other cupping my ass. Both hands explored and fondled QV from behind; his two lubricious fingers inside me moving to the slow rhythm of my fist moving up and down on his dick.

He drew me up against his lounging body stretched out along the sofa. With my leg canted up on his thigh, the hard length of his erection in my hand was added to the mix of his fingers and thumbs. Forehead tilted against mine, it took Luke only a few deliberate, rubbing strokes for the friction against my clit to send me on my way to orgasm heaven. Tingling, I stiffened. Clenching spasmodically around his fingers, I tried not to cry out, tried not to move. Luke kissed me with a deep thrust of his tongue. The rippling waves of pleasure kept building throughout my body, even as I craved to feel the large fingers inside me replaced with his thicker, much larger erection.

My mind-reader consort was still on my wavelength. He pulled his fingers out from inside me to tightly grip my bottom. He entered me with his cock, slowly thrusting in and out until he worked fully inside me. Then he stopped. I groaned against Luke's mouth at the incredibly tight, stretched almost-too-full sensation that was just what I desired. The waves peaked and crested. I came and came gloriously around him buried deeply

A Date with Fate

inside me. He growled low in my ear how the feel of me gripping and clenching around his dick was driving him crazy.

Luke and I froze at the same moment. We both reared back a few inches to stare into each other's faces in mutual, shocked disbelief. He was inside me to the hilt, skin on skin and unprotected.

I couldn't tell from Luke's still face and quickly lowered eyes what he was thinking, but I was dazed and freaked. I have never allowed a man's penis to penetrate Vicky unprotected, not even as a virgin queen with Mike McClain. I wasn't kidding when I said I wasn't a trusting soul and was never *that* young or *that* innocent.

Sam Sheedy chose this inopportune moment to erupt on the floor like the reenactment of Mount Vesuvius destroying Pompeii.

Jazy sat up and threw her pillow at him while shouting, "THAT'S IT! I have had it, you damn, snoring fuckhead! Wake up, Tre! Come on, we are leaving this hell-hole!"

My sister stood up and swiped a kick at the spluttering, befuddled Sam in his sleeping bag, grabbed her things off the end table, and marched off down the hall towards the bathroom. She yelled over her shoulder, "Anabel, get up---we're out of here in five!"

I quickly pulled my long T shirt down in front as best I could. Luke's face was against my neck. His shoulders silently shook and his dick throbbed inside me and his hands still squeezed my ass and he held me close.

I didn't know if he was laughing or crying, but flustered, I pushed at his shoulder. I hissed under my breath, "I can't believe we did that! Let me go!"

His hair was a disheveled mess from my hands. His sensual mouth was twisted with sexual frustration, but as Luke leaned back, the eyes that met mine were tear-free and lit with laughter. He slid his hands up from under the covers and respectably cupped my shoulders. With a smile as slow as his withdrawal, Luke didn't take his eyes off my face as he pulled out of me inch by inch. My hands clasping his forearms, I closed my eyes and went still at the sensation. The receding aftershocks of my personal seismic activity continued to shake me up inside. It caused me to clench and grip him harder, instinctively wanting him to stay put.

"Stop it, Anabel." He ordered softly on a laughing groan.

"No." I murmured, not opening my eyes.

Tre J sat up, swinging her legs to the floor and pulling the blanket over her lap. Yawning wide she asked, "What's going on? Was that Jazy yelling or was it a dream?"

As Luke circumspectly adjusted his boxers, Sam sat up right behind me.

"That's what I want to know! I was sleeping when she woke me up with her bitching." Affronted, he whined, "Can you believe she kicked me?"

I slid up to a sitting position until my back was leaning on the rolled arm rest of the sofa. Luke sat up beside me and brought his longer legs to the floor beyond the end of Sam's sleeping bag below us.

"Hey, watch what you say about my sister. You're lucky I don't kick you, too, the way you snore like a banshee." I threatened Sam without heat, lazily aiming my foot at his shoulder while running my hands through my hair and working out the tangles.

Sam avoided my foot and glared at me. "What? You women are nuts--I don't snore!"

I raised my brows.

He was starting to protest more volubly when he caught sight of Luke's hand slicing the air. Correctly reading the dark look on his face, Sam Sheedy wisely decided to shut up. I was going to have to learn that part karate chop-part snarl move for at the store with unruly customers.

Tre J went for her turn in the bathroom just as Jazy opened the door and came out. Jaz was dressed and no longer resembled the scary medusa of a few minutes ago.

I got up on my knees and reached over the back of the sofa to close the open window letting in the draft of cold air. I turned back and caught Jazy flipping off Sam Sheedy before continuing her way into the kitchen. My little sis is definitely the grudge holder in the family.

Unable to avoid it any longer, I looked over at Luke.

We stared at each other warily without speaking. Sam stood up, grumbling under his breath, and gathered his belongings. We were alone a minute later when he stomped off to wait his turn in the hallway for the bathroom.

Silently, Luke put on his jeans. Looking down to fasten his belt he said gruffly, "Listen, about…" he straightened up and made a waving motion at his groin area, "earlier. That's never happened before, but I'm okay with it. We should probably talk about some things." His face was serious when he met my eyes. "I trust you."

My amazed, "Really?" burst out before I thought to stop it.

Luke's eyebrows were meeting in a black frown when the door to the upstairs opened and Reggie came whistling into the living room.

"Good morning, friends and family! Looks like those dickheads got the weather report wrong again; there is not one flake of snow outside. Frigging unbelievable, isn't it? To get paid the big bucks to be so routinely wrong."

My brother wakes up like me; disgustingly, cheerfully chipper in the dawns early light. Or more accurately, like I used to wake up.

A Date with Fate

"Junior, when do you want to get going? Jazy said I have first shift, so my Sunday is cleared to make sure you don't get murdered today before three o'clock."

I was grateful for Reg's typical, bull-in-the-china-shop entrance. I was touched he was going to keep me from dying; at least during first shift.

I jumped up eagerly and scrambled into my slacks. I'd go anywhere at this particular moment to avoid talking with Luke. It didn't take a genius to get he might be feeling a tad disappointed with me again. I had inadvertently implied he couldn't trust me. I was too confused over my own actions and feelings to want to get into it now.

Reaching on the floor for my purse, I opened an inside compartment.

I answered my brother, equally chipper. "I'm ready to go when you are, Reg. I have a ton of stuff to do this morning at home." I babbled on, "Except for needing to make a grocery grab, my plan is to stay home today. If you want, we can hang out at the apartment and watch football this afternoon."

Reg was taken aback at my enthusiasm to get going so fast, but his expression showed immense relief at my proposed plans. "Sure, I'll need a little time to do a couple things, but then we'll go. An afternoon of football sounds better than a sharp stick in the eye."

Eyeing him thoughtfully, I realized I should have led him on first and said I wanted to go shopping at the Mall of America. I really was rattled. I popped a piece of cinnamon gum in my mouth. It would have to do until I got home to my shower and toothbrush.

I looked up to offer Luke a piece.

He quickly gave me a neutral, inquiring look, but he wasn't in time. I pretended I hadn't noticed the quick exchange of smirking grins and self-satisfied nods between Luke and Reg. Throwing him the gum, I shook my head at their conspiring together over their covert protection plans.

'Did it seem like I wanted to die? Did they ever think to tell me straight out what the plan was and why? Men can be such idiots.'

I really wished now I'd take a minute to string Reggie along and make him work up a sweat to get me to follow their plan. I shrugged it off with my own private smirk. One thing I could count on; there would never be a loss of opportunities to terrorize the men in my life for my own viewing pleasure.

Luke announced he had things to do today and needed to get going. I felt relief he was leaving, and relief he didn't seem mad at my avoiding any talks. It was nice he'd shown me his medical report weeks ago, and nice that he trusted me, but my head was still spinning. I could not believe that I forgot myself enough to let a naked Lawrence of Mylabia anywhere near Vicky. Or that Luke had forgotten himself.

Snagging his leather jacket off the hall tree, Luke shrugged into it while I walked him to the front door. We were alone again. Everyone was busy in the bathroom or kitchen. I heard the welcome gurgling of a coffee maker.

I gave in to curiosity. "Do you think Candy will still be at your house with your guest, John?"

He snorted. "Candy being on Pluto has a greater chance of happening."

I liked that answer.

He gave me a lingering cinnamon kiss and then stuck his hands in his jacket pockets. He regarded me a moment before asking, "You're cool staying with Reggie today? You feel safe enough?'

"Yeah, I'm sure it will be fine, but thanks for asking." I was a little surprised he hadn't offered to spend the day with me, but it was probably better this way. It sounded like we both had things to do.

I didn't tell Luke, but I had toyed with the idea of closing the store for today. I was nervous as hell with The Hammer running around out there plotting my demise. Last night before we left The Rock's parking lot, Jack said two plainclothes cops would guard the doors inside Bel's for the Sunday store hours. Even with the police presence, I still thought I'd be doing my employees and customers a disservice by opening today versus closing the store. I could always cite a broken water pipe needing repairs.

The problem with this line of thought was what if it took days to catch Hammerschmidt? I couldn't stay closed for more than today—even one day would impact my profit line unfavorably. Not that an employee, or customer, or yours truly getting killed wouldn't have a somewhat negative impact on the business, as well.

I needed to man up, go on the offensive, and be bait to help facilitate The Hammer's capture. Closing up shop and hiding was tempting, but it wasn't the answer. It didn't mean I would parade around town with a big target on my back. I figured since he was out of jail only recently and had immediately tried to attempt a kidnapping and murder, brains wasn't his long suit. For some reason, Gustav Hammerschmidt had set his psycho mind on me last night. He knew where I lived and worked. If I didn't make myself publically available as an easier target, he'd come to me at my home.

I reminded Luke dinner was at five. I grinned and invited John to tag along. Luke smiled at that and said he'd pass on the invite, but wasn't sure of John's plans.

He didn't leave, but stood staring down at the floor. When he raised his eyes and I saw his implacable expression it made me uneasy at what was coming.

A Date with Fate

"Listen, Anabel. We are going to talk."

'I knew it! Damn.'

He tilted my chin up and stroked a thumb along my cheek. "Tonight after everyone leaves your apartment, I plan on staying over for second and third shift guard duty, alright? We'll talk then. I promise it won't hurt," he nipped my bottom lip, "much."

I tried to smile while keeping my eyes closed, waiting for another kiss and less talk.

Luke snickered. "Anabel, Anabel, my strange and different woman. I want you to think about two things today for me, okay?"

I opened my eyes, curiosity winning out. He softly tapped my chin. "One, I *know* you. I've recognized you since the minute I first laid eyes on you in your store last spring." He paused, smiling faintly. "Why do you think I stayed away for months?"

His steady gaze held mine while his surprising declarations twirled through my head. I turned my cheek into his hand while nodding again without answering. I didn't know what to say. I admit to experiencing a romantic thrill at his unshakeable tone of confidence. What woman wouldn't want to be told they were known in such a way, by such a man, and only moments after returning from subspace at his touch? I hadn't given much thought to why I hadn't seen him from the first glimpse last April in my store until late September at my brother's house. I was speechless he'd stayed away deliberately. I couldn't help but wonder why he had, and what made him change his mind. Maybe talking later could be interesting, but I felt too confused to say anything now.

His words did send a longing through me. Maybe he was a man who could want and accept me as I truly am. Maybe he had been showing me all along how he knew me, and I was only now starting to be able to see. Maybe he did *know* me.

It would be nice to be known.

Luke pulled his other hand from his pocket. It held a sealed, white envelope with my first name scrawled across the front in a black, bold script. The envelope was the size of a small birthday card. I was only the teeniest bit curious about what was on the inside.

"This is the second thing I want you to think about today." His eyes were gleaming dark with secret promise. I was struck anew by how attractive I found Luke, even though I knew many men much better looking. He slowly waved the envelope to and fro. "This is my turn."

I sighed with the boredom of it all. With careless unconcern, I reached for the envelope.

Luke held it aloft out of my reach. The tricky man effortlessly held it higher when I unashamedly climbed his body quicker than a spider monkey and jumped for the card. Twice.

White teeth flashed as he laughingly shook his head. "Not so fast. In order to receive this envelope, you have to agree to some basic conditions."

Standing back with my hands on my hips, I felt my own smile blossoming wider. "I can't believe you had that in your pocket all evening! I can see you may need frisking in the future. Okay, I'm listening."

"Anabel, to accept this card, you must first give me your word you will follow these rules." He tapped his finger on the envelope in emphasis. "You will not open the card until I tell you to open it. You will do precisely what it says to do, and follow any and all instructions. No exceptions." Luke eyes were intent on mine. "Will you do this?"

My eyes widened in return. I realized I was a little apprehensive what his fantasy might be from these terms he listed. I licked my lips nervously as visions of Torquemada's dungeons danced through my head—and not like sugarplums. There's no way I was getting racked, or branded, or hung up on a hook somewhere like a side of beef. I had images of tools, and knives, and Makita drills. If my tough brother cried like a woman over a finishing nail, I didn't stand a chance against a scalpel or an electric cattle prod. Luke had seemed a little too casual over the subject of spankings yesterday. If he thought he could smack my ass until it chafed and me with no petroleum products, he had another thing coming. These sorts of tortuous fantasies did not put me in a positive frame of mind for fun and frolics, or oath swearing.

I gathered my hair and twisted it on top of my head as I thought. I desperately wanted to ask for my caveats, get my reassurances nothing would hurt, or be told of a safety zone. I wanted to rip the envelope in half to end my fears, and then I wanted to grab it and rip it open to begin his turn.

Then I was thinking of the first thing Luke wanted me to think about today.

He claimed to *know* me.

I believe I know him, too.

If you know somebody, you put their motives, needs, and desires ahead of your own in certain situations. You let go and trust them a little bit not to be a torturing psychopath.

This was Luke's turn. This was his secret fantasy I was going to find out. For him, the fantasy had all ready begun in the way he was delivering the envelope.

I let my hair fall. I stepped closer into his arms, sliding mine around his neck. I looked up into the challenging gaze of his green eyes. I knew mine were glittering with promise back at him when I solemnly answered, "Yes, Luke, to everything. I give my word."

Chapter XVII
"A Man's World" by Joss Stone

Sunday, 11/18/12
7:20 AM

    I was sipping coffee at Reggie's dining room table while staring warily at the square envelope with my first name on the front. I probably was imagining things, but the card seemed to be staring back and taunting me. It appeared Luke is also an experienced expert at taunting. Thinking of his level of experience made me vaguely uneasy. Were these the sort of games he played with every woman? I wasn't sure if I wanted to know.
    I was alone. Everybody had left within minutes of drinking a cup of coffee. Reg was taking a "quick shower" before we left to go to my house. I had been sitting here waiting for the slow-poke for over twenty minutes. This was after he'd sat and browsed the paper while he drank three cups of coffee before ambling off to his upstairs bathroom.
    Jazy and Tre were taking their guard duties seriously. They decided to pick up the groceries on my hastily written list rather than allow me go shopping in a public store. After their horse chores and errands, they were meeting us at the apartment to drop off the food.
    I could tell this day off was going to be much more relaxing than yesterday. The lovely way it had started guaranteed it couldn't be worse, that was for sure. Then I frowned recalling how it ended on the sofa.
    Ultimately, I take full responsibility for my own body. Having unprotected sex comes down to having complete faith in another human being. You are betting your health, and maybe your life, your partner is one hundred percent trustworthy and honest. Not only right then, but every time you have unprotected sex going forward in your relationship. Even if they are honest, they could have a disease and not know it. Anyway you look at it, I don't like the odds.
    Luke made the bad judgment call to enter me unprotected. He did so without my express permission, or even reassurances that I was safe. I should have stopped him. I was very troubled over his actions, and mine. I am actually extremely dismayed at the reality of exposure I was now subjected to from our risky behavior.
    While it's true I am safe, this seemed way out of character for a pragmatic man such as Luke to say he trusted me with no basis in fact. While I believe he is safe, having unquestioning faith that a man will never

lie or cheat is not an attitude I will probably ever possess again. I'm okay with that.

My phone buzzed, surprising me out of my brooding reverie. Picking it up, I read Crookie's name on the screen.

"Morning, Crook."

"Anabel, can you talk?"

His tone of voice had me sitting up straight. "Sure. Are you okay?"

"Yes, I am, but Cheryl's body was found last night. She is dead. She was murdered."

"Holy freakin' buckets! Oh, Crookie, I'm so sorry!"

"I know. Thank you..ah...thanks." Crookie stuttered nervously. "I was leaving to go work out and the police pulled up. They informed me of the news she had been found and was dead. They did not have any answers to most of my questions." He cleared his throat. "The Edina cop I mentioned married to my friend at work? He is going to be calling me sometime this morning with more details. At this time, I only know she was found in her car in an abandoned barn somewhere outside Northfield by two teenagers. She must have been dead for some time because I do not have to identify her body, or whatever the police procedures would be in the situation of a," he paused, looking for the right words, "recognizable corpse."

"Ah man, how awful it must have been for those poor kids that found her body. Crookie, I'm shell-shocked here. I mean, I know she's been gone two months, but I only found out yesterday about your married life with her. Now, she's dead. Murdered! It's one thing to talk about it, but the reality is…" I trailed off. Seeing a positive light in the gruesome news I asked, "Since your cop friend is willing to share details, does this mean they don't think you're a suspect?"

"It was nothing really, but I helped this couple out of a personal bind and we all became friends." I smiled at his humble attitude. Crookie is a good friend to have in your corner. "Even so, I would not expect him to tell me anything if I was under suspicion for murder. My friend implied they did not consider me a suspect. I was with many people that entire Saturday and Sunday after I saw Cheryl last, so maybe that lets me off the hook. I think I told you yesterday the locksmith was over early on that Saturday, and then I was at Ecolab." Crookie's voice turned contemplative. "Although, I am curious what proof exists to indicate she died that day, or that weekend. That was the only weekend I gave the police a detailed alibi for my whereabouts when I reported her missing. I had gone over the details so many times, it was easy to recall specific times and dates. I cannot believe they have had time to perform an autopsy and report the findings this fast. Can I call you back after he contacts me with more details?"

A Date with Fate

"Sure. Would you prefer I keep quiet about her death until then?"

"No, I do not mind if you tell people. As far as any details learned from my friend later, I will have to let you know. I would not want him to have any repercussions on the job for confiding in me. Umm, Anabel, do you still want me to come over later?" Crookie sounded tentative and lost. He's another only child, and has no family close by. I know how the shock of death makes you want to be with people who care. You may not want to talk, but you want the warmth and the reassurance of normalness.

"Yes, I absolutely insist you come here. I'll be holed up at home all day, so please come down whenever you're ready."

Crookie didn't pretend he wasn't relieved and eager. "Thank you, I will then."

"Were your plans to stay in town for Thanksgiving, or got to Florida?"

"No, no, I had no plans to leave town." Crookie sounded bemused. "Is Thanksgiving soon?

I laughed softly. "This Thursday, Crooks." I thought quickly for a second and then suggested, "If you'd like, why don't you pack a bag and stay with me for a few days? I have a guest bedroom with your name on it. We'll be helping each other out like in the old days."

Crookie jumped at the idea. "Oh, Bel, if you are sure, I would be really happy to stay. I have been dreading the thought of doing this alone with no moral support. I will be taking off several days from work to deal with all the formalities." He sighed loudly. "I guess there will have to be some kind of funeral service. I am still legally next of kin. I will have to call Tina next and meet with her this week in Northfield." He groaned. "Anabel, this is surreal. Cheryl is dead."

"I know, and I can hardly believe it. I'm trying real hard to not be a hypocrite here, but we never seriously wanted her dead, just gone from your life." An anxious feeling was stirring in my guts again. There were now two murderous people out there running around connected to my life. Surreal was right. Sunday morning was going downhill fast. "I don't mean right this minute, but are you going to be okay, Crooks?"

"You know, I think I am." He replied slowly in his thoughtful, serious manner. "Yesterday, when you said the Cheryl that I fell in love with never actually existed, you were so correct. I think I always knew this at some level. I no longer loved her, but I never wished her harm." Crookie blew out a deep breath. "Once the anger dissipated over all the lies, pity was all I had. It must have been terrible for her going through life endlessly using people and lying constantly." I murmured something noncommittal in agreement. "She was a broken human being, Bel, and I cannot hate her for that. She probably only desperately wanted to be loved, just like the rest of us. But, man, she was so wrong how she did it." Crookie laughed ruefully. "The thought of the publicity I can now expect due to Cheryl's sexual proclivities because of her murder fills me with anxiety. I have hives, Bel."

I exclaimed in sincere, laughing sympathy over the hives. "Try not to stress over things out of your control. It might not have anything to do with an affair. It's possible she was the victim of a random act of violence by some passing weird-o." I offered up this up not really believing it myself, but you never know. "You sound like you have your shit together, Crookie, and you're a generous man. I'm glad for you. Cheryl was a pathetic woman, and what a terrible epitaph that is to sum up a life. No matter what happens, you can count on me to help you, okay?"

"That means a lot, thank you. Wait a minute, Bel, explain how my staying over is helping you out?"

I laughed a little at my forgetfulness. It was becoming harder to keep track of who knew what about all the crazy shit happening in the last day. "Oh yeah, I guess you haven't heard the latest. Before you decide to stay, you should know a serial rapist tried to kill me and the girls last night. He's still on the loose. If that makes you too nervous to come here, I'll understand."

Crookie exclaimed incredulously, "What? A serial rapist! I received your text about your employee's ex-husband, but there was *more*?"

"Yep, it was the ex-husband's jail partner. He tried to run us off the highway last night. Nobody knows why. I guess I pissed him off. Imagine that, huh?"

He demanded, "He tried to kill you all and he is still on the loose? How did you get away?"

I recapped the bare bones details of last evening to catch Crookie up on events.

He was freaked over our narrow escape and adamant he was coming down. "Thanks for the warning, but it does sound like I definitely would be helping you out by staying. We will be each other's keepers." He added dejectedly, "Although, I should be nervous. The way my life has been going, if anyone ends up getting raped and killed by this man I am sure it will be me."

I tried to stifle my giggles at this image, but Crookie wasn't fooled. He protested he was a seriously depressed man at this moment and his luck had been totally crappy. I promised him The Hammer would have to get through me to get near his bum.

I shoved Luke's teasing, taunting envelope into my purse while I thought about Cheryl Crookston. After all my joking with the girls yesterday, somebody really had murdered her. I know she was terrible, but who would hate her enough to actually commit murder? Possibly it was someone I knew in Northfield; another unbelievably weird thought.

A Date with Fate

So that's what Jack's emergency call had been about last night when he took off abruptly from following our car. It gave new meaning to his very thick blue line between police and civilians.

I sighed, dispirited with Jack's insistence on keeping me out of the loop. This was getting ridiculous. I truly got the cop angle, but it wasn't only me being a civilian that caused his attitude. I was also a female; his little Angel, no less. Chief Jack's male chauvinism was alive and well. It was deeply ingrained, not only from his generation and upbringing, but from the natural inclinations of his personality type. I could usually blow it off and laugh, he didn't really affect me. This weekend, whatever his reasons, his issues were proving to be a major pain in my rectum.

Reggie swung around the corner carrying a long shotgun case in one hand, and a smaller, padded case that held his handguns in the other.

"I'm bringing three weapons total--a Ruger for you, my .357 and my 12 gauge shotgun. You'll have the varmint gun if anything happens, but you can't get into any trouble with the law in the mean...Whoa! What's wrong?"

I stood and faced my brother. On a hunch, I pointed to my cell. "I heard the news about Cheryl Crookston." Choosing my words carefully I added, "Not that Jack gave me any real information, I only know that she was found dead."

When I saw the fleeting look of comprehension pass over Reg's face before he glanced down to set the gun bags on the table, I knew my hunch was right. He had heard the news about Cheryl.

It's demeaning to be protected and patronized because of my gender. It's worse to realize I'm never going to change Jack's view point. Possibly a female police officer would be allowed into the inner sanctum boys club, but even that was doubtful if he has a choice. It was bitterly ironic a possible suspect like my brother gets the courtesy of a heads-up because he is the male in my family, but not me. Then the idiocy of Jack's logic tickled my bizarre sense of humor, despite my disgust.

Reggie was busying himself loading .22 caliber bullets into two magazines for the Ruger. This also allowed him not have to look me in the eye.

I laughed. "What the hell, Reg. Why wasn't I told when it's obvious you've heard of her death?"

Reggie held his hands up in mollification. "It's not my fault. I wanted to tell you. Luke told me Jack called not long after you got here last night. They thought you'd dealt with enough crap yesterday. Luke told me I couldn't talk about it. Besides, I don't know any details other than she was found murdered in a barn in her car. That's it, Bel."

I stood motionless. It *had* been Jack's voice I overheard on Luke's phone when we were in the hallway last night.

Talking more to myself, I repeated quietly, "Luke thought I shouldn't know, too, huh." I regarded my brother. "Murdered how?"

Innocent eyes the color of a clear, summer sky opened wide and Reggie shook his head emphatically. "Truly, I know nothing more."

I laughed shortly. "Come on, let's go."

Reggie slapped a full clip into the Ruger and put it back in the bag, along with the spare magazine and bullets. He kept his loaded .357 out for the drive. He grabbed all the gear and followed me at a trot to his truck. I slipped on my sunglasses while he hurried to tell me what went down.

"When you girls went into the living room last night, Luke told me about Cheryl. Jack wanted him to fill me in on the news. I was under the impression Luke and Jack decided none of us should say anything to you since you'd been through a rough day, what with Larissa's ex and the van man."

Now I wanted to maim someone. Preferably a man named Luke Drake. Jack being Jack was one thing. Luke being Jack was another. I silently climbed into the truck after Reggie clicked open the door locks. He handed me the handgun bag, but placed the shotgun case in the back.

Luke had looked me in the eyes after Jack's call and not said anything. He may not know of my friendship with Crookie, or all the pertinent details of my involvement, but he knew enough to agree to keep it from me. The tired, little woman was strong enough to get her head bounced off a wall as he virtually did everything but screw me against it, but couldn't be trusted with the news of Cheryl Crookston's death due to her rough day? When and why did Jack and Luke exchange cell numbers and start their let's-protect-Anabel-from-herself bromance?

I drummed my fingers on the console between our seats.

This overprotective behavior had to go. Jack and Luke teaming up was not a positive development, it was a catastrophe. Chief Jack was a terrible influence on a man like Luke. I was having a hard enough time getting Luke to jump through hoops, and now Mr. Man from LaMacho was coaching him? They must not be allowed to play together.

Reg ventured, "Luke seemed to know the whole story about Crookie and Cheryl, but I'm guessing it wasn't you who told him, eh?"

I shrugged dismissively in answer. That tidbit only made it worse Luke didn't tell me about Cheryl. I continued looking out my passenger window and thinking of my own plans. Reggie went on talking to himself.

"It must have been Jack who filled him in."

At my lack of response, his tone of voice got wheedling. "Come on, Anabel. No shitting you here, you're the most reasonable of my sisters. You know Luke was only looking out for you. What's so wrong with that? You got a good night sleep, and they told you this morning."

I faced my brother then. "I didn't say "they" told me. "They" told me nothing."

A Date with Fate

I snorted at his "Oh Shit!" expression.

I made a face and lifted a shoulder. "Somehow, I'll manage to take care of myself despite those big-balled, buttheads cramping my style. I'll tell you what; those stupid men shouldn't plot to deliberately keep information from me. It only hinders me. So, you said you wanted to tell me last night. Why, Reg?"

Starting the truck, my brother slanted me a grin. "Because you scare the living crap out of me when you're mad at me?"

Not smiling, I waited.

He put the truck in gear and started down the driveway. "Okay Junior, I get why you are disgusted. It must blow to be a girl." He smiled sheepishly over at me. "Don't tell Jack or Luke because I will lie and deny it, but I'm on your side about this nondisclosure crap. Yesterday, you kicked a dude in the balls, and then shot at a man trying to kill all you girls. Damn right, I think you should be told things. I snuck away from the game to tell you about Cheryl last night, but you were passed out on my couch with my brownies smeared all over your face." He thought a second. "I guess I should have said something before I went to shower, but I was thinking about what guns to bring today, and I must be one, cold bastard, " Reg laughed ruefully, "because Cheryl's murder didn't cross my mind."

"You're not cold." At his glare after this comment sunk in, I reached over and pushed his shoulder. "You sneaky, adorable, ratfink of a brother, do you swear to God you came to tell me last night?"

Reggie promptly put a hand to his heart and flashed me the infamous MacKenzie double dimples. "I hereby swear to God."

"Then thank you for that. By the way, the brownies were delicious. Oh, and Reggie," I pulled my sunglasses down on my nose to give him some sister-brother eye contact, "do you think by now you've given Jack and Luke enough time to search my building to be sure it's safe?"

Chapter XVIII
"Born This Way" by Lady Gaga

Sunday, 11/18/12
8:00 AM

Reg performed some groveling along the way to Northfield. Well, I consider it groveling when someone repeatedly calls me 'a damn bloodhound' with a certain tone of admiration in their voice. We made it to my apartment without incident. I didn't say anything more about not being clued in on the events concerning my own life, but Reggie must have felt bad.

Approaching my building on Division Street, Reg brought it up again. "Jack called and told me some of his cops were searching the building before you went home. My orders were to wait for his all clear. Luke wasn't involved in this, as far as I know." He glanced over at me to see how I took this confession. "I never thought about if Jack was wrong or right to do the search without telling you, I was only damned relieved he was making sure it got done.

"Jack mentioned the ex has lawyered up and isn't talking. Hansen won't say why his ass-wife, Hummerschmidt, is after you." Reggie then scoffed, adding in his forthright manner and sounding an awful lot like Jazy, "It seems obvious to me the fucker's nuts, and so who cares about the why. We only need to concentrate on trying to keep you alive until he's caught."

"Super. By all means, let's try."

The definition of the law of averages would indicate sometime today a piece of news I receive will have to be good. I didn't bother mentioning that Jack was able to enter my building without my consent because I gave Luke the codes to the doors yesterday. I consider Luke involved.

Now that I was thinking about it, what *did* Luke have to do today that was so important he had to take off instead of staying with me when a homicidal rapist was on the loose? Disgruntled, I imagined he was taking his houseguest out to breakfast, so his man-whore friend could find another woman to line up for a hit and run over some pancakes.

Sure, I was perfectly fine staying with Reggie. But if Luke was so concerned about my emotional well-being and physical safety; you'd think he would have insisted on sticking around. On the job, he prevented and

A Date with Fate

secured. It may be his weekend off, but if anybody could use a little preventing, it's me.

Was I wrong to believe I am worth the unpaid overtime?

I don't think so, either.

I wallowed in my pity party for a minute more while Reg parked directly in front of the entrance to the shop. Then I blew it off to concentrate on my goal of the day--staying alive. Glancing up and down Division Street reaffirmed this early on a Sunday there was little traffic and plenty of parking spots.

Reggie interrupted my progressively crankier thoughts. "I know what it means when you get quiet. Tell your little brother, what are you planning in that pointy head of yours?"

"Hard as it is resisting your suaveness, I'll tell you in the lobby. Let's go inside."

"Not so fast!" He reached behind for the shotgun case, and awkwardly maneuvered it into the front seat and across my lap. "Here, you carry both these bags in so my hands are free."

Reggie came around to my side and opened my door. He reminded me of a secret service agent in his sunglasses. His head was scanning the street while his right hand was in his jacket pocket. He crowded behind me when I carried the gun bags, my jacket, and my purse to Bel's front entrance. He used his larger frame as cover until I unlocked the door and we were inside. Using his body as a shield to protect my life almost made up for his earlier treachery, but not completely.

The main doors were locked behind us, and I plunked everything down on the bench near my apartment door.

"Can I have the gun you brought for me, please?"

My amiable brother complied, taking out the pistol from the padded gun bag. When he handed it over, I automatically checked the safety before relaxing with the gun in my hand.

He inclined his head, indicating the Ruger at my side. "The clip is loaded with ten rounds. This gun will feel about the same as your Glock to shoot."

I examined the weapon. "I have to say, this Ruger is quite cute. This skinny, little barrel is sexy. Maybe I can keep it?"

"Guns are not cute or sexy, Anabel, you little freak. They are tough and masculine. No, you can't have it, that's my varmint gun." His smirk disappeared and he frowned in worry. "I thought it was smarter to give you a gun closer to your Glock, instead of my .357, but I'm really stupid sometimes. We should have stopped at Luke's pasture on the way here and let you practice shooting a few rounds."

"Don't sweat it; we're only being precautionary here. You have the big guns, and we're sticking together, right? I doubt a little practice would make much difference in the scheme of things. Besides, I've been target shooting at the range and become pretty accurate with my Glock, so if they aren't that different," I shrugged, "I should do okay."

"I guess you're right." He pointed at me in warning. "You remember I get first dibs on shooting any fuckers that get in our way today, and we'll be fine."

I meekly gave my word. I then told him my plan.

Frowning in confusion, he rubbed a palm over his unshaven chin. The scraping sound was loud in the quiet of the lobby. "Jack all ready had the building searched. Why do we have to do it again?"

Patiently, I explained. "We know every crack and crevice in this whole building. You want to bet our lives Jack's cops checked the old dumbwaiter behind the cupboard door in Bel's staff kitchen? Or the hidden storage room in the basement behind the shelving? Unless we call Chief Jack and verify those cops searched in every nook and cranny I can name, I sure as hell don't."

Shaking his head in laughing frustration, my brother begrudgingly agreed. "Let's make it quick then, I'm starving." He brightened. "Will you make me some pancakes or scrambled eggs when we're done? Or wait, how about French toast?"

"Perhaps that could be negotiated." I cautioned, "Now don't have a kitten, but I'm carrying this gun ready to shoot."

Reg's face grew serious at my statement. "Damn right you are. I'd be freakin' out more if you didn't, Junior. While we search, I want you to stay on my left side and not behind me." He took the revolver from his pocket, shrugged out of his jacket and laid it on the bench. Out of the duffle he removed extra bullets for the .357 and the spare clip for the Ruger. He put the bullets in his jeans pocket, and handed me the spare clip. He unzipped the long bag and took out the Remington 12 gauge shot gun. He checked the safety, loaded the magazine tube with five shells, racked one in the chamber, and put the sling strap over his neck. Loaded for bear, he stuck his cell in his shirt pocket.

"Just remember that I'm a friendly, practice muzzle control like you've been taught, and be aware you will be prosecuted to the fullest extent of the law for brother-slaughter."

"You act like I haven't shot you before and don't know the drill."

My brother gave me a dirty look, but we were both chuckling while I set my weapon and spare clip down for a second. I slipped out of my high-heeled shoes and socks. Barefoot, but more slip-resistant; I was longing for a shower, my sweet smelling lotions, and my cosmetics bag. I felt about as appealing as something the cat dragged in. Then I had to deal. The cream colored slacks and pink blouse I still wore from last night had no pockets. I was nonplussed where to carry the extra clip for the Ruger, and also my cell. Shrugging to myself, I agreed with Plato's practical words, "Necessity, who is the mother of invention". In went the extra clip

A Date with Fate

of bullets under the tight waistband of my slacks, and down sideways went the cell phone into my cleavage.

Reg blinked, but was smart and said nothing. He gave me a few tips about stalking game quietly together and using simple hand signals while I listened attentively. Then we entered Bel's Books, relocking the door behind us, and started searching.

Silently as possible, we thoroughly searched the basement and then the first floor. Reggie did mouth the occasional grumble to be duplicating the cop's efforts. I firmly believe there was still a dab of admiration in his tone when he whispered I was 'a damn paranoid, little tyrant' for the fourth time.

After clearing the second floor apartment, Reg and I agreed the guest bedroom would serve as the Axelrod's last stand, if it came to that. We stored the gear there. Unlike my room, this room has a sturdy lock on the door. There was a heavy dresser against the wall if we needed to push it in front of the door. I took the rope ladder from under my bed and left it next to the guest bedroom window. This side of the building was a sheer drop down to Fourth Street.

I have a sizeable balcony off the back of my apartment. The balcony was higher than a normal second story due to the lofty proportions inside my building. It has a retractable, fire escape ladder attached to the side. I stood on alert while Reg, after scoffing in brotherly disgust, secured the ladder with a swaddling of duct tape. I wasn't taking any chances with areas I could control.

The back door onto the balcony has a safety bar lock and only a small window. The laundry room window looked out onto the balcony, and was large enough for a man to enter. It was locked and wired to my security system. Our reconnoitering had me mentally adding several more items to my personal, self-defense check list. Nothing like a little brush with death to make a girl reevaluate her security needs. An arsenal of guns and ammo, a bar lock for my bedroom door, and permanent bars for the laundry room window were now at the top of the list.

On the bedroom side of the apartment, the long hallway dead ended at a door leading up to the third floor. At the top of the steep, straight staircase, a long storage room ran back the length of the apartment over the bedrooms below. The high, loft-like ceiling throughout the other side of the apartment prevented the attic from spanning the entire third floor.

This attic storage room has finished white walls and dark stained plank flooring. It's an easy space to search and not your typical scary, cobwebby attic. It's possible to see over the entire space in a glance. There were the same original tall windows along three sides of the room as throughout the rest of the building. Covered only with light-diffusing, sheer curtains, the morning sunshine poured through the bank of east facing windows at the top of the staircase. When we reached the top of the stairs, it was bright and cheerful. The overhead lights I'd flipped on automatically were redundant.

At the opposite end of this very long attic, on the northwest corner above Division Street was the turret room. It was a three-sided appendage jutting out of the building with a wide, six-foot tall window set in each portion. The open, cross beamed ceiling above the turret area soared high into the shadows.

Another reason it's an easy space to search is because NanaBel was not a hoarder. There are shelves built along the south wall on the left. The shelves are wide enough to hold a series of clearly labeled, small storage boxes. Aside from a few odds and ends of furniture stacked neatly against this wall further down, the space is entirely empty. I'm more of a collector than my grandmother, but haven't overflowed up into the attic yet.

Guns hanging loosely at our sides, we looked around. This space would make a very cool workroom for some of my future projects.

Reggie voiced echoed when he wondered, "How come we never did anything up here when we were growing up? This is an awesome room."

"I was just thinking the same thing. I guess NanaBel kept us too busy down in the store." I gave my brother a droll look. "Either that, or she was working our tails off cleaning something in the apartment."

He chuckled as he walked further down the room, peering at the furniture. "Yeah, she's a wily one. I'm thinking about doing a Chore Chart for my own work crews." He pulled out an elaborately carved, heavy wooden chair. "Can I have this?"

"Sure, if I can have Miss Sexy here." I answered, holding up the Ruger.

Reggie shot me a "Get real" look, and I shrugged an "Oh well, then" look back at him.

He placed the chair back in position against the wall. Following him to the front windows, I ignored his pouting and asked his opinion on something I'd been thinking over.

"Do you think I should I cancel the dinner here tonight because of The Hammer?"

Reg scratched his head. "If everyone coming knows about this Hammershit loser, and they park in front where the streetlights are bright, there shouldn't be a problem."

He went on to say, "No asshole ass-bandit is going to keep me from doing what we always do. If it'll make you feel better, I'll go down and man the main doors around five." He grinned and toggled his revolver. "Since I'm the one packing heat, baby."

A Date with Fate

I laughed at Reggie's confident swaggering. "Thanks, it would. I won't cancel then."

My friends and family could always choose to stay home. With a swallow, I silently reminded myself I was bait. If it was The Hammer's intention to specifically attack me again, the more coming and going he saw, the greater the chance we'd draw him out. He needed to think it would be easy to come after me.

I parted the curtain with the barrel of the gun and peeked down on Division. I noticed traffic was picking up and a few walkers were on the sidewalks scurrying to their destinations. It was sunny, but the balmy weather of yesterday was a distant memory. Today was in the low teens with a nippy wind. They were still predicting a big snow, but no way would I get Reg going on that subject again. Weather forecasters make him irrational.

Reggie meandered towards the turret room on our right. "Man, these are some amazing windows!"

About to reply, I noticed a man with a bald head wearing a bulky, light colored coat across the street. I stiffened to attention and unconsciously tightened my hand around the gun. Nervously, I made sure my finger wasn't near the trigger, and then looked out again. The guy was sitting on the marble park bench facing my building, and directly across from Bel's front doors. He appeared much more focused towards the front entrance of my store rather than the newspaper in his hand.

Without taking my eyes off the man, I called out, "Reggie, check this guy out across the street on the bench. Does it seem weird he's sitting outside today? I can't say if he's Hammerschmidt," Frustrated, I had my face glued to the window trying to decide if the man could be the same dude I saw yesterday in the van and in the mug shot, "but should we do something?"

Reggie leaned down to look out the left turret window to get a view of the park. He teased, "Do something like shoot him? It's a good thing I'm the one with the shotgun or you'd probably have the man in your sights. You mean the guy with the paper?"

"Keep talking like that and I'll have you in my sights. Yes, Einstein, I mean the guy with the paper since he's the only person sitting on a bench..."

I broke off giving Reg a hard time when I saw something go swooping by out of my right peripheral vision. I had the impression of huge, black moth flying down from the turret's ceiling. Startled, I turned. I let out a surprised shout of confusion when I saw what appeared to be a bulky comforter blanket land on my brother's back and envelope him. It landed with enough force he was smashed against the glass of the window with a resounding CRACK!

The culminating crescendo of glass noisily splintering and shattering in the attic had me screaming Reggie's name and instinctively running towards him.

I couldn't see the top half of his body from this angle, but I saw his boots on the floor underneath whatever the hell had fallen from the beams and covered him. I was terrified it was his head that had broken the window and shattered the glass.

In my bare feet, I abruptly halted a few feet away. I screamed his name even louder when I saw his boots were still. I hesitated a moment going closer, scared I'd find his neck stuck through on a pike of sharp glass under the massive bulk covering his body from my view.

I quickly glanced upward, but I could see nothing in the rafters above him. When I looked back at Reg only a microsecond later, the comforter bulk on top of my brother's still form was rising up. I was close enough to recognize the covering was some sort of down-filled sleeping bag, but the fact it was moving while my brother's boots stayed still had me rooted in place in puzzled, growing horror.

The bulk turned my way, and I screamed out, "HOLY FUCK!"

The Hammer stood straight and flung off the sleeping bag.

Time stopped. My stunned, petrified impressions were that he loomed enormous. His head, his trunk, his legs—everything was gigantic. He had on a bizarre T-shirt that was so tight fitting across his over-developed arms and chest muscles, and so short over his hairy stomach protruding out like a watermelon, that it appeared he had put on a child's size by mistake. His jeans were baggy and drooped low under his gut that looked hard as a rock even though it stuck out like he was nine months pregnant. A wave of the foulest smelling body odor hit me, causing me to gag as I breathed in frightened gasps. Even in my complete terror, the thought flashed it was unbelievable we hadn't smelled him long before he jumped down from the beams.

I was paralyzed. I was staring into those malignant eyes that had horrified me in the mug shot. They were bloodshot red, bulging out of his head, and crazed with aggressive hate. The man was a monster. I could see a thick, snaking vein throbbing in his forehead. His pale face was mottled with purple. Then he opened his mouth wide and roared in fury. The raging echoes filled the attic and were the most terrifying sounds I have ever heard in my life.

He didn't pause when flinging off the cover, but charged me.

He was twelve feet away, incredibly fast, and coming at me like a freight train.

I let loose shrill, ear-piercing screams as I backpedaled away, tripping over my clumsy feet and trying to stay upright.

My heart was beating so fast I thought it would burst from my chest. I was in a confused, mind-numbing panic over everything occurring

A Date with Fate

so fast. One minute Reggie and I are talking, and the next moment my worst nightmare is a few feet away with my brother dead at his feet.

I fumbled to raise the Ruger in my left hand, and then my brain seemed to switch to slow motion like a slide show. I was seeing everything happening before me in sharply-etched detail. The rampaging man with widespread, enormously muscled arms inked with full sleeves of the crudest tattoos, the drops of spittle spraying from his screaming mouth fixed in a rictus smile of awful, yellowed teeth, and the sheer, linen curtain floating in the air current off to his side.

I was hearing the booming sound of a gun from far away. Each boom was distinct and hung in the air cloud-like, as if the deafening noise was manifesting itself physically. I was sure I was shot, but I felt no pain anywhere.

Just as suddenly as it had gone into slow motion, my mind snapped back into real time. My brain comprehended it was me shooting the gun. I swung the weapon up from my left side. Incoherent with frightened panic, I fired repeatedly. I was wildly out of control and reacting with no conscious thought. My arm continued rising higher after every shot instead of correcting. I was recklessly shooting without aim at the bellowing horror show bearing straight at me and now only a yard away.

Then Hammerschmidt was off his feet and flying through the air. His protruding, hairy stomach smashed into me first with bone-crushing force.

Instinctively, I flinchingly twisted away to my right while protectively throwing up my hands before he hit me. My body was flung backwards into the room from this massive body blow. I landed hard on my butt first, captured under his stinking, sweat-soaked body. Momentum from the smashing blow continued thrusting me backwards in motion. Upon my back's impact with the floor, the wind was knocked out of me with a WHOOSH! At the same time, the spine-jarring landing caused my elbow to crack sharply against the floor. An excruciating pain screamed down my left arm, and my hand holding the gun went numb. An instant later, my head was forcefully bounced off the floorboards.

Everything went black.

Chapter XIX
"Fact and Friction" by The Nearly Dead

Sunday, 11/18/12
8:45 AM

I heard a voice gasping in a painful chant, "Oh, my head, my elbow, oh, my head, my elbow."

A few seconds later, I realized it was me.

I heard another voice to my right say, "Your head and your elbow? My head is ready to come off!"

I didn't want to open my eyes. "Reg, is that you? Are we dead?"

A third voice right above me stated, "Axelrod's don't die from getting their thick heads thumped."

I recognized that low voice. I felt a gentle hand sweep the sweat-soaked hair from my perspiring face. I lifted my eyes open to see Luke glaring down at me.

I murmured, "Hello, Mr. Secretive. How was breakfast? Were they serving women on the menu?"

Again from my right, a fourth voice asked, "She concussed, or what?"

My brother's voice stuttered. "Of course she ca...can cu...cuss."

I giggled and then winced. "Shit!"

"See."

"Stop making me laugh." I beseeched plaintively. "It hurts too badly!"

"No, I'll tell you what hurts too bad. It's searching a building with you that the cops have all ready searched—now that hurts bad."

My brother and I both started laughing and groaning.

Holding the back of my head, I tried to sit up more. I gave up the attempt for now when a stab of pain pierced my skull. I settled back, closing my eyes. My left elbow really hurt, but I tested and could flex my arm and fingers. I didn't know if that meant anything, but it made me feel better.

Giving me a slight squeeze, Luke's amused voice answered the fourth voice. "No, she's not concussed; she's always this way." He stated firmly, "You'll both live." To me, he murmured, "We'll talk about the secretive comment later--in private."

His tone was even and composed, but I opened my eyes and dredged up a tiny grimace of a smile to alleviate the anxiety I'd seen on his

A Date with Fate

face. Then I stuck my tongue out about the talk later in private part. Having my brains scrambled regularly must be making me extra-immature, but it made me feel better, too, and said it all.

I was on the floor in the attic. Luke was sitting with me in his arms. I was half in his lap, but my legs were sprawled out. My toes were pointing to the bank of windows in front of me.

Green eyes clouded with worry searched mine. Luke ignored my smart-alecky tongue and asked quietly, "How are you feeling? Should I take you to emergency? When I got here you were unresponsive to my voice, but flailing to get out from under Hammerschmidt. Reggie said the bastard landed on you like a ton of bricks."

"I'll be fine. No hospitals are needed." I assured him firmly of this without any basis in reality whatsoever for reaching this conclusion. On general principle, I have a rule to avoid doctors and hospitals unless I was at death's door, or stitches were involved. It tees me off so much to wait around forever to be seen, I'd rather cure myself or die first. I moved and wriggled various body parts. This was a close one, but I'd survive. My diagnosis was I'd be bruised up, but nothing a shower and a couple of aspirin shouldn't fix right up.

I turned my head slowly to the right, and felt a drop of sweat roll slowly off my cheek. Reggie was slumped on the floor several feet away from where I was lying. He was on his back, his legs bent at the knee, and feet flat on the floor. He was cradling his head as if preparing to do a crunch. I was incredibly relieved to see it was still connected to his neck.

Standing next to him was the bald-headed man from the park. He was shifting from one foot to another, nervous energy coming off him in waves. Our eyes met for a second. He gave a slight nod and an encouraging smile. Up close, I could see he was much shorter and really bore no resemblance to The Hammer at all, except for the shaved head. The man standing before me here could be Middle Eastern, complete with golden skin, dark, liquid eyes and a hooked blade of a nose.

'Well, damn. Anna was so wrong; clearly I did need glasses!'

"The Hammer!" I cried out, feeling like an idiot I hadn't asked immediately. "What happened? Where is he?"

Luke's calming fingers stroked my cheek. "Relax, Anabel, he can't hurt you. Hammerschmidt's over there, dead. Shot about eleven times." He added dryly, "I think it was Reg's shot through the back of the head that might have finally decided matters."

The bald stranger chimed in, speaking in a fast, clipped voice. "I don't know, Luke. I'm partial to the nice grouping in the groin area myself. From the amount of blood gushed; the femoral must have been hit."

My brother's voice was emphatic. "John, if you're speaking of having a femoral partiality that would definitely be Anabel's work."

Luke laughed shortly while I gave Reg the finger. Thankfully, I could manage that without too much effort. Introductions must have been performed while I was unconscious. Since John was the nasty man doing my nastier cousin Candy last night, and I was all ready feeling nauseated enough from the lingering stink of the dead Hammer, I didn't mention their lack of manners when they didn't introduce us.

I turned my head to the left. A few yards away lay the enormous body of Gustav Hammerschmidt. He was draped under the sleeping bag he'd been wearing when he jumped on my brother like Moth Man. My terror hadn't exaggerated the enormous size of him, or the rank smell. I shuddered, bile rising in my throat.

It sunk into my brain that Reg and I had been moved away from the windows and broken glass, but it appeared the Hammer lay right where he must have landed on me.

Luke followed my gaze. "Jack will be here any second to take over the crime scene. You were only out for a minute."

I nodded slightly and looked away from the dead man. In the turret room, the curtains on the shattered window were snapping to and fro in the cold, morning breeze. Crushed glass littered the floor.

Questions crowded my mind. Why were Luke and John here before the police? How had the Hammer gotten into my building without leaving a trace of breaking in? How come my brother's head wasn't sliced off, or at least bleeding? Most importantly, did the falling glass hurt anyone on the sidewalk below?

For once, I was too overwhelmed to ask. I was filled with relief Reggie and I survived the ambush. I was even more ecstatic the stinking, homicidal Hammer hadn't. I lay back and nestled my aching skull into the warmth of Luke's chest, letting his fingers lightly rubbing my temple do their magic. I hurt everywhere, but the drumline banging away in the back of my head was the worst.

The apartment doorbell starting ringing, the shrill, buzzing noise distinctly audible even up here.

Luke stated, "Circus time begins. You two ready for this?"

Reg and I groaned, but we both agreed we wanted to get it over with immediately.

John strode off quickly and went downstairs. The three of us sat quietly in the lull before the shit storm heading our way arrived. Over the last twenty-four hours, I'd become an old pro at handling police investigation procedures.

A minute later, Luke's cell buzzed. When he answered, Jazy's yelling voice could be heard clear as a bell. "I don't care who you are, you damn well better let me up these stairs. Anabel! Reggie!"

Reggie started laughing. My head rose and fell with Luke's chest when he sighed loudly in irritation.

A Date with Fate

His response was a deep rumble against my ear. "It's the sister. Let her up, but only to the top of the stairs so she doesn't fuck with the crime scene." I could hear John's voice raised in question. "Yeah, it's the friend. Let her up, too. Yeah, John, she's gorgeous. Yeah, sure, like Zena, Warrior Princess is about right." Luke ended the call on a muttered, "Christ."

Reg snickered. "Tre J has that effect on all men, don't worry."

Luke gave a snort. "You'd better worry. He was talking about your sister, Reggie."

Then we were all snickering and snorting, Reg and me interspersing our mirth with the occasional moan of pain.

Jazy and Tre were at the top of the stairs in no time. John had to use his body and outspread arms to ban them going any further towards us. Luke added his warning to the mix, and the girls settled down after seeing Reg and me in one piece, more or less, lying in the sunlight at the other end of the room.

I had to sit up and turn around to face them. Groaning under my breath, I made this slow maneuver. Actually, it felt better moving around. I carefully flexed my shoulders. Even with all the extra padding, my butt ached almost as much as my head.

Peering around the human fence, Jazy took in the scene before her. She glared at John accusingly and shouted, "What the hell? I thought you said she wasn't hurt!" Jaz called down to me, "Anabel, are you shot?"

I reassured her quickly. 'No, we're banged around some, but only The Hammer got shot. He's dead."

Whistling in admiration, Jazzy sang out, "Hallefuckin'luelah!" Then her voice turned wondering. "Tre, take a look at Bel. That's gotta be The Hammer's blood and guts totally covering her. How cool is that!"

"Waaay cool!" was Tre's enthusiastic reply.

I vaguely heard Tre in the far recesses of my mind. I was looking down the length of my body. I heard more yelling start from the direction of the stairs and my mind registered Chief Jack had arrived, but only from a far-off galaxy in another world.

Woozily, I was staring in growing horror at the sight of myself. There was wet, gooky stuff on me everywhere I could see. I twisted painfully to get a better look. It was on my chest and stomach, and continued down the length of me to my bare feet. My slacks were dark purple-red with it. I could not begin to imagine the origin of what some of the slimy chunks may be.

I was dizzy and gagging in disbelief that I had been laying here oblivious to the effluvium of the bloody gore I was coated with while we chit-chatted about concussions and whatnot. I swiped my dripping, sweating forehead with a forearm. Glancing at the glob of bloody, gelatinous substance now smeared on my bare skin, I started making tiny, gasping, squeaking noises. Tingling and swaying, I was comprehending it wasn't sweat or perspiration I had on my face, in my hair, and drenching my body. It was the brains and blood and guts of Gustav Hammerschmidt.

Everything went black.

Chapter XX
"Haven't Got Time For The Pain" by Carly Simon

Sunday, 11/18/12
3:45 PM

    I survived the police investigation…barely. The yelling I'd heard was Chief Jack kicking Jazy and Tre out immediately from the third floor. Under escort, they were allowed to deliver and put away my groceries on the second floor. Once the evidence techs checked out the apartment, the two girls helped fainting me into the shower.
    Yes, I have to face the unbearable truth and admit I freaking fainted. The men upstairs are lucky I did that instead of tearing them apart from limb to limb, and then beating them over their heads with their own arms. It is seven hours later, and I am still shaking my head over Luke or Reg saying nothing about the filthy crud covering me from head to toe. John doesn't count. Luke let me touch him, and actually held me in his arms. He voluntarily touched my hair and my face. I may have to reexamine the whole concept of thinking I know men, much less like them.
    After taking Advil, I sat on the ledge seat in the shower under the hottest water I could stand. Above the noise of the pounding water, I told Jaz and Tre about The Hammer, and about Cheryl Crookston's murder. I needed to be distracted from the slime I swear was still circling down my drain while I compulsively washed my hair for the fourth time.
    When I was done, the girls left. They gleefully promised to contact Mac, Anna, Stella, Kenna, and Billy to share all the news occurring since last night. The store would be closed today, but I was still planning on having our family dinner at five. I did beg them to tell everyone not to come over any earlier than four this afternoon. I needed to be alone and recharge my batteries. Then I'll be ready to celebrate surviving another Final Destination attempt this weekend and give friendship support to Crookie; even if it kills me.
    Happily, I was right about the shower diagnosis. After finishing scrubbing myself so shiny clean I squeaked, and after the pills kicked in, I was feeling more human. Then after repeated gargling, vigorous teeth brushing, and lavish applications of Japanese Peony body lotion, I finally got my sniffer back in order. I've discovered the hard way; actually not smelling death every second is necessary before you can start not thinking about it every second.

Chief Jack was ominously silent after shouting his orders at the girls, but anyone knowing him could tell he was in a towering, black rage. The cops and assorted personnel were busy on the third floor, but it was a solemn, carefully quiet busy.

In the organized confusion of the first hour after the police arrived; Luke and I were separated. With his special talent of observation, I knew he always had his eye on me wherever I was, even if we didn't speak.

The County Attorney, Wade Patterson, showed up in my dining room to listen to Reg and I give our statements and answer questions on the shooting death of Gustav Hammerschmidt. Mr. Patterson is a high strung, anxious gentleman. When he saw Luke, a stranger leaning a shoulder against the wall and quietly listening, the head prosecutor of crimes in Rice County peevishly suggested Luke wait somewhere else.

Luke straightened up, pulled a chair out beside me, and quietly informed Mr. Patterson that he was representing me until it was determined conclusively that I didn't need to hire a criminal attorney. This is how I found out Mr. Secretive has a law degree.

This announcement was a double-dipper of a good time for Chief Jack. His grim countenance lightened up briefly for the first time since arriving at seeing the stunned look on my face at Luke's reply to Wade's invitation to leave. Plus, Luke had no way of knowing Wade Patterson has been in love with my grandmother since before we were both born. Mr. Patterson is an old sweetheart, and while he'd probably draw the line at letting me get away with cold-blooded murder, even that is debatable if NanaBel was in town. Shooting a full clip at a known bad man in self-defense while being attacked in my own home is a slam dunk, even with a weapon not registered to me. I learned chances were high it was Reggie's bullet that killed him first. As Chief Jack liked to say, this meeting was strictly for crossing the fucking T's.

Once they were done with my interview, I made no effort to speak with Jack. He seemed to be avoiding me, too. I was okay with being alive due to my decision to trust my own instincts. I didn't give a rat's ass about his emotional well-being due to professional embarrassment, or whatever else was causing his mood. His insistence to keep me in the dark had almost accomplished that permanently. This was one of those times that my silence would speak much louder than any words.

My brother will try to lord it over me the rest of our lives that he saved me with one head shot compared to my ten fired below the belt. I informed him this would be true except for one fact. I was aiming based on my theory that most men's brains are in their pants. He proved my theory by only needing one bullet in the man's head. He was still thinking that over when he left.

I assured Reggie, in fact I insisted, that he should go home to shower and relax. I wasn't up for cooking any breakfast right now. He said

A Date with Fate

he'd be back for dinner and took off as soon as the cops were done with him. Turns out his head wasn't sliced to ribbons because it never hit the glass, it was his shotgun that broke through the window. His head had been smacked hard against the wooden frame of the window when Moth Man landed on him. It stunned him insensible for a few seconds. It probably saved his life. The Hammer didn't mess with him anymore, but came right after me.

Luke and John left soon after my brother. They were the first on the scene within seconds because they weren't out ordering women for breakfast like I had grumpily imagined, but had been keeping my building under surveillance. It was too bad Gustav Hammerschmidt didn't get the memo he was supposed to come from the outside to attack me.

Luke saw the turret window shatter. He was on the stairs when the first shots started. It was over by the time he burst into the attic. Like he'd told me earlier, he knew right away I was still alive. I was doing the croppy on the floor. I was wriggling like a fish out of water while trying to get my wind back and squirm out from being half buried under The Hammer's revolting body. That image is nearly as pleasant for me to contemplate as fainting twice this weekend.

I don't know what Luke was thinking about today's events. He was closemouthed on the subject of The Hammer being overlooked in the police search when Reg brought it up. He was silent in general, he and John staying in the background as the police took over the scene. I was also keeping silent. This wasn't the time or place to discuss any personal issues. I had a feeling this near death experience may drive home to Luke the necessity to lighten up on the macho madness with me in a way no casual discussion could ever get across. If not, he was too thick to ever get it.

When I was done being questioned, John waited by the stairs to leave while my unsolicited Solicitor took me aside in the foyer.

I didn't say a word, but Luke held up a hand as if I had barraged him with a firestorm of questions. "I need to take care of some business, and then I'll come back in an hour. We'll talk about everything then."

I shook my head. "No, please don't come back before five tonight for dinner."

Brows meeting in surprise, he rapped his knuckles against the arm of the church pew bench while digesting my blunt refusal.

"I know we have things to talk about, Luke, but I am simply not up to it. I'm all yours later tonight after dinner. Frankly, I'm not feeling very cooperative or compliant. You won't be happy with anything I have to say right now." I frowned up at him. "I know I won't be happy with anything you have to say to me right now, that's for sure." I almost patted his jacket arm. "I'd love to really kiss you good-bye, but I know you are disgustingly smeared with dried gook in spots under your jacket. Please have a heart, get the hell out of here, and let me be alone a few hours."

For some reason, Luke's face lit up and he grinned broadly at my words. I heard a muffled snicker from the stairs and shot a questioning glare John's way. His face was bland and he shrugged innocently. I sniffed. We still hadn't been officially introduced, but I begrudgingly thanked him politely for his efforts on my behalf, fruitless as they were. He bowed slightly in return. Luke laughed as they departed down the stairs.

By eleven o'clock everyone was gone but the police. While the police followed their protocols and did their thankless, routine work; it felt good to keep busy doing my own thankless routine of work around the apartment.

The housecleaning service came on Fridays, but any woman worth her salt can always find a load of laundry that needs doing. I changed the sheets on my bed and did a pass of the guest bedroom before Crookie showed up. I found myself humming as I slowly worked. My head still hurt a little and I was going to be one sore, whining baby tomorrow, but it's interesting how having a death threat off the table makes you appreciative of the mindlessly mundane.

Finally, the police left after taping closed the door to the attic. A few hours went by, and keeping busy also helped me sort my muddled thoughts. Not that I came to any great conclusions because I am still me. I don't really want to change the status quo of having no definitive status quo in my life. Regardless of where Luke and I were headed, I knew I couldn't take the "protect me for my own sake" attitude. It was a matter of trust, in my opinion, and nonnegotiable. I realized it may take some time, but Luke had to be willing to compromise on this--and mean it.

Anna texted her plan of the day was to break it off with Jim Mardsen this afternoon. Mum was the word on that score; Anna wanted to see Reggie's face when he heard. Today, Mum was my middle name, so no problem there.

Kenna texted she was happy we were still alive as of ten o'clock this morning. She was at a friend's in White Bear Lake and not coming to dinner.

This led to me calling Mac about Candy. That led to a thirty minute conversation about The Hammer and Cheryl Crookston, but talking with Mac was good. We've always been sounding boards to each other and talk over life's issues together. My sis can be depended upon to be practical and level-headed—except for the going crazy every eighteen years part. The upside to our conversation was her reaffirmation I probably wasn't in any imminent danger of catching some foul plague from the grossness plastered all over me upstairs. I don't think I ate any of Gustav's guts, or absorbed any through my eyeballs, open sores, or Queen Vicky.

A Date with Fate

The downside to my call was that it led to me being blackmailed into doing a dessert for tonight. I was making an apple crisp with a crumble topping about three inches thick. This was Diego's favorite dessert. It was also the vig for Mac agreeing to get Candy over here sometime before five—no questions asked.

If I needed any further proof Mac is wild about her husband, her choice for dessert said it all. She's a chocolate girl all the way. This was giving it up for love in action.

I worked in my home office for an hour on store business. Thankfully, no pedestrians were nearby when the glass fell from the turret window down onto the sidewalk. The mess was swept up and the window had been boarded shut. Due to my freakish need for control, I was happy to be the one taking care of any store related issues concerning The Hammers's death. So what if I basically followed the same format as Luke had yesterday. The splitting hairs detail that it was me handling the issues had a way of making everything sunshiny in my world.

Jazy and Tre had done themselves proud and didn't miss an item on my grocery list. I cranked the music and got busy cooking. If I was banging pots and pans around a little louder than I normally did in the kitchen, it was for a good cause.

"Beat a Pan, Save a Man" was my new motto.

Not knowing how many would show up tonight, I'd decided on soup, salad, and breadsticks for the menu. I finished the chicken wild rice soup, with a smaller pot of mushroom wild rice soup for the non-flesh eaters. My salad greens were washed and chilling, I whisked together the raspberry vinaigrette, sliced strawberries, red onion, and a Gouda cheese, made cracked black pepper croutons, and toasted some walnuts in a little honey. I prepared rosemary breadsticks ready for the oven, and. I whipped up several pots of herb butter.

Cooking is zen-like for me. I wouldn't want to cook three squares a day for a large brood, but I loved having dinner parties and entertaining in my apartment. As I whisked and diced and boiled and stirred, I let my mind free fall where it would.

'Geez Louise, we have long phone conversations. What could possibly be the reason for Luke keeping a law degree hush-hush? Did he have so many talents and degrees he couldn't keep track of them all? Who can keep secrets like that, anyway? Most men bragged their butts off until you wanted to pay them to stop! He was a damn, tight-lipped freak of nature--was what he was.'

Peeling and cutting up the Honey Crisp apples, I absently munched on a juicy slice as I then recalled a comment I wanted Reggie to expand on from yesterday. It niggled and wouldn't stop, so I called him.

He was vegging out watching the game but it was a commercial break, so I was absolved. Courtesies were exchanged. We agreed we each felt much better now. We agreed we would refer to The Hammer's murder as a joint effort to keep the peace between us.

Then I asked, "What did you mean yesterday in reference to Cheryl Crookston when you said she was a 'ditch-digging whore'?"

"Ah, yes. How erudite of me. Jack nailed Cheryl for a DUI awhile back. She got fined and sentenced to do some community service hours. It was picking up trash in the ditches on the side of roads. She tried to get out of it."

I smiled at that scenario. I also complimented Reg on his impressive usage of last Friday's "Word-of-the-Day". Jazy had jokingly given us all the same calendars last Christmas in our respective stockings.

"Oh yeah, how did that work for Cheryl?"

"I think she offered up her services to Jack in another capacity. Well, you know ol' Jack," Reggie's voice was ripe with innuendo, "the job always comes first. Cheryl did her time in the ditches."

I snickered, but my hands stilled for a beat in the process of combining the crumble topping ingredients. I thought of my brother's streaked blonde hair and husky, muscular build. I couldn't believe where my Law and Order SUV voice in my head was leading me. No wonder his comment had niggled in the back of my mind.

Reg's hair is like mine. It's streaked with different colors from the darkest brown to whitest blonde. The white blonde streaks dominate the more sun we get. Since he works outdoors throughout much of the year, his top layer of hair is often bleached platinum blonde by the sun.

"Huh." was my less than erudite reply. I got busy again cutting in the softened sticks of butter with the flour, brown sugar, chopped pecans, and spices. This was going to be the mother of a huge pan of apple crisp happiness.

I asked casually, "Off topic, do you ever lend out your truck to friends? For instance, speaking of Jack; does he ever borrow your work truck to get supplies when he's doing projects around his place?"

"Tell me you aren't thinking of borrowing my truck?"

"You're a funny guy."

Chuckling, he said, "Sure, he's used my truck lots of times. Why do you ask?"

With perfect timing, I heard a roar of cheering from the television in the background. "I hear the game's back on, so I'll talk to you later. Bye!"

'Was I really thinking Jack was the man in bed with Cheryl Crookston the night Crookie spied on her?'

I didn't want to even contemplate Jack could be Cheryl's killer. I shook off that disquieting thought after telling my detective voice it had better shut up, or we would tangle. However, if he was the man Crookie saw it sure explained why he was so determined to control what information I received on her murder. I could easily see him writhing in embarrassment if I found out he had been screwing her. She was a girl my age, not only married to one of my friends, but a woman that he had also arrested.

My smile outdid a Cheshire cat. *'Jack, Jack, Oh Jack.'*

With a lighter heart, and singing along with Sara Barilles because she begged me from my iPod, I cautiously danced around and cleaned up. Finished with KP duty, I went to change out of my flour dusted yoga pants and T shirt. I had fun over the next hour doing girly-girl stuff.

I scrutinized my closet offerings. I chose a royal blue, gauzy peasant blouse stitched with black velvet embroidery. The shirt has an empire neckline and sheer, black embroidered sleeves. It was an exotically fanciful shirt; and it billowed when I twirled. I felt like a pregnant, gypsy queen. A perfect choice it you planned on eating a lot, or dancing around a campfire. I wove my clean, shining hair in a loose side braid that hung down my front, and tied off the end with a black silk ribbon.

Going with the gypsy theme, I put on make-up to accent what I consider my best features; my eyes. Not only have I been blessed with two of them, but they're a dark blue color with touches of gray. I have long black lashes and dark, naturally arching brows. Otherwise, I like my face, but it's nothing extraordinary to write home about.

NanaBel and her friends say I have the look of a young Ann-Margaret. Most people my age have no clue who a young Ann-Margaret is unless they've watched old Elvis Presley movies. I don't know who I resembled, but I would best describe my looks in more modern terms as the girl-next-door type, only with a D cup.

Putting on dangly earrings made of lapis lazuli, I heard the sound of the apartment door bell. Checking my cell, I saw it was 3:45 PM. It was Reggie and I buzzed him up.

He arrived at the top of the stairs with two six-packs. "I was bored after the game, and I decided to come over early to bug you."

"Oh, lucky me." I scooted past his half-hearted swipe with a laugh, we were both still moving a little slower than normal. "Do me a favor? Go taste the soup and tell me if it needs anything, would you please? I'll be right there." I called back over my shoulder, "But do not add anything yourself, Salty Sam, or I'll go for your femoral."

"You can try, but it may be awfully hard with the back of your head blown off." Reggie responded as he went to taste.

From my bedroom, I heard the TV flipped on in the living room. Sports blared. My alone time, rejuvenating afternoon was officially over. I was leaving the bathroom when the doorbell rang again. Reggie beat me to the master station.

He threw me an odd look as he spoke into the intercom, "Hang on a minute." He motioned me over with his head. "Junior, come here." He stepped aside for me to peer at the small screen. "Is that Mike McClain?"

I took a quick glance and saw a tiny image of Mike McClain for the first time in almost ten years. My first reaction was to stand back, as if burned.

I recovered from my shock. "He's moved back to town recently."

"Hey, that's great! Should I buzz him up?"

I heard the note of eagerness in Reg's voice. When he was in his teens, my brother had hero worshipped Mike. He was the older brother Reg never had, but always wanted.

I had triumphed over a murdering rapist today, Mike McClain was small potatoes. "I guess."

Reg pressed the intercom. "Mike, this is Reg. I'm buzzing both doors unlocked. Come on up, man!"

I waited at the top of the stairs, but Reggie went down to the landing in his excitement at seeing Mike. Their hearty greetings and backslapping echoed loudly in the stairwell. It was strange hearing Mike's voice again in my apartment after all this time. Luke's voice was low and deeper, a baritone. Mike's was a tenor. He still sounded laid back and friendly, a man at his ease in any social situation.

"Reg, look at you! Good job, man, you aren't a shrimp like your sisters." He and Reg laughed together and bumped fists. "It's great to see you. What are you up to these days?" When his eyes looked up to see me at the top of the stairs, Mike stopped speaking. A smile burst across his face. He recovered his stride and came up to where I was standing. I didn't return his smile, but waited politely.

"Hello, Bel." he said softly.

Mike's about six-feet tall, athletic, solid and muscular. Anna would be happy I could see for myself he was neither fat nor balding. The scumbag looked great. He had fully matured into the man he was just promising to become at twenty. Back then, he was considered boy-band worthy by my girlfriends. Mike was one of those rare golden blondes with dark brows and a dark brown beard—not blonde or red. I could not watch the TV series "LOST" when it aired, even though Anna and Mac raved over it and never missed a week for years. Mike was a dead ringer for the character Sawyer. The resemblance was too eerie and too much of a reminder.

"Mike." I replied evenly, stepping back a little.

Mike ran a hand up the back of his head. His hair is shorter now and more golden-brown than blonde. He probably didn't spend the summer outdoors working construction anymore. The nervous gesture was familiar, though, and I felt a tug of remembrance before I shut it down.

A Date with Fate

He flashed a self-deprecating smile. "Thanks for agreeing to see me today. I know it's rude to stop by this way, but I couldn't wait to talk to you. I took a chance you'd be here, or in the store. I noticed the store's closed early today."

His glance moved past me. He was taking in the yellow police tape on the attic door at the end of the hallway.

"Not too big a chance you wouldn't find me here." I ignored his inquiry about Bel's hours. I looked at Reggie, standing off to the side and clearly curious. "Listen, Mike is only here for a few minutes to talk about something." I raised my brows at Mike. "I assume you want your five minutes of talking in private?"

Mike gave my brother's shoulder a friendly punch. "I did come by to see your sister for a minute, but let's you and me get together later this week. Does that work for you?"

Reggie grinned broadly. "Sounds good, Mike. I'll have you out to the lake house. It's getting cold as a witches tit out there, but we're men and can still grill on the deck, am I right?"

Mike laughed and agreed. Reggie fished out one of his business cards from his wallet, and then went back into the living room to watch football. My brother wasn't being disloyal to me, it had been too long for him to give the past a thought. He and I had never talked in detail about why Mike and I broke-up. He had been on a camping trip up in the Boundary Waters at the time and missed the gossip. I never brought Mike up, Mike's parents moved, and Reggie got on with his busy, teenage life. To him, Mike McClain was just a fond memory of one of his sister's boyfriends.

"Follow me." I didn't wait, but went down the hallway. I passed my closed bedroom door. The next room on the left was Reggie's old boyhood bedroom, now serving as my home office.

I could feel Mike's gaze on me as I lead the way. It figured that I was wearing my pregnant, gypsy shirt and jeans, instead of something tight or short. He probably thought I'd gone to fat. Not that I cared what he thought, but this weekend really sucked.

I opened the door and waved him into the office. As Mike passed me by, I caught a whiff of the clean scent integral to him that always reminded me of a sunny day outdoors.

Suddenly I felt sad and drained; I wanted this next five minutes over. Mike could take his prosperous, golden boy looks and get back to whatever life he'd been leading these last ten years. It wasn't going to shake up my life he'd chosen to move back to Northfield.

Mike waited politely until I sat in my desk chair before he took a nearby chair. After I endured a moment of his silence while he stared at me without speaking, I frowned and motioned for him to get on with it.

He sat forward, hands lightly rubbing up and down on the tops of his thighs. "I'll get right to the point. I have come across some information that reflects on what happened all those years ago…" I started to get up, but he talked louder, "No, wait Bel. I know we never spoke of that time and you don't want to now, but please, hear me out completely. Please?"

Reluctantly, I sat back down and lifted my chin. "Hurry up, then."

Mike didn't visibly react to my impatience. His voice was calm. "I have a lawyer friend that works for the D.A.'s office back in Atlanta where I have been living for the past five years. She called me a month ago, and in the course of our conversation was telling me about a recent rape case she was prosecuting. What made it unique; she was prosecuting a woman accused by the man of raping him. Apparently, with the rise of easily obtained date rape drugs, this is not unheard of." He nervously got up and leaned back against the closed door, stuffing his hands in the pocket of his jacket. I'm such a terrible hostess; he still had his coat on. "The more details of the case she divulged, the more interested I became." He met my eyes with a direct look, and I realized with wariness his were burning with some emotion other than nervousness, and that I really hadn't been listening much to his actual words. "I've always been stymied at what possessed me to cheat on you with Candy MacKenzie. I didn't like her, and I seriously did not harbor some secret, sexual desire for her. Point of fact, it was the direct opposite."

Mike moved from the door and came over to stand by my chair. Gazing down at me, there was a sincere expression written all over his smoothly-shaven, handsome face. My snarkiness disappeared. It was replaced by a roaring in my head. Now that I was really paying attention, it was clear this story could only be heading in one direction.

He shrugged one shoulder and faintly smiled. "I was in love with you. I've lived with the knowledge that I cheated on you, someone I loved and admired and hoped to marry. At twenty, I pictured our future together. You were going to own this store and I was going to be the next Alan Dershowitz." His voice went quieter. "You were going to have my babies and teach them to read inappropriate novels by age three. I'd teach them how to skateboard and ride bikes because you'd kill yourself, and them, if you did. We'd both teach our kids how to cheat at cards, but only so they'd recognize cheaters." He paused, and I had to look down. I stared at my clenched hands as he continued, "I've beat myself up for years for destroying our life in a moment of weakness I don't even recall. That night was a blurry nightmare. I haven't touched a drop of alcohol since that weekend. How could I? What if I did it again, and had sex with a stranger or attacked some woman unknowingly?"

Mike sat on the edge of my desk, facing me. His long legs were next to my forearm resting along my thigh. Honesty radiated from his voice and filled the air around me. "Anabel, all these years it's never made

A Date with Fate

sense. I thought it had to be because I was black-out drunk, even though I could have sworn I didn't have more than three or four beers. Why else would I have done such a ridiculously stupid thing? I am now convinced, without a doubt; Candy drugged my beer. I think I have proof."

Mike once again stopped talking. This time it was because I stood up and did something in one fluid motion that flabbergasted us both.

I kissed him.

I didn't need proof. Instinctually, I knew with a conviction born of certainty everything he had said was the absolute truth. It all clicked into place, and it was that simple. After ten years of my world being sideways and wrong, it was suddenly righted.

All during that day from hell, and the weeks and months that followed, my heart and my gut screamed at me it couldn't be true. I wanted desperately to be justified in my belief of Mike's honorable character, but how can you doubt the evidence of your own sister's eye witness account from two feet away? Instead, I had to deal with the repercussions that someone I chose to love proved how mistaken I was to trust in my own instincts. I had felt worthless and degraded. I could only now imagine what Mike had gone through back then.

Like Mike, there wasn't a shred of doubt in my mind Candy had drugged him a decade ago on that fateful weekend. She'd viciously instigated the joined path of our young, happy lives to go careening off course in separate, miserable directions.

It was the smallest of innocent kisses, no more than a soft, tender lingering of my lips against his. There was no carnal intent. The impulsive kiss was a healing balm meant to sooth our shared years of sadness, and to demonstrate a connection that I, too, felt an anguish our life together he'd lovingly described had been so maliciously destroyed.

It was a kiss of forgiveness for us both.

Somewhat numb, I sat abruptly back on my chair.

Mike stayed still as a statue. He leaned on the desk next to me while his warm, caramel brown eyes searched mine in growing wonder.

He started smiling, and it kept spreading until it took over his whole face. His voice was rough with emotion when he stated, "You believe me."

"I do believe you."

He jumped up and threw his fist, punching the air. "My God, that's fantastic! I can't believe it was that easy." He paced the small room. "I was prepared to present my whole case with every shred of proof, and I thought you'd still end up doubting me." He frowned anxiously. "You're not pretending so that I'll leave faster, right?"

I pointedly looked at the clock. "You have two minutes left."

Arms outspread; Mike threw back his head and started laughing ebulliently. He came over and reached for my hands, pulling me out of the chair.

Whirling me about, he was beaming. "I love it! You're still a smart-ass!"

I smiled at his joyful demeanor at my faith in his words. It was incredibly strange to be facing Mike without thinking he was The Betrayer. The twists and turns life can throw your way are astounding. One minute, Mike McClain is a distant memory of a cheating asswipe I was stupid enough to believe in. The next minute, he is standing before me a grown man. He's not only redeemed, but was a victim of a personal betrayal at a level worse than mine. The unexpectedness of it all had me spinning in my head, as well as around the office with Mike.

Suddenly, he stopped. He gripped my elbows to steady me when I stumbled against him. He didn't let go, but pulled me in closer.

"Before you decide not to hate me any longer, I'll tell you what action I am seriously contemplating as my next step. I've decided after seeing you again, it's important to me that you agree I'm doing the right thing."

Uncomfortable with being so close, I stood back a step out of his embrace and crossed my arms over my chest. I met his eyes. "What action?"

Mike's face hardened. "I've been advised to bring a civil suit against Candy. I'm planning on suing her for rape."

It was my turn to laugh with ebullience. I twirled him around the room.

Chapter XXI
"We Are Family" by Sister Sledge

Sunday, 11/18/12
4:00 PM

  The dining room table I'd reluctantly inherited from NanaBel when I bought the apartment is monolithic. Without leaves, it seats fourteen. When fully extended, it opens to seat twenty-four comfortably. I cannot carry the heavy leaves on my own. I'd have to hack the brute to pieces with an axe to get it out of the apartment.
  I don't do anything formal for my Sunday night dinners. It was all about coming together for comfort food and relaxing. Tonight, the long sideboard in the dining room was set up as a self-serve buffet with wineglasses, plates, bowls, cutlery and napkins.
  My only rule at these Sunday dinner parties is no fighting. I laughed to myself as I loaded a few dirty dishes into the dishwasher. I had a feeling I'll be breaking my own rule tonight.
  I turned back to the crowd sitting on stools around the granite island in my kitchen. They were keeping me company while I finished preparing our dinner. They were munching on chips and salsa from a CoOp in Apple Valley. Crookie had brought it, swearing they made the best salsa in town. Reggie and Jazy, mouths stuffed full, were in fervent agreement.
  Crookie's arrival had ended my time alone with Mike McClain. I avoided them meeting today since Crooks called from the back lot when he parked. Mike and I had agreed to get together on Tuesday after the store closed at eight to talk more details, and to catch up on our lives. After giving me a long, tight hug, he'd left out the front door.
  I was grateful Crookie showed up because as happy as I am Mike's exonerated from being an evil dickhead; it's a lot to take in. With everything else going on, I needed time to process. My mind can only handle so much mayhem and I needed to prioritize. My current top priority was slowly savoring the thought of my cousin Candy being sued publically for rape. I was hugging this thought close to my heart like a girl with a secret love letter.
  'Wait, I had one of those, too!'
  Thinking of the envelope now stashed in my dresser drawer, I came to the conclusion maybe this weekend didn't completely blow after all.

I had gotten Crookie and his gear squared away in the guest bedroom, and was listening with half an ear to him and Reggie getting reacquainted. He seemed to be in good spirits.

Crookie, being a logical guy, wanted to wait until everyone arrived to tell us all at once what his cop friend discovered about Cheryl's murder. The details didn't need to stay secret, but he and I agreed we wouldn't say it was a cop friend who had told him. It was easy to ramp down my curiosity for now. I was still pretty freaked at the thought of Jack with Cheryl, and was almost afraid to hear anything more pointing to Jack as a suspect. I wasn't sure how Chief Jack was going to take Crookie discussing details of an open murder case, but last I checked it was still a free country.

Tre J, Jaz, and James Byrd were talking on my right. They were getting to know Stella's friend, but not yet a boyfriend, Eric George Jasnik. He was younger, only about twenty, but laughed in all the right places and carried himself with a friendly maturity and confidence.

Stella was sitting closely at his side, eyes sparkling. When not batting her eyelashes in his direction, she was shooting me little, questioning looks. This included tilted head nods and flaring eyes towards him. I may have mentioned subtleness is not her strongest suit. I had all I could do not spitting my wine out in laughter watching her facial movements become more grossly exaggerated the more I pretended confusion as to her meaning.

Eventually, I had enough of my own private fun and relented, signaling he was a real cutie. Finally satisfied, she smiled back up at him. The look of shining adoration passed between them made me hope I did need glasses. I didn't want Stella to find the man of her dreams at eighteen. Thirty-eight was a nice round number. I thought it'd be very educational if she spent her J terms going to school in Europe being chased by frisky Italian and French men—maybe even a swaggering Spaniard or two. It's the epitome of my Bel Curve Mind, Body, and Soul concept in action.

James Byrd made me uncomfortable with his speculative gaze following me around. It felt like I was providing the night's secret entertainment for him. This guy could say more with his silences than most men talking nonstop, but I shrugged it off and kept busy. I don't know why my sister brought him to dinner, but Jazy never kept a man around for long--not even one as hot as this dude. Chances are I'd never be graced with his presence again after tonight. I'd give him this; the man did have great hair--if you happen to like long hair on a man the color of midnight with the texture and shine of the most luxurious satin.

I poured myself another Riesling and relaxed.

Amidst the conversation flowing around us, James leaned towards me and said quietly, "Jasmyn told me about the man attacking you again this morning. You seem to be coping fine, but I hope you know in here,"

A Date with Fate

James put his hand to his chest, "a man like that deserves death. He seeks death. He was driven to end his own existence. I'm only sorry it was you, and your brother, that drew that unpleasant task to perform today."

I took a sip of wine while thinking over his odd words. Skeptically, I wondered if he was some sort of Indian Shaman wannabe. Killing someone rated stronger words than 'unpleasant task'. For me, an unpleasant task is taking out the garbage. Shooting Gustav and being physically smashed under him, and his stinking body fluids, will wake me up gasping in terror for years to come.

James was right, though, in some respects. It *had* felt like Hammerschmidt kept coming after me against everything logical. I'd probably never know the why of it, nor did I care. I only knew the load off my mind that he was no longer a threat to me, or anyone else, was immense. I felt like I had carried the weighty menace of him around my neck for twenty-four years, and not just the twenty-four hours since I glimpsed him in my parking lot yesterday.

I smiled politely at James over my wineglass. "Thank you for your sympathy. Maybe you can tell me how I can get out of ever drawing *that* short stick of a task again?" I shuddered.

His eyelids lowered seductively. "Maybe I can be persuaded."

My eyelids blinked from the effort of not rolling them into the back of my head. Just when I thought maybe Mr. Gorgeous wasn't a total douche bag.

When Reg buzzed Mac and Diego up a moment later, I ran to the top of the stairs. I wanted to get the first battle of the night over with immediately. I saw them round the staircase landing. Diego was carrying a bulging bag and I caught a glimpse of several bottles. What I didn't catch a glimpse of was my cousin Candy's bulging eyes.

Seeing my face, Mac spoke first. She sounded irritated. "I know what you're thinking, but she wasn't at home when we swung by. Aunt Carol and Uncle Trevor are out of town, so nobody was home. I just now got a text answer to my 'Where the hell are you?' with an 'Oh yeah. Something came up'. So, sorry kiddo, she's not coming." She reached me and gave me a quick hug. "On top of all her other wonderful qualities, she's got the manners of an inbred."

Talking of manners, I waited until Mac and Diego had left the foyer to go get a beer before I let loose with a "Fuck! Fuck! FUCK!"

Reggie snickered at my mini temper tantrum, but was confused why I cared Candy wasn't here. It was customary to be thankful for her absence at family functions.

I waved my brother off while saying distractedly, "Oh, I just wanted to discuss her stealing my gun."

"Discuss?" He grimaced knowingly. "Discuss her one for me, the thieving bitch!"

Sometimes it's rather nice having a little brother.

I knew what had come up. Candy was going over to Luke's house again to have gross sex with John. I did not like that man. He'd done nothing but cause me trouble this entire weekend. Plus, I was getting irate that my cousin was spending so much time at Luke's house. I didn't want her anywhere near him or his property.

It was schizophrenic to be overwhelmed with happiness Mike had been drugged, but then be filled with rage he had been drugged. I'd held it banked inside waiting for this moment to confront her. I've never hated anyone in my life before. I can honestly say that I hate Candy. I was elated at Mike's plan for public retaliation against Candy for her rape, but I'm a hands-on kind of girl. I prefer the personal touch and needed to confront her.

Once back in the kitchen, I took a deep breath and let it out. I guzzled some wine while agreeing with the vengeful voice in my head. I'll hunt her butt down if needed, and then rub her face in some yellow snow as a starter. Candy has a phobia about getting her face wet. Probably afraid it could cause a mud slide.

I made myself think on the positive side. The good news about her no-show; I could now enjoy my night surrounded by a majority of people I liked, and look forward to a nice, normal evening. I try to have the wine glass half full mentality whenever humanly possible.

The doorbell started ringing nonstop and I waved Reggie back to his seat. As I crossed the apartment to the intercom, I was positively ecstatic how great it felt to not worry that a killer was out hunting *my* butt.

While I waited at the top of the stairs, Reggie came up beside me. "I'm still not cool sitting back without keeping an eye on things, you know?"

I slung my arm over his shoulder. "I do know. All of a sudden I'll tense up, and then relax when I remember I have nothing to be a scaredy-cat about anymore."

Jazy came sliding across the hardwood floor of the foyer in her socks like when we were kids. She halted near us at the stairs. "I'm feeling left out, you two. Who's here now?"

Grinning, I put my other arm around Jaz and gave her a squeeze. "Miss Anna Lynn."

Reggie tensed up at her name. He walked casually over to the master station of the intercom and started being busy.

Jazy shrugged after my brother with a questioning look at me, but then she and I were diverted when we heard loud clomping coming up the stairs. We also heard heavy, labored breathing.

"Is Anna sick?"

A Date with Fate

"Not that I know." I saw Anna turn onto the landing. My mouth dropped when I caught sight of Aunt Lily behind her, breath heaving in and out like the bellows for a fireplace in hell.

Jazy's whisper was appalled. "This is fucked up!"

My lucky sister slid quietly away from me and disappeared.

Reggie took a step and peered over the ledge. He then shot me an accusing look as if I was to blame for this oddity.

Anna saw me waiting and gave a shrug of helpless apology; a smile flitting on and off across her face. It wasn't that Aunt Lily had never before come to dinners at the apartment; it had just been a long, long time. Long enough that I had complacently thought my apartment was a Behemoth-free zone.

Anna reached me and gave me a hug, saying into my ear. 'I know what you're thinking, but she insisted. You could have picked me up off the floor. My god, I have so much to tell you!" She pulled back, checking me over hurriedly. "You doing alright? You look great, but I know you've got to be hurting after getting tackled. You did the right thing to shoot him, Junior, don't ever doubt that."

I brushed off her sympathies; we had too much ground to cover to worry about my sore butt, or the state of my immortal soul for having committed a co-murder today.

I squeezed her back while whispering, "I have so much to tell you, too. Hell, I have forgotten some of it all ready—THAT"S how much has been going on since you went home last night."

She grinned. "Well, okay then. Me first!" She kept her back to my brother still standing over by the intercom. "Ask me where Jim is...hurry."

After her urgent order to me, Anna trilled with laughter, not a care in the world. She angled herself so she had a clear line of sight over to Reg out of her peripheral vision. She was wearing tight jeans and a shirt showing off plenty of plumped-up cleavage. My brother didn't stand a chance.

Hearing Aunt Lily clomping closer as she sucked the oxygen out of the stairwell, I hurriedly played along with Anna and asked brightly, "So Anna, where's Jim tonight?"

In a suggestive move I could only admire, Anna threw back her head and shook her brown hair out. All while wiggling her shoulders back, pushing her breasts out, and posing with a hand perched on her hip. She opened her mouth to answer with whatever Reggie-devastating response she had memorized, but Aunt Lily beat her to it. The Behemoth had reached the top stair and leaned her bulk against the half wall.

She shook her cane at my head. "That pawing beast was sent on his way with his tail between his legs when I caught him forcing himself on Anna in our front room." She paused to catch her breath. Her chest was rising and falling rapidly under her shapeless winter coat. She roared, "I will NOT tolerate that kind of lewd behavior under my roof!"

I don't know if seeing Reggie doubled over with laughter was the reaction Anna was hoping for, but I could only stare back at Aunt Lily in disbelief. Lately, she'd been treating Anna more and more like a young virgin needing a chastity belt instead of a grown woman pushing thirty. In my current mood at being thwarted from ripping off a piece of Candy's beef jerky hide, I was not feeling tolerant.

"Remove that cane out of my face."

Anna quickly reached in front of me, pushing Aunt Lily's walking stick down while saying, "Oh, Aunt Lily, lighten up. It wasn't like Jim was attacking me. We had just broke-up. He was simply giving me a final hug good-bye."

Anna was looking towards Reggie, but I didn't take my eyes off Aunt Lily. When Anna said the word 'hug' the woman was distracted from glaring at me. Her sour lemon mouth puckered into such a parody of extreme disgust, I realized she really was off her rocker when it came to men/women relations.

Crookie came into the foyer calling out Anna's name. He opened his arms. Smiling, she ran over to him and was enveloped in a huge, swaying hug. Anna patted him and said consoling phrases while at the same time shaking his arms and telling him how much she had missed seeing him.

The doorbell buzzed, and I darted a quick glance at my brother. He had been watching Crookie and Anna with no hint of his previous laughter. Reg hit the button, shot me a thumbs-up, and then stalked by the laughing couple to go back to the kitchen.

My attention was pulled away when Aunt Lily hissed in a venomous undertone, "His murdered whore of a wife recently found dead, and this is how he acts?"

I rounded on her. I looked into her hard eyes and threatened in a low voice, "Let me be perfectly clear. Anna's my friend, while you--not so much. You will keep a civil tongue, and you will be polite, and you will not talk bad about any of my guests, I don't care if it kills you. If you can't do this for one evening—GO HOME."

I held her murderous glare. Aunt Lily heaved off the wall. She didn't say a word, but her scowling face was a caricature of twisted fury. She thumped off, and started muttering once she was past me. She approached the oblivious, chattering Anna and Crookie. Without a pause or apology, she jarred Crookie with a heavy shoulder in passing.

Rubbing his arm in surprise, Crookie looked after her retreating bulk in bewilderment. Resuming their conversation, he and Anna followed her into the living room.

A Date with Fate

I shook my head. *'There went someone else that didn't have a problem hating.'*

A throat cleared. Luke was standing on the landing. He had a shit-eating grin on his face.

I folded my arms and frowned down at him. "And that goes for you, too."

Luke laughed and bounded up the last few steps. I met him at the top and threw my arms around his neck. I was happy to see him, and it didn't escape my notice he had a gift bag in his hand.

After I gave him the really big kiss promised earlier today, Luke demanded, "Who in the hell was that woman?"

I didn't lift my head from the crook of his neck. It was quiet in the foyer. I was enjoying my one minute respite before rejoining the fray. "Evil Aunt Lily."

Luke whistled above me, "THAT was Anna's Aunt Lily?"

"The one and only."

"Christ!"

"Pity him. I know I do." At Luke's shout of laughter, I grinned, too. "Come on, let's go get you introduced around and then I have last minute dinner stuff to do."

I started to walk away. Luke pulled me back.

His eyes scanned my face, "Hey, everything okay?"'

I snorted, laughing a little. "Honestly, some things are okay, and some things are not okay. None of which we need to discuss right now."

Luke's hands ran up my arms and cupped my face. He leaned down and kissed me again, very slowly and very thoroughly. He pulled away.

Smiling a little at my dazed expression, he asked, "What do you want to discuss right now?"

I sniffed. "Certainly not the large gift bag with the pretty, silver bow." I laughed shortly. "I remember the gift bag you brought me on our first date. Do you really think those tactics would work twice, Counselor?" I practiced Anna's move with the hair and threw my braid behind my shoulder, wiggling. "I'm not that easy."

His eyes glinted. "I like your top."

I reluctantly pushed at his roving hands. "That's because, Mr. Attorney, your hands can travel unimpeded underneath. Now quit; I have serious hostess duties that need tending."

"I like your braid, too." He ran his hand down its length, until his fist was resting over my right breast.

"Thank you." I tossed the braid behind my shoulder again, dislodging his hand. "I have plans to whip you with it later on."

His smile was growing as he put his hands on my hips and pulled me closer. "I like that you're a planner."

I felt the shiny, black, gift bag with the glittery, pretty, silver bow nudging my thigh.

I brushed off his hands and stepped back while laughing in amusement. "Oh, do you now? I'll be holding you to those words for a long time, Luke Drake, Esquire."

"You can hold anything of mine you want, Anabel."

Rolling my eyes as he laughed, I put my palm up towards him. "Oh, okay. I'll open my present, just to make you happy."

He ignored my wiggling fingers and walked around me. He set the gift bag on the church pew in the foyer, and slipped off his black jacket. He carefully draped the jacket over the gift bag, covering its beckoning, siren light from my view.

He then gave me a teasing, sideways look from under his brows. "I never said it was for you."

Walking back towards me in dark jeans and a white shirt, Luke crackled with vitality and energy. Since I saw him last, he'd shaved off his beard and his coal black hair had been cut short. No more Dirtbag.

"But if it was for you, it would be a present to open sometime when we're alone."

Spell broken now that the gift bag was safely out of sight, I ignored his taunting and complimented him. "I like your shirt."

"Do I have to be scared you are going to whip me with it later on, too?"

"It's always safe to be scared of what I may do."

I took his hand, swinging it between us. I don't know why the man has such a problem sharing things like his past, his present, surveillance plans, advanced degrees, and condoms, but I like him more often than not.

How could you not highly respect a man astute enough to bring gifts when it wasn't for the typical, boring occasions of my birthday, or quelle horreur, Valentine's Day? I despise that awful holiday designating when we should express love and affection. A man smart enough to figure that out on his own without a peep from me deserved to be cut some slack with a very long rope. Before I used that long rope to tie him up or whip him, of course.

"Jack asked me to tell you that he's unable to come tonight."

"I see. Thanks for the message."

'Dammit, tonight was going to be fun. The possibility Jack was a Cheryl-screwing killer, or Luke's best buddy, could wait. We deserved a fun night together.''

Still holding his hand, I started walking with Luke through the foyer. "Hmm, that's too bad. Guess that means you'll have to sit in Jack's big boy chair at the head of the table."

"You're referring to the big boy chair of the highest respect and consequence at the table, correct?"

A Date with Fate

"Uh...sure." I agreed, dubiously. I brightened. "More importantly, it's the chair next to Aunt Lily and nobody else will want to sit there."

I squealed when Luke sat down on the church pew and swung me onto his lap. I squirmed when he tickled my sides and kissed loudly down my neck.

"Admit it's the big boy chair of respect."

Laughing, I grabbed his shoulders to hold him off. "Not even if you kiss me for hours, strip off my clothes, tie me up, tickle me with a feather, insert foreign objects into my orifices, and then use your tongue to lick every square inch of my body will I ever admit such a thing."

Luke paused and stared at me.

"Well, Anabel, the mystery is finally solved why an ugly, little thing such as you gets so many dates." Mac's dry comment came from a couple feet away.

Luke's crack of laughter echoed sharply in the foyer as he stood up, depositing me on my feet.

He stuck out a hand to Mac. "You could only be Stella's mom."

"Luke, meet my number one sister, Mac."

Mac smiled and shook Luke's hand briefly. "I think she introduces me that way so she can say Kenna is her number two sister and get away with it." He laughed again and Mac looked back at me. Her blue eyes were twinkling mischievously under the light from the chandelier. "I was wondering where you were. Do you want some help with dinner?"

"You know it's not Mexican food, right?" I teased, slipping my arm through hers. As she laughed and shook her fist, I motioned to Luke. "Come on, let's go eat. I need me some vittles!"

Within fifteen minutes, everyone was around the table and serving themselves family-style. Some people consider thirteen an unlucky number and I did consider asking Aunt Lily to leave for this reason. I settled for sitting her far away on the opposite end of the table. Luke stayed glued to my side until we were all safely seated. Poor James and Diego got the honors of being Aunt Lily's chair partners tonight. If those two perfect examples of male magnificence couldn't keep her speechless with wonder, nothing could.

We'd barely dipped into the soup when Jazy leaned forward to address Crooks on her right. "Okay Crookie, if you don't want to talk about it--I get it. We all get it. Otherwise, I'm shamelessly asking, do you know anything more about Cheryl you can tell us?"

Mac exclaimed, "Jazy, quit being so shy and sensitive!"

Crookie was on my left, with Anna between us. He replied seriously, "No, Jazy is perfectly fine, Mac. A guy never has to worry about what she is thinking." He smiled at her. "I like Jazy's plain way of speaking."

Everyone laughed at this understatement, even Jazy. She shrugged, comfortable in her own skin. James smiled slightly from his chair next to her, and I realized I'd never seen him touch my sister, or even flirt with her. I guess being super good-looking and inscrutable was all the effort he needed to put forth with the women. Too bad he hadn't had reasons to develop some interesting qualities in his personality to make him more genuinely appealing for the long term. I've concluded extreme physical beauty was more often a curse than a blessing.

When Crookie cleared his throat and started talking, everyone stopped and listened attentively. Even Aunt Lily sat forward in morbid anticipation.

"So there are no misunderstandings, I am not a suspect in Cheryl's murder," Crookie's voice cracked a little on her name. "The police routinely operate on keeping information out of the public domain for their own reasons. Please do not name me as the source where you've heard these details I'm about to tell you. I trust all of you." Crookie paused, and looked at James. "Well, I do not trust you since I do not know you, but it appears you are a reserved man and not a chatty type. You are not from Northfield, correct?"

Smiling, I met Jazy and Tre's eyes. They both loved Crookie and were openly grinning. Reggie snorted into his beer bottle.

James nodded and answered calmly, "Correct on all accounts."

Crooks nodded back. "Good." He spoke to Aunt Lily down at the foot of the table. "Ma'am, I do not know you well, either, but as Anna's aunt it stands to reason you must be a good person."

Reggie laughed softly this time. Anna shot him an emphatic bird with her left hand while she forked up salad with her right. I giggled, and Luke squeezed my thigh under the table in shared amusement.

Aunt Lily slapped the table loudly with an open hand. The unsuspecting Diego startled. His breadstick dropped to land in his soup with a small splash. His spoon went clattering to the floor.

Diego's eyes widened comically in dismay when Aunt Lily turned the force of her dark glare on him and shouted, "Pick it up, pretty boy! Don't they teach you table manners where you come from?" Without taking a breath, she looked over at Crookie and sneered with a mocking gesture of disdain. "Good person, good schmerson. I'm a Christian woman and gossip is a sin."

In the vacuum following this outburst, Crookie cleared his throat. Appearing doubtful, he nevertheless answered amicably, "Very well. Eric George?"

Luke squeezed my thigh again, but when I peeked up at him, he was sitting back and listening with fascinated amusement.

A Date with Fate

Stella's friend leaned forward and smiled shyly across the table at Crookie. "No problems, man. I'm not Christian, but say what you want. I can keep my mouth shut."

Stella squeezed his hand at his answer, and Eric George smiled down at the Junior Jezzie with worship in his eyes. Mac was soothing an angry Diego, but she and I exchanged rolling eyes and grins at Eric George's expressive face. Luckily, Eric George missed the sight of a scandalized, angry Aunt Lily staring his way. Good thing he wasn't sitting closer to her, or she'd snap his blasphemous spine in half as easily as one of my breadsticks.

Crookie turned to Luke last. He grinned shyly. "Anyone here knows if Anabel asked you to dinner, you must be…" Crookie paused, at a loss for words.

Mac supplied a straight-faced, "Superman?"

Stella dimpled at Luke. "Steve Jobs."

Anna's laughter was deep. "A secret agent!"

Tre J winked. "Strong."

Reggie, his mouth full of salad, pointed a fork at Luke and stated decisively, "Nuts. You're brave, man, but certifiably nuts."

We all laughed at that, but I think Luke's cheeks were actually a little pink.

I leaned over and spoke low in his ear. "How strange, but it's really true. Men *are* always right."

Aunt Lily couldn't contain herself and erupted. "You fools, look at him! He's Satan incarnate!"

Eleven heads at the table swiveled in Luke's direction to see what they'd missed. Make that twelve. I had to look, too.

Anna cried out in embarrassment, "Aunt Lily, what's with you tonight? Please, stop! Luke, just ignore her. I'm sorry. We know you're not Satan."

As Anna argued over proper etiquette with her crazy aunt, I struggled to contain my laughter at Luke's carefully blank expression. I well remember the first time I was scathingly called Delilah at age eight for encouraging a classmate to get a Mohawk within hearing range of the Behemoth. Luke's reaction to Aunt Lily's bizarre accusation was no reaction. His eyes were narrowed in thought as he gazed down the table in her direction.

I squeezed his thigh. I should say, I tried to squeeze his thigh but it was rock hard. I stroked his thigh. "In some cultures the elderly are known to be always right, too." I nodded seriously when he switched his gaze to mine. "It's a known fact she's not an idle gossip or a sinner."

We smiled at each other.

Tilting my head, I tapped my pursed lips while I looked him up and down appraisingly. Meeting his amused eyes once more, I nodded.

"Personally, I'd name you more of a demon versus a devil. Yes, I think Baal fits nicely."

He arched a black brow slowly. "I thought you were a heathen?"

I scratched my fingernails up his inner thigh and warned under my breath, "Don't be raising that brow at me at the dinner table. Where *are* you from, hell boy?"

Luke was snickering as I went on to answer him. "Yes, it's true I'm not religious, but not from lack of curiosity or illiteracy." I took a sip of wine, and shrugged a negligent shoulder. "The concept of faith isn't easy to swallow when you're older, if you aren't fed it first with mother's milk."

He put his big hand over mine on his thigh. "My father is going to really like you."

I laughed and looked away, confused but warmed by his words.

Everyone around us had started talking at once to rush in and fill the awkwardness, but Aunt Lily's fanatic ways were familiar to most of us here and taken with a grain of salt.

Reggie called a halt to the chatter by dinging his wine glass with a spoon. "Can we let Bob tell us what he found out about Cheryl, please?"

Stella spoke up, smiling shyly from on Luke's right. "Yes, we'll be quiet, Uncle Reg, but only if Luke will promise me something first." I knew that look. She'd learned it at my knee. I watched her suspiciously. "He has to tell us all about his first date with Anabel when Crookie is done."

Mac chuckled wickedly and dinged her glass. "Hear, hear, I second that motion."

Luke's easy, smiling expression as he listened to Stella's request didn't change by a flicker, but I felt him tense up at my side. I laughed silently in my soup. He swiftly recovered.

"I'm sorry, ladies, but you'll have to ask Anabel about our first date." He shrugged with a "Gee, shucks" grin. "Men never get that sort of thing right, no matter how hard we try." He stroked his chin in thought. "I'm sure it must have been a fun, first date. When she begged me to take her out a second time, I obviously agreed."

My family and friends were laughing uproariously even as they complained at his answer.

Anna's voice was the loudest, "No fair pulling the "I'm a man" card, Luke. Everyone here knows Junior won't say squat. No offense, but she probably doesn't even remember your first date."

Tre J was looking at me like I had two heads. "You *begged* him, Bel?"

"I think she remembers." Stella smiled at me around Luke. She asked sweetly, "Will you tell us, Auntie Bel?"

A Date with Fate

I finished my bite of soup, and lay down my spoon. Ignoring the man with the straight face at my side, I smiled back. "I would love to, Stell, but it's X-rated, so I can't tonight."

Jazy didn't doubt me for a second, but raised her wine glass in grinning salute.

Stella giggled. "Oh, don't be a hold out. It was your first date. It can't be that bad!" She smiled quickly at Eric George. "Besides, I'm not a baby."

"Of course it wasn't bad. Didn't I just say it was X rated? And of course I didn't mean *you*, sweetness." I gave a nod towards Aunt Lily slurping up her bowl of soup at the other end of the table. I made a throat-slitting motion, crossing my eyes.

Eric George laughed. I smiled at him thinking maybe he was a keeper.

Anna muttered a "Yeah, right." on my left while Stella narrowed her eyes at me on my right.

Mac was laughing, even as she impatiently shook her head. "Stella, honey, no matter how tempting it may be to beat it out of her, you can't force your aunt to tell. You must learn to barter."

My niece opened her mouth for a rat-terrier rebuttal, but suddenly stopped. A small smile played on her lips. Although it may be used against me at a later date, it's always fun to see our Stella learning the ropes. I still shot the grinning Mac a glare that promised revenge. After all, she had announced a trade secret in mixed company, which broke all sorts of sisterhood rules.

Tre J and Crookie laughed together at this byplay, and then she gave a little elbow to Crooks to continue.

I took this opportunity to pinch Luke hard under the table. He didn't flinch, but his lips turned up as his gleaming eyes met mine. I wasn't lying. Our first date really was rated X. Luke wasn't lying, either. I wouldn't call it begging exactly, but it was true that I was the one to ask him for a second date first.

Luke leaned in and spoke low. "You remember every minute, Anabel."

With a small smile, I turned away from his look of masculine confidence to give Crookie my attention.

"Here is what I know. Cheryl was found by two teens about ten o'clock last night when they went to a conveniently unoccupied farmstead to probably have sex in the barn." Crookie had come a long ways socially in ten years. He didn't even blush. I heard Aunt Lily revving up a deep grumble at the word "sex", but didn't take my eyes from Crooks. "They discovered the car with Cheryl still in the driver's seat."

There were groans around the table at this revelation. Tre J, being one exception to my beauty-is-a-curse rule, covered his hand with hers.

She nodded encouragingly with a small smile. Her Nordic blue eyes were soft with sympathy. Crookie smiled sweetly in return.

Nibbling on a soft breadstick, I paused in speculation while marveling at the two of them together. '*Good god, the potential! Their offspring could be beautiful, kind, ass-kicking giants with monster brains—practically a new species of human.*'

"Thankfully, these were decent people." Aunt Lily grumbled under her breath but we all ignored her. "They called the police immediately, and didn't touch or take anything from the car. Cheryl's cell and her purse, with the cash inside, were recovered. In her purse they found a receipt dated and time stamped from a Saturday morning in September. It was the fifteenth, the day after I had seen her last. The receipt was from the Northfield Bakery. The bakery owners were questioned earlier today, and they remembered her even two months later." Crookie shook his head remorsefully. "Cheryl had been terribly rude to the woman owner. She came in early, about seven in the morning on that Saturday, and bought coffee and rolls. Then she claimed their Cruellers were stale, and made a scene demanding her cash back. They do not get too many customers calling them "motherfuckers" at the bakery."

At his wry tone, we all groaned and chuckled in sympathetic disbelief. Aunt Lily shook her finger at Crookie. Watching her from my end of the table, it was obvious she was riled up. Her whole chest rose and fell with each breath.

"How dare you curse on the Sabbath? There will be NO profanity at this table!"

Anna was trying valiantly to be patient. "Crookie's not swearing, Aunt Lil, he's repeating a story."

Crookie ducked his head and shrugged apologetically in Aunt Lily's direction. "Cheryl always kept her phone charging in her car, and that is how I am cleared. When she was stabbed…" at our collective sounds of shock his eyebrows raised. Then comprehension dawned, and he rushed to clarify while running a hand through his light brown hair. "Oh, I am sorry! Yes, that is how she was murdered. Her heart was punctured by a sharp, unknown weapon--most probably a knife of some kind. I apologize again; it has been a long day. I do not mean to sound callous, but I have had hours to become accustomed to this news." He leaned forward to look down his right at Luke and I. "The police found her phone between the seats. They interviewed the person she called last. I don't know who it is, but the report is they had heard strange, gasping noises, but then ended the call after a few seconds when there was no other response from Cheryl. This person had one earlier conversation with Cheryl at 7:05 AM. I was not told all the pertinent details, only that somehow these calls cleared me." He shuddered. "I am definitely not arguing with that conclusion."

A Date with Fate

Tre J squeezed his hand in agreement. Nobody spoke right away. Around the table, everyone seemed lost in their own thoughts. I didn't know how much he knew beforehand of Crookie's latest details, but Luke was silent on my right. I could discern little from his closed expression. I was hoping he'd share his insights later when we could speak freely.

I turned back to my left and asked Crooks, "What time was the second call, do you know?"

Crookie's forehead wrinkled. "Yes, it was right before seven-thirty that same morning."

Jazy asked, "Did your friend tell you where the farm is located? Was it out my way south of town?"

"No, I am not sure where it is located, but east off Highway 19 was mentioned. I do not know the names of the teenagers, so I have no point of reference."

Surprisingly, James spoke up. "What would cause a woman to leave a bakery in Northfield at approximately 7:00 AM, make a call on her cell at 7:05 AM, and drive to a deserted farm in the country east of town, only to be murdered in her car while making a call to that same person by 7:30 AM?"

Reg nodded vigorously. "Couldn't have put it better myself. Cheryl wasn't a country girl, that's for sure, right Crookie?"

"That is definitely for sure. Cheryl hated anything to do with the country."

Tre asked tentatively, "She wasn't raped?"

Aunt Lily made a loud, snorting explosion from her nose, but before she could speak Crookie rushed to reassure Tre. "No, nothing like that happened. I was told there were no signs of an attack, or a struggle. Only the single stab wound." He picked up his fork again, sighing quietly. "That is all I know. It is no secret that my marriage to Cheryl was over. My only hope is the police catch the murderer quickly, so I can put this behind me and move on."

After a moment of silence, I raised my glass of wine. "Here's to peace for Cheryl and closure for Crookie."

Everyone seconded the toast and took a drink, except for Aunt Lily who didn't look up from her soup and salad.

Reg raised his beer. "Here's to police proficiency. Good luck with that!"

We all laughingly cheered and took another drink.

I nodded towards James. "Your statement made a strong case for someone hijacking her out to this barn to purposely kill her, since nothing else was stolen. Or she went willingly, and was killed by someone non-threatening to her."

"Thank you, Anabel." James replied, expressionless as always.

I didn't respond to his lightly mocking tone but looked out towards the living room, my gaze turned inward. "It's interesting the killer didn't take her phone. Having it found under the seat makes me question if the killer was aware of the last call. I wonder if it was an attempt for help, or if she was all ready calling when the killer stabbed her and she then dropped her cell. Does anybody know how quickly you die if you're heart is punctured?"

Over a mouthful of soup Tre J immediately mumbled, 'Seconds to minutes, depending where in the heart you are stabbed. It also depends if the weapon is left in, or pulled out."

I blinked at her unhesitating answer, but then Jazy caught my interest when she said to Crookie, "Okay, I've been thinking. Cheryl's killer could be the man you saw her with at Tina's, don't you agree?"

Crookie thought it over. "It could be him, but Cheryl," his head shook in sad reflection, "was too indiscriminate to pin it on that particular man without knowing more facts."

Visibly shaking, Aunt Lily shouted from her end of the table. "She was the great Whore of Babylon!" She stood up, her cane rising in the air. "And there came one of the seven angels, and talked with me, saying unto me, Come Hither; I will shew unto thee the judgment of the great whore that sitteth!"

Everyone was stunned speechless as Aunt Lily stood and spewed out these words. It was extremely strange behavior even for her. She seemed overcome with violent emotion, but I doubted she even knew Cheryl, except maybe in passing.

Luke showed off his bible study talents when he said in an undertone, "Interesting. She's misquoting Revelations 17:1."

"Hush, Baal, or anyone could think you were a pastor's kid."

A large hand sliding high on my thigh, and squeezing with no problem, was his response to me. Luke was chuckling softly at hearing Crookie's placidly agreeable response to Aunt Lily.

"Yes ma'am, that is probably as good as description as any to describe Cheryl's unfortunate behavior."

Standing at the end of the table, her features brutally hard, Aunt Lily regarded Crookie in silence for a long moment. Then her voice started low and rose in volume with every word until she was screaming, "You should be thankful she is dead! The scripture said she deserved to die! She was an Adulteress, a terrible wife, and she broke every sacred commandment!" She stopped abruptly, leaning both hands on the table before her and gasping. She looked up under her heavy, caterpillar brows and hissed, "She made Anna cry."

Unlike discussing the details of a murder--religion, politics, or being publically named a Crybaby are not relaxing topics for the dinner table. Anna's face was stricken. Even Crookie was at a loss how to

A Date with Fate

respond courteously to this latest proclamation. Everyone was uncomfortably silent, and a few mouths were hanging open. I glimpsed Diego crossing himself and reaching for my sister's hand.

Her words had brought to my mind Aunt Lily's special visit to Bel's yesterday with the same bakery item to lord over Anna. Since I am an admitted tormentor that does not rest, even on a Sunday, I spoke up to lighten the mood.

"Speaking of terrible things, I told you their "Crullers" were terrible at the Northfield Bakery, Aunt Lily. Even the great Whore of Babylon could figure this out after one bite."

It flashed through my mind the date of Cheryl's death was the same day I met Luke at Reggie's house. Not that I had recorded that September date in my Dear Diary, but our first date later that night was rather hard to forget since it was rated X. I recalled Aunt Lily had brought us a bag of cookies that morning to the store right when we opened at ten. I had taken the cookies to Reggie's house knowing he'd eat them.

I opened my mouth to pour salt in the wound and remind her of the "dry, tasteless cookies" also from the Northfield Bakery, but Aunt Lily had grabbed her cane again. She was whacking it on the floor beside her in time to her thundering, bellowing words. "Those Cruellers were not stale, Anabel Axelrod! The Pastry Chef went to school in New York City, not some two-bit…"

The Behemoth's yelling continued unabated, but I heard Anna's gasp next to me. She was ignoring the latest ranting from her relative because she must have been thinking the same thing I was. The date for her was probably etched in her heart since she and Reggie broke off their new relationship because of the murdered Whore of Babylon the previous night.

Aunt Lily's cane slamming and whacking was taking place on James' side of the table. He slid his chair far to his right side and crowded Jazy to save his feet. He glared reproachfully at me for riling the Beast. I couldn't hide my grin fast enough behind my wine glass. I wondered if he was happy he'd joined us for our little family dinner.

I observed James, Jazy, Reggie, Tre J, and Crookie on one side of the table, along with Diego, Eric George, and Stella on the other. All of their heads were swiveling back and forth in time to the conversation coming from either end of the long table like they were watching a tennis match broadcast from Hades. They all had round eyes the size of their soup bowls.

Anna's loud voice interrupted Mac's appeasing attempts to calm down Aunt Lily's screaming, incoherent tirade on culinary schools and whores. Jack was really going to be bummed he'd stayed away tonight.

Anna bellowed to be heard over her aunt's screams. I could practically see Anna thinking out loud. "Hold on a minute, wait a minute!

SETTLE DOWN, AUNT LILY!" Miraculously, Aunt Lily quit screaming although she was still furiously wielding her cane. "Didn't you bring cookies to the Fare that day from Northfield Bakery? I know it was in the morning." Anna bounced forward enthusiastically in her seat. She spoke even louder in her growing excitement. "Don't you go to the bakery early before Saturday church? Oh, my god! THINK, Aunt Lily, did *you* see Cheryl there at the bakery that morning before she was murdered?"

I felt Luke stiffen beside me and murmur, "I'll be damned."

Aunt Lily's face drained of color before us. Her small, black eyes, burning with spiteful hate, looked everywhere but at Anna while she mumbled, "I did the right thing. The Angel came…she made Anna cry..that whore deserv…"

Her cane stilled, and then fell out of her clenched hand and onto the floor with a thud. She stared wildly around the table, her mouth opening and closing with no sound except the gasp of her heavy, labored breathing. Skin ashen gray, her eyes then rolled into the back of her head until only the whites showed. I thought she was about to speak in tongues—which to be fair to myself—she has been known to do upon occasion.

This time, she let out a long, unearthly groan. Hands pressing convulsively against her chest, Aunt Lily dropped heavily with no warning. Her chair was previously pushed back behind her. We all heard the horrible smacking sound when her skull connected with the wooden edge. She was out of my sight on the floor.

James, Diego and Mac reached Aunt Lily first.

Mac's even, calm voice declared, "I think she had a heart attack. I can't find a pulse. Somebody call 911. Here, Diego and James, help me turn her slightly."

Before Aunt Lily had even hit the ground, Luke had shot out of his chair with his phone to his ear. He strode swiftly around the table. "I'm calling, Mac. Nobody touch her cane."

He plucked a few linen napkins off the sideboard and bent over. Straightening up with the cane wrapped in the napkins, he took it over and laid it carefully on the sideboard. He rapped out clipped instructions to 911 into his phone. He stepped a few feet away and observed Mac's ministrations as he made another call.

Anna and I were right behind him. He said quietly to us, "I'm calling Jack."

In the confusion of the next moments, I stood silently arm-in-arm with Anna. She was rocking back and forth in agitation while we kept watch on the activity occurring around the stricken Aunt Lily. Every few seconds, we'd look at each other with the knowledge of what we suspected in our shocked faces. My mind kept repeatedly playing the last few minutes before Aunt Lily crashed to the floor.

A Date with Fate

My brother came up on the other side of Anna and put his arms around her. With a cry, she turned gratefully into his sheltering warmth.

Our eyes met. I nodded in approval at his move.

He mouthed in disbelief, "Aunt Lily killed Cheryl?"

Shrugging, I mouthed, "I think so."

I realized we were all arriving at the same conclusion. Luke only reinforced our belief when he'd snatched up the cane and put it aside as the probable murder weapon.

I looked around me at the drawn faces. Everyone's attention was on the life and death drama occurring on the floor before us. Jazy and Tre J stood silently across the table from us. They had Crookie between them, each holding onto an arm of my tall friend in protective support. His mouth was a tight, grim line. Crookie and I shared a look of understanding. He could be getting his closure faster than we ever dreamed possible. The surreal was becoming commonplace.

Stella and Eric George stayed seated down on my left, but huddled together. I went to stand by my niece. I squeezed her shoulder in soft question and patted Eric George's. They nodded they were fine, Stella reaching up to rub my hand in return. After a final pat, I turned away.

I walked back over to Luke. "I need to do something. I'll be over opening the doors for the ambulance."

He was watching Mac and Diego performing CPR. James knelt next to them, ready to assist if Mac gave the word. I could tell by her voice as Mac worked that my sister knew Aunt Lily was dead, but was following the correct emergency, medical procedures for a heart attack victim.

"Good idea." Luke walked with me.

At the intercom, I unlocked the doors for the EMT's and police.

Luke pulled me close. "Her cane really is a sword stick, huh? You mentioned her slicing and dicing a few weeks ago. I took it as a joke until tonight. Then it hit me when Anna asked her if she was at the same bakery that morning."

"Yes, it is." I swallowed. "I've haven't seen the blade in years, but it's something we've always known. Do we really think Aunt Lily stabbed Cheryl Crookston and killed her?"

Luke tightened his arms and replied, "I'm leaning that way based on what I've heard tonight. The police will investigate, but that's my take. Do you think she murdered Cheryl?"

"It makes a weird sense. Too bad she keeled over before finishing her last sentence. She appeared to be heading in the confession direction. Something about Anna being so hysterically upset late the night before triggered it, would be my guess."

Luke bent his head to mine for a lingering, soft kiss. "How are you holding up?" His voice was dry. "Still think our dates are ho-hum?"

I pressed against him with a short laugh. I thought over how I was holding up. "Maybe I should be more shocked. I should at least be sorry she's dead, but I'm neither." We were so close together, I had to tilt my head back to see his face when I confided quietly, "I've always considered her an evil troll and I'm not going to pretend I'll miss her just because she's dead." I frowned at my next thought. "I do feel bad for goading her tonight if she was ill." I ran my hands distractedly through Luke's short hair on either side of his face. "I didn't realize how off the deep end she really was until recently. Was it obvious to you?"

Luke's gaze was warm as he smiled down at me. "I can always count on an honest answer from you, can't I?" Before I had time to answer that tricky question, Luke continued speaking. "She was out of control long before you said anything, so don't worry over that, Anabel." His warm hands massaged my sore, lower back. "Yes, the more she yelled, it became pretty damn clear she was eight up. I'm not surprised she had the heart attack. Her stress levels had to be off the charts."

I arched my back under his capable hands. I was sure if he'd only continue touching me like this, I'd never worry again about anything. I was about to ask Luke what 'ate up' meant, when his cell vibrated. He released one arm around my waist to answer. Looking at the message, his face darkened and he swore softly. His head came up and I knew.

I joked halfheartedly, "I want to meet the schedule-Nazi on the other end of these texts. Their timing is becoming ridiculously annoying."

He closed his eyes briefly. Opening them, he sighed and nodded. "Christ, I'm sorry. I wish..." He stopped and his mouth tightened. "Listen, I don't know how long I'll be gone, but there was a lot I planned on talking with you about tonight."

'I knew there had to be a silver lining somewhere in all this.'

Holding my hand, he started walking over to the church pew where his jacket waited.

"Hold on there, Luke Bond. You are not going anywhere until you answer one question. Make that two."

He smiled slightly, and let go of me to shrug into his coat. He placed the gift bag on the floor. "Shoot, Princess."

"First, are you taking the little predator with you?"

Luke snorted. "Yes."

I nodded in satisfaction. "Good."

He patted his pocket for his keys. "Second question?"

I slid my arms up around his neck and widened the baby blues. I whispered, "I know I'm shallower than a wading pool, but I don't have to wait until you are back in town to open my beautiful, black gift bag, do I? After all I've been through this weekend?"

Luke's dimple appeared. "Yes."

I smiled. "Yes, I can have it?"

A Date with Fate

"Yes, you have to wait."

At my disgruntled pout, his mouth kicked up. "Think of it as a joint gift. You won't appreciate it without me." He slid it under the pew with his foot until it was tucked away.

His black brows met and he warned, "I'll know if you peek, Anabel."

"Yeah right, mean Santa."

Leaning down, he kissed the pout off my lips while pulling me tightly against the full length of him. Our bodies touched from my head to my toe. He ran his hands slowly over my ass, up my back, and along my upraised arms. Taking my hands in his, he unclasped them from around his neck. He kissed across my knuckles on one hand, and then the other. He put me away from him.

"Now, no begging me or whining. It's beneath you."

He ignored my disgusted cry, kissed my cheek, and gave my ass a final squeeze before heading towards the stairway. Watching him walk away, I thought I heard a siren outside. Pausing momentarily, Luke turned back. Gleaming green eyes traveled over me while his fingers drummed along the top ledge of the half wall. He appeared to be having an internal debate. He looked so hot when he was so serious.

I blew him a kiss.

He held my eyes for a long moment. He started down the stairs.

I was just turning away when I heard his voice call back.

"Forty-one thousand five hundred and thirty-four."

I cocked my head to the side. I ran to the ledge and saw only the top of his fast descending head. "Was that new with no trade-in, you demon bastard? If it was, I want to bow at your feet in eternal worship!"

"And eighteen pennies!" His deep laughter echoed back up the stairwell to me.

Grinning most inappropriately considering the circumstances, I turned back to the foyer and went to rejoin my family and friends. The ambulance was here, and Chief Jack wouldn't be far behind. Call my mean mommy voice uncaringly practical, but she was right. I know men and I know women. After all the excitement died down, they were going to be starving. I should get the apple crisp in the oven to serve warm later on, and make some coffee.

Passing the church pew sheltering the smug, shiny gift bag, I stopped long enough to say, "Oh, be quiet. That wasn't me begging him. I was simply stating a fact."

Chapter XXII
"Raise Your Glass" by Pink

Tuesday, 11/20/12
11:56 PM

I was aware of a vibrating, buzzing sound annoyingly loud near my ear. It continued relentlessly until I rose up on my elbow, grabbed my phone, and turned it off.

I felt a hand cup my bare shoulder, slightly shaking me. A muffled voice a little slow on the uptake said, "Bel, answer your phone."

Confused, I glanced back and saw only a wide, masculine shoulder and a golden-brown head buried in a pillow next to me.

I looked down at what I was wearing and groaned. I fell back on my pillow with a moaning curse. The evening came rushing back.

It was Tuesday night, and what had started out as Mike McClain coming to the store to talk over the details concerning his plan for Candy had turned into a Welcome Back party. Mike had been well-liked when he lived here, and Anna and Billy were excited to see him. Trent, Stella, and Eric George were there in the store, too. Stella remembered Mike a lot more than I thought she would. Tre J had stopped in for coffee and studying an hour before the store closed, so she joined in the partying. Crookie had been there until he left to go meet Tina. Mac and Diego, coming to pick up Stella and Eric George for a late dinner, had ended up staying and adding to the impromptu fun.

It had snowed double digits on Monday, but tapered off by the evening. This was great. I got a day to recoup from the weekend with very few inquiring minds in the store. Crookie hung out with me. He had fun working on reports. By Tuesday morning all the roads were plowed. By early afternoon most people had dug themselves out and it was business as usual. Mike had been over to Reggie's. They bonded over meat on the grill before coming to the store later in the evening. Reggie had tagged along with him to meet up with Anna.

On Sunday night, Anna had stayed overnight with Crookie and me at the apartment after the ordeal with Aunt Lily's death was over. Surprisingly, Chief Jack had not been one of the police at the scene. We were told he was busy elsewhere. After the hullabaloo was over, everyone left but Reg. To distract my slumber party friends from their individual doom and glooms, I hooked them up with second helpings of apple crisp ala mode. Then I told Crooks, Anna, and Reg all about Mike's visit and

A Date with Fate

Candy's nefarious deed. I kept the possibility of the pending civil suit action to myself. Since these were the two friends that had been the stalwarts in my life back then, it seemed like fate they were the first people I told all these years later at a sleepover.

It worked as a distraction. They were blown away by the news. Anna thought it was incredibly romantic for Mike and me to reconnect after all these years. In a weepy state anyway, she tearfully demanded to be part of the posse to help me hunt Candy down. Passing her tissue after tissue, I hurriedly agreed she could drive. Crookie, thankfully, shed no tears but was truly incensed. He offered me several good ideas on how to get Candy's face wet. Boys truly do think differently than girls. I never would have thought of the toilet. Reg thought we should just drown her and be done with it.

By the time I crawled into bed Sunday night, I was drained completely dry of energy from my weekend off. I didn't let myself dwell on the fact I had co-killed a man that day, even if he had tried to kill me first. You start thinking about the right or wrong of being responsible for ending a life and it becomes a slippery slope. So I didn't start. I slept like a baby all night. Not even one selection from the menu of nightmare possibilities from my weekend off surfaced to deny my exhausted brain and body their much needed rest.

After Crooks and I went to our rooms, Reg and Anna had their talk. Word is they're a thing again.

Earlier tonight at the store, Anna was giddy with running the full spectrum of emotions over the last couple of days. She'd gone from losing her only known relative to death and facing she most likely had killer blood running through her veins, to finding her way back to Reggie. Now she's worrying if they ever have children what mutants the Axelrod/Johnson gene pool could produce. She'd been through the wringer. She decided breaking out a couple bottles was the ticket. The shots started flying. When someone turned on some music, our last minute party really got going. I was soon feeling no pain. I'd passed my usual one drink in a night several shots ago.

Watching Mike laughing and joking with my family and friends was cathartic. It wiped away any lingering pain lodged in my heart until it disappeared completely.

I never dreamed it would feel so wonderful to be able to reclaim the lost years we'd been a couple. I'd done too complete of a good job erasing from my mind any of the fun and romantic memories of that time. I was getting back an important piece of me and I could be whole again. Listening to them all reminisce about those times was bittersweet, but in a lovely way.

I could easily see Mike's an impressive man. He's everything I always knew him to be years ago, only ten years better. He's the total, mature package of what I admire and respect in a man--smart, confident, and funny. He has an easygoing, open and affectionate personality. Mike's refreshingly real and unaffected despite being so desirably good-looking and built. Every time our eyes had met, I smiled in secret happiness to myself. I could almost feel the healing taking place deep inside me. Or maybe that was the vodka. Either way, he'd never been the dishonorable man I thought him to be all these years. Like mine, I'm sure his feet are made of clay up to the knees, but that was a fact I was never in doubt about. It was always the damn disloyalty showing the true lack of character that was my deal-breaker.

After a couple of hours, my cheeks were rosy hot, a sure sign I was beyond tipsy. Starting to see double was the second clue, and way past time for me to cut myself off. Amongst everyone's boos of me being a spoilsport, I laughingly kicked everyone out and rounded up the grinning Mike to go upstairs to the apartment.

Crookie had left only a short time before to meet with Tina after her late shift at her job. He would probably be gone for hours yet. If Mike and I were actually going to talk in private--now was the best time. My revenge on Candy took precedence over anything in my mind these days, even when smashed and smiling like a goofball.

In retrospect, it probably wasn't one of my better plans.

My mind stopped there when the ringing of the doorbell penetrated my muddled, drunken thoughts.

All the lights were on in my bedroom, so it was no problem seeing my phone. Being able to focus was a different story. Pushing the waves of hair back off my face, I held my cell away from my eyes and then brought it closer. The time was 11:58 PM.

I stared at the short text. Then read it again. I stared over at the man sprawled next to me in my bed.

My apartment doorbell kept shrilly buzzing.

I read the text a third time. It finally sunk in.

Open the envelope

ABOUT THE AUTHOR

Meet Tracy Ellen.

Tracy wishes she could tell you she has super-impressive credentials to be an author, but she tries hard not to lie. She does have half a brain, an insatiable hunger for books, sparkling conversations with the voices in her head, opinions on everything under the sun, opinions on the sun itself, true grit and determination, a strange sense of fair play, a stranger sense of humor, and the ability to laugh at herself. The latter has turned out to be quite a good thing since she often has reasons to do so.

A Date with Fate is Tracy's first novel. She's seriously, passionately hooked on writing. As you read this, she's happily listening to music that inspires chapters while typing away on her next book; regardless of attempts to tie her up.

She would love to hear from you. Did you know newbie indie authors thrive on attention? It's true. Your thoughts, questions, and opinions matter, so drop by and visit Tracy on her blog or face book.

www.tracyellen01.wordpress.com
facebook.com/tracyellen01

Made in the USA
Charleston, SC
16 November 2012